J.T. Bock's

A SUREFIRE WAY

An UltraSecurity Novel

PepperLip Press

www.jtbock.com

Manufactured in the United States of America

Cover Design by Mike Parkinson
Interior Design by Mike Parkinson
Edited by Stacia Kelly, Karen Corkran, Barb Reed, and Kerri Nelson
Cover Art by Mike Parkinson © 2012

Published by:

PepperLip Press
Virginia

ISBN: 978-0-9888362-1-1

www.jtbock.com

For my husband, Mike. He is my superhero.

For my very special dog, Ashley, who sat by my feet for long hours while I worked on this story. I miss you.

Special thanks to my editors, critique partners and everyone who took the time to read my manuscript and offer me feedback. Without their help and encouragement and belief in me when all hope was lost, this book would never have happened: Mike Parkinson, Stacia Kelly, Karen Corkran, Chris Prochaska, Laurin Wittig, Barb Reed, Jessica Darago, Kerri Nelson, Karmela Johnson, Maya Rodale, Laurel Wanrow, Laura Bolea, and Elizabeth Johnson.

Thanks to all my friends and family—especially my mother, ma, mom, and dad—for asking over and over again, "Is it done yet?" Thanks to Von and Paul for letting me take over their vacation home for a few days to finish the story.

Thanks to the Washington Romance Writers for offering fantastic workshops and support for published and pre-published writers.

For the Aztec ball game, history, and mythology, I used several resources. I took some liberties with Aztec mythology for this story, but I attempted to portray any historical references, the ball game, and language to the best of my ability based on my research. For more information on ancient Aztec culture, check out the following:

www.aztec-history.com
www.ballgame.org
www.aztec-indians.com
Mythology of the American Nations by David M. Jones and Brian L. Molyneaux

Chapter One

Bad guys should never be this hot, Surefire thought before she slipped on the crossbeam hanging high above the warehouse floor.

Her next thought, she vocalized. Repeatedly.

"Shit . . ."

She was running along the rafters, jumping from beam to beam in close pursuit of Raven—the annoyingly hot thief—when her knee gave out. Her outstretched foot missed its landing by inches.

Time stopped. Her stomach lurched and her heart screeched to a halt. For a nanosecond, she seemed to float. But that was only an illusion.

She was falling. Fast. Her heart pumped out a last-ditch beat. She flailed her arms and stretched her upper body, groping for the next beam.

"Oof!" Her chest caught the edge, knocking the breath from her lungs. She wrapped her arms around the beam and hugged it tight to her now throbbing chest.

Surefire looked down at her feet, dangling forty feet above the floor below.

Big mistake.

"Oh, God," she uttered. *I can't fail now.*

"Need help?" Raven called out from a few beams over.

Surefire's mouth fell open. She must have misheard him.

Raven jumped, as if on springs, from crossbeam to crossbeam back in her direction. He stopped on the beam across from her and stood with his head cocked, waiting, it seemed, for her reply.

Surefire's gaze trailed up his body from his rock-climbing shoes to his rock-solid abs.

No, she decided, a transhuman baddie needed a bizarre deformity—metal teeth, yellow skin, neon eyes, a joker face—something. Not a second-skin black suit that showed off the body of a Grecian athlete.

It was way too distracting.

Not that she was distracted one bit. She was an UltraAgent—a trained law-enforcement professional. She was always in control and always focused, and she always completed her mission. In this case, capturing the thief directly across from her.

Her falling had nothing to do with being distracted. Her bad knee had buckled. That was all.

His eyes locked on hers from behind the two holes in his Zorro-like mask, and he asked again, "Do you need help?"

Under her own mask, she blinked, registering his question. Did he think she was an idiot?

Surefire repositioned her arms for a better grip. Anger now replaced her fear. "Isn't this the part when you run away? Or toss me to my death?"

"I can't and won't have blood on my hands," he replied.

"Glad you have some principles. It'll help you in court."

He shook his head as if she didn't get it. "I can give you a hand—"

"Stay where you are." She emphasized each word so he didn't mistake her meaning.

Never moving her eyes from his, she hauled herself back onto the beam, inch by painful inch. Swinging her leg over, she pulled herself up onto unsteady feet but remained in a squat for better balance. She took a deep breath then winced as pain sliced through her ribcage.

Just great. A bruised rib.

If Raven noticed she was hurt, he didn't give any indication. He casually stood on the beam across from her. Over his shoulder, he held the burlap sack containing the statue he had stolen from the museum.

Surefire raised her right arm and aimed the small dart gun attached to her wrist. She concentrated on keeping her hand from trembling as she locked on the masked space between his eyes.

Then she hesitated.

She couldn't shoot him this high up off the floor. He'd fall, and the priceless artifact he had slung over his shoulder like a bag of dirty gym clothes would crash to the ground.

Surefire lowered her gaze, and the bastard grinned.

"You okay?" he asked, not fazed by the weapon pointed at him.

"I'm fine."

He snorted as if he didn't believe her. Her finger tensed on the trigger button hidden in her palm.

"The police and the FBI will be here any minute." She swallowed to strengthen her voice. "I suggest we climb down and—"

His lips puckered into a kiss before he dropped onto the concrete floor as if it weren't a forty-foot fall but a leap off a balance beam.

Dammit!

Not hesitating again, she flicked her wrist toward the ground and depressed the trigger.

Click. Click. Nothing.

She inspected the tiny dart gun, shook it, and tried again.

Click. Click. Again, nothing.

Oliver was so dead when she got back to the UltraSecurity office. She hadn't had time for a weapons check this evening, and Oliver had sworn he had tested her weapons earlier in the day.

"Having a wardrobe malfunction?" Raven called up to her.

Surefire glared down at him. He stood below her with his hands on his hips and his face tilted up at her. Moonlight filtered through the smudged windows lining the top of the building and cast a dim spotlight on his infuriating grin.

She rolled her eyes. He had something up his tight sleeve, or he would have escaped when she slipped.

Then again, maybe he wanted to see what else she'd mess up.

Hands down, he was the most arrogant criminal she'd been assigned. Not that she had encountered many. He was only her fourth assignment since joining UltraSecurity, known as U-Sec, over three years ago. And the first assignment she headed up since her elevation from rookie to full-time agent. The last two agents on the case had been reassigned. Inferno had lost his cool and seared a museum's storage center trying to stop Raven. They had found the last agent, Tara Kard, tied up on Marie Antoinette's bed at Versailles, a priceless vase missing.

So by now, Raven probably thought UltraAgents were pathetic amateurs, and he had become cocky.

Hence, the not running away part.

Either that or he hoped to win her trust and disable her as he had done to Tara.

Whatever his motive, she'd show him.

Surefire grabbed a metal tube the size and width of her index finger, hidden in a small pouch on her belt. She aimed it at him and depressed the release button on its side. A net shot out but didn't deploy evenly. It drifted onto the ground next to him, a limp parachute.

He nudged it with his foot. "Cute. Should I throw this over my head?"

"That would be helpful."

Surefire sighed. Between the weapon malfunctions and her slipping, he deserved to get away, and she deserved to have her U-Sec badge revoked.

"Nah, I'll let you work for it. I don't want you to think I'm easy." He darted away into the shadows of the aisles.

Surefire spun around, straining to hear his fleeing steps in an effort to pinpoint his location. But the building housed metal crates, which bounced sound around like a pinball, making him nearly impossible to track.

"You know . . ." His voice sounded from down below to her left. Or was it from behind? "I don't think you want to catch me. I'm probably the most excitement you've ever had."

"Don't flatter yourself," Surefire yelled, angrier than she intended.

"Then why all the mistakes? Are you trying to screw up?"

She threw down the empty metal tube with a clang.

How long had she been on this case? Three months. And how many times had she almost caught him? Three near misses. And how often had he tried to provoke her? Three times, of course. Three signified the final strike, the final out—the charm. She had begged her bosses for this case. If she wanted to make a name for herself at U-Sec—and if she wanted a raise—then she needed Raven.

Well, she needed to *catch* him.

She scanned the boxes below for one stacked high enough to jump onto but found none nearby. She was a sure shot and a trained gymnast, but she was only human, well, a transhuman. She hated that label the media used for people with extraordinary abilities. She could hit any target—when her weapons worked. But that was the extent of her talents. Looking down at the long drop to the floor, which Raven had taken with such ease and no broken bones, she wondered whether he was something more than a transhuman.

Most transhumans were gifted with one ability. Very few had two distinct talents. Raven possessed several that U-Sec was aware of. Bullets slowed but never stopped him. He toted off statues weighing three hundred pounds as if they were plastic mannequins. Then, during his previous heist, he had walked through the walls of a sealed vault, adding "phasing out" to his list of talents.

Why he didn't use that skill now, Surefire couldn't guess. However, she was grateful. She was close to capturing Raven or at least uncovering his thefts, and failure was not in her family's genes, as dad loved to remind her.

But first, she needed to find Raven again or at least distract him until her backup arrived. They were late, and Surefire was too focused on her target to question why.

Eyeing the rafter angled just above and to her right, she lifted her left arm, aimed a small compact box secured to her wrist, and shot out a line to the next beam up. The small weighted grappling hook, attached to the end of a cable, spun twice around the beam then latched onto the edge. She tugged on it and the hook held. Her gaze shifted to the floor below, finding the perfect spot to land. The drop didn't seem so frightening when she wasn't dangling over it.

Surefire swung down and dropped onto solid concrete.

The hard landing jolted her body. Renewed pain surged along her ribs. She doubled over as she struggled to breathe past the searing sting. She pulled two capsules from a belt pocket and popped them into her mouth, breaking them open with her teeth. Seconds later, a soothing liquid slid like hot Irish coffee down her throat and to her stomach. The sensation branched out to her limbs and dulled the pain but not her senses. For another hour, she wouldn't feel a thing. These Happy Pills, as the other agents dubbed them, were the best innovation by U-Sec's lab geeks.

She ejected the thin, strong cable from the box on her wrist then heard the click of another hook and cable loading inside the small contraption as backup. Though she certainly wasn't in any condition to imitate Tarzan again this night.

Regrouping, she quieted her breathing. Cargo containers loomed above her. Giant Legos stacked in countless rows. She listened for a footstep, a misstep, anything.

And heard nothing.

Surefire slumped against a crate. If Raven were stashing his stolen goods in this warehouse, as she believed, he wouldn't go far. She considered her options. She'd rather not reveal her position. She'd prefer a sneak attack, but the warehouse was so large the only way to find him was to get him to start talking.

Not the typical protocol, but Raven seemed to enjoy showing off his verbal gymnastics, especially when it came to mocking her. Only one way to find out. Desperate, she straightened up and opened her mouth, when Raven's voice resounded above her.

"Did you do that?"

"Do what?" she replied, caught off-guard.

"Nothing. It's probably nothing."

What the hell was he talking about? Her face cinched in confusion under her mask.

Whatever it was didn't matter. The hairs on her arms stood on end. He was close. Very close. His voice was loud, clear.

"Maybe if you describe it, I could help," she offered.

She eased a small stun gun from her utility belt, pressed her back against the cold steel of the crate, bit her lip, held her gun high in the air, and then—

"Doubtful," his voice echoed loudly.

Surefire jumped back. His voice was too close, like he was speaking next to her ear. She whirled around and looked up. Above and to her right, Raven peered over the edge of the top crate. His lips flashed an oh-too-perfect-smile before he backed away from the edge.

She pulled the trigger to at least graze him. Again, another empty click.

What the—?

She flung the gun down and attempted another tactic—not exactly a typical tactic, but worth a try, since Raven was an atypical criminal.

"Come down here, and I'll show you how helpful I can be." She tried to deepen her voice and make it sexy. "Tried" was the operative word.

He laughed a rich, sultry laugh that she was certain he had practiced to get just so. "You need to work on your bedroom voice. You sound like a man, and I don't swing that way. Ask Inferno."

"Inferno?" Surefire frowned. "What do you mean?"

"What do you think?"

She mulled this over. "You're wrong."

"Why do you think he burned down the storage center?"

"He lost control. It happens to the best of us," she said, defending her friend. A retired Navy SEAL, he hadn't officially exited the closet.

"Hell hath no fury like a man scorned." Raven chuckled, and his amusement bothered her more than this conversation, which was supposed to distract him instead of her. He had both men and women bumbling over him. Surefire was certain the same thing had happened to Tara Kard, even if she had never given specifics. Tara had hated turning over the case to Surefire, who assumed it was because she had been embarrassed for having failed. Now Surefire wondered if it were something more.

Egotistical bastard. If sex appeal were another one of his powers, he needed to save it for his cellmate.

Surefire jumped when the crates to her left creaked. She caught sight of Raven landing on another box farther down the aisle before he disappeared. She ran down the aisle and vaulted over the metal rails of a forklift.

Think of something. *Anything* to annoy him.

"Maybe your outfit annoyed Inferno," Surefire shouted before rounding a corner.

A small crate teetered and swayed above her. She could see Raven's outline against the filtered light.

"What's wrong with my outfit?"

Surefire suppressed a laugh. He actually sounded offended. "Looks like something a mime would wear, and Inferno hates mimes."

"I'm miming something right now. Too bad you can't see it."

"Come down here and show me."

He coyly changed the subject. "I'm liking your leotard. Doesn't leave much to the imagination. I assume it's for distraction?"

Surefire blushed. Ever since she'd moved in with her sister six months ago, Heather's cat, Prada, saw fit to use Surefire's uniforms as her own special bed. Tonight, Prada had made Surefire's only clean uniform into a litter box, and her backup had been lost by the dry cleaners after a previous Prada incident. So Surefire had had to find a new outfit quick—one that allowed ease of movement—and found her old gymnastics leotard. Apparently, her breasts and butt, though mostly her butt, had grown in the past ten years.

"Obviously, it's not working or you'd be down here taking a closer look."

"The view's just as good from up here," he countered, and Surefire didn't think her face could flush any hotter. "But where did you get that mask? A luchador yard sale?"

She balled her fists. Ditto with the mask. Prada had used that as a hairball receptacle. Surefire had dug out her Halloween costume from four years ago when she'd dressed as a Mexican wrestler. Not a good look, but it hid her identity.

"At least I'm wearing underwear," Surefire goaded him again.

"I did that for you." He skimmed along the windowsills. "Was wondering if you'd noticed."

Her body tensed in frustration. She needed to get Raven down to the floor now, and not for the reasons his tone suggested. Her mind raced through her portable arsenal. She had another weapon that released a net—if it worked.

Damn Oliver.

Instead of focusing on work, he was too busy focusing on U-Sec's newest agent and call center manager, Pixie Chick.

They were going to have a nice long chat about the problems with interoffice dating when she returned.

Red and blue flashing lights skimmed across the dirt-encrusted windows at the top of the warehouse. Sirens grew louder as police cars surrounded the building. She glanced at her watch.

About time they arrived.

Nearly forty-five minutes had passed since she'd first called the police after she spotted Raven climbing down from the roof of the Walters Art Museum in downtown Baltimore.

Outside, car doors slammed shut and hard soles beat a path across the ground. She had five, maybe ten, minutes until the cops gassed the place, which was their preferred MO for dealing with transhumans like Raven. And her. Last time they had given her an assist, she'd almost gone down in friendly fire.

Technically, she shouldn't be in here. Shouldn't have entered the building without backup. The warehouse doors were locked, and she hadn't wanted to lose sight of Raven; she'd had to scale a semi parked underneath an open window to get in.

It was a stupid, impetuous, and ultimately dangerous move. However, she'd assumed the police would have arrived sooner. When Raven had entered the warehouse, she'd known she'd lose him again if she didn't follow. Her bosses at U-Sec had to understand. And if she brought Raven in—no, *when* she brought Raven in—they would more than understand.

Maybe even give her a promotion.

She glanced at her communicator, a secure U-Sec cell phone, clipped to her belt. It was her direct link to the U-Sec office and police. She'd silenced it before entering the warehouse. Usually, a dull green light blinked if there were a message. She unclipped it and looked at the LCD screen. No missed calls.

She had spoken with Pixie at the U-Sec call center before she'd notified the police. Oracle—her sergeant and mentor—should have contacted her by now. Despite the officers outside, she preferred to have someone from her own team as backup. Most officers were not thrilled to work with U-Sec or, as they called it, the Freak Squad.

Something clanged to her right. Just above her, Raven jumped onto another crate and then to another window, possibly searching for a weak spot in the perimeter.

"Give up," Surefire called out to him. "The building's surrounded."

"Never stopped me before."

Surefire kept her eyes focused on Raven. Across from her, the doors rattled.

Suddenly, Raven's foot slipped. He fell a short distance and then caught himself on the windowsill. Pulling himself back up, he wagged his head as if to clear it. "You don't feel that?"

"No," Surefire replied, though she couldn't explain the uneasiness prickling up her spine.

A gruff male voice shouted orders outside. Then the police tried to open the nearly floor-to-ceiling doors with a resounding bang. Surefire edged closer to the doors. Her gaze shot to the iron handles. She did a double take.

The doors were chained from the inside.

Something on the far end of the warehouse slammed shut. She looked up and saw Raven staring in the sound's direction.

She grabbed her communicator and tried to control her nervous fingers as she dialed her police contact.

"Detective Matthews," she whispered into the small phone. She held it to her ear but heard nothing. The LCD screen faded to black. The battery was dead.

She hooked the phone back onto her belt and ran toward the exit to warn the police the doors were chained.

A tingling sensation skimmed across her skin. She paused in mid-step. Vibrations, like a mild electrical current, hummed through her veins. Crates creaked and shifted above her, and the floor started to shake.

"What the—?" Surefire grabbed the handle of a cargo container just as a crack snaked through the middle of the concrete floor. Above her, metal containers shifted and scraped together. Across the aisle, a few wooden crates fell and splintered apart onto the floor. She aimed the rappelling gun on her left wrist, but it was too late. Before the cable could deploy, she slipped and fell next to the fissure.

She sprang to her feet and darted away from the widening crack.

This couldn't be another earthquake. In twenty-seven years, she'd experienced only one in Baltimore a few years ago. And then she'd hardly felt anything while driving on the beltway.

Something creaked above her.

"Watch out!" Raven shouted as he jumped from the window to the top crate and landed with practiced ease next to her. Wrapping his arms around her waist, he tackled her to the ground. He rolled with her several times before they stopped with him on top, leaning over her in a provocative straddle— leaving her breathless.

Surefire's carefully packed gadgets on her utility belt cut into her lower back. She couldn't breathe, couldn't concentrate, and needed to get up. She jabbed both palms hard against his chest, but he didn't budge. A loud rumble interrupted her struggle. The sound rose and filled the warehouse, ending in an ear-splitting crash.

The cargo container she'd been standing underneath seconds ago fell to the floor, sending up a cloud of dust and dirt. The metal sides and corners buckled like an accordion.

Her heart thumped wildly. She glanced up at Raven, who was staring at her with a fierce intensity. Under normal circumstances, she might have been frightened by a criminal looming over her. But she was too shocked from her near-death experience to care.

"Thanks," she stammered.

The side of his lips lifted up in a smile. "Anytime."

She noticed he no longer held the sack. "Where's the statue?"

He shifted, elevating his weight from his left side. He inclined his head toward a crawl space between two containers. "I threw it out of the way—"

With her right arm free, Surefire used her thumb to flick a switch in her palm. A dart ejected from the gun on her right wrist, and she jabbed the needle into his neck in one swift movement.

He raised his hand in astonishment and pulled it out. He frowned at the needle. "This is the gratitude I get?"

She shrugged and smiled smugly under her mask.

"Typical woman."

"Typical man," Surefire countered.

He planted his hands on either side of her. His eyes glazed over as the drug took effect. "My body is going to reject it. I'll shake it off in seconds."

"I had this one made especially for you. You left behind more than a fake fertility statue at your last robbery."

He groaned. His arms buckled.

The floor shook again and started separating underneath her back.

She slammed her palms into his chest. "Move!"

But it was too late.

Chapter Two

Raven's eyes rolled back. With a thud, he fell unconscious on top of her—over 180 pounds of dead weight by her estimate. She couldn't budge him. Maybe it hadn't been a good idea to knock him out while he was straddling her. Live and learn.

The floor trembled again and the crack expanded, dropping both of them down a few feet. Raven's weight crushed her and choked out her breath. Once more, pain cut along her ribs.

She leveraged her hands under his chest and tried to push him off, but the fissure was as wide as the two of them and there was nowhere to roll him. His weight pressed down on her. She could barely expand her chest to breathe. Black spots floated across her vision. His face rested on her shoulder. And . . . what was that? Was he snoring?

Great. Just freaking amazing.

What an UltraAgent she made. Crushed under the body of her target. Her arms were pinned in front of her chest, and what was left of her utility belt was trapped underneath their combined weight.

"Wake up." She smacked her forehead into his. Why had she made the serum so strong? Maybe because she hadn't expected him to be on top of her when she used it. She would never live this down when the police found them.

Raven moaned. He wriggled his body as if trying to make himself comfortable. And whatever poked her leg had better be a weapon hidden under his pants.

"Mmmm," he moaned again, as if enjoying a pleasant dream.

"Off." She squirmed.

He raised his head. Slowly, he opened his eyes.

"Uhhhh . . ." His groggy voice trailed off. His eyelids fluttered shut.

"Off!"

He opened his eyes again and then frowned. "What are you—?"

"Now . . . can't breathe," she said, grateful the serum wore off quicker than planned.

His dazed expression cleared. He cracked a lazy smile. "Oh, yeah. You drugged me."

He leaned down so his face was inches from hers and lifted his upper body off her chest.

Surefire gulped at the air, and something sweet like chocolate wafted over her tongue. His warm breath caressed her chin, her lips, and the cocoa scent became stronger. She stared at his mouth, way too close to her own, before raising her eyes.

From outside, a bright light flicked on in front the warehouse's entrance, cutting through the smudged windows and landing across Raven's face. He shot an annoyed look up at the intrusive light before glancing back down at Surefire.

Her breath caught in her throat. She'd never seen blue eyes as dark as his, almost violet, made even darker by thick lashes.

He stared back into her eyes and gave the barest squint under his mask, as if he were trying to register something that didn't make sense.

Surefire knew what caused his confused look. "Get off me."

"Say 'please.'"

Was he joking?

The floor churned underneath Surefire. Raven sat back, pulling her with him, and tried to ease them both out of the crack, but it was too late. The concrete crumbled and fell away beneath them. Surefire's stomach dropped along with her body through the floor, and she began falling into a seemingly bottomless dark pit with Raven on top of her.

He wrapped his arms around her, pinning her arms between them. Mid-fall they swung around in the air. A second later, they slammed onto the ground with Surefire on top.

His arms fell away from her and landed limp at his sides. She lay with her head on his chest, listening to him breathe. She couldn't hear his heart, probably because hers was pounding loud enough to wake the entire city. She lifted her head, still swimming from the fall. So much so, it didn't register that she was cowering on top of him—this felon she'd been hired to capture and take to jail—because he somehow seemed safer and a lot warmer than their cold, dark surroundings.

"Are you okay?" he rasped.

She blushed, embarrassed to still be lying on top of him and embarrassed by the fact that she didn't want to move. She rolled away onto the dirt floor and shivered.

"I'm good." She was surprised her words didn't shake like her insides. Because, actually, she wasn't doing so well. Dropping into a pitch-black underground cavern—or wherever the hell she'd landed—alone with a transhuman criminal counted as the opposite of good.

SOL . . . *Shit out of luck* came to mind.

Surefire scooted across the sandy dirt floor out of his reach. She ran her hands over her chest, her stomach, her legs. No severe injuries, just a few scrapes and bruises. She took a couple of short breaths, relieved the Happy Pills continued to work. The rib pain had subsided again. She rubbed her arms against the dampness. Dirt, water, and a rich mineral scent filled her lungs and left a metallic taste in her mouth.

Her eyes continued to adjust to the dark as she watched Raven's shadowy form lying a few feet away from her. He didn't move. Just remained on his back. Hesitantly, she lifted her gaze from him and tilted her head back. Dull beams of light filtered through the crack they had fallen through in sharp contrast to the blackness surrounding them. A twenty-foot drop at least. She shivered again, and it wasn't because of the cool, dank air. She could've broken her back or her neck or worse.

Raven had saved her life—again. He had taken the brunt of their fall and was still alive and asking about her well-being.

"What *are* you?" Her voice echoed through the darkness.

"That's an odd question to ask now. Kinda cliché." His words came out between wheezing breaths.

"No, it's not." She stuck an index finger into the small, square compartment attached to her right wrist. It came out gooey. The tranquilizer darts had busted.

She slid another foot away from him. "Are you a transhuman?"

"Is that what you call yourself or what others call you?" He gasped.

Good grief. Her asthmatic grandmother sounded better than him. He might be hurt worse than she'd realized.

Maybe she wasn't shit out of luck after all.

"Just answer the question." Surefire patted the smashed pockets of her utility belt.

"You should know." He let out a dry, hollow cough. "Didn't you use something of mine to make that knock-out juice?"

"We retrieved blood from a bullet embedded in the wall after the police shot you at the museum." During his last theft in DC, he'd run toward a police barricade outside the exit. They had tagged him in the leg and shoulder. He hadn't even flinched, and he'd phased out before he'd reached their barrier.

"Humph. I almost forgot about that."

Surefire ignored his comment. "We tested your blood, and the tests came back different every time. Human or unknown. And sometimes animal. I made the serum strong enough to knock out a rhino."

"A rhino, really?"

"Answer the question."

She heard him take a shallow breath before replying.

"I'm the Raven. Only this, and nothing more."

She paused to consider his words until he started to chuckle. Then she realized his joke. His chuckling turned into a choking cough.

Served him right.

Surefire poked around the pockets of her belt, hoping for something, anything that could help her out of this situation and keep Raven disabled: penlight, butterfly knife, some thin but strong cord, handcuffs, and a few other odds and ends. But her communicator and most of her main weapons were missing or broken.

She turned on the penlight and shined it in his face.

"Did you cause this?"

"Do you mind?" He raised his hand and turned his head.

"Answer me."

She stood. Her left hand held the penlight steady while her right reached for the handcuffs.

"Do I look like I caused this?" He squinted at her.

She edged nearer him. Keep him talking. Keep him distracted. Disable him and then find a way out. At the moment, that was her plan. It sounded doable, if she didn't think about it too much.

"What's your game?" She leveled her gaze at him and inched forward.

"Game?"

"Yeah, game."

"I have no idea what you're talking about." He coughed.

She shuffled closer. "You keep saving me, when it's my job to arrest you and—"

"Glad we got that straight. I was beginning to wonder."

She paused when he shifted and rotated his shoulders. Something popped. He winced.

"Are you hurt?"

"Nothing that won't heal."

She hesitated again. His voice sounded stronger. No more brittle rasp. More like a rough version of his smooth, deep tone. Like he had a sore throat and no longer a collapsed lung.

The metal handcuffs dug into her tense fingers. They may not hold him. But she had to try before he gained more strength. She was not about to get this close only to lose him again.

She could do this. She was strong and capable. Plus, her backup was just above them, outside the warehouse doors. This was her chance to succeed. Her chance to prove her worth. She'd bring him down where others had failed.

Maybe she'd finally get a medal after all these years.

"As an UltraAgent contracted by the United States of America in matters of transhuman crime," she recited, "I'm informing you of your right to remain—"

"Are you kidding me?" Raven's face pinched in disbelief.

"Silent," she continued. "Anything you—"

"You can't stop me. Your only weapon that even slowed me down leaked out all over my shirt when we fell." He sat up and bent his legs.

Surefire took a few steps back and reconsidered her options. According to his record, Raven was nonviolent.

So far.

From what she'd seen on surveillance videos, he had the strength to snap her in two and toss her across the room like a discarded doll. But he hadn't attempted to harm her yet. In fact, he'd saved her life—twice.

She straightened her back and swallowed the fearful lump in her throat. If she screwed up this opportunity, it would prove to her boss, her colleagues and, most importantly, her father that she couldn't succeed. She wanted this arrest. This victory. On her own. By herself. Without anyone's help. She just needed to get these cuffs on him.

Raven jumped to his feet. In two long strides, he stood in front of her. She whipped the cuffs around to hit him across the face, but he grabbed her wrist and forced it down. Then he took her other arm and angled it up, like he was posing a mannequin, so the beam of the penlight she was still holding hit the ceiling.

In the distance, the large warehouse doors banged again as the police attempted to open them. Yelling for help wouldn't solve her problem right now; the police would never hear her from this far underground.

With one easy leap, Raven launched upward and grabbed onto a rock jutting out from the bottom of the crevice about ten feet above her head. He dangled for a second before swinging his legs from side to side to get a foothold.

Panic cinched her gut. This couldn't be happening. He couldn't escape now.

She started forward, and her foot touched a rock. She eased to the ground to retrieve it.

"Throw me a line," he called down to her.

"What?" The rock slipped from her hand.

"I'm assuming you have rope or something helpful in your fanny pack."

"Utility belt."

"Whatever. Just toss it to me, so we can get out of here."

"You're going to help me?" The words came out before she could stop herself. Was this a trick?

He sighed. "As I told you before, I won't have blood on my hands. That includes leaving you down here as rat food."

She grabbed a hook from her belt pocket and began to tie the cable. But before she could throw it, the room shook, followed by a violent grinding sound. Raven lost his grip and slipped. He landed next to her with a dull thump. The fissure closed up, snuffing out the weak warehouse light. The penlight flickered once more then died, leaving them in total darkness.

"Huh . . . you don't see that every day," he said.

Surefire inched closer to him until their hands brushed. She snapped a cuff onto his right wrist and attached the other cuff to her left forearm above the rappelling gun.

He blew out a breath. "Tell me you did not do what you just did."

"You're not getting away again," Surefire said with a victorious smile. Third time was definitely the charm.

"I don't think you're aware of our situation, sweetheart. We're stuck in an underground cave. Unless you have night vision shades tucked away in your bra, I can't see a thing, let alone escape."

"Insurance." She held up both their arms. "So I know you won't escape."

Pop. Pop. Pop. Lights blared to life around them.

Surefire squinted against the harsh glare. She blinked several times until she could scan the room without seeing orange orbs everywhere.

They were in a small cave ringed by light stands. On the opposite wall hung a wide-screen monitor. Seconds later, a picture flickered across the screen and a face materialized.

Curious, Surefire strained forward, pulling Raven along with her, and what she saw made her worst nightmare seem like a perfect spring day.

Half of the face was human. The other half had the features of a bug.

A cockroach, to be exact.

Now that is what a bad guy should look like.

Chapter Three

Raven had to be hallucinating.

Minutes ago the warehouse floor had cracked open and deposited him into an underground cavern—strange enough. Now Ari, his cousin and old partner in crime, with a half-roach body, stared out at him from a flat-screen television.

That was some drug Surefire had injected him with. Maybe he should ask for another dose.

From the TV screen, Ari addressed him in a quivering but strong voice. "James, I'm glad you could drop in."

Yeah, he definitely needed another dose.

"I'm Raven now. James died years ago. But you should know that, Ari, you were there."

"Is that what happened?" Ari arched his human brow. "My mind is a bit disjointed."

Raven shook his head and then said, with mock seriousness, "You got a little something on your face. You may want to see a doctor about that. Looks like it's spreading."

Ari glared. At least the left side of his face did. On the other side, the antennae gave an angry twitch.

"You haven't lost your keen ability to note the obvious," Ari said in a jittery, high-pitched tone.

"It's a gift." Raven shrugged and tried to appear nonchalant, but his blood ran cold at the sight of Ari's deformity. He didn't know why his cousin could be a mascot for Raid. Though he wondered if Ari had plugged into a source similar to the one that fueled his own abilities. It would explain why his powers had faded in the warehouse and why he couldn't phase out and escape. Even now Raven felt tired, weak, and human, as if Ari were somehow feeding off him.

But a roach, why was Ari a roach?

Out of the corner of his eye, Raven glanced at Surefire, who was way too quiet. Under the ridiculous wrestling mask he could see her odd eyes—one blue, one green—round as hockey pucks. Her lips were stuck in an O shape, which, he wasn't ashamed to admit, he found very enticing despite their circumstances. And this led him to a disturbing thought: it had been far too long since he'd been with a woman if being confronted with a giant man-roach couldn't keep him from wondering what kind of lip gloss he had smelled on her lips—berry cherry or strawberry delight.

You'd think he would have learned his lesson by now.

"James," Ari shouted.

"What?" He snapped back, unable to shake the nagging feeling he was about to be dragged into something way over Ari's grotesque head.

Ari eyed him for a moment as if making sure he had Raven's full attention.

"You're probably wondering why I brought you here."

"I figured you missed me." Raven gave him a broad, boyish smile. "Maybe you wanted to catch up on old times. It's been what? Five years?"

Ari's human face dropped into a scowl. He leaned forward and tilted his head to stare at Raven with the cold, disturbing bug eye. Raven took an unconscious step back. Surefire shuffled closer to him. Her shoulder touched his bicep. He slid forward a few inches to block her—shield her. And this reaction bothered him a bit more than Ari's transformation.

He edged away from her, as far as the handcuffs would allow. However, before he could ask Ari what had happened, Surefire spoke.

"I know you." She moved in front of the television. "You're that magician. Master Stephanos."

"I am no common magician. I'm a mentalist and a telekinetic."

"You're a fraud," Surefire stated.

Raven choked back a laugh, not expecting her to call Ari that which angered him the most.

"They exposed you on the *Late Night Show*," she continued. "Your own assistants came clean about your tricks. Then the Fantastic Farrell recreated your act in that HBO special."

Ari made an indignant sound and settled back from the screen. "He is a fool, and he wanted to make me look like a fool as well. He was envious because I have the true power all magicians aspire to achieve."

"The power to scam people?" Surefire leaned forward within striking distance of the TV.

"If they are that naïve, then they deserve to be scammed." Ari lifted his human shoulder.

Surefire's lips parted then shut as if she couldn't find a good enough response to Ari's quip. Then she asked, "Why did you set all this up? And did you cause that earthquake?"

Ari merely responded with a self-satisfied nod.

"The most important question is," Raven cut in, "what do you want with us?"

"Originally, it was just with you," Ari replied. "But she will be useful."

"She has nothing to do with this."

"Wait . . . just . . . one . . . minute." Surefire angled her body to stand with her arms spread out between the television and Raven. "I have one job here and one job alone. To bring you in and find the rest of the artifacts you've stolen. So wherever you go, I go, because you're not getting away again." She held up their wrists, still cuffed together.

Raven snapped both their wrists down and drew her closer. She was sorely mistaken if she believed being cuffed to him meant she had him.

"You have no idea what you're getting into." Her bravado, though cute, was not worth risking her life.

Surefire met and held his gaze without a flinch. "Then enlighten me, because you're stuck with me, *sweetheart*. So get used to it. And Kafka over there," she pointed at the screen, "had better have a damn good and legal reason for this show, because right now U-Sec and the police are above us searching the warehouse, and they will find us."

Ari laughed. "Kafka." He continued to chuckle. "How apropos. She's witty. I like her. Too bad she's on the wrong side."

Surefire started to reply, but Raven beat her to it.

"What do you want?"

Ari paused, and in the clarity of the plasma television, Raven could've sworn that what was left of Ari's Adam's apple bobbed up and down in a nervous twitch.

"I have them. The crystal skulls. Twelve of them. I just need the last one to complete the collection."

"How did—?" Raven began, but Ari kept talking.

"It's not the *how* that matters. I have them, and the human race can finally receive the answers to which we are entitled. From where did we come? What is our purpose? Is the world to end? Mankind can have infinite knowledge. I just need the last skull to make it work."

Raven fought the urge to scrub his hand over his face, a gesture Ari would recognize as a sign that he was worried. He fought to maintain a neutral appearance. He fought to remain calm despite the creeping dread that told him he had to stop Ari—even if it meant killing him and breaking his cardinal rule. He'd finally have blood on his hands.

"According to legend, when humans are ready, all will be revealed," Raven replied. "If you can't find the last skull, then the world is not evolved enough to acquire it." *And you are not meant to have them all,* his tone implied.

"The world may not be ready, but the world's survival depends on it," Ari said with all the gravity his vibrating voice could relay.

"I'm not following."

"Look at me."

"I'd rather not."

"Oh, I forgot, you hate insects." A smirk tugged on the edge of his lips. On the other side, a flap over the roach's mouth flipped out sideways and back.

Raven's arms itched with a sensation of tiny maggots crawling over them. He crossed them to keep from scratching at his skin. He doubted Ari had forgotten his disgust for roaches and insects in general. Ari had the uncanny ability to retain and recall everything—a human Google—which is why he could dupe people with his supposed psychic powers. But, most importantly, Ari remembered weaknesses. And even with the powers Raven now held, he had other Achilles' heels that had nothing to do with his physical form.

"Do you not wonder how I became like this?" Ari asked.

"Justice? I'm assuming you were mixed up in something beyond your ability."

"Nothing is beyond me. However, I do admit that a miscalculation was made."

He settled into his chair and folded his hand and roach leg across his chest. Bile rose in Raven's throat each time Ari's spiny limbs moved, especially when the two hooks on the end touched his human skin. Ari was shirtless and fortunately for Raven and Surefire, he was sitting so only his face and chest were exposed. Behind Ari's chair hung a red curtain like the kind used on a theater's stage, which did nothing to complement Ari's new features.

"What did you do this time?" Raven demanded.

"Remember the Pyramid of Quetzalcoatl?"

On their last assignment together, the one before Raven left APS—Artifact Procurement Specialists, a euphemistic name for upscale grave robbers—Ari had performed an ancient ritual at the center of a Mesoamerican temple. Their mission had been to "procure" several golden Aztec idols discovered by a team of American archeologists. They had worked undercover on the dig for days. The final night, Ari had persuaded Raven to sneak back into the site to pocket a few additional pieces. Then Ari had started the ritual, which caused the temple's interior chambers to crumble like a stack of blocks. Ari had escaped, but Raven had been crushed inside a burial chamber.

"Vaguely," Raven lied.

Ari rolled his human eye. "I had the wrong place. It was the wrong tomb and the wrong god."

"Common mistake. Those ancient gods all look alike." Raven shrugged.

To his right, Surefire stifled a smile, and for whatever reason, it encouraged him.

"I was misinformed." Ari's voice rose higher, straining against his jittering vocal cords, so Raven had to concentrate to hear his words. "I trusted someone who I thought was on the level. He wasn't. I brought him down a few notches. You've heard how persuasive I can be."

"Unfortunately," Raven replied, this time with sincerity.

Raven had never seen him in action but had learned about Ari's sadistic practices long after he had left APS for greener and purer pastures. Along with his love of magic, Ari had an infatuation with torture devices, which he displayed in his museum in Baltimore. The visitors and his museum staff never suspected these centuries-old exhibits had seen recent action.

"I discovered a hidden entrance to an Aztec temple still buried outside Mexico City. A few locals keep the old traditions and perform sacrifices on the site. Though they use only animals."

Raven pressed his lips together to stem the nausea inching up from his gut, and this time it had nothing to do with Ari's appearance and everything to do with what he was alluding to.

"Did you kill someone?"

"The ritual calls for it. Besides, it's not really murder but a sacrifice, an offering and a blessing to those being offered. How many can claim they died so a god may live?"

"Was I meant to be your sacrifice?"

Ari lifted his human shoulder. "I had slim pickings. You weren't my first choice if it makes you feel better."

"Can't say it does."

"Ah, well. Easier to ask forgiveness than permission." Ari flipped up his hand and two of the roach legs mirrored the movement.

"What did you do?" Raven jerked closer to the screen, putting his face inches from Ari's distorted mug. Surefire tripped behind and then bumped into his side. In his anger, he had forgotten she was there.

"I woke the god Tezcatlipoca, and now he wants me. He wants to use my body as a vessel. It wasn't supposed to happen this way." Ari's voice trembled, and this time it wasn't because of his warped vocal cords, it was with fear. "I was supposed to capture his power, not be possessed by it. But now he's preparing it. Transforming my body to take it over. I can't stop him. I need your help, and the only way to do it is with the skulls. They hold the key. They can send him back to hell."

♥ ☠ ♥ ☠ ♥ ☠

"What are these skulls?" Surefire interjected, tired of being kept out of the conversation.

Initially, she had fought the urge to gag when confronted with this gruesome train wreck of human flesh and roach parts. Of course, seeing Ari on the television screen helped a bit. Made her think it could be a trick, could be special effects. However, the more she heard, the more she saw this as an opportunity for a case bigger than Raven. A case all her own. A case even her father would appreciate when she saved the world.

Okay, so the "saving the world" part was up for review. She wasn't clear what Ari meant by Aztec god. She didn't think those beings were real, and she certainly didn't understand what Raven meant about having died years ago. However, whether Ari was imagining this god or not, he had confessed to murder. And he'd somehow caused the earthquake that had landed her in this bizarre scene. She had to learn more about his plans and stop him before anyone else got hurt.

"Well? What are these skulls?" She looked at Raven.

Raven returned her gaze with a blank stare. Below his imitation Zorro mask, his cheeks had paled along his dark stubble. She turned her attention to Ari. Even through the screen, she could see Ari's human face glistening with a nervous sweat.

"Not much is known about them, but most have been found in South America. Two others turned up in Europe," Raven finally responded, his tone reluctant. "Archeologists believe they are hundreds, if not thousands, of years old. They were used in rituals to speak to gods, though psychics have other theories."

"Like?" Surefire prodded.

Raven's eyes narrowed. "According to legend, there were thirteen skulls scattered across the world. The skulls contain silicon, like the element used in computer chips today. Psychics believe the silicon in the skulls retains the history of the universe, and when brought together, the skulls act like an ancient memory stick."

"How can these skulls stop a so-called god?" Surefire asked, and Ari gave a little grunt.

"I don't know," Raven replied as they both turned to face Ari. "How will the skulls stop a spirit with a superiority complex?"

Ari's human face was so clenched in anger it seemed as if it would crack. The antennae on the roach side swished, and the mouth flap whipped forward and back. "The psychics were wrong."

"What a shocker," Raven muttered.

"And they were right," Ari said.

"An even bigger shocker," Surefire said with a cynical smile.

"I need you to take what I am telling you seriously. The world is at stake, need I remind you?" Ari admonished.

"So you say," Raven retorted. "This coming from the man who got me killed."

Ari continued, undaunted, "True enlightenment will take mankind into the next stage of evolution. The skulls will give humans infinite knowledge of their origins and meaning for their pitiful lives. But it will also give man the power to defeat evil."

"How do we find this skull? Do you know where it is?" Surefire asked.

"Raven knows. It's where the Old Ones dwell." Ari inclined his head at Raven, whose body had gone perfectly still. For several heartbeats, he didn't move. He just stared at Ari and Ari at him.

"Who are the Old Ones?" Surefire shook her hand to rattle the chain attached to the cuffs.

Raven broke from his trance, inhaled deeply, and dropped his eyes from Ari's.

Ari spoke first. "They're Raven's employers."

"Employers?" Surefire exclaimed. "Then I'm game. Bring in several birds in one fell swoop." She tugged on Raven's arm. "And if we recover most of the stolen artifacts, I'll make sure you get reduced time." And she'd challenge anyone to mention her past mistakes again.

Raven bowed his head and let out an exasperated breath. Ari started chortling, which is the only way Surefire could describe the wheezing, vibrating noise coming from his human mouth.

"What?" Surefire demanded.

"I'll let Raven field that one," Ari buzzed between breaths.

"They're immortals," Raven said. "They're the ones who came before everything we know. They're not subject to our rules. You can't just arrest them. Besides, I haven't seen them since the night at the pyramid. They don't travel in this world the normal way. I can't call or text them."

"We don't need them. We need the skull. Just slip into their world, take it, and slip back out," Ari said. "If you can pilfer a mummy from the British Museum, then you can steal anything."

"You were behind that heist?" Surefire asked. Three years ago, someone had stolen a mummy and several Egyptian artifacts from the British Museum. Mysteriously, the objects had turned up at the Egyptian Museum in Cairo a week later. No one in Egypt claimed responsibility, but no one was willing to return the artifacts either.

"It's not that easy and you know it." Raven disregarded Surefire's question.

"You hold their mark, and with it you can open the portal," Ari argued.

"No."

"I don't think you realize what you're saying." Ari gave a patronizing shake of his head.

"We cannot bring that skull into this world," Raven stated.

Surefire shifted her attention from one to the other, trying to make sense of everything she'd heard. If what Ari had said about the final skull was true, then it could stop Tezcatlipoca. But its very presence could end the world. Her logic rebelled against this idea. An ancient god trying to possess Ari, causing the world to end? Then she had Raven to consider. What exactly was he? And how was he involved in all this?

Apprehension gripped her chest. The more she dissected this curious conversation, the more she didn't want to go down this rabbit hole alone. She needed backup.

"I can call my boss, Pax," Surefire interjected, keeping her voice calm. Hoping they wouldn't suspect how nervous she'd grown. "Let me get U-Sec to help. With our resources, we can set this right."

"No," Ari boomed, and for the first time his voice sounded normal, human. "And let you put me away for good? I just confessed to murder. You're not going to let me off."

"I think saving the world is more important than you going to jail," Surefire countered.

"Have you ever been to jail?"

"Yes," Surefire replied, and Ari's expression reflected his shock at her answer. She felt Raven's eyes searching her masked face for an explanation she wasn't about to give.

"I'm sure where you stayed was a night at The Palms compared to where they'd send me."

Surefire thought about the common jail cell, communal toilet, mushy cot, and rather stout woman named Danger Dee, who'd kept sneering at Surefire and running her tongue over her one and only gold tooth.

"Probably." Surefire shrugged. "But isn't it worth it to save the world?"

"Frankly, it's not," Ari replied blandly.

"Then we're at an impasse," Raven said.

"Are we?" Ari looked amused. "Then I'll have to resort to the final plan and make you an offer you can't refuse."

"Next you'll tell us this is business, not personal." Raven sighed.

"It always is," Ari said.

"What are you talking about?" Surefire shot a scathing look at the screen.

"There is only one way out of this cave—through that door." A floodlight turned on at the other end of the cave, illuminating a solid stone carved door twice Surefire's height engraved with a large, leafy tree. The wall surrounding the door was smooth stone, not the rough cavern surface of the other sides.

"Hell, no," Raven exclaimed. "We're not doing this."

"I can't open it. The key is within you. If I could cut it out of you, I would. But we're wasting time. His power is spreading, and my hold is weakening. Tezcatlipoca becomes stronger with each passing day. Twenty-four hours from now, on the twentieth day, there will be a new moon. Then he'll be fully in our world, and the balance you've strived to maintain with your thefts will be for naught. And the world, as we know it, will end."

"I don't believe you. This is a setup," Raven said.

"I agree," Surefire added. "This isn't right. There are other ways."

Ari raised his one dark eyebrow. "If you don't believe me, maybe I can persuade you in another way."

"What?" Surefire and Raven asked in unison.

"Synthia St. John. Code name: Surefire." Ari regarded her, and Surefire couldn't stop her mouth from flopping open when he said her given name. "Vanessa St. John, mother, a former Olympic gymnast who teaches at a school in Owings Mills. A place not too far from her home in Westminster, which she shares with Stephen St. John, retired general, who has a contract with—"

"How do you—?" Surefire tried to interrupt but he continued speaking.

"Lockheed as a consultant and is the PM of U-Sec's contract with the Department of Defense. He and your boss, Pax, fought together in Afghanistan. Isn't this correct?"

Shock froze her tongue. How could he know this? The systems at U-Sec were supposed to be more secure than the Oval Office.

Ari carried on without waiting another beat. "Heather St. John, sister, gold medalist in the uneven bars and parallel bars; silver medalist in—"

Surefire's face heated with anger, which thawed her tongue enough to say, "Okay, you can stop."

"Floor routine—"

"Stop now."

"Wheaties model, CoverGirl model, spokesperson for The Humane Society—"

"Stop," Surefire said again, louder.

"Engaged to Hunter Thompson, starting quarterback for the Ravens. Resides on Light Street in a two-thousand-plus-square-foot condo overlooking the city."

"Shut up!" Surefire rushed at the screen, forgetting she was attached to Raven, and jerked backward when he didn't move. She shot him an irritated look before she tore off her mask, which had long before become too hot and constricting. She didn't need to hide her identity anymore. Ari knew everything about her, and this revelation was like a cold, dead weight pressing down on her gut.

"How do you know these things? The U-Sec systems are supposed to be secure. Our identities safe."

"Not secure enough, it would seem." Ari leaned forward so his face—human and otherwise—filled the screen. "My, how you look like your sister, yet not. There's something a little off."

Surefire scanned the top and sides of the TV screen, looking for the camera. She was going to smash it.

Raven shifted closer to her, but she kept her eyes on the screen. She didn't want to see him staring at her in appraisal and then eventual disappointment as so many others had done before, as Ari was doing now.

"Your eyes are oddly mismatched. And your nose, there's a slight bump above—"

"Enough," Raven spoke up.

Surefire noticed, with a start, he'd taken off his mask.

"Do you want me to point out your faults? Because if this is a competition, I'm betting you'll win," Raven said.

"And be here all night?" Ari laughed. "You're right, I digress." He settled into his chair. "Your family and your friends all dead, if not by my hand then by the god Tezcatlipoca's. Do you want that?"

Surefire could only respond by narrowing her eyes and wishing over and over again that she could kill with a thought.

"Well, your sister you'd probably be happy without."

"Enough already. We get the point," Raven said.

"Good, then I don't need to mention to you, James Stephanos, what you have to lose."

Stephanos? Surefire reeled around to face Raven. Was he Roachman's brother? She could see some similarities in their deep-set eyes—well, Ari's one human eye—and low, dark brows. However, Ari looked more like an old-school magician or maybe Dracula, with slicked-back dark hair that curled at his neck, high cheekbones, and a long, pompous nose. While Raven had black hair that fell in choppy waves to his ears and rugged features that belonged on the cover of an extreme sports magazine.

Raven lifted his hand as if to rub his face, then dropped it back down to his side.

"I don't know what you mean," Raven replied in a low, tight voice.

"Kat," Ari said with smug satisfaction. "She's what I mean."

Surefire watched Raven for any reaction. His clenched jaw was the only indication that Ari's words affected him.

"You always tried to protect her," Ari went on. "But I found her tucked away in a house on Crete. I know what you gave up so that Kat could have a normal life. It would be a shame if you lost her."

Ari and Raven stared at one another, neither speaking, neither blinking, neither moving a muscle. Surefire shifted away and crossed her arms. Only to remember again that Raven was cuffed to her wrist. She'd inadvertently brought his hand up to her chest. He broke his gaze with Ari and shot an unhappy look at the chain connecting them and his hand close to her breast. Surefire dropped her arm.

"I'll do it." Raven's cold tone prickled Surefire's skin. "But if that god doesn't kill you, I will."

Chapter Four

"Where's Matthews?"

Levi Paxton—known as Pax to everyone but his mom—stood in front of the ruins of the warehouse doors. On the other side, detectives and officers milled about the wrecked scene, chatting, collecting evidence, ignoring Pax. A few nonchalantly ducked behind a crumbled crate in the middle of the aisle.

Idiots.

He had lost his temper once outside the precinct, and now he was persona non grata. Of course, it didn't help that he had accidentally ripped the door off a squad car right after said temper loss.

Nothing different from snapping a pencil in frustration. Right?

Pax his jaw and tried again. This time he zeroed in on a skinny, bug-eyed officer lighting a smoke outside the doors.

"Where's Matthews?" he demanded.

The cigarette dropped from the startled man's stubby fingers. His eyes rolled back and forth like an animated dummy before settling on Pax's chest. He stepped back into the wall and bumped his head.

"Down there." He pointed a shaky finger past the ruined crate, never once meeting Pax's gaze.

If Pax didn't know better, he would think the man cowered away in disgust, not fear. As if Pax would infect him.

Infect him with what, Pax had no idea. But the man edged away, making a concerted effort not to touch him. Pax didn't know whether to feel angry or insulted, so he opted for angry. Always the more comforting emotion.

"Take a breath, Pax. Relax." Oracle, one of Pax's top agents, eased next to him. "Remember what Lily taught you."

He scowled at her. She retaliated with a dazzling white smile. Even though Oracle was blind, she could somehow sense his expressions and knew how to respond to set him straight.

Unable to stay angry when Oracle wielded her model-perfect smile, Pax took her advice and inhaled a deep breath through his nose and exhaled through his mouth like he had learned in Lily's yoga class.

A class he loathed, since he was as pliant as a rock. But it did teach him techniques to control his temper.

Oracle's smile widened, and she patted his arm. "There, much better."

"If you say so," he grumbled.

"Give me your hand, so I can see what's happening." She stood eye-to-eye with him, matching his six foot four height in the heels she wore. He preferred her in flats.

Pax took her slender fingers in his hand, and the mild shock she emitted twitched the muscles in his arm. Her pupilless and iris-less eyes swirled with the dull colors of the scene before shifting back to a grayish white.

"Thanks for the perspective." She turned back to him. "Now, will you behave?"

Pax shook his head, but said, "Yes."

She stared at him hard, as if she saw past his lie. "We'll find her, I promise."

Oracle repeated what she'd been telling Pax since they'd received the call that Surefire had gone missing. But her words felt empty, contrived. Surefire was his former commander's daughter. He had promised to keep her safe when she joined U-Sec. He had not only lost an agent but also broken a promise. He sure as hell didn't appreciate Oracle making promises she couldn't keep.

"Whatever you say," Pax said, unconvinced. When Matthews had first notified them about Surefire trailing Raven without backup, Pax had planned to ream her out, throw U-Sec's handbook at her, demote her. Then came the call that she had disappeared, and the night's agenda went from disciplining an overly eager agent to finding a missing agent—or possibly worse.

"Let's talk to Detective Matthews, shall we? And then we'll render judgment." Oracle stepped through the crumbled doors and into the warehouse.

Pax trailed behind her, watching as she breezed through the warehouse as if she could see as clear as anyone else. She tilted her head, honing in on voices to guide her down aisles lined by large crates. A few times she grazed the hand of an officer to get an image flash of the area from his or her perspective. She used these images to guide her like a light flicking on and off in a pitch-black room.

Most stopped their conversations and stared openly at her tall, lean figure striding by, her black hair flowing straight and smooth down her back and her eyes like gray-white marbles against her dark skin. A few whispered derogatory transhuman remarks as she passed, not realizing that Pax trailed behind her. He bumped these jokers out of his way, even if they weren't technically in his way.

"Oracle." Matthews greeted her from where he crouched on the ground. He set down the stone statue he held in his gloved hands.

"Detective Matthews, nice to see you again," Oracle replied, and they shared a smiled at her joke.

Since when had they become so chummy? Pax cleared his throat, and Matthews tore his gaze away from Oracle. His smile disappeared as he turned to Pax and put out his hand. "Hey, Pax."

"Where's Surefire?" He ignored Matthews's outstretched hand.

Matthews plowed his disregarded hand through his reddish mop of hair.

"She's gone. I don't know where. As I told you on the phone, she called to report that Raven had robbed the Walters Art Museum." He nodded toward the statue on the floor. "But we missed her call and got here too late."

"How, again, did this happen?" Pax inquired, holding back his frustration with great effort. "That part is still unclear."

"We don't know," Matthews replied. "It's under investigation. But, apparently, Surefire's calls were routed to another officer in a different department. We only learned of these calls because a sergeant overheard this officer talking on the phone about Raven's case and became suspicious."

"The officer went missing before we could interrogate him. So we retrieved his phone messages and found several from Surefire," Matthews continued. "We traced her cell to this location and soon after received a 911 call from a security guard who spotted someone breaking into this building."

Pax considered how an officer from another department could have received Surefire's call. Matthews was the detective in charge of transhuman cases. All U-Sec calls automatically routed through his department. If a call got transferred to another officer, then there was flaw in their system.

"What happened to those doors?" Pax motioned toward the front of the warehouse.

"All entrances to the warehouse were chained from the inside."

Pax's brows shot up.

"Suspicious, I know." Matthews nodded. "The night watchman had no idea why. It isn't their standard procedure to chain doors. Not to mention, there was no way back out, except through the windows after the doors were chained. So we forced our way in, using a Mack truck that was parked outside. After the earthquake hit, we had no other choice."

"Earthquake?" Oracle exclaimed.

Pax looked over his shoulder at the smashed cargo container in the center of the aisle. Then he noticed a few policemen squatting over a crack that ran across the floor under their feet. Had an earthquake caused that? He hadn't heard anything on the news about an earthquake hitting the city.

"Yeah, I know." Matthews lowered his voice and leaned close to Oracle, touching her hand. "No one believes us, because it didn't hit anywhere else but here. Though, trust me, the ground shook twice. Several seconds each time.

The quakes were about five or so minutes apart. After the second one, we lost a lock on Surefire's cell signal, which is why we busted open the door."

"Interesting." Oracle knelt down and ran her fingertips over the cracked surface.

"When we entered the building, they were both gone. We found the stolen statue in a sack by this crate. And a U-Sec–issued stun gun on the floor. But no Raven and no Surefire. It's like the earth swallowed them."

"Maybe it did," Oracle said. "I need to see if I can find her."

"Is that a good idea?" Matthews asked before Pax could.

"We have to start somewhere." She closed her eyes, and Pax knew she was dropping her telepathic shields to seek out Surefire's thought patterns. Rarely did she do it, especially in crowded environments. It could be too overwhelming with so many people—and errant thoughts—in close proximity.

He moved to stand behind Oracle when her body wavered, but Matthews beat him to it. Oracle sunk back against Matthews's arms.

Pax tensed and looked away, annoyed with himself for having such a petty feeling as jealousy with Surefire missing or even dead. Years ago, he had ended his affair with Oracle. He didn't need a relationship clouding his judgment, distracting him from his job.

But it didn't hurt any less to see another man supporting her.

Oracle groaned. Her eyes flew open.

Pax shoved Matthews away and grabbed her.

"I can't sense her." Oracle tried to stand. Her legs wobbled, and she fell against Pax.

"I was hoping you wouldn't say that," Matthews muttered.

Oracle shivered in Pax's arms. Her toffee skin turned an ashen brown. Her glossy lips paled.

Pax squeezed her to his chest. He whispered her given name. "Cassandra, what's wrong?"

Her face contorted. She lifted her hands and dug her nails into her scalp as if fighting off a sudden migraine.

"There's something else here. Below us." Her voice came out hoarse. "Something dark. Cold. Empty." She shuddered and buried her face in Pax's shoulder.

"What's underneath us?" Pax craned his head to where Matthews stood behind them, keeping his distance.

"According to city records, there's nothing underneath the building. Not even a sewer line. Should be solid."

"It's bad, Pax. I've never felt—" Oracle's teeth clenched in pain, cutting off her words.

Pax scooped up Oracle, who was too weak to protest.

"Something's down there," Pax said. "Get a drill in here. I don't care what it takes. I want to know what's there, and I want to find Surefire. It's the least your department can do, considering how you fucked up."

Pax charged toward the exit with Oracle fading fast in his arms.

♥ ☠ ♥ ☠ ♥ ☠

"You'll kill me?" Ari looked amused, too amused. In fact, he seemed to have a hard time containing the ugly half-grin that spread across his human face. Not exactly the reaction Raven had wanted.

Ari wheezed out a laugh. "Oh, you'll have—"

The screen's picture wavered and zigzagged. Ari's mouth clamped shut. He sat rigidly in his chair and stared straight ahead as if in a trance.

Seconds later, the screen returned to normal. Ari frowned and twisted his head. His human eye darted up and down as if looking for something. Then Raven felt the lightest nudge. Not on his body but in his mind. In his soul.

"Seems there's a disturbance in the force," Raven commented. Whatever magic Ari had used to trap him and Surefire still surrounded them. An invisible dome sucking lightly at Raven's powers like a metaphysical mosquito. But someone or something had tried to poke a hole through it. He was betting a U-Sec agent was behind it.

Surefire narrowed her eyes. "What's going on? What just happened?"

"I think someone at U-Sec is trying to find you," Raven explained.

"Oracle," Surefire said softly.

"I can assure you, she won't be doing *that* again," Ari said.

Surefire rushed at the monitor, catching Raven off-guard and jerking him alongside her. She slammed her palms on either side of Ari's image. The picture wavered again. Raven grabbed her arm with his un-cuffed hand to stop her from hitting it again, afraid she would crack the screen and cut herself.

"Get off me." She twisted out of his grip and whirled back toward Ari's face. "What did you do to her?"

"The same thing I'll do to whoever stands in our way," Ari replied.

"You son of a bitch," Surefire spat. "She better not be hurt."

"I would worry less about Oracle and more about yourself right now. Within minutes, this cavern will fill with water from the harbor. I suggest you try the door as soon as possible. Otherwise . . ." He lifted his human shoulder. "I doubt your abilities include breathing underwater."

"You have twenty-four hours to deliver the skull before the new moon. When you retrieve the skull, you'll know how to find me."

The television shut off, along with the lights, except for the one illuminating the door.

"You all right?" Raven asked when Surefire remained frozen in place, seething at the blank screen.

"Fine." She tore herself away from the screen to look at him. "What's the plan?"

"We go through the door."

Something crawled over his foot, followed by a few more somethings. Raven fought the bile inching up in his throat.

"Roaches." Surefire moved her foot back and forth, kicking them away. A few of their bodies cracked as they hit the wall.

Then something bigger ran over Raven's foot.

"Rats." Surefire stumbled into him.

Rats, he could handle. However, the lot of them streaming across the cavern floor and into the crevices meant only one thing.

He felt it before he saw it. A trickle of water coursed under and around his foot. He pulled Surefire over to the door. She stumbled behind him trying to match his long stride. He forgot she stood barely to the height of his shoulders.

"I need these cuffs off."

"They stay," she replied and tripped once more. He grabbed her arm to steady her and again she twisted out of his grasp.

"I can't do this with the handcuffs on," he stated.

"Do what?"

"Open the door."

"I'm assuming this doesn't open like a normal door."

"You don't see a doorknob, do you?"

"No." She leaned close to the door. Her eyes followed the lines of the engraving.

The sound of rushing water filled the cavern. Small rivulets of water soon turned into shallow streams.

"How do you open it?" she asked.

"Unlock the cuffs and you'll see."

She looked at him with unabashed skepticism. "No."

"You won't trust me on this?"

"I don't trust you, period. For years, you've knocked off museums across the world. You've incapacitated a U-Sec agent and caused another to lose control. So I'm going to err on the side of intuition and history."

"Have it your way." He trudged to the side of the door, to the cavern wall. Surefire struggled to keep up. He picked up a large rock and flattened his hand against the wall.

"What are you doing?"

"Since I lost my ability to phase out, I need to break my hand to get out of these cuffs."

"You wouldn't."

He met and held her eyes, so she would see his sincerity. Then he turned to his hand, hers dangling underneath. His fingers splayed over the cool stone with his palm pressed hard against the gritty surface. It was going to hurt, bad. His natural instinct for self-preservation was the only thing holding him back. Bad time to lose his phasing ability.

Water splashed around his ankles and submerged his feet. He pulled back his right hand and looked the other way.

"Wait!" Surefire jerked her cuffed hand down, though she only succeeded in moving his hand a centimeter at best.

She reached up and pressed her thumb against a small black circle in the bottom of her cuff. Immediately, he heard a click, and the cuffs released both their wrists. She hooked them back onto her belt.

"You're insane," she said.

"It would've healed."

She shivered, her face contorted in disgust.

"Can you get us out of here?" She stepped in front of the door.

He tapped Surefire's shoulder to edge her back. She shot him a don't-touch-me-glare before crossing her arms and inching away.

Really? Did she have to keep pulling away from him as if he was infected with Ebola?

He scanned the mammoth door. It was about ten feet high, made of solid grey stone polished to the smooth sheen of a marble floor. A carving of a leafy tree, like an ancient oak, extended from the base to the top of the door. He counted five obsidian spikes protruding from the tree: three dotting the center of its thick trunk and two slightly higher within the branches. They reminded Raven of tips from giant sharpened pencils. As he inspected the spikes, he noted their placement in comparison to his body. One aimed at his gut, another at his heart, and the last between his eyes. If he stretched out his arms to mirror the tree, he could smack the remaining two with his palms. The spikes' points were hollow, forming large needles set to drain blood.

His blood.

Dread slid up his spine. He wished he didn't need to do this, but a sacrifice was always required to enter the other realm. He just hoped his sacrifice was enough to let Surefire through the door as well.

Water surged up around his knees.

"Can you open it?" Surefire shot a panicked look back at the cave and then at the water sloshing around her thighs.

"Yeah, but I'm not sure if you can make it. I've never done it this way. The last time I crossed over, I died."

She pulled back. "Died?"

"I'm hoping it won't be the case for you."

"There's got to be another way." She squinted into the pitch-black cave and back up the wall, as if searching for a foothold to scale the cavern's surface. But there was no way out, only solid walls and a ceiling surrounding them.

He wanted to say something to comfort her, to make her believe that everything would be fine. But he had never been good at giving false hope.

"This is it." He threw up his hands.

She stared down at the water rushing around her, climbing higher to encircle her waist. She inhaled a long breath and when she looked up at him with her mismatched eyes, he was amazed at her composure. Her lips, though pale, were set tight across her teeth.

"Whatever happens, happens. Let's get this over with."

He nodded and faced the door. He spread out his arms and allowed the points of the two farthest spikes to pierce his palms. Another pierced the center of his torso.

He cried out. Acid coursed through his veins. He fought the urge to pull away. Three spikes inserted. Two more to go. One pressed between his eyebrows and the other stuck into his chest at the heart, cutting through his shirt and into his skin.

Icy water now encircled his waist, and he knew without turning that it almost covered Surefire's chest.

"Push me," he said between gritted teeth.

"I can't," she protested.

The water surged several more inches. Surefire sputtered then coughed.

"Fine, I'll do it. Where should I push?"

"My back." He forced himself to speak through the pain. "And head."

He felt one hand against his lower back, now submerged underwater, and another brace against his head.

"Push," he yelled.

She cursed, and he felt her cringe. Then she slammed her body into his, shoving with all her strength. The world became blindingly white before it went black.

Chapter Five

Ari watched Raven and Surefire disappear into the stone door.

"They made it." He closed his laptop.

"Excellent," a voice boomed inside his head, vibrating downward and spreading throughout his bones.

Ari sat back in his chair, satisfied that everything had fallen into place. His theatrical production had taken months to set up below Raven's stash of stolen goodies, but it had been worth it. Ari wanted Raven to understand he had the resources and power to move the earth itself to get what he wanted. Sacrificing a plasma screen and staging those lights in the cavern had been a bit much, he knew. However, the grander the stage, the greater the awe of the audience— and the more distracted they are from what is really behind the magic.

Deception is an essential tool of any performer.

Ari leaned farther back in his chair, set in a dilapidated office building across the street from the warehouse Raven and Surefire had just left. The back of his head skimmed the red curtain hiding the broken desks and overturned chairs in the abandoned, dust-encrusted room.

With his human hand, he tugged on a leather cord strung around his neck until a shiny obsidian stone hanging behind his back flipped forward onto his chest and burned against his skin. Clutching the heated pendant, he screwed his eyes shut, and an image took shape behind his lids. It first appeared as dark grey smoke, then slowly solidified into a white skull with metal orbs for eyeballs and a band of turquoise painted around its eyes and mouth.

"May I get my body back now?" Ari asked aloud to the empty room.

"Soon." Again, the deep voice originated from inside Ari's mind and caused ripples of energy to blanket his limbs.

Bronze skin formed over the skull but couldn't quite cover the nose or forehead. Lips partially formed over menacing white teeth that ground together in frustration.

"Will the woman cooperate?" the voice asked.

"I don't know."

"Then we will need to make certain. What does she fear most?"

Ari let go of the pendant and opened his eyes. He leaned over and picked up Surefire's missing uniform from the floor next to his feet. It still had the dry cleaner's tags stapled to its collar. He grasped the cloth and let go of his mind, his body, his spirit. Gave himself over to the dark power. Smoke poured from the pendant and coated his body. The stench of sulfur mixed with moist dirt assaulted his nose. He arched forward and snapped his teeth together to keep from crying out, but it didn't help. Powerful energy like a thousand little static shocks picked their way over Ari's skin. He wailed in pain as his body reformed from a roach into something entirely different.

Chapter Six

"Ugh!"

Surefire landed on Raven's back after they fell through the door.

She pushed herself off him, and her butt plopped onto thick, soft grass. Her head spun and pounded and the world became a kaleidoscope of earthen hues. Orange, green, brown, and red swirled together into a child's finger painting.

Falling back onto strange feathery grass, she closed her eyes and rubbed her temples. Nausea overwhelmed her. What did her old gymnastics coach say when she felt sick before competition? She tried to remember, but her memory was foggy and her mind remained unfocused.

She took a deep breath. Pleasant scents of jasmine and lavender infused the air. The queasiness in her stomach dissipated.

"Focus," she said out loud, reassured by the sound of her voice.

She eased up and leaned forward with her head between her knees, which were surprisingly dry, as was her leotard. She wiggled her toes. Her shoes were dry, too, as if she hadn't waded in chest-high water moments ago.

"Breathe in and out. In and out."

The dizziness subsided. She opened one eye. When the earth remained stationary, she opened the other.

"Oh my God," she gasped.

They were in a clearing, a perfect green circle in the middle of a dense forest. Flowers grew on the periphery. Tulips larger than water pitchers. Irises with stalks taller than her. Bright flowers of yellow, red, and orange. Dainty white buds dotted vines like pearl buttons. Above her, the sky melted into various shades of yellow, orange, violet, and a dark purplish-blue much like the color of a certain someone's eyes.

"Raven." Surefire had forgotten he was lying next to her. She reached over and tapped his back. "Are you okay?"

He didn't respond. In fact, his skin was cold.

Dread twisted her stomach. He couldn't be dead. But after what she had witnessed in the cavern, she didn't know how he could be alive. She reached across his back and grabbed the edge of his torso to roll him over, but she couldn't budge him. Scooting back, she wedged her feet under his chest and shoved until he flopped onto his back.

"Raven, wake up." She ran a finger along his jaw, then gave it a little slap.

No response.

She leaned closer and hesitated with her hand just above his face. Lightly, she traced the spot between his eyes where she knew a stake had pierced, but the skin held no laceration. No scab or scar was visible. She grabbed his hands, and his palms were unblemished, without even a callus.

"What *are* you?"

Her eyes trailed lower to the two holes in his shirt where the spikes had torn through and into his chest and abdomen. She peered up at his face to see if he was awake, then she poked her finger through one of the holes and felt the smooth flesh underneath. Again, no blood, no wound.

Was this a trick?

A loud grunt made her jump, and she scurried backward. The sound resonated again from Raven's chest, and then he began snoring.

"On edge much?" A nervous laugh escaped her lips.

At least he was alive. And hearing him snore humanized him, even after he had used his body as a human meat skewer to open the door. Speaking of which . . .

Surefire glanced around. Where was the door? More importantly, how would they get back?

She let out a long, exasperated sigh. No amount of U-Sec training had prepared her for this. Whatever this was. Wherever she was. Was she still on Earth?

She had to find a way to contact U-Sec and let them know what had happened—and that Ari had compromised U-Sec's database, that none of them were safe. But could she let them know without tipping Ari off? And would he make good on his threat? She'd never been threatened with death before, never had her family threatened by a crazy half-roach man. That chapter had been left out of the U-Sec handbook.

She threaded her fingers between blades of grass as green as a professional golf course but softer and plusher like faux fur. Her nails dug deeper into moist dirt. She broke off a piece of grass and twirled it between her thumb and index finger. It looked like normal grass.

But it wasn't. Everything here appeared real, appeared the norm. The scene was perfect, yet off. Maybe it was too perfect.

There is no such thing as being too perfect. Her father's words floated through her mind. He'd probably love it here.

Surefire snorted at the thought. Then she stood and flexed her arms and legs. Her previous vertigo and nausea were gone. She felt rejuvenated, as if she'd woken from an afternoon nap. No rib pain. No soreness. No bruises. The Happy Pills should begin wearing off by now. She kicked her right leg back and forth, stretching out her knee. It still stuck a little but felt better than it had in years.

She was relieved some discomfort remained. She preferred the physical reminders of her past mistakes.

Her eyes landed on Raven, who continued to sleep soundly and snore loudly. A few pieces of ebony hair fell across his brow when his head rolled to the side. Dark stubble lined his cheeks, his chin, and around his lips, which even in sleep held a hint of his obnoxious smirk. He was definitely good looking. Rugged, with a boyish charm mixed in.

Boyish charm?

She checked herself. About as charming as an eel and just as slippery. Besides, there wasn't anything boyish about him.

When she noticed the bump on his nose, she lifted her hand and rubbed her own. Though she doubted his was caused by a fall off a balance beam. More likely he had been on the wrong end of a fist.

Her eyes lowered to a strip of colorful flesh just above his pants. His shirt had lifted to reveal patterns of blacks, reds, yellows, and blues over the lean muscles of his lower stomach. She bent over him and peered more closely. Tattoos. Loads of them from what she could tell. She reached out to lift his shirt higher and see what the designs formed underneath.

Her fingers skimmed the edge of his black spandex shirt. Her pulse quickened.

She stopped, wrenching herself away.

What am I doing?

It would be inappropriate if he awoke and caught her peeking at his abs, especially since she was an agent sent to capture him. She really needed to date more if this guy got her leotard in a bunch. Not that anything was particularly bunching now, but he did keep her off balance in a weird fluttering-in-the-stomach sort of way. She didn't know what it meant, and she didn't care to find out.

Snap. Crack.

Surefire spun around and peered into the thick foliage to pinpoint the sound.

She eased toward the border of the clearing. Again she heard the same sound, followed by a rustling noise. Instinctively, her hand reached down for the gun on her belt. It was gone. She had tossed it away in the warehouse.

She crept closer to the trees and lifted her left arm. Maybe her rappelling gun still worked. She could scare away whatever it was with a hook in its eye.

Over her thudding heart, she began to hear a murmuring sound but couldn't pinpoint it. The noise increased with her every step forward. Soon it became a loud vibrating hum like a huge generator. Then she realized how silent the forest had been before she'd heard the sound. Not even a bird singing or a bug buzzing.

Several branches pitched forward. A tree reached out for her. The humming stopped, replaced by the snapping and creaking of branches.

Surefire depressed the release button in her palm. Nothing came out. The tree pitched forward more steeply. Skeletal mossy arms reached out to her.

Surefire sprinted back to Raven and dove onto the ground by his side.

"Wake up!" She slapped him.

♥ ☠ ♥ ☠ ♥ ☠

Wake up. Wake up. Wake up.

Raven heard a voice call out, echoing down from the top of a bridge while he floated in the cool waters far below it.

"James . . . Raven . . . whoever you are." The voice became stronger, higher pitched. "Are you okay? Answer me."

Was he okay? He wasn't sure. He was still floating just out of reach of the voice, and it felt nice, too nice. No pain. No worries. No problems. Just peaceful bliss.

A slap across his face.

What the—?

Another slap.

Pain brought him careening back into reality. He opened his eyes to find Surefire reaching back to strike again.

His hand shot up to clamp around her wrist before it swooped down again.

"Enough. I'm awake."

"About time." She tugged her wrist out of his grip.

He tried to sit up, but his head throbbed and the world spun around him. He needed to take it slow. He closed his eyes and reclined back onto the ground.

He pinched the bridge of his nose then depressed it with his thumb. There was no hole, no bleeding. Didn't he remember a spike piercing his skull?

He felt lower, over his chest and his abdomen. Nothing. No wounds and no pain. He cracked open his eyes and stared at his palms. Not even a scratch. He opened his eyes wider and saw Surefire kneeling next to him, looking exasperated.

"Where are we?" she demanded.

"How should I know? I've been unconscious." He squinted at her and propped himself up onto his elbows. "How long have I been out?"

"I don't know," she blurted in a disgusted tone, though he could've sworn her words carried a drop of worry. "My watch stopped."

He settled back on what he realized was cushiony grass. Quite comfortable. He closed his eyes again. Taking another snooze wouldn't be so bad. He felt drained.

Of course, it could be that five spikes had just drained his blood.

Surefire poked at his shoulder, and he opened one eye. Maybe now was not the time to catch up on his beauty sleep.

"We need to go." She shot a nervous glance around them.

"What's wrong?" He sat up again, this time more carefully. "What do you see?"

"I'm not sure. The trees seemed to move."

"The trees actually moved?"

"Well," Surefire hesitated. "I don't know. Maybe not. Maybe an animal was on the branches and it just looked like . . . Oh, forget it. But I did hear something."

A loud rustle came from the carpet of dry leaves in the brush. They both turned toward the sound.

"That's what I heard, and it's getting closer."

Surefire jumped to her feet. Raven sprang to his, then regretted the sudden move. The world spun and teetered like a vomit-inducing carnival ride. He leaned forward with his hands on his thighs.

"You okay?"

"Stood up too quickly." Raven took a long, deep breath. A lavender scent greeted him, and within moments his dizziness subsided and his vision cleared. He rose again to his full height and stretched, feeling refreshed.

"I'm good now."

Surefire nodded in response, but continued to eye him as if she didn't believe him. And he didn't blame her. If he'd seen someone get stabbed in the torso and head and survive, he'd be suspicious as well.

He looked around and saw they were in a perfect circle of Crayola green grass surrounded by what appeared to be a dense, dark forest. He didn't recognize the clearing. He did, however, recognize the forest. Except it wasn't a typical forest but one formed by shoots off an ancient, overgrown banyan tree. He looked through a circular hole in the branches above, which narrowed like a cone to a sky streaked with red, orange, and hints of dark blue, creating the perfect sunset. But this was a trick as well. They were underground. Inside the earth where the sun never shone.

"How did we get here?"

"We landed here," she replied.

He gave her a puzzled look.

She raised her hands, palms up. "As soon as I pushed your back and head into the spikes." Her face pinched, and she shuddered. "The door was consumed by this blinding light. Before I knew it, we dropped into this clearing."

"Dropped?"

"More like, we fell flat on our faces."

"Sorry I missed the show." He looked behind them at several rooted trunks snaked with vines and small, white flowers.

Surefire crossed her arms. "Now, tell me. Where are we?"

"We're where the Old Ones reside."

"Your employers?"

"That's one way to put it. But I'm not paid in the conventional sense."

"Okay, so how do we find the skull?"

"I'm not sure."

"What do you mean you're not sure?"

Raven shrugged. "Ari said I could find the skull here, and as far as I could tell, going through that door was our only way out."

"Out?" Surefire huffed. "We got out all right, and now we're in . . ."

Her two-toned eyes darted around the clearing as if searching for a clue to where they were. Finally, she flipped up her hands.

"What is this place? A forest? An alternate dimension? Heaven? Hell?"

He bobbed his head. "Depending on how you view it, all the above. But it could be worse."

"How's that?"

"You could be dead."

She raised her eyebrows and pointed a finger at his chest

"How do you know I'm not? Didn't you have to die to get into this place the first time?"

He grabbed her finger and gathered her hand in his. Surprisingly, she didn't resist as he placed her palm against his chest. He watched her face for a reaction. At first she pressed harder. Then she squinted, and her mouth puckered in disbelief. Next she pressed her ear against his chest. Her dark blond hair fell forward and veiled her face.

He breathed in, and underneath the fishy scent of harbor water clinging to her leotard, he smelled light floral powder along with a hint of sweet berry. He breathed deeper, his arms lifting around her.

Wait! What the hell was he doing?

He nudged her away, uncomfortable with her closeness. Or maybe he just felt too comfortable. He was having trouble thinking.

Man, he was off his game if this sprout of a woman caused him to squirm. He relished making women feel embarrassed with his teasing remarks and innuendos. He relished being in control. But he didn't relish this strange gooey longing she aroused in him.

It wasn't natural. Or maybe it was, and that's why it felt so weird.

"Unbelievable. You have no heartbeat."

He edged further away. "Now feel for your heart."

She hesitated.

"I'm happy to do it, if you like," he said, half-jokingly.

She blushed and stepped back.

Good. Now she *squirmed.*

"No, I'm fine." She put out her hands. "Just keep your hands to yourself."

"No huggin' and no kissin'. Got it." He winked.

"I can feel it pounding without touching it." Though her hand did graze over her chest as if to reassure herself.

When he saw her face redden from his teasing, he couldn't resist provoking her more. "Got you all excited being so close to me."

"If my heart's thumping, it has nothing to do with you. But how is it possible that you don't have a heartbeat?"

"Like I said, I'm dead. I'm an ex-human."

"But how?"

"The Old Ones keep me alive."

She studied him, confusion clouding her face.

"Their spirit." He gave his shirt an irritated tug, which widened the rips where the spikes had gone through it.

She tilted her head and knitted her brow.

"Their powers are keeping me alive. Their energy is what fuels my body, makes my blood flow, gives me my abilities." The more he told her, the more it bugged him. He wasn't sure why. Maybe explaining it to her reminded him how far from human he had become, how different he was from her.

He hadn't discussed his situation with anyone except for Kat.

Surefire's arms tightened around her chest. "Who are the Old Ones?"

"You'll see soon enough." He started walking into the woods, then turned back to find her staring at him with an odd look. "I need you to take my hand and stick close. Don't touch anything in this forest."

He offered his hand to her. She hesitated and pulled away as if suddenly afraid to touch him. Reaching out, he snatched her hand and dragged her forward.

"Hey!" She stumbled, falling against his arm.

His grip tightened, and he trudged forward despite her protests. Branches hung so low they had to move in a crouch for several feet at a time. One nicked the top of Raven's head. As they travelled deeper, he heard a moan, followed by a low groan, and knew without turning that the sound hadn't come from Surefire. It came from one of the trunks.

Vines drooped down like withered, dead snakes. The branches and vines above crisscrossed so thickly they blotted out the sky, but some light filtered through at points, allowing them to see.

He glanced back at Surefire. She was looking back and forth from trunk to trunk with a dazed expression. He knew what caused her puzzlement. The farther they ventured, the louder the voices. Some were shouting. Others were singing. A few echoed with children's laughter. Then one trunk vibrated with a growl that wasn't from any animal alive on Earth today.

Raven quickened their pace. A face peered out from the center of the aged wood, and Surefire gasped. He slowed down so she could catch her breath, then he started forward again even more quickly.

"I can't—" She sidestepped a root then rubbed her right knee. "I can't keep up. You're going too fast."

He stopped suddenly, and momentum carried her into him. He put his hands on either side of her shoulders and moved her back.

The scent of grass and sweet fragrances of flowers mixed with moist bark and dried leaves nearly overwhelmed him. The air was so fresh it made him lightheaded. He'd been living in the city far too long. It would take time to get used to clean, pure air.

"I keep seeing things, hearing voices. Tell me I'm not going crazy." Her words came out between raspy breaths.

"You're not crazy. You're surrounded by portals. You're hearing voices from the past."

"You mean these trunks can take you back in time?"

She walked over to the one closest to them. Shouts, screams, a guitar tuning resounded from it. She put out her hand, mesmerized. A face materialized. A face of a crying woman. Raven grabbed her hand and stopped it just inches from touching the bark.

"If you slip through one of these portals, you may never return."

She jerked back.

"If this is where the Old Ones reside, where exactly are we on a map, metaphysically speaking?"

"We're inside the Earth. Where life began. And what you see all around us is the Tree of Life." He swept out his arms.

"Tree of Life? As in the Garden of Eden?"

"That's one version." He lowered his arms and shrugged. "There are several. I'll be happy to explain everything to you later. But we need to get out of here."

Shouts, explosions, and machine gun fire came from a trunk at Surefire's right. She whirled around toward the sounds. Above her a branch cracked and fell loose, whipping down at her.

"Watch out!" Raven yelled, but he was too late. The thick branch smacked Surefire in the back and sent her careening into the trunk, which opened like a sideways mouth and swallowed her with one gulp.

"It's never easy, is it?" Raven uttered. He grabbed a vine, tied it around his waist, and dove in after her.

Chapter Seven

"For the third and final time, I am fine." Oracle pursed her lips and shot Pax her I-dare-you-to-say-another-word-about-this look.

"All right, I won't ask again." He lifted his hands in resignation.

"Good." She unscrewed the cap on her bottled water.

"I'm just concerned," he added, if only to have the last word.

She sighed, long and deep.

Pax knew her tough-girl stance was an act. Despite her assertions, she wasn't one-hundred percent. Her skin still carried an ashen tint, and her hand quivered when she lifted the bottle to her lips and took an abnormally long drink of water, almost downing it in one gulp.

After her collapse in the warehouse, Pax had carried her to his truck and then raced down the road to the hospital. The farther he had driven, the more lucid she had become until she had insisted that they return to the scene. He had argued with her, but she'd held firm, and being too worn out from this whole disaster of a night, he ultimately had given in.

So an hour later, Pax continued to keep a watchful eye on Oracle as the warehouse employees moved half the crates outside. They planned to drill into the concrete floor. The warehouse and shipping managers were not happy. But when a life is at stake, there's no time to ask permission. Not to mention that the shipping company was now under investigation. Several pieces from Raven's local museum heists had been found crated and hidden within shipments that contained legal exports. It was in the company's best interest to cooperate.

The loud grinding of the drill filled the warehouse. Oracle placed her hand on Pax's arm to see the production through his eyes. They finally got another lock on Surefire's cell, and the tracking signal indicated she was below them. Pax could guess by Oracle's rigid posture and the tight set of her jaw that she took Surefire's disappearance personally.

She was Surefire's mentor and U-Sec contact. However, it wasn't Oracle's fault that Surefire had never called her for backup. In fact, Surefire hadn't contacted the U-Sec offices at all. Protocol dictated an agent contact U-Sec along with Matthews's squad before shadowing a target. But the U-Sec switchboard hadn't logged any calls from her. The oddness wasn't lost on Pax. Although Surefire could be impulsive at times, displaying her father's drive, she always followed the rules. He wondered if U-Sec had been compromised along with the police. An issue he planned to deal with as soon as they found her.

From Surefire's last phone message to the police and the security guard's 911 call, they estimated she had entered the warehouse at approximately midnight. About twenty minutes later, the police had arrived, just before the mysterious earthquake had struck and Surefire and Raven went missing.

Now it was three in the morning. It had taken time to move the crates and call in a few late-night favors. But there was still hope they could save Surefire if she was trapped underneath.

"Let me try searching for her again," Oracle shouted over the drill's loud shrieking.

"No." Pax couldn't risk Oracle dropping her shields again. Whatever negative force she had tapped into could still be there.

"But . . . "

"No." Pax stood firm. "I'm not risking another agent's life. You promised you wouldn't do it again. That's the only reason you're here now."

Oracle turned away from Pax and didn't force the point anymore. Score one for him.

The drill's grinding stopped about five feet down. A gush of water sprayed up.

"Pull out!" A man with a hardhat waved his hands at the woman operating the drill.

She tugged on several levers, and the drill reversed out. When it was clear, a fountain of water flowed from the hole and flooded over the floor. Police and FBI agents, who had recently arrived on the scene, scampered outside. The warehouse managers offered a few choice curse words and yelled for those operating forklifts to move the rest of the crates out of the way. The workforce manning the drill searched for something to divert the water to the harbor outside.

Every muscle in Pax's body tensed, fed by the realization of what he had just witnessed. "She's dead, isn't she?"

"We don't know for certain," Oracle replied in a soothing tone, losing the previous edge to her voice, as if she could temper Pax's anxiety by swallowing her own fear. She placed a gentle arm on his shoulder to bring him into a hug.

He pushed away from her and trudged through the rushing water to where several policemen stood with the manager of the drilling company, whom Pax had met earlier.

"I want someone down there now," Pax ordered.

They stared at him as if he had sprouted a second head.

"In there?" The manager jerked his thumb toward the child-sized hole, which continued to spurt water.

"Yeah, down there."

"Once we get this water pumped out, we can see what we got underneath. But I ain't making any promises."

"I didn't expect any." Pax glared at him until he got the hint and excused himself to call in another team to help.

"Pax," Oracle shouted to him from across the room.

He turned to find Matthews standing next to her with his hand resting on her bare arm.

"Pax!" she yelled louder and waved him over.

He ignored her and stalked out of the warehouse. His soaked tennis shoes squished with every angry step. He had no desire to talk with Matthews or Oracle or anyone for that matter. He wanted to be alone.

A stiff, chilly wind blew across his shorn head and exposed neck as he strode outside to the docks. His skin prickled in response. He shoved his hands into the pockets of his jeans.

Goddamn climate change. How could it be thirty-odd degrees in the middle of May? He tried to focus his mind on something as benign as the weather so he wouldn't think about what they'd find in the water underneath the warehouse floor. Nearing the edge of the dock, he coughed, assaulted by the smell of slightly salty water and dead fish along with a few drowned rats. He absently touched his back pocket, looking for his pack of cigarettes. A habit he'd given up years before, which always resurfaced in tough times. Instead he pulled out a pack of cinnamon gum and prayed that Surefire was still alive.

♥ ☠ ♥ ☠ ♥ ☠

What just happened?

One minute Surefire was staring at a tree trunk that somehow emitted gunshots. The next, she was in a total free fall into pitch-black nothingness—and she'd believed this night couldn't get any worse.

Wind blasted past her ears, whipping against her skin and through her hair. The sounds of gunfire and explosions grew louder the longer she fell. But still she saw nothing but total blackness. Then she heard shouts and men screaming and she smelled an acrid scent: burning wood, oil, and the ocean mixed with a disgusting odor of sulfur that made her gag. Next, a pinprick of light cut through the darkness in front of her.

"Hold on!" someone shouted. Were they behind or in front of her?

"I'm almost there," the disembodied voice called out again.

She couldn't turn far enough around to look behind her. She could only remain squinting, looking forward at the ever-expanding light, which had grown to the size of a flashlight beam.

"Gotcha." A strong arm wrapped around her waist. She jerked to a stop and her head bounced back and hit something soft.

"Ow. That was my nose."

"Raven?"

"Yeah." He sniffed. His hand rubbed what she assumed was his nose near the back of her head.

She raised her voice over the wind roaring past them and the gunshots resounding below. "What happened?"

Raven's arm tightened around her waist, pulling her against his body as they dangled in the noisy darkness. "You fell into the trunk."

"I was pushed." She tried to turn to see him but only succeeded in spinning them around on the line.

"Don't look at me. A tree branch did it," he said next to her ear.

"A branch?" Then she remembered the limbs reaching out to her in the clearing and figured he was telling the truth. "At least I know that I wasn't seeing things earlier. How do we get out?"

"Can you climb a rope . . . er . . . a vine?"

Surefire looked up and squinted. The weak beam from below cast a muted light on the intertwining vines forming a thick rope-like material, which disappeared into the black void above Raven's head.

"Of course, I can."

Using the arm still wrapped around her waist, he hoisted her up onto his shoulder. She reached above, grabbed the vine, and pulled herself up. As she climbed, the smells slowly faded, the wind dropped to a mild breeze, and the sounds abruptly stopped as if someone had muted the volume. She braced herself for a long, muscle-aching climb. However, after a brief period of climbing, she found herself at the mouth of the trunk. She could've sworn she had fallen at least a hundred feet, possibly more. But she climbed only about twenty feet before she worked her way out of the pliable trunk and landed onto the soft dirt of the forest floor.

Raven slipped out of the trunk and dropped onto the ground beside her. He untied the vine from his waist.

"You all right?"

She crossed her arms so he wouldn't see her trembling hands.

"I'm good. But I don't understand what happened. I was falling for a while. It should've taken more time to climb out."

"Physics change as you cross dimensions. It distorts your perception." He stood and offered his hand to help her up.

She took it, unsure if she could stand up on her own yet, and not wanting to touch another tree, branch or root in this particular forest.

Surefire crossed her arms again as her entire body started to shake, not with cold but with the thought of what had happened. "So, that was a time portal?"

"Yes."

"It was a portal to a war."

"Sounded like it." He moved closer.

She glanced down at her feet and refused to meet his gaze, mortified he'd had to save her once again.

"Thanks," she quietly said.

He didn't reply but continued to stand directly in front of her. Finally, she lifted her eyes to meet his. He smiled, and this time it wasn't an obnoxious smirk but a genuine I'm-glad-you're-okay smile. Warmth spread across her stomach. Her body stopped shivering, though she wrapped her arms more tightly across her chest, uncomfortable with the expression on his face. He leaned closer as if he wanted to kiss her; his eyes searched her face as if looking for validation that she wanted him to.

She licked her lips, and a strange tickling sensation blossomed in her chest when she met his eyes, laced with an emotion she couldn't read. Desire? Sadness? She opened her mouth to ask him why he was staring at her.

Raven quirked his brows, and his eyes again shone with a playful glint.

"Don't mention it." He lifted his hand and patted her head then walked away.

Her mouth fell open. She didn't know what was worse—his condescending pat on the head or her total misreading of his intentions.

Her hands clenched. "Where are we going? Do you even *have* a plan?"

He turned to her, and the annoying smirk was back on his face, though it dropped away when he met her scowl.

"To find my employers, as you like to call them. And, no, I never have a plan."

"Typical. Well, I like to plan things out. Have an idea of what we need to do."

He shook his head. "Once we figure out what they have to say, then we plan. Will that make you happy?"

"No, it won't."

Surefire had no idea where they were going or how they would return home. She was being forced to put her faith in a man who wasn't technically alive, which brought the weirdness level up another notch. A man who just minutes—or was it hours at this point?—before had been number one on her public enemies list.

Now he was leading her farther into some sort of Middle Earth realm surrounded by the Tree of Life. Next he'd say Frodo was his employer and maybe throw in an elf and a dwarf for good measure.

"You'll have to trust me."

"Doesn't look like I have a choice."

"You always have a choice. For example, you can stay here with the man-whipping tree limbs and face whatever is trailing us."

"What?" Surefire's stomach dropped. She looked behind them but saw nothing except the dark forest interior. "Then something *is* following us?"

"As far as I can tell. Or you can come with me and try to find a way out of this mess."

"Fine. Lead the way. But remember, I don't have your ability to avoid roots and branches with a single bound."

"I can always carry you. Sling you over my shoulder. Give you a piggyback ride." He grinned.

Surefire glared at him, and his grin faded. Just because she was small didn't mean she liked being tossed around like a doll or carried like a child.

"I can walk. I'm not helpless."

"Never thought that for a second." His grin was back, but this time it seemed less naughty and more sympathetic. "I'll take it easy. But maybe you should check your fanny pack for anything you can use. Then toss it for less resistance."

"Utility belt," she corrected him, again.

"Sure it is."

It took a second for his words to fully sink in, but when they did, she flushed with frustration. And it wasn't from his smart-ass remark this time. Her own target had to remind her to check for weapons. She chastised herself for making yet another potentially fatal mistake.

Where was her training? Where was her focus? Where was her common sense? It was the Olympic trials all over again, when she'd blown her chance to join the gymnastics team with her sister Heather. One distraction, one slip up, be it on a balance beam or during a mission, and your life was ruined.

She didn't need her dad's coldness or her sister's accomplishments to remind her of that every day. They didn't believe in second chances. She did. U-Sec was her chance to set things straight, blaze her own path, capture her own gold medal.

If she didn't screw up once more.

Raven touched Surefire's shoulder. "Are you ready?"

She jerked back from his touch, realizing she'd been staring into space. "Give me another minute."

She stepped away and began checking through the compartments of her utility belt. Her broken communicator must've dropped out somewhere in the cavern. And the cable in one compartment had somehow become knotted. She took a small butterfly knife out of one pocket, turned her back to Raven and slipped it inside her bra.

Next she removed the rappelling gun from one wrist and the dart gun from her other. The vials of serum she had used to knock out Raven had busted during their initial fall. Her tube of cherry lip balm was still intact. A lot good that would do as a weapon, except against chapped lips. She slipped it into the tight sleeve of her leotard.

She unhooked the belt and let it drop to the ground. At once she felt vulnerable, and this just fed her agitation. However, when she faced Raven, he gave her comforting smile, as if he sensed her fear and wanted to put her at ease.

This only made her feel more vulnerable and agitated, because a part of her wanted to like him at that moment for trying to make her feel better.

"Let's go." She pushed ahead of him.

Without another word, he came up from behind, took her hand, and led her farther into the woods.

He kept his promise to take it easy, though she was sure it was hard for him to do, because whatever had followed them continued to trail at a slight distance, which meant it was either toying with them or just curious. Surefire prayed the latter was true.

Eventually they came to another circular clearing, larger than the one in which they had landed. This glade was on top of a hill and gave a spectacular view of the area below.

The forest seemed to stretch out forever in every direction with a dense growth of vines and limbs. Enormous green leaves grouped with what appeared to be red fruit in the center littered the canopy. Some of the leaves were large enough for her to lie on. Peeking out from several of the branches were more flowers. Some were different from those she'd seen earlier—as large as magnolias but more colorful and much more fragrant, if that were possible. Some appeared tropical in neon pinks and yellows. Others looked like large pink and white pom-poms, reminding her of a Dr. Seuss drawing.

Surefire studied the sky with its beautiful array of colors, an oil painting that had captured the perfect sunset. They didn't have much time before nightfall.

She considered this last thought and became even more baffled, which she didn't think was possible.

"How are we seeing the sun? I thought we were underground."

"We are." Raven dropped her hand and paced away from her as if agitated.

She wasn't sure if it was her question that annoyed him or they were lost and he didn't want to admit it. They had been wandering for what seemed like an hour at least. Their respite in the clearing allowed her to catch her breath, but she had hoped to find a stream or some kind of water source. All their trekking around had made her thirsty. But in this lush paradise, she hadn't seen any water either. Almost as strange as not having a sun.

"Seriously, how are all these plants able to survive without the sun?"

Raven scanned the area, averting his eyes from her probing stare. "They've been preserved. Frozen in time. The power of the Old Ones keeps them alive."

She lifted an eyebrow. "Like you?"

"Yeah, like me." His shoulders drooped a bit, and he walked away. He stood on the edge of the clearing with his head hung.

She wasn't sure what she'd said or done to make him appear so sad. Oddly enough, she felt bad for whatever had caused him to feel this way.

She changed the subject. "We're lost, aren't we?"

He glanced at her then scanned the landscape below again.

"I'll take that as a *yes,*" Surefire murmured.

"Last time I came here, they were waiting," Raven said. "I didn't wander too far. But we entered through a different portal, and it dropped us off at a different spot."

"Is there a way to contact them? I mean, you must communicate with them. How do you get your assignments?"

He furrowed his brow. "Assignments?"

"How do you know what to steal?"

"I'm not actually stealing but returning."

"You're taking things that don't belong to you. How is that not stealing?"

"You're partly right. I'm taking things that don't belong to me, but they didn't belong to the so-called owners either."

"Then who do the artifacts belong to? The Old Ones?"

"No, they belong to the descendants of the humans who created the objects."

Surefire took a moment for this revelation to sink in. "So, I'm guessing we shouldn't waste time looking for the numerous pieces you've stolen, because you've sent all those relics back to the heirs of the original owners or to the countries and places where these artifacts originally resided."

"You got it. But you're welcome to contact any of the tribes or countries or villages that received their *rightful* inheritance back and ask them to return a piece of their heritage because they had never purchased or dug up these objects that should, by all rights, belong to them. I doubt the 'finders, keepers' logic will go over well."

Surefire didn't know how to respond. A part of her knew it was illegal. Stealing was stealing, and he had damaged property and cost museums and private collectors millions of dollars.

However, another part of her found what he was doing noble. She could almost understand. Maybe she could get the charges reduced or even dropped. Maybe if he promised to use the proper legal means to return the artifacts, the judge might cut him a break.

"Do all artifacts need to be returned?"

"No, just the ones that contain the essence of their ancestors. Those pieces had an energy specific to that culture and place, and when those things were removed from their homeland, a delicate power balance shifted in the world, which has been leading to mankind's not-so-pleasant end."

"Why do the Old Ones care what happens to us?"

"They are the ancestors to all humans. Our exponential great-grandparents. Besides, if the world is destroyed, they'll be destroyed as well. Even immortals can die under the right conditions."

"Can you contact them now?"

"They usually contact me."

"How?"

He reached down with his arms crisscrossed and grabbed the edges of his shirt. Surefire pulled back, unsure of his motives.

One side of his lips quirked up in a half smile. "I'm not going to do anything naughty. I'm just going to answer your question."

"Okay." Surefire remained skeptical.

He pulled the shirt over his head.

"Wow," she uttered.

Pictures covered his back, chest, and arms with bolder, richer colors than any tattoo she'd ever seen. She stepped forward and unconsciously stretched her hand out, longing to touch the images, to trace the beautiful detail.

"Go on," he prodded. "I don't mind."

His skin twitched where she touched him. She pulled back when she heard him take in a quick breath then release it.

"Ticklish."

She nodded and reached out again. Her face heated, which matched the heat radiating from his skin. She'd expected him to be cold to the touch, as he had been in the clearing when they first came through the door. But now he felt hot, almost feverish. Her fingers grazed over his patterned skin, smooth and soft in contrast to the well-honed muscles underneath.

I shouldn't be doing this.

But I'm only doing my job, gaining more insight into this case.

The more she understood how Raven operated, the more information she could impart to U-Sec, and the more she could help Raven now.

However, why every nerve in her body tingled when she touched him was another story. She ignored her body's reaction and moved closer to inspect a golden bird on his shoulder.

Of course, her body could be reacting to the tattoos. Every man she had dated since college had tattoos. Maybe because it ticked off her father. Maybe because the men who wore them were the opposite of her father, who thought only criminals and weirdos got ink. Unless, of course, it was a military tattoo, which was in a league of its own. Raven was just the kind of man her father would hate.

Oh dear God, where did that thought come from? She pulled her hand away. *Keep it professional.*

Hormones aside, she was here to do a job.

She cleared her throat and focused again on the golden bird on his shoulder. It had an abnormally long neck and bulbous chest and held in its feet flowered vines that trailed onto Raven's back to entwine with a stone statue of a kneeling woman. She recognized the statue from an ad in the city newspaper detailing the Aztec exhibit at the Walters Art Museum.

"Is this the statue you stole earlier?"

"Yes." He craned his neck to look at her as she traced the image with her fingertip. Along with that picture was a figure of a voluptuous woman with a green patina and melon-sized breasts hanging down to her stomach. The fertility statue he had stolen the last time she had nearly caught him.

"Amazing."

He flexed his pectoral muscles as she came full circle around his body to the raven across his chest. Goosebumps prickled along his skin as if in reaction to a cool breeze, though there wasn't any breeze.

He sighed. At least, she thought he did. When she glanced up at him, he coughed and turned his head.

She moved closer, overwhelmed by an intoxicating scent of earth and leaves and something that quickened her pulse and that she couldn't quite pinpoint.

Her lips were inches from his chest. She wondered if the colors on his skin would each taste different.

Again, she forced her hand away. She really hoped he couldn't read minds. And she really needed a good girl's night out if this Robin Hood wannabe was doing it for her.

She cleared her throat more harshly this time and stepped back.

"Absolutely amazing."

"Thanks." His warm, cocoa-scented breath caressed her forehead, and her body tingled again. She took a few more steps back.

"The artwork." She was grateful her voice didn't quiver like her insides.

"Ah, sure," he replied, sounding disappointed. "I have some a little lower, if you want to see."

Crap. Maybe he can read my mind.

"No, thanks."

She pointed to the magnificent bird on his chest. "What about the raven?"

"That one is mine."

"You had a raven tattoo before this happened to you?"

He nodded.

"A big Ravens football fan?"

"Hell, no." He pulled a face. "Pittsburgh Steelers all the way. Don't insult me."

She raised her hands in surrender. "Sorry, didn't know."

"You're forgiven this time." He tugged his shirt back on.

"Then why that particular tattoo?"

He shrugged. "When I was kid, I read a story about a raven being the first thief, and it stuck with me. So when I worked for APS, I took Raven as my alias, and that stuck with me, too." He turned over his forearm to show her a smaller tattoo of a raven with a yellow sun hanging from its beak.

"You were a part of APS?" She pulled back, shocked. "Artifact Procurement Specialists?"

Allegedly, they had infiltrated archeological digs throughout the Middle East and Central America, stealing millions in artifacts. Authorities worldwide had been trying to shut them down for years.

"That was a long time ago." He dropped his eyes from hers, but not before she saw regret in them. "Since then, I've returned what I could."

Surefire stored this information away for later. "These pictures form on your skin when it's time to hunt down a new object?"

"Yes."

"Does it hurt?"

Raven shrugged again. "Kind of tickles."

"Any tickling sensations now?"

"Nothing."

A loud snap made both of them jump. The trees rustled behind them. The humming noise she'd heard earlier filled the air around them and pulsed against her skin.

"What is it?" Surefire whispered.

Raven stepped in front of her and faced the noise. Surefire reached into her bra and took out the butterfly knife she'd hidden there.

"Who's there?" Raven called out.

Into the clearing walked the most beautiful woman Surefire had ever seen.

Chapter Eight

"Pax, over here," Graham, U-Sec's head of security and recon, shouted from near the hole.

Pax sloshed through a shallow puddle left after the water had stopped spewing. They had pumped most of the water out. However, the hole was too tight for an average person to fit through, especially with scuba gear, and the amount of water underneath in the unstable cavern made it dangerous to even try. Instead, they'd pushed down an extra-long plumber's snake with a light attachment that sent video images to a monitor on the surface.

"What did you find?" Pax asked as he neared Graham.

"Looks like a broken communicator. Surefire's maybe?" Graham pointed to a small, rectangular, cracked object floating across the screen.

"Must be." Pax glanced back at Oracle, sitting in a folding chair near the entrance. She gave him a sympathetic shake of her head as if she had heard.

"Huh. Looks like there's also a flat-screen monitor." Graham tilted his head while he studied the monitor.

Pax bent closer and squinted. "Son of a bitch. What's that doing down there?"

"And these look like light posts." Graham circled a tall image on the monitor with his index finger.

"Any bodies?"

"Just dead rats."

"Keep looking." Pax straightened and rotated his tight shoulders.

Helena, Pax's assistant, walked up and handed him a coffee.

"Anything?" she asked.

"Rats."

She stared at him hard. "You need rest."

"I'm fine."

"I've seen smaller bags hanging in the window of Saks than what are under your eyes. You may be forty, but that doesn't mean you shouldn't take care of yourself."

"Thirty-nine," he grumbled.

"Pardon me?"

"I'm thirty-nine."

"Not for much longer."

Helena shot a look at Oracle. Pax followed her gaze. Oracle wore a vacant expression on her face, one he had seen many times before. But Oracle wasn't resting or lost in her thoughts. She had let down her telepathic shields, even though he'd ordered her not to. Before he could yell for her to stop, she popped up in the chair. Her head whipped to the left as if surprised by an odd sound.

Matthews meandered over to her with a drink, interrupting whatever had stirred her attention. She took the offered cup and gave him a smile in return.

"Did you hear me?" Helena demanded.

"Uh, no . . . I'm a bit distracted."

"Yes." Helena shot another unhappy glance at Oracle. "I can see that."

She turned back to Pax and inclined her head. Her thick silver hair was cut in a Jackie Onassis style that somehow still gleamed in the yellowish lights of the warehouse. Her deep brown eyes, made deeper by her lightly powdered skin, regarded him with amusement and condescension. He ran his hand over his face. Most days he regretted hiring his mother's best friend. Just because she'd changed his diaper as a child didn't mean she could talk to him, or even look at him, as if he still was one.

"What did you say?" he asked.

"I suggested you go home and go to sleep. Let someone else take over for a few hours."

"I'm fine." *For the fiftieth time.*

"You won't be in a minute," Helena said into her drink. She motioned with her pinky toward the doors of the warehouse where Surefire's sister, Heather St. John, and her fiancé strode through the police barricade and into the warehouse.

"Don't say I didn't warn you," Helena said over her shoulder as she made a beeline in the opposite direction.

♥ ☠ ♥ ☠ ♥ ☠

Surefire's hand tightened around the knife she held behind her back.

Ever since she'd fallen through the crack in the warehouse floor, things had kept getting more and more curious and just plain weird. Little Miss Perfect strolling toward them in a sheer purple drape she considered clothing upped the ante on the strange meter. Not to mention the trail of blue and yellow flowers that sprung up wherever she stepped and an entourage of butterflies and hummingbirds fluttering around her—an acid-induced fairytale.

Surefire's skin tingled as the woman sauntered closer. The vibrating hum pitched louder before it fell silent in the wake of this woman's entrance. Gold adorned the woman's head, neck, wrists, and feet and glittered with its own light source, giving her an angelic appearance despite her gauzy dress. A gold hoop hung around her neck attached to a large gold plate, round and shimmering as the sun, engraved with a marigold. The obnoxious-sized plate settled in the rise of her breasts with the sheer fabric gathered underneath it. A gleaming gold band embossed with flowers wrapped around her head, over glossy ebony hair straight from a shampoo ad. From that band, two long, narrow, blue-green plumes stuck out and curled a foot above her head like feathery antennae.

The tingling sensation increased. Surefire's body buzzed with a primal energy that moved from her arms and chest and then lower past her stomach.

She shifted on her feet, uncomfortable with her body's reaction to this woman, who oozed sexuality and not in the metaphorical sense. Pheromones leaked from her pores like gas from a broken pipeline.

Raven kept his back to Surefire. But from the way his muscles twitched and he crossed his arms tightly across his chest, she knew he was affected as well.

"Sho-chi, we've been looking for you," Raven said.

Sho-chi? Where had Surefire heard that name before?

"I know," the woman responded in a sultry voice tinged with an exotic accent Surefire couldn't quite make out.

Then Surefire remembered the name. She hadn't heard it spoken, she'd read it in the museum's brochure next to its phonetic spelling: Xochiquetzal. Raven had used a shortened version. Surefire tensed and remained rooted to the ground, as Xochi, the same woman whose likeness Raven had tattooed on his back and whose statue Raven had stolen from the museum, sauntered toward her with a defiant look she'd seen many times before.

This woman, this goddess, was sizing her up.

This woman with hair that fell in a straight, jet-black line over her shoulders, with black eyes in a perfect almond shape. This woman with flawless skin the color of honey without a wrinkle or a freckle to mar it. This woman with angled cheekbones and a straight, elfish nose with each nostril perfectly flared.

This woman gazed steadily at her as if Surefire posed a threat.

She couldn't help but stare back into Xochi's bottomless eyes, even when every ounce of her wanted to run screaming. Xochi's raw sexuality became more intense, more primal, and turned into something darker that overwhelmed Surefire until her breath came out in gasps and her heart thudded in her chest.

Power rolled off Xochi in stifling waves. Surefire felt like she was being pounded repeatedly by heavy surf, but this was metaphysical surf, and Xochi, so petite and angelic-looking, had all the metaphysical force of a hurricane.

"I followed you here." Xochi stopped a few yards from Surefire.

She held up Surefire's discarded utility belt and waved it once. The leather belt became a green stalk, and the compartments morphed into bell-shaped yellow flowers. She flicked her hand, and the birds and butterflies flew away and disappeared into the forest.

"Then *you* were trailing us." Raven blew out a breath, his back still to Surefire. "Could've given us a heads-up at least. Where are the others?"

"You are my responsibility, so it is I who have come."

She placed the new flower onto the ground, where it planted itself. Then she stared at Surefire as if daring her to perform a better trick.

You've got to be kidding.

Surefire tried to move her legs but found them literally rooted to the ground. Tall grass snaked around her calves, holding her in place.

Raven looked back and forth between the two of them. "Xochi, this is—"

"I know who she is," Xochi purred.

The grass grew higher, tightening around Surefire's knees and digging into her skin.

"A human should not be here," Xochi stated.

Raven's eyes widened with fear when he finally noticed Surefire's legs.

"What are you doing?" He dropped down to Surefire's feet and ripped the growth away, but it only grew higher and tighter. Her legs throbbed. Her knees buckled. She couldn't speak, as if the grass tied up her tongue as well.

"You're hurting her," Raven hollered at Xochi.

"No human can enter our realm without a sacrifice," Xochi responded, monotone.

"I was her sacrifice. Wasn't that enough?" Raven desperately clawed at the dirt to dig at the roots.

Surefire fell and landed on top of Raven's bent back. A too-sweet floral scent burned up her nose. Her throat constricted. Shadowy spots floated across her vision.

Raven shouted again at Xochi to stop. He wrapped his warm, sturdy arms around Surefire to hold her up. The grass wound its way to her hips.

What's happening? How is she doing this?

Xochi continued to stand away from Surefire with her head held high, her lids lowered, and her mouth curved in a defiant smile.

"No!" Raven let Surefire go, jumped to his feet and ran at Xochi. She swatted her hand in the air, and Raven pitched to the side, tackled by an invisible force.

Desperate, Surefire squeezed the cool handle of the knife she still clutched behind her back. If Xochi wanted a show, she'd give her a show.

She forced in a ragged breath, and everything fell away. Even the pain in her legs, bleeding from the ropes of grass cutting into her flesh. She dropped into the target zone, as she had dubbed it, a trick she used when she needed to focus on a challenge. Only two things remained: the weight of the knife in her hand and the small indentation between Xochi's perfectly shaped brows. Her muscles tensed, fueled with the knowledge of the force needed to pierce Xochi's flesh and the angle needed to hit it.

Her hand whipped back then forward, releasing the blade with a snap. The knife struck between Xochi's eyes. They rolled back into her head, and Xochi collapsed onto the ground.

The grass dissolved away from Surefire's legs. She dropped to her hands and knees as the sounds, smells, and sights of the world came rushing back. A moment later, she heard Raven's feet pound across the clearing to her right. She glanced up as he squatted next to her.

"You all right?" He wrapped his arm around her waist.

"I'm good," Surefire replied in a weak whisper. She rubbed her legs, which miraculously held no cuts or scratches, just dried blood.

"Can you stand?"

She nodded and gripped his shoulder for support. He eased her onto her feet, his arm strong and safe around her waist. So much so, she relaxed her head against his bicep while her heart's spastic rhythm slowed to a normal beat.

Only when he reached up and smoothed his palm over her hair did she realize how long she'd been resting against him. With a blush, she stepped out of his embrace.

"She's not dead, is she?" Surefire motioned to Xochi, prone on the ground. Her stomach trembled at the sight.

"Doubtful." Raven cocked his head toward Xochi, though he didn't move to check on her.

"Figured her weakness was in her chest. Maybe her heart, considering her plate-sized necklace, so I aimed for her head. Hoped it might stun her at least, considering I didn't think she was human."

Surefire stared up at Raven for assurance that this was true.

"Trust me, she's far from human. I'm positive you didn't kill her."

Kill her?

The trembling in her stomach spread out until her whole body shook. She had sent a knife careening into this woman's forehead. Granted, she was scared and in pain, and Xochi appeared to be the cause of it. But she'd never used her ability to try to kill someone before.

"That was some shot to the ole glabella. Never seen anyone do that before." Respect lit up his face.

"Glabella?" She went on, uneasy with the admiring look he gave her, "That's a two-hundred-dollar word."

"At some point, I wanted to be a doctor." He shrugged. "Found I had other talents."

Yes, things did keep getting stranger.

"Cenca cualli. Very well."

Surefire and Raven spun toward the voice to find Xochi rising from the ground with the knife sticking out between her eyes.

"I assumed you could do it with some prodding." Xochi pulled the knife out. Her torn flesh knitted back together over the wound.

Relief calmed Surefire's quaking limbs. Xochi was alive. She hadn't killed her. Then Surefire tensed again, as she processed Xochi's words.

"You set me up?"

Xochi gave her a nonchalant shrug and handed back the knife. "I was right. You need to be more than human to make it into my realm."

Surefire folded the knife and stuck it back inside her bra.

"What do you mean?"

"Exactly what I said." Xochi took Surefire's hands in her own and stood eye-to-eye with her. She smiled, a loving smile that touched Surefire's heart. A smile that cut through Surefire's fear and confusion over what had happened, over Xochi being a flesh-and-blood Aztec goddess. A smile a mother would bestow on a child she was proud of.

"But you." Xochi dropped Surefire's hands and whipped around to Raven. She ran a finger across his chest and over to his heart. "I gave you life, yet you stood by while Synthia tried to take mine."

"You can't die, but she can."

She flattened her hand against his chest. "Does not this man who lives by my power belong to me?"

♥ ☠ ♥ ☠ ♥ ☠

Raven stood as still as if Xochi had a loaded gun pointed at his chest instead of a small graceful hand placed over his heart. A hand that could break through his sternum and claw the life out of him if he did or said anything more to offend her.

"Of course." He struggled to sound sincere.

She slit her eyes.

"I belong to you."

He glanced over at Surefire. She gazed at him with wide, disbelieving eyes. Anger mixed with embarrassment raged inside. At that moment, he wished Xochi would kill him. He hated for Surefire to witness the power Xochi held over him. And most of all, he hated for Surefire to think that he wanted this—to be Xochi's property, her plaything.

His answer must've satisfied Xochi, because her essence surged through him, recharging him. Her power buzzed through his veins better than an energy drink. His anger dissipated in the wake of the warmth blanketing him. Heat that led straight to his groin—an unfortunate drawback when someone received powers from the goddess of physical love.

He took a step back and thought of dead puppies, fish guts, and then a naked Ari.

Ahhh . . . that did it.

"We're here on a mission." He moved from Xochi to stand next to Surefire, who pointedly stared at her feet.

"You seek the final skull," Xochi said.

"Yes."

"You know it is not time."

"I know."

"You know the consequences."

"I know."

"It will take a sacrifice."

"What doesn't?" he asked.

She paused at his sarcasm before saying in a deep tone that vibrated the air long after she spoke, "Are both of you willing to make it?"

"You know the answer," Raven replied, and Surefire nodded.

Xochi stepped closer to Surefire. They were about the same height. The same build.

"I'll do whatever it takes to stop Ari," Surefire said.

"Even sacrifice your own body?"

"Whatever."

"Easy to swear when your life is not threatened, but will you make the same choice when it is?" Xochi's empty eyes bore into Surefire's. Raven had to give her credit, Surefire didn't flinch.

Xochi reached out and brushed back a lock of hair from Surefire's face, and every alarm went off in Raven's body. He didn't want Surefire too comfy with Xochi; there was always a price to pay when a god got cozy with you.

"I will help you." To his relief, Xochi walked away from Surefire toward a low-hanging branch. "Because you know the consequences if I do not."

Raven trailed behind Xochi. "Then what Ari told us was true. He has raised the god."

"Yes and no." Xochi turned her head and gave him a tight smile. "Tezcatlipoca cannot fully enter your world without the final skull. He resides half inside the magic man and half in limbo—partway between our plane and yours."

"Then Ari lied," Surefire interjected and moved to stand beside Raven. "He said the god would possess him on the twentieth *if* we didn't retrieve the skull."

Xochi let out a soft, cynical laugh. "Tezcatlipoca has an affinity for liars, like himself."

"But the skull will send Tezcatlipoca back to your world, right?" Raven asked.

"The skull can dispel him from the human, yes. The magic man is wielding a fraction of Tezcatlipoca's abilities, which will intensify as the twentieth feast day nears. But he has tricked Ari, making him believe he'll possess all his godly powers, when Tezcatlipoca will use the skull to possess Ari instead."

"If Tezcatlipoca wields the crystal's power," Xochi continued, "then he will fully possess the vessel."

"It's a Catch-22," Raven interjected. "The skull can stop Tezcatlipoca or allow him to pass into our world."

Xochi's smooth features pinched in puzzlement. "I don't know this *catch* you speak of. However, you are correct. The skull serves a dual purpose. With it, Tezcatlipoca can fully cross over, and his presence would destroy the world's balance. We are in this place for a reason." She let out a breathy sigh. "He was always breaking the rules, which is why we kept him locked up, secure within the ground here. Or so we thought."

"How do you know him?" Surefire asked.

Xochi touched the branch, and immediately dainty purple flowers bloomed in a trailing vine that matched the violet of her dress. "He is my husband."

"Husband?" Surefire looked to Raven for an explanation.

He shook his head, stunned at the revelation as well. Years ago, while in APS, he had studied Aztec lore to glean information on lost treasures. It wasn't until Ari had mentioned Tezcatlipoca's name that Raven recalled the legend, but legends could be spotty at best. Raven had never met a husband of Xochi's, nor had she ever mentioned a husband. He had assumed the story was wrong. Now he remembered why he should never assume.

"I will help you." Xochi turned fluidly on her heel and faced Raven. "But I need something in return."

"I didn't expect anything else."

"Do you have the statue?" She held out her delicate hand.

"I did."

She waited with her hand held out.

"But I lost it."

"Then I can't help you." She lowered her hand.

"Can't or won't?" Raven asked.

Xochi simply glared at him with those inky black eyes.

"They probably took it into evidence," Surefire offered. "I know where they'd store it at U-Sec. I can get us in."

"We need to get in and out. We can't get caught," Raven said.

"I can do it. But how do we get back to our world?" Surefire asked.

"That, I can help you with." Xochi beckoned them to follow her.

Several steps into the forest, Xochi stopped in front of a trunk overgrown with vines, which looked like every other trunk in the forest.

She pointed at it. "You go through here."

"Where will it take us?" Raven asked.

"To where you need to go."

Raven crossed his arms. "Can you narrow it down a bit?"

"The closest available portal to where you need to be."

"Okay," Raven replied although he didn't feel okay about this, and he still didn't know exactly where they would end up. *Why did gods have to be so cryptic?* "Do I need to make a donation to return?"

"You will need to verify your identity through a sacrifice."

"Didn't you ever hear of retina scans? Maybe fingerprints? Something less invasive?"

She didn't respond, only touched her hand to the outside of the vine-covered trunk, which opened with a snapping of branches, like dry bones popping and grinding against one another.

Raven eyed Surefire, who stood cautiously between the trunks, arms tucked at her sides. He wondered whether he could trust her not to contact the authorities as soon as they were home. She had to be freaked out, scared out of her mind. In fact, even he was concerned. According to legend, Tezcatlipoca was a mean SOB, and Raven had no doubt that Ari, with the god's help, would make good on his promise to kill everyone they knew if they didn't comply.

Raven debated knocking Surefire out and tying her up while he retrieved the statue. Of course, the thought of her tied up led to another idea. A less wholesome one.

Surefire quirked her left eyebrow at him, probably wondering why he was staring so hard and so long at her.

He scrubbed his hand over his face.

"When we get back," Raven said, "you don't contact anyone."

"I know. You can trust me."

"We'll see." He started toward the trunk.

Xochi's arm shot out and stopped him from entering.

"She goes first." Xochi grabbed Surefire's wrist and flung her like a rag doll into the portal.

"Surefire!" Raven reached out, straining against the forearm Xochi had braced against his chest.

"Why did you do that?"

The corner of her plump lips lifted. "You like this being."

"She's going to escape."

"She can't. She won't."

Raven tried to settle down, but he worried that Surefire would hightail it to the nearest police station. And he also worried about whether she made it to the other side safely. The contradiction wasn't lost on him.

"How do you know she won't escape and run as soon as she enters the other side?"

"She likes you as well."

Raven choked out a laugh. "Your feelings are wrong."

"You need her help, and she needs yours. You are not to leave her behind. For now, she is . . ." Xochi raised her hand to his face, stood on tiptoe, and leaned close as if to kiss him. "Useful."

Raven tried to pull back, but a pleasant current of energy—soothing as a warm ocean breeze—surged through him and held him to the spot like an invisible harness.

"However, when her usefulness is over, I will not tolerate sharing that which is mine with another."

The pleasant energy turned cold and then burned like dry ice encasing his skin. His muscles seized up. He began to double over, but Xochi held him upright, increasing the pain. His jaw clenched shut, and he lost himself in her eyes, now swirling like two black holes.

"Always remember," she whispered, her lips inches from his. "My feelings are never wrong."

She shoved him backward through the trunk.

Chapter Nine

Who the hell called Heather?

Pax stretched to his full six foot four height.

And why was she here?

Since Surefire's family was in the public eye, she worked hard to keep her identity secret and her family safe. Heather showing up put her, as well as Surefire, in jeopardy.

Heather's fiancé, Hunter, trailed behind her like an obedient puppy. The quarterback with the current NFL record for pass completions looked like he'd been sacked one too many times, and Pax guessed it wasn't on the football field.

Five-inch heels clacked against the concrete, echoing throughout the warehouse, announcing Heather's arrival. With designer jeans painted onto her girlish body and a flimsy top that looked taped on, Pax could've mistaken her for a woman from the Block, Baltimore's famous strip bar and prostitution area. And judging by the way the policemen and agents gaped at her, Pax guessed they felt the same. A few took out their phones and snapped some not-so-discreet photos.

Her choppy bob, obviously cut by a blind man, gave her young face—which was too overdone with makeup for Pax's taste—an edge and a look very different from the clean-cut, poster-girl gymnast she used to be. She also looked surprisingly awake, given that it was past three thirty in the morning. They must have interrupted her night out, and considering the frigid sparks shooting from her psycho-cat green eyes, she was not pleased at the interruption.

"Where the hell is my sister?" Heather shouted before she reached Pax.

"I—" he began, but she interrupted.

"Is that where she is?" She pointed to the hole. "Is my sister in there? Because I swear to God, you are going after her if I have to squeeze your ass into that hole myself."

She halted in front of him, barely coming up to his chest, but her presence filled the space between them so much she might as well have been an Amazon.

"We haven't—"

"Oh, you haven't found her body yet? Is that what you're about to tell me? Is that supposed to comfort me somehow?"

"She knew—"

"I know she knew the dangers of her job."

How does she know what I was about to say?

"Do I have to remind you of your promise to my father?" Her eyes drilled into him.

Oh, hell. She didn't.

"Did you—"

"Yes, I did. He cut his vacation short, so you better have some answers by . . ." She looked pointedly at her watch. "Six hundred hours."

Pax clamped his jaw shut and ground his teeth. He didn't want to confront her father—his former general—until he had concrete answers. The last thing he needed was his old commander looking over his shoulder, blaming him for his daughter's disappearance, making him feel guiltier than he already felt.

Her father knew there were no guarantees in this line of work. Besides, Surefire refused desk duty; she wanted to be in the field. And her perfect aim was one of the most useful skills any of his agents had. With more trans-crime happening, they needed all the trained agents they could get. Surefire was still green, trying to prove her worth like most new agents, which is why she had begged him to be given this case where other agents had failed. He'd agreed, but only with Oracle as her backup. Not to mention, Raven wasn't violent compared to other cases.

"We'll have something by the time he gets in."

"You better. Because when my father—"

"Yeah, I know. Probably better than you do."

"I doubt that." She arched her thinly plucked brows. "Now what can Hunter do to help?" She shoved her fiancé in front of Pax.

"Stay out of my way." Pax marched away, ignoring the nuclear burn of Heather's eyes boring into his back. Behind him, he heard a couple of officers approach Hunter and ask for his autograph.

"Any luck?" He rested his hands on the back of an empty metal chair next to Graham, but he didn't sit down, just rolled his shoulders to stretch out tense muscles.

"Haven't found Surefire, but we did find a door." Graham adjusted his Orioles baseball hat and pointed to a grayish mass on the screen. "Can't make out the markings but it looks like it's made out of stone with spikes protruding from it."

"Could she have gone through it?"

"Possibly. It's split in half, though. Maybe it happened after she went through." Graham extended his arms above his head until his back cracked. "Not sure what's behind it, but it's the best lead we've got."

"I want someone down there. Let's see if we can pump more water out and make a larger hole to find a way in."

"You got it, boss." Graham reached for his cell phone. Before he could dial out, the phone began buzzing and then let out a sound like an air raid siren.

"Yeah," he answered. Pax heard a voice babbling on the other end but couldn't discern what he or she said.

"Are you sure?" Graham rubbed his forehead, pushing back his hat and squeezing the front of his bald head. "Do what you can to fix it and then trace whoever did it. I'll tell Pax." He hung up and glanced up at Pax, though his eyes refused to meet Pax's questioning stare.

"What happened?"

"Our firewall has been breached. Someone gained access to our servers."

Pax crushed the back of the metal folding chair, and it crumbled like a piece of aluminum foil. He didn't think this morning could get any worse. "What did they see?"

"They snagged a few employee records before our safeguards shut them out."

"Whose records?"

"Surefire's and also Oracle's."

The tightness in Pax's gut told him this wasn't a coincidence.

He threw the chair to the side, and it skidded across the floor and banged into the warehouse wall, crumpling the chair and making a large dent in the siding. A few people jumped at the commotion but kept their attention averted from Pax. Oracle called his name from where she stood near the entrance. Matthews touched her arm then whispered in her ear.

"Stay here and see what you find. Keep me posted," Pax ordered.

"Sure thing," Graham replied.

"I'm heading to the office," he told Oracle and stormed outside to the parking lot.

He didn't say a word to Matthews, and he didn't wait to see if Oracle followed. But he heard her tell the detective goodbye, and he hesitated before opening his truck's door just long enough for her to catch up.

♥ ☠ ♥ ☠ ♥ ☠

Not again.

Surefire screamed as once more she fell through a tree trunk into black nothingness.

Cold wind whipped across her skin and beat so strongly against her body that her arms blew up and out to her sides, forcing her into a skydiver pose. Unlike the last time, no sounds of gunfire or shouts greeted her—only the whizzing of the air by her ears.

Adrenaline surged through her veins. Her muscles braced for a not-so-pleasant impact. Fear twisted her insides. Her eyes watered. Again, a pinprick of light formed below her. However, this time it expanded to the size of a basketball then grew exponentially larger. She shut her eyes against the light's rays and forced her arms down to block her face and protect her head from certain collision with whatever was waiting for her at the bottom of this stomach-dropping fall.

She slowed down. The wind rushing by her ears decreased. Her body jolted to a hard stop. A second later she floated on her stomach through a dark chamber and onto a gritty floor.

Immediately, she flipped over and scampered back until she hit a wall. Seconds later, she heard Raven land in the same spot.

"That was fun. Want to do it again?"

"I'll pass." Her insides were so distorted she braced herself for an encore performance of her dinner. She blinked several times, adjusting her eyes to the darkness. She could make out Raven's grey outline from a minuscule amount of light seeping in through cracks in the stone walls.

"Nice of her to give me some warning." Surefire rubbed her arm where Xochi had nearly torn it from the socket.

"And where would be the fun in that?"

Surefire rolled her eyes.

He stood and ran his hands over the surrounding walls. She stood as well and wiped the grit from her legs and leotard. From what she could tell, they were in a square chamber a bit larger than a walk-in closet—though not as large as her sister's closet. That was the size of the average person's apartment.

"What is this place?" Surefire coughed from the dusty, stagnant air.

"A tomb, judging by the skeleton I just manhandled."

She heard what she assumed were bones rattle onto the floor.

"Let me see." He seemed to be talking more to himself than to Surefire. "There should be a lever somewhere over here."

A grunt followed by a high-pitch whine of old gears springing to life filled the chamber. Slowly, light poured in as one of the walls gave a jerk and slid halfway open.

Too blinded and shocked by the bright light, Surefire didn't get a chance to ask why a tomb would open from the inside.

Raven stuck out his head first. Surefire squinted then rubbed her eyes. She peered under his arm and was struck speechless.

Raven was right. They were in a tomb. A five-hundred-year-old Aztec tomb, according to the plaque situated in the corner of the platform where the chamber sat—a plaque that also read "Smithsonian National Museum of Natural History."

He stepped out, and she followed him onto the platform, which was surrounded by a black velvet rope. Behind them, the tomb's wall sealed shut.

"Don't move." He put his hand in front of her and motioned to the red beams of light crisscrossing a foot in front of the exhibit.

She scanned the room. Various glass cases containing pottery, statues, gold jewelry, and other Mesoamerican artifacts dotted the antechamber. Several banners in brilliant colors hung from the ceiling, calling out important dates in Central America's history. She looked up at the track lighting shining down upon the display cases. Her eyes panned to the left and right into the lens of a security camera.

"Crap."

Raven followed her gaze.

"Crap," he echoed. "We've got to go. Security will be here . . ."

Shouts resounded from the rotunda outside the room, followed by shoes scuffing across the marble floors.

"Now." He jumped down from the exhibit through the red beams, setting off a shrill alarm.

Surefire hesitated. They had seen her. They had her image. They would know she was helping Raven. Reality struck her across the face, and she reeled from the shock of what this meant.

"No. No, this can't happen. We need to tell them. I need to—"

Raven scooped her up and threw her over his shoulder.

"What are you doing?" She clawed at his back.

"Stopping you from making a bad decision." He spun around and raced toward a back staircase.

Surefire leveraged her hands on his back and pushed up and craned her neck to look over his shoulder and then wished she hadn't.

When they reached the top of the stairs, he crouched down and jumped.

She flattened herself against his shoulder and back. He landed, and her head bounced off his lower back as the impact reverberated through his body to hers. But he didn't seem to notice her head smacking his spine. He continued to run and leap again, spanning about twelve stairs to the next landing. The stairs spiraled down and wrapped around two large totem poles. The carved figures bobbed in front of her eyes: a large-nosed face mocked her with a smile; two square, stoic faces glowered at her; and . . . was that a raven smirking at her?

"Don't even consider screaming. I will knock you out, and I'm certain you don't want that."

As if she could even make any sound besides a weak gurgle. She held her breath with every leap he made, waiting for her inevitable face plant on the edge of the steps when he slipped. Blood rushed to her head. The world teetered and swayed. She wondered what Raven would do if she threw up on his backside. A thought that would've been funny in any other circumstance.

Raven paused at the bottom. Above them security guards shouted, and a multitude of feet pounded down the steps. He moved forward again. She lifted her upper body and craned her neck to see where he was taking her. In front of them was a set of glass doors that led outside.

He hit the handle on the door. A chilly breeze blew across her thighs. She shivered.

Raven ran out and looked to his right. At the same time, a Smithsonian guard puffing a cigarette stepped out from under a tree to their left.

"Watch out," Surefire began, but it was too late.

Raven spun around and sprinted into the surprised guard. Raven fell, still gripping Surefire's legs to his chest. She flipped backward over his shoulder and smacked her head on the pavement. The impact knocked the breath from her lungs. Stars flitted across her eyes. She rolled onto her side to see Raven spring back up and punch the guard in the face.

"Sorry, buddy." Raven snatched the unconscious guard's revolver.

Smithsonian security spilled out from the glass doors. Raven raced over to Surefire and dragged her to her feet and off the sidewalk. She stumbled over a low stone ledge and onto a grassy lawn under an old, sprawling tree. His fingers dug into her upper arm.

"What the hell are you doing?" She tried to wrench away from his iron grip, but he whipped her around and pushed her in front of him. "Ow! You bastard, that hurts."

Raven shoved the cold barrel of the gun into her temple. She froze. "Ah, Raven."

"Don't come any closer." He flattened her against his chest.

Five guards fanned out along the path in front of the doors. Two pointed guns at them. Two had their radios out. The last one's hand hovered over the pepper spray on his belt. Sirens resounded down the city streets, becoming louder with each passing second.

"Now, son." A fifty-something guard, who could've passed for Burt Reynolds's brother, moved closer, his gun held steady in his hand. "Drop your weapon. There's no need for violence."

Raven edged back, pulling Surefire with him.

"Uh, what are you doing?" she asked as calmly as she could between clenched teeth, even though she really wanted to smack him. Instead, she remained wedged between his kung-fu grip and the barrel jammed into her temple with his finger tightening on the trigger.

Raven ignored Surefire's question and answered the guard. "Why don't your men drop their weapons? Then I'll consider losing mine."

The guard motioned to the others to lay down their guns. As they carefully placed their weapons on the ground, Raven whispered to Surefire, "This will feel weird."

"What?"

Raven's hand slid from her arm to the bare skin of her throat. A second later her body tingled as if she had hit her funny bone, except the tingling began in her neck where Raven held her and traveled to her head and to her shoulders and then down to her toes until every cell in her body pulsated.

The guards snatched up their guns and jerked around. Their faces contorted in varying degrees of confusion.

"Son of a bitch." The Burt Reynolds look-alike squinted his eyes and moved closer to where they stood.

"Where'd they go?" A young guard walked up behind him.

What are they talking about? Surefire looked down at her body then did a double take. She didn't have a body, and neither did Raven. He had phased both of them out.

Two guards walked closer. The older man reached out his hand and put it right through them. A warm tickle sent a ripple through her body, or whatever was left of her body as particles parted and then reformed themselves. At least that was what she assumed was happening. What her brain could process. Of course, where was her brain? Did she still have a brain?

Something tugged her away, and she floated backward as she watched the guards fan out and begin searching the area.

"How?" The word didn't come from her mouth but the air around them.

"Whatever I touch with my bare skin, I can change the molecular structure and fade out for a short time. Xochi rebooted my abilities, but it takes a lot of my strength to maintain you as well." Raven's explanation flowed through her, so it wasn't as if she heard his explanation as much as it was transmitted to each floating cell that translated it into words.

Totally trippy. Her friend and co-agent TimeTrap would love it. Surefire, not so much.

She gazed forward as they turned up Pennsylvania Avenue and then up Eleventh Street.

"I don't like this feeling. It's like . . ." She struggled to find the words to explain something this odd.

"Like you're going to float away into a thousand fractured atoms?"

"That sums it up."

"Don't worry. I'm holding us together."

"Reassuring. But where is the 'me' that you're holding together?"

They drifted past a group of young professionals returning from a club. Several turned toward where Raven and Surefire floated, probably wondering if they had drank too much to begin hearing voices.

"You're all here. Mixed in a bit with some of my cells. May have to redefine our relationship after this."

Was he joking?

It was hard to tell when he was joking. Though she had to admit, this did feel a bit intimate. His voice vibrated through her every time he spoke, as if they were joined. As if they shared the same body and mind. It was discomforting. Yet, not. Maybe she was getting too used to him. Or maybe it was just hard to keep her guard up with her molecular structure all faded out and jumbled with his.

They continued another block up Eleventh Street and floated across another road.

"Where are we going?" she asked.

"To the U-Sec offices. Isn't that where the statue is?"

"Yes, but how are we going to get there? It's in Baltimore."

"By car." They rounded a corner and floated up a different street. A rat the size of most house cats scuttled across their path. They phased through it, and a shiver pulsated through her.

"But where are we going now?"

"You ask a lot of questions."

"And you're not very open with your answers."

"I'm a guy. That's how we communicate."

"Then you'll get twenty questions, because that's how I communicate."

They turned up a narrow alleyway between a restaurant and a hotel. Then they stopped in front of a garage door in the center of a wall with the faded remains of an eighties-style Coca-Cola ad painted on it.

"I'm going to phase you back in. Get ready to grab onto something. It's disorienting."

Slowly, feeling came back to her. The uneven alley below her feet. Her close-fitting leotard. The cold air blowing along her legs and across her face. The bruise throbbing on the back of her head from her most recent fall. Raven was right. Phasing back in was disorienting, like waking from a dream—not in a strange bed but in a strange bathtub in frigid water. Her knees wobbled. She dug her nails into the gritty brick wall to keep her balance. She gulped at the air as if she'd just resurfaced from a deep dive. Then she considered that thought. Had she been breathing while phased out?

She ran her hands over her torso and checked out her arms and legs. Yes, everything was in place. Nothing missing. No limbs sticking out her back. She crossed her arms. Her body quivered, either in response to the unseasonably cold air or to the sudden understanding of what had happened.

Raven leaned his head against the wall for a moment and took in a few deep breaths. His arms hung at his sides. One hand still held the gun. His body gave a shudder. He shook his head twice then pressed a few buttons on a keypad hidden behind a dumpster. The door rose to reveal a shiny black Mercedes-Benz sedan.

"Subtle," Surefire murmured.

"Have to be some perks to this job." He grabbed her wrist and yanked her inside. He pressed a square button on the interior wall, and the garage door closed. He let go of her wrist and squeezed the bridge of his nose.

Surefire whipped her fist around and decked him in the jaw. Raven dropped the gun and staggered back. He rubbed his cheek.

"What the hell?"

She snatched the gun from the floor with her now throbbing hand. Hitting Raven's jaw had hurt more than she'd expected. Did he have marbles underneath his skin? She switched hands and pointed the gun at him.

"How does it feel to have a gun pointed at you?"

His gaze flicked from the gun up to her eyes. "Not good."

"Exactly." She motioned with the gun. "Now open the door."

"No."

Her finger rubbed the trigger. "I've seen you get shot once before, so I know a bullet can puncture you." She watched as Raven lowered his hands to steady himself on a workbench lining the wall. "But I have a feeling that it's going to slow you down this time."

"It isn't loaded."

She cut a look at the exposed chambers and saw they were empty. She released the lock and pushed down the barrel on the top break revolver. No bullets.

"Told you." He rested his butt on the workbench.

Surefire slumped against the car. Couldn't one thing go her way tonight? At least Raven hadn't pointed a loaded gun at her head. That knowledge made her somewhat less upset.

"And you're welcome, by the way."

"For what?" She snapped the gun back together.

"For making those guards believe I took you hostage. That's why you hesitated in the museum, right? You didn't want them to think you were helping me."

She sighed. Was she that transparent? She rubbed the knot forming at the back of her head and winced. There was a little bit of blood, but not too bad. Though an ice pack would help with the swelling and her headache. Her eyes took in the garage; cans of paint, empty oil bottles, and various tools were scattered across a worn wooden workbench. She felt Raven studying her as she eyed the tools.

"That is why you hesitated back there, isn't it?" he asked again.

"I wasn't hesitating."

"Don't lie to me."

She took a deep breath before admitting, "Okay, you got me. I was going to turn us in."

Her head pounded. She rested her hand on the car to steady herself while guilt washed over her. It was as if she had broken a bond of trust with an old friend.

Raven stepped closer, and her breath hitched in her throat. For a split second, a dark violet hue swirled around his irises as his eyes bore down into her own.

"Ari wasn't joking when he threatened our families."

"I know." Surefire crossed her arms.

"No." He crossed his arms as well. "I don't think you do."

He continued to stare down at her as if waiting for an apology that Surefire would be damned if she would give. She tried to return the good ole stink eye he was giving her, but she wasn't feeling it, especially with her throbbing head.

"I've known Ari my entire life." He leaned against his car. "He was always driven to be the best even at the expense of others. I don't know where it came from. He had the kind of parents that I could only wish for." He took a deep breath, and his eyes shifted from her to stare blankly at the workbench in front of him.

Surefire wasn't sure how to respond, or even if she should. So Raven hadn't grown up in a Brady Bunch world. They had that much in common, and that tidbit brought him back down a notch after seeing him doing something extraordinary like phasing both of them out.

"He loved magic," he began again then shook his head. "No, he was obsessed with it. He wanted to be better than Copperfield. When he was around fourteen or fifteen, he was in this local talent competition. There was this kid who was an amateur magician and actually good enough to beat him. His name was Spencer. We broke into the kid's house. We were only going to sabotage a few of his tricks. But Ari killed the rabbit he used for his act. He picked up a paperweight and then . . ." Raven slammed his fist into his palm. "Smashed its head in. Just like that."

"That's horrible." Surefire couldn't imagine how someone could go to that extreme to win anything. In all her years of gymnastics competition, the worst she had done was have a stare down with another girl, or maybe give a well-placed cough during someone's dismount.

Then again, there was her sister Heather. No, she hadn't killed an animal or a person to get where she was now. But she'd definitely had a hand in crushing Surefire's gymnastic career.

"What happened when Spencer found out?"

"He had a breakdown and ended up in the hospital. Apparently, the rabbit was his best friend. He wasn't exactly Mr. Popular at school." He shrugged. "Came out on top, though. Owns a strip club on the Block. Love Bunnies, I think."

She choked back a laugh. "You made that up."

He gave her a quick smile. "Truth is stranger than fiction. But the moral of this fractured tale is that was Ari fifteen years ago. He's moved up from bunnies. He killed me." His irises again swirled and darkened to a purplish black. "His cousin. And by some freak twist of fate, I ended up with these abilities. Considering how he literally moved the earth to capture me, he is even more obsessed with attaining this god's powers."

"But that's what I don't get. Why the big production? Couldn't he have just taken you at any time?"

"Production is the key word here. He's a showman at heart. He wanted to show off his power."

He paused, and his eyes glazed over with a faraway look. "But you're right. Why now?" He focused back on her. "Unless . . ."

Her mild headache took that moment to explode into a raging migraine. Surefire rested her forehead on the roof of the car.

"What's wrong?" Raven's voice dropped with concern.

She pointed to the back of her head. "Smacked my head on the concrete when you tripped over the guard. It's nothing." She flicked her hand dismissively.

His fingers brushed the bump. "Let's get you some ice and an aspirin. Plus, I need a doughnut."

"A doughnut?" Her head popped up too quickly. The garage teetered then tottered as a sledgehammer pounded across her brain. Before she could stop herself, she grabbed his arm.

"Sugar powers me up. My health goes down a few notches when I phase or heal." He put his arm around her shoulder to steady her. "I'm especially drained now. I've never phased another person before, and it took its toll even with Xochi's recharge."

He bent closer and brushed her hair away from her forehead. Something a boyfriend would do, a particularly thoughtful one, not an enemy. She couldn't get a grasp on her feelings toward Raven. Was he a thief? A target? Her kidnapper? Someone she could trust? He went from shoving a gun in her face, to phasing her out, to taking care of her. Her emotions were in a jumble, not unlike her head.

She winced. Her headache had moved beyond a sledgehammer to the constant grinding of a jackhammer.

"Can you walk?"

"Yeah." She didn't want him carrying her again. The steps he led her to looked way too steep to be carried up. Especially if he was still weak. Though Raven's weak was probably stronger than most men.

The wooden steps creaked under their combined weight.

As they reached the top, her head stopped pounding enough for her to ask, "Is this where you live?"

"When I'm in town."

"Aren't you afraid to show me your place? I'll know how to find you."

He scooted past her onto the top step in front of a grey metal door. "Considering my cousin is about to unleash an Aztec god and end the world, you're the least of my concerns."

He opened the door and motioned for her to go through. She walked into the dark room as he flipped on the light.

The sudden brightness stung her eyes. She closed them and then attempted just a slit to test her reaction. When the pounding in her head ratcheted back to a dull throb, she opened her eyes fully.

"Oh." The exclamation fell from her lips before she could stop it.

The apartment was modest and normal, like her last boyfriend's home. What had she expected? A high-tech hideout? A playboy bungalow? A well-armed bunker?

She wasn't sure, but this wasn't it. This wasn't Raven. The car in the garage, yes. This place, definitely not.

Her disappointment must've shown on her face, because Raven seemed compelled to blurt out, "It's a hole in the wall. Just a place to lie low when I'm in town."

She walked past the galley kitchen last updated in the eighties with fake oak panel cabinets and into the living room with a two-seater couch littered with jeans, socks, video game controllers, and underwear?

Raven pushed past her, shoved the underwear behind the couch, and knocked the rest of the items off the cushions and onto the floor.

"Make yourself at home." He motioned to the sofa.

"Do you feel nauseated? Dizzy? Confused?" he asked. "I want to make sure you don't have a concussion."

"No concussion, I'm sure. Though I have a headache." She propped herself up against the partition wall between the kitchen and the living room. "You mentioned aspirin?"

"Yes." Raven jogged by her and into the kitchen. He opened a few cabinets until he found the pill bottle.

He slid it across the scratched beige countertop toward her. "Here."

"And water." He opened the refrigerator and took out two bottled waters and set them on the counter. "I don't trust DC tap water. Tastes like metal socks."

"And then ice." He threw open the freezer and grabbed two small cooler packs. "You need to ice that hand. It's starting to swell."

She looked down at her hand and extended her fingers. Sure enough, her knuckles appeared puffy, and her joints ached. She tossed the gun onto the counter.

"Like hitting Superman." He took a drink of his water. "I'm just glad you didn't break it."

"Funny. I see humility isn't your strong point."

She tried to open the bottle of aspirin, but her fingers could barely bend to grasp the cap. Raven took it from her, opened it, and then poured three tablets onto the counter.

"I'm only stating the obvious." He tossed her two towels.

"So was I."

She popped the pills into her mouth and downed half the water bottle, more thirsty than she'd realized. She wrapped the towels around the ice packs and perched one on the back of her hand. Bowing her head over the counter and closing her eyes, she positioned the other ice pack onto the ever-enlarging knot.

"Here, let me help," Raven said, his voice muffled by something in his mouth.

"Are you eating?"

He moved her hand away from the ice pack on her head. "A doughnut. You want one?"

Her stomach growled when she smelled the sweet strawberry jelly, her favorite. "Not yet."

"I'll leave them out for you."

"So you still eat food."

"I still do a lot of things," he replied between bites.

She ignored the innuendo in his tone. Obviously, he was feeling better. "Food regenerates you?"

"Just like food gives you energy, I need it to reboot the abilities I have. They become drained, like people's bodies are drained when they do a marathon or workout. I still sleep as well."

"Hmmm . . ."

"Have you ever played a video game?"

"A few."

"You know how there's this power bar in the corner of the screen that depletes as the character is hurt?"

She nodded.

"And in some games, you have to find special health packs to build their energy back up?"

"I guess."

"Well, food is my health pack."

"Huh. I think I get the metaphor. I used to watch my boyfriend play Call of Duty."

"Boyfriend?" Did she detect jealousy in his tone? "I never pegged you for having a life outside of work."

She took that as a compliment. "Had a life. We broke up last year. He couldn't take the hours I worked. Wasn't the center of attention. So, I moved in with Heather until I found a—hey!" She straightened up and snatched the ice pack from his hand. "Why am I telling you this?"

Grabbing what was left of her bottled water, she stalked out of the kitchen and into the small living room/dining room. Her head pounded a little less. The swelling in her hand had started to go down. She took in the pea-green couch with black cotton boxers strewn over the corner—which Raven had missed during his hasty clean up—and the wobbly oak kitchenette table with two chairs pulled out haphazardly next to it. She plopped down into one of the wooden chairs and reapplied the ice to her head as she tried not to think about how she had just told Raven more about her ex-boyfriend Tony than she'd confided to her family.

She heard Raven plod across the carpet and stop in front of her. "Hope it wasn't me."

"Excuse me?" She raised her head.

He looked down at her with an expression she couldn't quite read. Amused? Regretful? Sorry? "I hope it wasn't my case that kept you away from him."

She huffed. Why couldn't he let it be? This had nothing to do with him.

"Your case took up a lot of my time, but really, it's weird talking about this with you. Just drop it."

He folded his arms.

"Fine. If it makes you feel better." She had no idea why she felt it necessary to say, "It wasn't you. It was me. There, you happy?"

He smiled more with relief, it seemed, than amusement. "How did you find me tonight?"

"I'm not about to tell you."

Raven leaned down and planted his hands on the table next to her arm. She hadn't realized how large his hands were until she saw them next to her own. Long, tapered, strong fingers with small patches of dark hair on the backs of them.

"How did you know where I was going to be this evening?"

She raised her eyes to meet his.

"I didn't even know my next assignment until earlier today."

She considered lying, but the gravity of his expression made her reconsider. He was working something out, and her answer was key. "I knew you'd end up at the warehouse. I'd trailed you there the first time I lost you. Several guards claimed to have seen you there over the past few months. We assumed you had a stash in there, and some of the shipping manifests looked doctored, but we didn't have enough evidence for a warrant."

"Go on."

"I wasn't scheduled to work tonight. I hadn't planned a stake out at any potential museums or private residences I thought you might hit. Things had run a little dry, and then I got a call from Pixie."

"Pixie?"

"Another agent. She was manning the phones tonight and called to say they got a lead that you had broken into the Walters. Which made sense, since I had seen an ad for the opening of a new exhibit similar to your other hits."

"But who told Pixie?"

Surefire shrugged. "She never said."

Plus, Surefire had been too excited to finally have some action in the case to question Pixie at the time. It wasn't odd for anonymous sources to call in with tips on a case. Especially one as high-profile as Raven's had become.

"All right then." He scrubbed his hand over his face, a gesture Surefire had noticed he did when he was worried.

He strode over to the couch, where he picked up a duffle bag she hadn't spotted before. "I'm going to use the bathroom. You want to go first?"

"What?" She stood and dropped the ice pack.

He hesitated with his hand on the doorknob, then gave her an innocent expression, which didn't work on his not-so-innocent face. "I'm going to wash up. Use the potty, if you need to know."

"No."

"No? I can't use the bathroom?" He cocked his head.

"No, I mean, what was with the grilling about your case? How I found you tonight? There's something you're not telling me."

He took a long breath before opening the door. She was sure he was buying time, trying to determine what to reveal to her. "I think we were set up by someone working on the inside at U-Sec. Probably the same person who helped Ari break into U-Sec's servers and download your personal information. I think Ari wanted you in that warehouse tonight, but I don't know why."

He stepped inside the bathroom and closed the door before she could respond, before she could process what he'd said.

Then his words sunk into her aching, muddled mind. Ari wanted you. We were set up.

She ran over to the door and slapped her hand against it. "Why would Ari want me?"

"I don't know." His faint reply came over the whirring of the bathroom's exhaust fan.

"Then what should we do?"

"Can we talk when I get out? I'm . . . uh . . . thinking right now."

"What?" She furrowed her brow before she realized what he meant. "Oh, yeah. Bathroom." She backed away from the door and into the chair. "Gotcha."

Why would Ari want her? Before tonight, she hadn't known Ari was related to this case. She hadn't even known he was related to Raven. She hadn't known he was a criminal.

A psychic scam artist, yes.

Someone capable of raising a god and destroying the world, no.

Thankfully, the aspirin had kicked in, and she could finally hold a thought without pain slicing through her brain. Although her thoughts did nothing to shed light on the situation. Finding out her involvement tonight was possibly premeditated unnerved her to the core. Someone had controlled her like a pawn in their game. Someone close to U-Sec, close to this case had pulled her strings.

She needed Pax. She needed him now. Needed to tell him that U-Sec's systems were in danger.

Over the continuous sound of the bathroom fan, she heard the shower turn on.

She stared dumbfounded at the bathroom door. Raven was taking a shower at a time like this?

Oh, he really was vain.

Surefire didn't waste any time pondering his vanity. She sprinted toward the entrance and tried the door. Locked. She knelt, took out her knife, and eyed the doorknob. No lock, just a solid brushed nickel knob. Then she noticed the keypad next to the door, and the blinking red light above it.

She ran back into the living room and pushed aside two snowboards wedged behind the couch in front of a window. She threw open the orange polyester curtains. The windows were welded shut with bars on the other side. She scampered into the kitchen and opened the drawers and cabinets. She only found a pack of paper plates and plastic knives and forks. Not even a skillet or a pot. Not even a lighter.

Then she searched for a phone, anything that could help her contact the outside world. Besides a stale cheese puff, a dollar in change, mismatched snowboarding boots, and some random DVDs—including a collection of Buffy the Vampire Slayer, which was rather surprising—there was nothing she could use.

Of course, if Ari had planted a spy at U-Sec, then she shouldn't call the U-Sec switchboard or even send a text to Pax's cell. Ari might be monitoring all channels in and out of U-Sec.

She shoved a piece of jelly doughnut into her mouth then flopped back onto the oak chair.

A plan. She needed a plan. Some direction. The next step was to drive to Baltimore and retrieve the statue from U-Sec. After that, they return it to Xochi. Then what? They retrieve the skull and stop Ari. Though she was unclear on the "how" part of all this.

She chewed the last bit of the doughnut, then licked the jelly off her fingers.

At some point when they returned to Baltimore, she would find a way to contact Pax directly. If a U-Sec agent was working for Ari, then Pax needed to know. How to do that without Ari finding out and bringing the wrath of a god down on her family was another thing altogether.

Then again, she had forgotten about Oracle. She could read minds. Search out and find people based on their unique thought patterns. But Oracle needed to be in close proximity with a person to fully read his or her mind, and she'd have to focus on reading that person's thoughts. And she never opened her mind without proper cause and only under controlled situations. It was too dangerous for her.

Surefire laid her head on the table in resignation. There was also the problem of what to do with Raven. Which, technically, shouldn't be a problem. When all was said and done, he had stolen millions in art and artifacts. Albeit it was for a good cause—to save the world.

Damn it. She'd liked it better when he was just an obnoxious, slippery thief. Then she knew where she stood with him. Why did he have to be so . . .

Nice?

He'd saved her life several times. He'd pretended to kidnap her, so she wouldn't ruin her reputation. Then he'd made sure she got aspirin and water and even held an ice pack to her head. Seriously, if Tony had iced even one of her wounds—just once—in the year they were together, they would probably still be together. Hell, she couldn't even remember a time when anyone in her family had cared for her as Raven had done tonight.

She liked him. And she was beginning to like him a lot more than was appropriate considering he was on U-Sec's Most Wanted list.

Heather was right. She really did have bad taste in men.

Surefire lifted her head and downed the rest of the water. Out of habit, she glanced at her wristwatch, then did a double take. It read one thirty. Her watch was running again. When they were in—she furrowed her brow, not knowing what Xochi's home was called, then decided the the Garden seemed to fit—so, when they'd entered the Garden her watch had stopped at one. She knew it had taken longer than thirty minutes to make it from the warehouse through the Garden and then to Raven's apartment.

She turned to the generic black-and-white round clock hanging on the living room wall.

It showed the same time.

It had been midnight when she'd entered the warehouse after Raven. She remembered looking at her watch when the police pulled up outside at twelve twenty.

This meant one key thing: the statue was still at the warehouse. Since they went missing, she doubted U-Sec or the police had time to tag, bag, and transport any evidence from the scene.

If they hurried, the statue might still be there when they reached Baltimore.

♥ ☠ ♥ ☠ ♥ ☠

Raven strained to hear over the fan's whir if Surefire would say anything more. She didn't.

Good.

She was probably trashing his place right now—not that she'd do much damage—trying to find a way out or a phone. He was certain she'd attempt to contact U-Sec in spite of his tale of Ari and the bunny. Which didn't sound so scary when he put it that way.

Surefire was definitely hardheaded. And she had a hard left hook.

He rubbed his jaw. If he were still human, her punch might have left him stunned or at least slightly bruised.

Leave it to him to help a woman only to get decked in the face. What did they say about good deeds?

After sifting through his duffle bag, he took out his toothpaste and toothbrush. He leaned against the sink and brushed his teeth. He was exhausted. Still drained from phasing out. He needed something more substantial than a doughnut. A good eight hours' rest would work, but that wouldn't happen anytime soon.

He wiped his mouth with a hand towel. It was more than physical exhaustion. Mentally and emotionally, it all weighed on him. Everything that had been revealed to him tonight. Everything that had happened to him tonight.

Ari had raised a god. Ari had previously sacrificed Raven to raise a god. Ari was going to destroy the world.

Just one of those events would've been mind-blowing enough. Adding to this frustrating mix was Xochi's involvement. It wasn't a coincidence she'd sent him to steal her own statue tonight, a statue they needed to find the final skull and stop Tezcatlipoca. Xochi was more involved than she'd let on and knew more than she'd been willing to reveal.

A woman keeping a secret from him. What a surprise.

Was Xochi working with her estranged husband? He doubted it. However, before tonight he had doubted Ari would ever kill him. He'd thought the temple collapse was an accident.

He needed to work on his people-reading skills.

Then there was Surefire. Or Synthia. Or whatever she preferred to be called.

Pain in the ass came to mind.

A nice ass also came to mind.

He chuckled, remembering when he'd first seen her in the leotard and wrestling mask entering the warehouse earlier that evening. He'd almost fallen off the beam. Just to find out if his eyes were playing tricks on him, he had waited for her to catch up to him. She'd worn the absurd outfit with an unnerving confidence, as if it was her standard uniform. He always thought of her regular one-piecer as belonging to a Star Trek extra.

In all the commotion, he had forgotten to ask her what had happened to her uniform. Though he had to admit, the leotard did show off her tight body. There was no doubt she was an athlete, a gymnast. He wondered if she were still flexible.

He turned on the shower. Cold.

Not that he needed to consider her flexibility. He tore off his shirt. Not that he needed to consider anything more about her except how she could be useful to this mission—as Xochi had pointed out. He shoved off his pants.

Not that he could help himself.

When he'd first met her months ago, he'd crashed into her on his way out of the Baltimore Museum of Art. Tripped over her at the exit—a small girl with long, thick blonde hair sticking out from under a black Lycra ski-type mask that covered the top portion of her face. He'd thought it was a joke, or a college cheerleader playing vigilante dress-up. She'd looked like an anime cartoon come to life with her large eyes and heart-shaped face.

Then she'd pulled out a gun and called for backup on her communicator. He'd asked, "Does Ken know you left the dream house?"

She'd rolled her eyes, her soon-to-be signature reaction to him, and this had goaded him to comment, "Didn't know a dart gun was the new accessory. Shouldn't it be pink?"

She hadn't missed a beat when she'd said, "You know a lot about Barbies. Is there something you want to confess before I arrest you?"

He stepped into the icy shower and blew out a breath when the water hit his skin. He loved the initial shock of the cold beating down on him. Because when he turned the water to hot, it felt so much sweeter. Though this time he left it a bit chilled. The cool shower allowed him to think. Focus.

And the cold kept his body from reacting to her.

Surefire on the other side of the door. Alone. In his place. How many years had it been since he was alone with a woman? How many years had it been since he was with a woman?

A human woman. A flesh-and-blood woman.

Three years. It had been three years since the pyramid had crumbled and crushed him and he'd made a deal with Xochi. It felt like an eternity. With Xochi's threat hanging over his head, it would be an eternity until he was ever with another woman. She was not sharing what was hers.

His body flushed hot with resentment despite the cold water showering his skin.

He was used to his freedom. He had done whatever he pleased, whomever he pleased. Since he had become—whatever this was—he lived on the fringe. Away from nearly everyone. Alone. Save for one person. Kat.

Being this close to Surefire reminded him of what he had given up—in the physical and emotional sense. He hadn't felt the longing and the emptiness until she'd run her fingers over his tattoos, his skin. Then he'd held her tight after she'd fallen into the tree, and he'd smelled her perfume and felt her warmth in his arms. And just now, when he'd held the ice pack for her, and she'd talked and opened up to him, he'd felt a connection. A connection he hadn't experienced with another living soul in years.

This was only a tease. A preview of a movie he'd never get to watch. After this adventure was over they would go their separate ways. She'd go back to trying to hunt him or whatever other assignment she was given. He'd lie low for a while until his next assignment.

Life would go on. Everyone else's lives.

He missed his old life. He missed playing sports, especially snowboarding—one of his favorites. He'd even sponsored a team that made it to the Olympics. And he was pretty good, too. The wind whipping past his ears, the crunch of snow under his board, the pristine scenery represented a freedom he'd taken for granted at the time.

He'd thought his life would forever be that free. How cocky and disillusioned he'd been.

He missed his home near the slopes in Utah and the penthouse condo on the beach. He missed his business—the legitimate side—and he missed the women. But they had never really been his, and he had never really been theirs. Some probably had thought they were, acted as if he belonged to them. He'd been foolish enough to think there was time to find love, foolish enough to think he would never need it, never want it.

He turned off the shower and heard Surefire yelling through the door.

"We've got to go."

He toweled off. "I'm getting dressed."

"Ugh. Hurry up."

She was rolling her cute mis-matched eyes. He knew it.

He sprayed on some deodorant, then threw on his jeans and a T-shirt. He swung open the door. "What's going on?"

She pulled back. "You changed?"

"The tight clothes chafe." He shoved his hands into his pockets and leaned against the door jam. "And we'll have to get you something new. The harbor water cologne isn't for you."

She sniffed her sleeve and then crinkled her nose. "I don't have time to shower and neither did you, if we want to snag the statue before it gets put away at U-Sec. According to your clock and my watch, it's taken less than thirty minutes to go from underneath the warehouse to your apartment."

He looked at the living room clock and stuck out his bottom lip. "So it has. Even better."

He walked past her into the kitchen and opened the refrigerator door.

She followed him. "I don't understand how this could happen."

"Time operates differently there."

"This means we've gained time to get the statue. They may not have placed it in storage yet. It might still be at the warehouse, which will make it easier to take."

He grabbed a soda and closed the refrigerator door.

"We need to go now. It'll take at least an hour to get to Baltimore from here."

"Maybe a little less." He winked.

She threw up her hands.

"It's chilly outside. Don't you want to change?"

"Into what?" She motioned to his tall frame. "I'll get swallowed up in your clothes."

"The last time Kat was in town . . ." He trailed off as he walked across the room and opened the door to his bedroom. "Ah, here. She's somewhat taller, but it should work. And I just washed them."

He brought out a purple sweater and a pair of black leggings folded in his outstretched arms.

"Might be a little long on you, but you could roll up the leggings."

She took the offered clothes and looked at him with a question.

"You can change in the bathroom. I hung an extra towel and washcloth for you, which you may want to think about using." He popped open the can of soda and took a drink.

She stared at the clothes in her hand, her brows drawn down. "Who's Kat?"

Raven studied her, unsure what he wanted to reveal. If something went south, if U-Sec somehow captured him, he didn't want Surefire—or anyone at U-Sec—to know details about Kat.

"The only person I've ever cared about."

Chapter Ten

Ari paced inside the boarded-up brewery, wearing a path in the layer of grime on the floor of the abandoned bottling room. The smell of rancid hops and barley sickened his stomach, but the steel fermentation tanks and the iron beams lining the ceiling helped obscure his presence from any sensitive U-Sec agents at the warehouse—particularly Oracle. Her abilities were stronger than alluded to in her file. When he had arrived again on the scene, he'd felt her probing the area, opening up her mind, searching. Her telepathic tentacles had immediately latched onto him and tried to burrow into his mind like energized worms. He'd shut her out and fled to this building to wait for Raven and Surefire, who were taking way too long to arrive.

He checked his watch.

According to his sources, Raven and Surefire had returned via a portal in the form of a tomb on display in the National Museum of Natural History—without the final skull. Soon after, he'd received word that U-Sec had found in the warehouse the statue stolen earlier by Raven, which explained why he hadn't returned with the skull. Raven needed that statue to retrieve the skull. Ari had assumed Raven had the statue on his person when he and Surefire had passed through the stone door.

His temper rose along with Tezcatlipoca's power, burning a path across his shoulders to the base of his skull. Adding another layer of complications, his source had relayed to him that the portal under the warehouse was broken and the water had yet to recede. Hence the reason Raven and Surefire had traveled through the one in the museum. They would need to return to DC to cross back over, another waste of precious time.

He had considered nabbing the statue himself. However, the essence trapped inside the stone object belonged to Xochiquetzal, Tezcatlipoca's wife—the yin to his yang. Since Ari received his power from Tezcatlipoca, there was a chance Xochiquetzal's essence would negate Ari's powers and weaken him. Thereby exposing him to U-Sec and the police.

A chance he couldn't take. If anything were to go wrong, he wanted Surefire and Raven to take the heat. They would be his red herrings. U-Sec didn't need to know Ari was the director behind the scenes.

Now if only they would get here, so Ari could make sure nothing more went wrong.

He took out his tablet computer from the satchel flung over his shoulder. An hour ago, he had hacked into the security cameras in DC and spotted Raven's Mercedes cruising down Ninth Street toward I-395 north, so he knew Raven and Surefire were en route. He tapped open the maps application and was greeted with red flashes lining the major arteries leading out of DC.

Traffic. His hands tightened on the device, and the screen wavered. *Always traffic mucking up the best-laid plans.* He hated living in this area. Thankfully, that was about to change soon.

His phone buzzed in his pocket. He looked at the name on the screen and inwardly groaned. He was irritated enough at the moment without having to deal with her.

"Yes," he hissed.

"Sweetie, it's all set. I'm on the plane."

He cringed at her sugar-coated, girlish tone.

"I've never been on a private jet before," she went on, speaking so fast she didn't pause when Ari tried to interrupt. "It's amazing. Real posh. And they have steak *and* Heineken! Can you believe it? Talk about class. Anyways, the captain's ready to start loading it up. Where are you?"

Just one more night.

He needed her help for just one more night and that was it. "Change in plans. I want you back at U-Sec headquarters."

"No can do. Olie is coming by the office soon. I had to get *outie.* I cleaned the computer, though. Deleted all the major bits. I also called Surefire's sis like you asked. Man, was she ticked. She had to cancel plans in Atlantic City or something like that. I don't know. Wasn't paying much attention. She started freaking out on me about Surefire disappearing, so I hung up."

"But she's back in town now?" Ari asked in a measured tone.

"She was on her way a few hours ago. Should be there soon. But I tell you that Olie is a sweetie," she prattled on. "I think he was worried about little ole me. He was planning to take me to breakfast after my shift. Geez, I only went on a few dates with him, and it was only for you. It's really sad I can't get him to come with."

"I don't care about Olie."

"Awww, is someone jealous?"

He scowled at the phone. Energy danced along his skin like little fingers itching to break free and scratch the life from her.

"One more night."

"What was that, hon?"

"Nothing." He took another breath and considered his contingency plan. "I gave you an address yesterday. Go there and wait for further instructions. I want you to do one more thing for me before we leave."

"Anything for you." Her voice purred through the phone. *"Ma xipatinemi.* See, I'm practicing my Aztec."

"It's called Náhuatl."

"Na-ha-what?"

"Never mind. Just go."

He hung up the phone and felt the urge to regroup. Funny how an ordinary chit could be so taxing.

He touched the obsidian amulet hanging around his neck by a leather cord. The amulet was a chip off the obsidian slab in which Ari had trapped Tezcatlipoca's spirit. The palm-sized piece warmed in his hand, pulsating with an orgasmic power that sent his heart racing and every cell buzzing. This was just a taste of Tezcatlipoca's powers. When Tezcatlipoca ascended, he would fully possess him and his abilities. He couldn't imagine how stimulating it would be. How everyone would finally respect him, finally see he did possess true magic. Not like those mutated transhumans. Not like Raven, who existed on borrowed abilities. No one could compete with the power of a god.

He'd come a long way from a child of factory workers barely scraping a living in West Virginia. He'd always known he was meant for extraordinary things. Now it was time for the world to realize it, too.

He pulled a uniform out of his bag and then stopped when he caught his reflection in one of the windows. Thankfully, it was no longer a roach, though the face that stared back wasn't his. It was older, fuller, and more distinguished. He liked the authority it yielded. The square jaw, level eyes, low forehead. The deep, weathered voice. Maybe he would keep it for a while after this bit was done. After this show was over, and he ensured that Surefire would keep her promise, that she knew how real his threats were.

Chapter Eleven

Fighting a bizarre mix of sleepiness and unease, Surefire tapped her fingers on the polished leather armrest inside Raven's obsessively clean Mercedes sedan. It was taking longer to reach Baltimore than Raven had brazenly declared. DC highways were unpredictable even during the early Sunday morning hours. There was always construction or an accident or both.

This time it was both.

"Take Route 198." She flipped her hand at the upcoming exit sign. "We can cut over to I-95 from there."

"The radio said it would break up after this exit. Ninety-five is worse. Too much construction. I got stuck in it last week."

"Whatever. You're driving." Her vision dimmed with drowsiness. The sign blurred as they drove past. How could she be so tired, yet this anxious? Forcing her eyes open, she slumped in the seat and crossed her arms. Her right leg bobbed.

"Nervous?" He glanced at her then back to the road as traffic started moving again. The radio announcer was right. The backup ended at this exit.

"I want this over."

"It will be soon." He gunned the engine, and they sped past the final fire truck blocking the left lane.

She wasn't sure which he meant—that they'd soon have the statue or that this twisted adventure would soon be over. She was about to steal from her job, from those who trusted her. Those same people were in danger, and she couldn't even shoot out a warning flare.

Sitting up, she rubbed her eyes in a vain effort to rub away the tiredness. She pushed the sleeves of the sweater down over her hands, suddenly feeling chilled or maybe fidgety, because she couldn't get comfortable despite the heated, body contouring leather seat. Wearing clothes that belonged to a strange woman didn't help either. A woman whom Raven cared about deeply. A woman who apparently had generous assets and loved low-cut clothes, because Surefire had to wear the sweater backward or risk exposing her own not-so-generous assets.

Figures Raven would be into a woman like that.

"You're not having second thoughts, are you?" Raven asked.

Of course I am.

"Of course not."

He slammed on the brakes, and the car skidded onto the shoulder and fishtailed. Surefire bounced off the passenger window.

"You can't contact anyone while we're there," he stated sharply.

"Ow." She rubbed her shoulder. "No need for theatrics. I said I wouldn't."

"I don't believe you." He pivoted in his seat.

She looked down at her hands, dry and cracked from the cool night, and away from his accusatory gaze. "That's rich. A *thief* not believing me. Is that another one of your powers? Human lie detector? Do you have a magic lasso in the trunk?"

She peeked up at him from the corner of her eye through the veil of her hair. He stared straight ahead out at the road. A few cars whizzed by, and Raven's sedan rocked slightly in their wake.

He rubbed his forehead with his thumb. "No, I don't know if you're lying, but you hesitated before you responded. Since we're about to steal from U-Sec and breach the security of your employer, I assume you're having second thoughts."

Steal from U-Sec. Breach their security.

Those words hit a nerve sending a wave of anger through her body. On second thought, yes, she was lying.

"You know what?" She tossed up her hands then slapped them down on her legging-covered lap. "Yes, I am having second thoughts. U-Sec's systems have probably been compromised. I don't know how—or even if—we can defeat Ari by ourselves."

"And you're willing to risk the lives of your family for something you're unsure of?"

"We believe someone played me. Someone from inside U-Sec. If that's the case, I need to warn Pax. The lives of my family and co-workers are at risk even without my compromising the situation. They have the right to know."

He responded with a blank stare, as if he couldn't process what she was saying.

"Just a note." When yelling didn't work, a softer approach might. She touched his arm. He glanced at her hand resting on his forearm and grimaced, but she continued anyway. "I could slip a note into a car in the parking lot. If Oracle is there, I could possibly reach her telepathically."

"Absolutely not. We do this together without their help, or I do this alone with you tied up in my trunk."

"Wha . . . what did you say?" Surefire stammered. No, she'd heard him wrong. He hadn't just threatened to hog-tie her. Had he?

"You heard me." An ornery grin replaced his grimace. She drew back her hand. "Now, do I have to tie you up and stow you in the trunk until this is over or will you sit there, shut up, and continue to look pretty?"

"I won't do anything. . . ." Her words trailed off as her vision fogged.

"Didn't think you'd agree." Raven's voice drifted across her befuddled brain just before she dropped into a dead sleep.

She wasn't sure how much later it was when she found herself bound, gagged and awfully cramped in the pitch-black trunk of his car. Her hands and legs tied together behind her back allowed her to flail like a beached porpoise at best. Though a beached porpoise was probably more graceful—and less irritated—than Surefire. Thankfully she was flexible, or this situation would be even more uncomfortable.

The car slowed from mach-speed to something more reasonable on what she assumed were city streets. Then it stopped. She heard the release lever being popped from the driver's side, and the car door opened and then closed. A moment later, the trunk was lifted up.

"Are you ready to listen?" Raven leaned down and yanked her gag off.

"I can't believe you did this to me. I swear when I'm untied you are so—"

He slammed the trunk shut.

Oh, he did *not* just do that to her.

"No, open it. Come on. My leg's asleep." She strained fruitlessly against the nylon ropes and wondered where he had gotten the rope—and more importantly—how he had knocked her out.

He must have drugged her at his apartment. Maybe with the water. Maybe with the jelly doughnut. Something that didn't have any lasting effects and took time to get into her system. It would explain why she had felt sleepy in such a stressful situation.

As if that mattered now. What mattered was getting the hell out of these ropes and ending this mission and putting him in jail, a fortified one from which he couldn't phase out.

To think she'd actually considered him nice, had actually started to like him.

Despite his recent assignment to save the world, Raven was a career criminal used to lying and manipulating others to get what he wanted. What else did she expect?

He started the car. She banged her feet on the back seat. With her hands tied to her ankles, this stunt proved awkward and painful.

"Let me out." She twisted her neck to face the front of the car. "I'll do whatever you want."

She stopped and reconsidered what she had said, then clarified, "I won't try to contact them."

The car took off again. Soon they bounced along pothole-laden streets and over what she assumed were railroad tracks.

She jerked her shoulders back and forth to dislodge the butterfly knife resting against her breasts inside her bra. In her frustration, she had forgotten about it. The knife slid out then got caught in the bulky folds of the sweater.

"Damn it."

The car slowed to a stop, and the engine shut off.

The second time Raven opened the trunk, she was prepared. She bit her tongue so hard she almost drew blood. It was the only way she could stop herself from cursing him out.

"I need you to look me in the eyes and promise you won't contact them. I'd rather you come with me. I may need your help. But it's no skin off me if you stay here."

Surefire glared at him and bit out, "I promise."

He reached his hand down her sweater.

"Hey!" She squirmed.

He pulled out her knife and flicked it open. "Know that any type of communication could cost people their lives. If you do anything to compromise us, you'll wish I'd used a stronger dose and left you here."

"When this is over, you're so going down." She leveled what she hoped was an intimidating gaze at him.

He flipped her over like a stuffed piglet and cut the ropes. "Is that a promise?"

"You know what I mean." She wiggled her hands out of the ropes and pushed them off her legs. Raven stood back from the trunk, probably afraid that she'd kick him where it mattered. He was right.

She eased out of the trunk and then held out her hand for the knife.

"I'll keep it for now." He shoved it in his front jean pocket.

"Fine." She pursed her lips, unhappy that Raven had confiscated her only weapon. Losing the knife made her more vulnerable, and this added to her annoyance. "Where to?"

She recognized the sixties-style shipping offices around her and the boarded-up, gutted remains of a brewery. Old hops and barley formed a putrid mix with the salty, fishy water scent lacing the air. Several semis were stowed in a fenced lot adjacent to where they had parked on the street. They weren't far from the warehouse.

"This way." He nodded in the direction of a narrow alleyway.

They stayed in the shadows and stuck to the left side of the alley. They crossed a couple of roads. From between two buildings, she could make out the lights of the warehouse property and the high fence surrounding it. Raven stuck out his hand to stop her before she could cross the last street. He peered around the corner of the building. A truck barreled down the street too fast for these uneven, cracked roads. She poked her head out in time to witness her sister's red Hummer career by, kicking up dirt and rocks in its wake. She flattened herself against the building.

"That was my sister. What's she doing here?" Surefire whispered.

"Driving like an ass."

"Like you're one to talk."

She peeped around the building's edge as a large truck rambled down the opposite side of the main road. Surefire's silver Honda Civic bounced atop the flatbed tow truck.

Just great. She hoped they were towing it home and not to the impound lot.

They waited a beat while Raven tilted his head, listening for sounds of cars or other movement. Then he grabbed her wrist and led her across the street to an abandoned office. He kicked open a door.

"What are we doing here?"

"Getting a better vantage point." He pulled her inside the disheveled space and up three flights of questionable stairs.

When they reached the third level, Raven walked across a room littered with broken desks, bookshelves, chairs, and outdated computers blanketed with a layer of dust and dirt. In front of them, the floor-to-ceiling windows provided an unobstructed—except for the greasy smudges and random cracks—view of the warehouse lot.

Raven pulled out pocket-sized binoculars and scanned the area below. "Here." He handed them to her. "What do you see?"

She looked out past the fence below and over the grassy parking lot, where her sister had parked next to Pax's SUV. She focused the binoculars on the police cruisers and U-Sec's shiny new moving truck, which were parked along the side of the warehouse. Wearing U-Sec-issued flame-resistant black canvas pants and a hooded sweatshirt, Inferno carried objects from inside the building to the truck while two men each pushed a dolly up a ramp inside. His shorn head exposed along with his clean-cut, Irish-American good looks, Inferno didn't wear a mask like Surefire did. He didn't have anything to hide. No family to protect. He went by Inferno because it was a nickname his military buddies had given him.

"My boss is here. I saw his car." She lowered the binoculars. "That moving truck belongs to U-Sec. They use it to haul large amounts evidence. I guess they found more than Xochi's statue in that building."

Raven swore and kicked at a busted keyboard. "Months of work." He dropped his head and stood with his hands on his hips.

She scanned the scene again, and her heart jumped in her chest at what she saw. "Inferno is carrying the sack you left behind. The statue's still here."

She handed him the binoculars.

He peered through them. "Sure enough." He tossed her the binoculars and then disappeared.

Surefire spun around, amazed how Raven could phase out so quickly. Is that what the Smithsonian guards had witnessed at the museum? One minute Surefire and Raven had stood in front of them, the next minute . . . *poof?*

She had to admit, it was a cool ability.

Squinting out the window, Surefire wondered if she could pinpoint where Raven was floating. Several minutes later, Heather stomped out of the warehouse. Well, as much as she could stomp across grass and gravel in those heels, which looked suspiciously like Surefire's new shoes. As they bickered, Hunter trailed a few steps behind with his hands in his pockets. Surefire raised the binoculars up to her eyes. Actually, Heather was bickering and Hunter was trying to look everywhere but at his soon-to-be wife.

They jumped into Heather's truck and peeled away. Another few minutes went by without any sign of Raven or the statue. Surefire fidgeted and looked at her watch then back at the scene, tapping her foot against the grimy linoleum.

Once more she peered through the binoculars when she noticed Pax walk out of the building toward his truck. He paused before opening the door and cut a look behind him. Surefire refocused the lenses and saw Oracle making her way toward him. Suddenly Oracle stopped and lifted her head and stared right at Surefire.

She dropped the binoculars and skittered back. Had Oracle seen her? Surefire shook her head. *Don't be stupid. She can't see.*

Oracle must have sensed her. She must've opened her mind to search the area and picked up on Surefire's thoughts.

Surefire closed her eyes and closed off her mind. Then she reconsidered. She should do it. Raven would never know. She could reach out mentally.

She shook her head again. She couldn't. She had promised Raven she wouldn't do it. Her word, even to a criminal, had to mean something, or she wouldn't be any better than he was. If there was a chance Ari would find out and hurt her family, then she couldn't do it.

Behind her a piece of glass crunched and the floorboards creaked.

"Raven?" She spun around. Her mouth went as dry as the dust around her. "Dad?"

"Are you coming?" Pax called to Oracle, who was taking her sweet time walking from the warehouse to his car. He had tried to be nonchalant about waiting for her outside his SUV's door to see how long it took for her to leave

Matthews's side and follow him. Now it was obvious that he'd been waiting and that irritated him even more.

When she stepped onto the grassy parking lot from the gravel drive surrounding the warehouse, Oracle came to an abrupt stop. Her eyes closed tight, and her head dropped back.

"What is it?" He jogged over to her. He recognized the focused expression cinching her face. "I ordered you not to open your mind. It's too dangerous."

"I thought I sensed Surefire, but I wasn't certain. I can't hold onto it. Like something's blocking me."

"Is she blocking you?"

"No, I've felt people keep me out before, and this isn't it. It's like the force I felt in the warehouse when she first went missing. The air feels dense, heavy, like it's weighted down with a thick fog." Oracle scanned the far edge of the parking lot as if she were searching with her eyes and not with her mind. Her gaze wavered on a rundown building outside the fence opposite them.

She breathed in deeply. "There. It's gone again. Retreated. I don't know what caused it."

The lights around the parking lot flickered, and a few burned out. Pax and Oracle glanced up at the burned-out lights and then at each other.

"Did you feel that?" She rubbed her left shoulder and peered behind her at U-Sec's evidence truck.

"What?"

"Like something brushed past me. A spirit, maybe?"

"You're telling me there's a ghost here now?" As if Pax needed something else to complicate this evening. Not that he believed in ghosts, but he believed in Oracle. If she sensed a ghostly presence, he wasn't taking any chances.

"No." She paused, confusion lining her high forehead. "It feels like a spirit, but it's alive, yet not quite."

That made absolutely no sense to him. Maybe he should take Oracle to the hospital after all. Maybe her abilities were finally driving her insane. He'd seen it before and he couldn't—wouldn't—let that happen to her.

"You should go home." He reached for her hand, but she pulled away and headed to the warehouse.

"I need to go back in. See if it is stronger inside," she said over her shoulder.

Pax hesitated, unsure whether to follow Oracle. He had dealt enough with the police, the FBI, even his own agents. After what Graham had told him about someone breaching U-Sec's firewall, he wanted to get back to his quiet office and regroup and have several cups of very strong coffee.

As he continued his internal debate, he glanced over at the men loading U-Sec's newly acquired evidence truck—a medium-sized moving truck painted a nondescript black and fitted inside with armor. Raven had stashed more goods in the warehouse than they had realized. It was going to take at least a week to categorize everything.

He watched Inferno tote several small boxes to the end of the ramp. Then a lanky, baby-faced guy started waving his arms at Inferno. His voice rose an octave so Pax could make out a few choice words that set off every alarm in his body.

"Missing . . . someone took it . . . stolen."

An older fellow kept referencing his clipboard and began arguing with the young guy.

"What's going on?" Pax stalked toward the truck.

"Hey, Pax," Inferno greeted him and raised his eyebrows, struggling to look innocent and doing a horrible job. "We were just checking the inventory."

A fiftyish, squat man with no neck piped up, "Nothing. Everything's under control here, Pax."

"No, man, no, that's not true," the skinny, barely-out-of-high-school guy spoke up. No Neck shot him a killing look.

"Johnny, let's not get ahead of ourselves," Inferno cut in.

"It was here. Right here a minute ago." Johnny pointed to the palette with a crate stacked on top. "Now it's gone. I don't want to get blamed for this."

"What's missing?" Pax demanded.

"Nothing," the older man said stiffly. "Nothing's missing. It's here. Somewhere." He motioned with his thick head toward the back of the trailer. "It's already been packed."

"No, it's gone, Bill. I swear it hasn't been packed," Johnny's voice cracked. "Inferno handed the sack to me, and I placed it here a minute ago." His hand trembled as he pointed again to the palette. "It wasn't packed with the rest."

"If someone doesn't tell me what the hell is missing, then blame will be the least of your problems," Pax's voice rang out.

"*Youz* figure it out. I've got work to do." Bill threw up his hands then lumbered back into the truck with the clipboard.

"The statue Raven stole from the museum." Inferno's hands clenched into fists that started to glow a pinkish red. "We don't know where it is."

"We'll find it. It didn't just walk away." Pax placed a hand on Inferno's shoulder to calm him down. Inferno was still sore over losing control with Raven and enflaming part of the Smithsonian's storage center. This was his first time out in the field since the incident. Inferno's therapist recommended that he take it slow, and this was as slow as it got. Moving evidence from a crime scene. Pax figured nothing could go wrong. Yet another lesson learned this evening.

Johnny swiped his palms over the crate. "I placed it right here. Turned my back for a second to open a carrier box, and it was gone."

He leaned close to Pax. "They're not gonna dock my pay for this? I mean, that's gotta be worth like a thousand bucks, and I can't really swing that. I barely get paid enough for my rent, if you know what I'm saying." He took out a pack of cigarettes and lit one with nervous fingers.

"Yeah, I know." Pax turned to leave and motioned for Inferno to follow him.

As they walked away, Pax called out to Johnny, because he couldn't resist, "And it was worth just south of a million."

Behind him, Johnny made a strange retching noise.

"What do you think happened?" Pax walked Inferno past the police cruisers to the far end of the warehouse near the parking lot.

"It has to be in that truck." Inferno shrugged. "Johnny's a newbie. I think he's nervous around us. Probably just misplaced it."

Pax nodded in understanding. For a new hire at U-Sec, a crime scene was nerve wracking enough. Add a few transhumans to the mix and the stress level increased tenfold. Most considered transhumans unpredictable mutants, and a few lived up to that title. The press tended to focus on the rogue ones, not those who made a difference, who were just trying to eke out a living like the rest of the schmucks in this world.

But still, something didn't feel right about this. "*Could* someone have taken it?"

"Who?" Inferno rubbed the back of his shaved head. "No one here would risk their careers by stealing an obscure statue. Besides, there are other objects in those crates that are probably worth more on the black market."

Pax ran through the scenarios, but nothing made sense. Unless APS was involved. They were famous for planting undercover sleepers at archeological digs and in museums and other organizations to gain access to precious antiquities. It was possible and would explain why a statue not well known by the general public just disappeared.

"There's nothing." Oracle approached Pax and Inferno. "I tried reaching out to Surefire again but I don't know. Right now, I'm hitting a brick wall."

She touched Pax's hand, and her head swung from him to Inferno. "What happened?"

"An artifact is missing from the truck."

She searched his face with her pupilless eyes, which swirled with the dull colors of the scene around them. "The statue?"

"The one stolen by Raven tonight from the museum." He shrugged. "Some Aztec goddess. I don't know. Probably not important. We've had so many people in and out down here. The police did a shit job setting up the perimeter. I'm sure someone snatched it."

Oracle stepped closer and placed her hand under his chin, gently forcing him to look into her eyes, which were back to their grayish white. "Or it could be a clue."

"I think you're right." Inferno's hands fisted again and small flames danced along his knuckles to his wrists. "And I think we just found another one."

A tall, dark-haired man in jeans and a black T-shirt sprinted past Pax's truck with the stolen statue tucked in the crook of his tattooed arm like a football.

"Raven," Inferno uttered and let loose a fireball.

♥ ☠ ♥ ☠ ♥ ☠

Surefire's mouth dropped open. She wanted to ask what her father was doing here but she couldn't form the words, could barely form a thought.

His long, thick legs marched across the floor. His large hand grabbed her shoulder and shoved her against the wall. His other hand clamped down across her mouth.

She looked up into his pale, grey eyes, and her heart trembled. Tears ran down her face. Her back and shoulders ached from being ground into the decaying wall.

Why? She wanted to ask, but his hand tightened around her mouth.

"Synthia, you disappoint me, again," he said, though something was off. His voice was his, yet not. Like a ventriloquist operating a puppet.

She stared, wide eyed. Too shocked and confused to fight back—unwilling to harm her father. The air changed. It became charged, heavier. It became harder to breathe and harder to think, and she wasn't sure if it was from fear or something else. Perhaps some force outside her, making the environment denser, more oppressive.

"You were going to contact Oracle, weren't you?"

Surefire couldn't understand why her father was asking this. How did he know? Why would he care? Wasn't he on her side?

"Are you trying to get your family killed? Do you even care? But I would understand." His voice dripped with condescension. "Considering we turned on you, it would be fitting for you to return the favor."

Her father wore his general's uniform, and that didn't make sense. He was retired, and he only used it for special events—and this was not a special event. Surefire's eyes went to his shoulder strap, which displayed only three stars, not the customary four. Then she noticed his overseas service badge was missing, along with a few others.

She bit down on his palm. He flinched and snatched his hand away from her mouth.

"You're not my father." She kicked him in the groin.

He let go of her and doubled over. She fell to her knees. Her rock-climbing shoes, great for running and climbing after Raven, offered no protection to her toes. She struggled to stand, and her foot screamed in protest. He grabbed her ankle, causing her to fall face first onto a broken keyboard. The keys cut into her forehead. She kicked her left foot back and nailed him in the eye.

With a curse, he staggered back.

Her fingers knocked against a hard object. A glass paperweight. She grabbed it and spun around onto her back. The paperweight flew from her hand into the center of his forehead.

"Bitch!"

Her father's image shimmered then flickered like a poorly projected movie until it morphed into Ari, fully human with no discernible roach parts.

Surefire watched this transformation in awe. "What did you just do?"

"Ensure that everything goes as planned and you don't compromise this mission. Raven shouldn't have left you alone." Ari's breath came out in short spurts, as if he had finished a marathon. His image turned once more into her father's and then faded back to his true form. Outside, the lights over the warehouse lot flickered.

"Raven trusted me."

"He shouldn't have. He was always a sucker for a pretty chit in spite of everything."

Surefire wiggled her sore toes and carefully propped herself up onto a rickety desk. Her eyes never left Ari, who looked pale and withered, as if suddenly struck with the flu. If he was weak, then she could take him, tie him up and call for help from the U-Sec agents outside. Half their problem would be solved. Her family and U-Sec would be safe from Ari while they retrieved the final skull to remove Tezcatlipoca's power from him.

Sweat beaded on Ari's white forehead around a red lump and small cut from where the paperweight had smacked him. He tore open the uniform and pulled out a necklace with a large, shiny black stone attached. He grasped the stone in his hand, and immediately his breathing evened out. His color returned.

"Oracle is causing interference. She's hard to keep out of our minds." Ari winced.

Surefire sprang on him. She wedged her legs on either side of his biceps and tried to wrench the charm out of his clammy hands. She didn't know what that hunk of rock was, but she needed to get it away from him.

Surefire grabbed a phone and smashed it across his face. The plastic and electronic bits crumbled in her hands. He grasped her shoulders. His pupils dilated and swirled a deep, blackish red. His thin upper lip curled, and he sent her flying back into a bookshelf. The shelves tore into the middle of her back, the bookcase collapsing on top of her.

Moldy particle board fell around her, and she quickly covered her head. Before she could try to stand, Ari tossed the remnant of the bookcase off her and picked Surefire up by her neck. Around them, objects not bolted down began to float and spin with disjointed, choppy movements.

He drew her close to his face. His skin was smooth, akin to porcelain. His bottom lip was thicker than the top, which gave him a slight pout. They were almost like Raven's lips, but on Raven they were appealing. On Ari it looked disproportionate on his thin face, making his pointy chin look even pointier.

His eyes had returned to a burnt brown. When his hot breath spewed across her face, it smelled bittersweet, like dark chocolate.

She wheezed, only able to take in small spurts of air. Not enough to sustain consciousness. Her vision dimmed.

"Did you think you could stop me?"

She wrapped her hands around his arm and twisted with all her strength. He didn't cringe, didn't take his hate-filled eyes off hers.

"I see you did, idiot."

He let out a husky laugh. His hard expression melted into something much scarier on his face. Desire. He dipped his head until his cool, smooth cheek pressed against hers.

"It's been awhile since a woman was that rough with me. Maybe you'll be worthwhile in other ways."

The building vibrated. Orange and yellow flames lit up and then shot across the windows. The objects floating around them crashed to the floor. Ari released Surefire and ran to the window. She slipped and regained her balance. She leaned over a broken desk and massaged her burning throat.

"What was that?" Ari asked.

Without looking up, Surefire replied in a brittle voice, "Inferno."

She lurched forward and gazed past the black burn marks on the windows. Her body went rigid. Down below, Raven lay sprawled on the ground. The backs of his arms and neck were singed a light gray. Small tufts of smoke rose from his T-shirt and jeans.

"Raven." Helpless, she watched several officers draw their guns as Pax edged closer to Raven's prone form. He held one hand behind him to keep Inferno in check. Inferno's fists were engulfed in fire as he pushed against Pax's restraining hand.

"We have to help him." Surefire ran to the stairs.

Ari lunged forward and grabbed her arm and whipped her back around to face him.

"Do exactly as I say."

♥ ☠ ♥ ☠ ♥ ☠

Raven floated through the third-floor windows of the building overlooking the warehouse lot and then drifted above the barbed-wire fence. He shot a look back at the abandoned office and could make out Surefire cupping her hands to peer out between two large cracks in the windows.

Good. She hadn't moved. So far she was following his orders, keeping her promise.

He had hoped tying her up in the trunk would make her realize he was serious. Ari was dangerous. His threats were legit. Judging by his earth-moving stunt in the warehouse, he was extremely powerful as well. Possibly more powerful than Raven. Any slipup, any action that questioned their loyalty to Ari's plan could put themselves and those they cared about in danger. They had to follow Ari's plan—for now—and if that meant incapacitating Surefire until her usefulness came into play, then Raven was fine with that.

In fact, he kind of enjoyed it.

More specifically, he enjoyed annoying her. She'd press her lips together and glare at him with her two-toned eyes and try to look tough whenever he ticked her off. About as tough as a tiny mouse reaming out a mighty lion.

In other words, adorable.

However, it didn't mean he wasn't impressed with her spunk—she was a scrapper. Surefire had held her own with him, with Ari in the cavern, and then with Xochi by sending a blade between her eyes.

Forget little mouse. Surefire was more Mighty Mouse.

Except with a nice butt.

He focused his attention back on the moving truck, and his mood darkened. Months of work down the tube. He'd have to reclaim those artifacts again after the dust had settled and they'd stopped Ari. It wouldn't be as easy next time. They'd be expecting him.

"I can't believe he blew us off like that, after *they* called us here." A young woman tottered past Raven on pointed heels that sank down into the dirt with every other step. A man the size of a quarterback trailed behind her looking everywhere but at her.

Check that. He *was* a quarterback. Hunter Thompson. Starting quarterback for the Ravens football team. He'd given the Steelers's defense a hammering during the playoffs.

What is he doing here?

The Hummer beeped behind Raven as the alarm shut off.

Raven floated back toward their truck. He looked closer at the woman and found himself staring into Surefire's heart-shaped face.

Hunter opened the driver's door.

"Synthia is my sister for chrissake."

Heather. This was Heather. Surefire's twin.

Yet this woman and Surefire couldn't be more different. Heather's hair was chopped in an uneven bob, whereas Surefire's flowed passed her shoulders, thick and soft and highly touchable. Heather's mouth drooped at the corners, Surefire's was curved upward so even when she frowned it wasn't far from a smile. Though her sister's nose was straight, curved up at the tip, Surefire's looked more proportionate despite the bump in the middle from where it had been broken. Unlike Surefire's eyes, Heather's irises were both the same—an acidic green. A color, Raven assumed, that came from colored contacts, because no one's eyes were that obnoxious a shade.

"I'm sure she's fine," Hunter said in a reassuring tone, one used by the Dog Whisperer to diffuse an angry mutt.

"Really? So you're a psychic now? My *sister* could be dead." She hopped into the driver's seat. "If she dies, Pax and U-Sec will pay. She should never have taken this job. I knew it was too dangerous. Of course, no one listens—"

She slammed the door and cut off Raven and Hunter from her one-sided conversation. Hunter paused to take a breath before walking around to the passenger side.

No doubt, Surefire had inherited the better personality as well as the looks.

The Hummer peeled away, shooting into the air dirt and debris that cut through Raven's floating form and blew him back a few feet, forcing him to take a moment to regroup and refocus. Then he felt himself starting to phase back in. Something tugged at his powers, at the very center of his being, and slowly began drawing away his energy. It was a milder version of what he had felt in the cavern below the warehouse. Was Ari here? He wouldn't put it past him to keep a close watch on them. Raven concentrated all his strength on holding his invisibility. First things first, reclaim the statue and then find out if Ari was nearby.

Raven scanned the lot in front of him. A man wearing faded jeans and a black sweatshirt with a white U-Sec logo stretched across a chest nearly two times wider than Hunter's barreled forward with such intensity that Raven was sure the man had seen him. Raven swooshed out of his way and changed direction toward the shiny black and chrome U-Sec truck.

He continued forward several feet and then froze when he heard the heavyweight jogging after him.

He saw me. Raven's mind raced with how to escape, but every scenario ended with Schwarzenegger's long-lost cousin putting a fist through his head.

Then the man ran past him and up to a tall African-American woman, gorgeous enough to give a supermodel a run for her millions. Her eyes were closed, and her head tilted back.

The woman mentioned sensing Surefire but being blocked. Relief flowed through Raven. Surefire was keeping her promise.

He brushed past the exotic beauty, and his every cell shimmered and quaked from the touch. Her head pivoted to where he floated, and he met her pupilless, off-white eyes with shock. This had to be Oracle. Then Raven realized the man standing so close to her, staring at her with such concern, was most likely Levi Paxton, also known as Pax, Surefire's boss.

Pax was well known in the underground, not only for being one of U-Sec's founders but also for stowing away a ton of secrets about experiments done on soldiers under the public's radar by the U.S. military—and he had been their prime guinea pig. Pax leveraged this information to create U-Sec and keep the government out of the lives of his transhuman agents and score several lucrative government contracts as a bonus.

Sounded like a man worth knowing. Too bad Pax's job was to catch Raven. It put a kink in any possible friendship.

Raven left Oracle and Pax to their conversation and made his way to the evidence truck. After handing the sack over to a young man working a dolly, Inferno disappeared around the corner at the back of the warehouse. Raven eased forward. He couldn't help but feel guilty after what had happened between him and Inferno. He hadn't meant for Inferno to lose control and burn part of the storage center. How was he to know that Inferno was dealing with sexuality issues?

That would be the last time he made a crack about being a flamer to someone with a flamethrower for hands. Though he'd really lost it when Raven sang the lyrics to *Disco Inferno.*

The guy working the dolly, who looked too young to be up this late, deposited the sack with the statue onto a small crate resting on top of a wooden palette. The kid abruptly turned his back, opened a carrier crate, paused, and then walked away, lighting a cigarette in the process. He sauntered down the ramp and waved at a pretty female officer standing nearby.

Raven entered the truck. He phased back in and leaned with both hands on the crate in front of him for balance. When the initial dizziness subsided, he tore the statue from the sack and threw the sack behind some boxes.

He grasped the smooth stone statue, and a static charge tingled along his fingertips and up his arms and rebooted every cell in his body.

"Don't remember that happening before."

Of course, last time he had handled the statue at the museum, he'd been at full operating capacity. Maybe he hadn't needed a power charge then. It was as if Xochi's essence were trapped in the statue and bits of her power seeped through into his skin. Was this why Xochi wanted the statue?

If he had known about this potential energy boost back in the warehouse, he could've removed the statue from the sack and rebooted himself when his power faded just before Ari tore up the ground. Unless Xochi hadn't wanted him to know, hadn't wanted him to escape.

He eyed the likeness of Xochi, which was more of an abstract likeness if you asked him. Her body was very square-shaped, her mouth a bit too wide and cavernous. But the soulless eyes were spot on.

Behind him, he heard the metal ramp bang as someone pushed a hand truck up it. He clutched the statue to his chest, phased out his body along with the statue, and oozed through the thick armored sides of the truck. Seconds later, he heard the young man swear from inside the truck and call out to an older, beefy man for help. Soon Inferno joined the men, along with Pax.

Raven continued the mission. He was halfway there. Just the grass parking lot to traverse and then back over the fence. He looked up at the abandoned office building. Through the smudged and cracked windows, he saw a shadow in the room with Surefire. He focused and tried to move faster without expending too much energy. His power was depleting faster than he could draw it from the statue. As he passed onto the grass, he could tell the shadow was a man, and this man held Surefire suspended in the air by her neck. Objects spun around them in the room. The closer he got, the more he felt it. Another tug on his powers, a siphoning of his abilities, like a vampire draining his blood until he grew weaker. He drove himself forward. The uneven grass wavered beneath his feet, and he stumbled, then fell. He pushed himself to his feet, past the lightheadedness of phasing back in. With his remaining strength, he sprinted toward the fence.

He sensed it before he saw it. A scorching ball of fire at his back. He dove to the ground as if leaping for a touchdown. Except his goal line was yards away and in his weakened state, no amount of leaping was going to help him reach it.

The fireball brushed over him, singeing the backs of his arms, neck, and clothes. It melted a hole in the fence and slammed into the old building, dissipating before catching the rotting wood on fire.

He remained on the ground, the statue clutched to his chest. His cheek resting on the cold, dewy grass, careful not to make any sudden movements, he narrowed his eyes to slits and focused on Pax and Inferno, who moved closer to him. Let them think he was dead or unconscious while he figured out how to get away without twenty cops turning him into Swiss cheese. Plus, he had no idea what Pax was capable of. Raven was strong, but he had a feeling Pax was in a much higher weight class.

Pax eased forward and, fortunately, held Inferno in check behind him. Inferno's face burned a bright pink, and it wasn't just with anger. Flames covered his hands. If Inferno had his way, he'd barbecue Raven right then and there.

"Stop!"

Raven popped his head up. Was that Surefire's voice?

"Pax, please." She picked her way through the smoldering hole in the fence with her hands held up.

Several guns swung from Raven to Surefire.

"Surefire, where have you been?" Pax called out. "Are you okay?"

"I'm fine." She nodded then clamped her lips together as if to keep from saying anything else.

"What's going on?" Pax asked.

"I . . . uh . . . can't say." Surefire shot a nervous glance behind her.

She dropped to her hands and knees at the same time the ground shuddered and a crack snaked under Raven, ripping up the ground below Pax's feet. Pax fell, and Inferno staggered onto the ground next to him. Officers dropped their guns and scampered away from their cruisers and trucks. Car alarms went off. A woman screamed. Raven turned to see Oracle fall to the ground and grab her head. Pax crawled over to Oracle and cradled her to his chest.

Whatever was causing the quake was using Raven's powers, sucking away his energy and creating a vacuum around his body that began to suffocate him. He gasped for air.

A hand touched Raven's shoulder. He glanced up at Surefire, who was kneeling next to him, trying to keep her balance.

"In a second, this will stop. Then we need to get out of here—quick." She grabbed the statue from him. She reached underneath the sweater to inside the waistband of her leggings and took out a scratched-up glass paperweight with sand and shells suspended inside. Lifting her hand over her head, she swung it down into the middle of Xochi's chest. The statue caved in, and Surefire stuck her hand inside and drew out a necklace with an opaque round crystal amulet.

How did she know to do that? Raven's eyes swung from the statue to the large polished rock dangling from a gold necklace in Surefire's hand.

"Here." She shoved it into his palm. The earth settled around them, and the quaking stopped. The oppressive film of energy lifted from Raven.

He inhaled a deep breath. The soothing scent of lavender filled his lungs. The amulet burned bright purple in his hand. A warm current traveled up his arm and tickled down his spine. It was as if Xochi herself were touching him, restoring his powers.

"We've gotta go. Now. Phase us out." Surefire held out her hand.

"Raven, how about some flaming balls?" Inferno pulled back a bright red fist as if gearing up for a punch. "Surefire, get down."

Raven grabbed her hand. A small fireball blazed past them and missed Raven by inches as they phased from the scene.

Chapter Twelve

Raven's and Surefire's bodies faded away then tore upward toward the sky, faster than Raven had ever traveled while phased. They rose above the warehouse parking lot until Pax looked like a child's action figure and the rest like figurines spread out in a train garden.

"How did you know to smash the statue?" Raven floated them past the tops of the buildings and away from the chaotic scene below.

"Ari told me."

"Ari? He was in the building with you?"

"Yes."

"Did he hurt you?"

Surefire didn't reply. Her lack of response put him on high alert.

"He's waiting for us. He moved your car to the Canton Waterfront Park at Boston Street. Do you know where that is?"

"I have an idea. Did Ari hurt you?"

Raven thought she wasn't going to respond, until she finally said after a few long seconds, "I'm fine."

Which meant, "Yes, he did." He concentrated on holding their particles together when all he wanted to do was explode with the rage reverberating through his phased-out cells. He dared Ari to lay a spiny roach leg on her again.

"He's not a half-roach anymore," Surefire said when the park came into view. "He's something else."

Surefire didn't elaborate on what this "something else" was, and Raven didn't press her. He'd find out soon enough. They arrived at the park and drifted down to the ground next to a bench overlooking the water. After they became solid, Surefire flopped onto the wooden bench and hung her head between her legs as if she were going to faint.

"I'll need to take a pill before we do that again." Her voice wavered. "I was never good with flying."

Raven sat down hard next to her. The amulet was lukewarm in his hand. Its heat and power dimmed as if Raven had used up its force.

He sensed Ari's presence before he saw him standing on the grass under a tree across the brick walkway from where they sat. Tiny electrified fingers moved over and pressed into his skin then retreated, slapped away by an unseen force. He slung Xochi's necklace over his head and stood to face Ari.

Surefire was right. Ari wasn't a roach anymore. He was human. At least, he looked human in his black slacks, red silk shirt, and skinny black tie complete with a pair of checkerboard-printed Vans.

Magicians never had a sense of style.

"What are you doing here?" Raven stood and started forward.

Ari held up his hand. "Don't come any closer."

Raven's hands curled into fists. "Afraid I'm going to hurt you? Because you're right. I am." He bolted in Ari's direction. A few steps in, he bounced backward and landed on his backside in the middle of the brick path.

"What was that?" He sat up and rubbed his scalp to clear the weird buzz prickling along his skull.

"The closer you get, the more our powers feed off one another, almost canceling the other out."

Raven rose to his feet and reluctantly kept his distance. "You almost got me killed."

"I hadn't realized I was siphoning your abilities when I used my own." Ari shrugged. "I must be slightly stronger than you. The stronger power can always tap into the weaker one." He walked from under the shadow of the tree to stand below the light post and smirked.

Raven knew Ari was loving this. Ari sucked at sports and most physical activities where Raven excelled. Ari had always been picked last, always sidelined. Now, according to him, he had the physical advantage over Raven.

"Want to test that theory?" Raven itched to punch that slimy, self-assured smile from his face.

"I'd rather not. At least, not now, anyway. Your necklace comes directly from Xochi. It holds her essence, purer than what's running inside your veins. I can feel its energy trying to burrow inside me. It's possible that it contains more power than you." His smirk widened as he let his words sink in. "We should both keep our distance, so neither gets hurt. We need our strength for what's upcoming."

"Besides, I didn't mean any harm. I only wanted to check up on you. Make sure you kept your end of the bargain." Ari gave Surefire a pointed look, as she moved from the bench to stand next to Raven.

Surefire folded her arms across her chest and glared at Ari with such cold intensity that Raven knew without a doubt Ari had hurt her.

Badly.

Raven's stomach tightened into a knot. He tried not to imagine what had happened between them, but the images kept cutting through his thoughts, feeding his growing animosity for his cousin. His hands clenched again. His muscles twitched. When this was over, Ari would pay. But first things first.

Raven swallowed down his anger. "We don't have the skull yet."

"I know. There's been a delay." Ari adjusted his tie and propped a shoulder against the post.

"You're looking well." Raven flicked his hand at Ari's attire, wanting to bait him, insult him. It was the only way Raven could hurt Ari at the moment. "Thought you were being made into a cockroach or some kind of bowl."

"Vessel," Ari answered testily.

"Ah, yes, that's the word. Vessel. You're looking less vessel-like right now."

"And how do I look?"

"Like an unfashionable prick, as always."

Ari sneered. "Looks can be deceiving."

Both eyes swirled reddish black. Surefire edged back. Her arms dropped to her sides, her knees bent, her shoulders angled in a defensive posture.

Ari's left arm extended out of his shirt, no longer human, but a spiny insect leg. It stopped about two feet from Raven's face. Raven turned his head and swallowed the bile rising up his throat. His body trembled, no longer with rage but fear. Even with the power of a goddess, he couldn't shake the phobia of insects he'd had since childhood. A phobia made worse by his unconventional—and slightly insane—father, who'd sought to toughen up his young son by locking him in a room filled with large, creepy bugs.

It had backfired, of course, and Raven had hoped when his father died, the phobia would die along with him. It didn't, of course.

Surefire's hand reached into his front jean pocket.

"Hey." He pivoted his hips back, surprised by her groping.

She pulled out her knife and flipped it open. Lunging forward, she forced the blade up into Ari's roach arm. "Raven can't come near you. But I can."

She twisted the blade. Ari howled and snatched away his arm. It morphed back into a human appendage. The knife fell from his flesh and onto the brick sidewalk.

Ari cradled the arm to his body and smoothed his right hand over the wound until the skin knitted back together, the bleeding stopped.

"That's for earlier." Surefire leaned down and scooped up the knife.

When she stood, her hair flipped back over her shoulder, and Raven noticed the faint yellow-purple bruises lining her neck.

Ari would definitely pay for what he had done to her.

"Touché." Ari's lips slid into a sadistic smile, and Raven realized that Ari got off on Surefire's stunt. He'd always enjoyed it rough. Enjoyed physical pain inflicted on him by women, and he enjoyed giving it right back.

His anger boiled over, flushing his skin, tunneling his vision. Raven no longer wanted to hurt Ari; he wanted to kill him.

Ari averted his gaze to the ground as if he'd read Raven's thoughts. Then Ari's face contorted in exaggerated pain. He dropped onto the ground in a melodramatic flop.

"I'm sorry, James, but I can't stop it. I need your help. It's becoming stronger by the hour. I need that skull. I don't know what I'm doing. It's not me." Ari's eyes faded to a muddy brown and he tried to don the innocence of a puppy dog, but he looked more like a meth addict trying to convince his family that he was clean.

Surefire's face pinched in bewilderment at Ari's total one-hundred-and-eighty-degree personality turn.

Raven rolled his eyes. "Quit the melodramatic bullshit. We know the truth."

"What truth?" Ari's voice quivered.

"That Tezcatlipoca will use that final skull to take over your body."

"No, that's not right. It will stop him from possessing me."

"That's not the word on the street. You see, a little hummingbird told us that the skull works both ways. It could stop Tezcatlipoca *or* allow him to possess you. Trust me, you'll need more than an exorcist to get him out."

"I don't know what you're talking about."

"I believe you. I don't think you do." Raven nodded thoughtfully. "I think you're vain enough to think you'll be the one possessing this god. But consider this, why would a god give his power to someone like you?"

The question must've struck a sore spot, because Ari reeled back as if Raven had slapped him. He climbed to his feet and lifted his pointed chin with a mixture of contempt and indignation.

"Because I deserve it." Ari jabbed a finger at his own chest. "I was the one who trapped him. The only one smart enough to trick him."

"Trick him?" Raven let out a brittle laugh. "You're the one who's been played, my man."

Raven started forward, then stopped when Ari's ice-cold power pressed against his own like a blast of arctic wind. "Tell Tezcatlipoca that we'll get him the skull. We'll keep our end of the bargain as long as you keep yours—and leave our families alone. Because when he fully enters our world, I'll be there to personally send that has-been god back to hell."

Ari's body went rigid. His head dropped back, and his arms fell flaccid to his sides. A scream tore through his throat that began human but turned into a deep, sinister bass. Deeper than any human voice Raven had ever heard.

Once again the air thickened, more suffocating than before. The light above Ari burnt out, and soon the others lining the walkway flickered then fell dark. Raven was ready this time. He knew what was about to happen. He concentrated on wielding his own power deep inside and keeping the darkness out. He stumbled back from the effort. Surefire grabbed his arm to steady him. She angled her body closer and forced him to move away from the grotesque display in front of them.

Ari's head flipped forward. His skin receded from his face until all that remained was a gleaming white skull and black swirling holes where his eyes had been.

"Xochi's power has made you arrogant. Your death will not be swift, I assure you." The otherworldly voice vibrated the air around them, stinging Raven's eardrums.

Surefire flattened her palms against her ears.

"Blah, blah, blah," Raven intoned. Tezcatlipoca's power pressed against his flesh. Invisible, icy tentacles tried to hook him, but Xochi's amulet fed on this power, deflecting Tezcatlipoca's energy and keeping Raven safe, making him brazen.

Of course, his brazenness was also fueled by having a real-life Skeletor threaten him—a bit surreal and almost cartoonish.

"Come up with something more original next time," Raven challenged.

Ari's eyes stopped swirling. "How about this?"

His body fell apart onto the ground, melting into a thick stream of roaches, black flying beetles, and other nasty critters that Raven didn't stick around to identify.

He grabbed Surefire's hand and ran in the opposite direction, yanking her along with him. He glanced behind and saw the black swarm arch in the opposite direction and disappear into the water.

"Are you okay?" Surefire panted.

"I'm fine." He dropped her hand and continued to his car, which Ari had parked in the adjacent lot in front of a boat ramp.

A line of police cruisers flew down Boston Street and passed in front of the parking lot. He took out his keys. They jingled in his hand because he couldn't stop shaking.

"Here." Surefire put her hand over his. "Let me drive."

♥ ☠ ♥ ☠ ♥ ☠

Surefire figured it was better not to think and instead tried to focus on the road. Because every time a thought popped into her mind—Ari appearing as her dad, Raven nearly getting scorched, Ari's face ripping apart, Oracle screaming and clutching her head—she found herself pressing down the accelerator, wanting to get back to Xochi that much quicker. She wanted answers. Needed answers. Needed this night to be over with so her life could return to normal—as normal as an UltraAgent's life could be.

However, as she drove farther down I-95 away from the city, away from Pax and U-Sec, she knew deep down that things would never be the same again. *If* Pax let her return to U-Sec after the stunt she had just pulled. *If* she didn't go to jail for helping a wanted criminal escape custody.

Raven lounged back in the passenger seat and took a drink from his bottled water. His color had returned after eating three protein bars stashed in his glove box and downing an energy drink before breaking out a bottle of water. The burn marks on his arms and neck faded away, though a patch of dark hair on the back of his head was shorter than the rest.

Back at the park, she had worried about Raven. Either the phasing out or Ari's presence had weakened him, she wasn't sure which. He had turned several shades of green before his light olive skin had become a muted white. After collapsing into the passenger seat, he murmured only one sentence, "Don't wreck my car."

A comment she let slide, considering his condition. However, the longer he stared blankly out the window without so much as a smartass remark about her driving, the more she wondered if he really was sick.

Raven shifted in the seat and the weight of his gaze made her skin twitch. Her eyes darted from the road to him then back to the road.

"What?" She was uncomfortable with him staring at her, examining her. She hazarded another glance at him and noticed his gaze resting on her bruised neck. She pulled her hair over her shoulder.

"Ari did that to you, didn't he?" His voice was hoarse.

She nodded and squeezed the steering wheel. "It's okay."

The plastic water bottle crinkled under his grip. "No, it's not. He's going to answer for that. For this whole clusterfuck of a night."

She glanced over at him. His jaw was ground shut, his mouth set in a firm line. Anger streamed off him in waves. She suddenly felt hot. She turned down the heat.

"What happened in there?" he asked.

"I'd rather not talk about it."

"Please, I need to know."

She let out an exhausted breath. She knew by his determined tone he wouldn't stop until she answered. "About five minutes after you left, Ari entered the room. He looked like my father."

Saying this out loud caused a dam to burst inside her. Outrage filled every crevice of her body. Then she said louder, "He fucking turned into my father."

"So he can shapeshift?"

"Apparently."

"Then what?"

"I figured out it wasn't my dad and fought back. He grew weak before he removed this black rock from inside his shirt and squeezed it. It seemed to recharge him."

"Was it like this one?" Raven held up Xochi's amulet.

"Rougher. Not polished and well cut. Like it had been chipped off from a larger piece and then tied to a cord."

Raven fingered the round, purple-colored stone hanging outside his shirt.

"If Ari can change into my father, then that means he can get close to my family and into U-Sec. I can't take the chance."

She sighed and then admitted in a small voice, "You were right."

"Come again?" The edges of his lips perked up into a smile. "Did I just hear a woman admitting a man was right?"

"Don't look too pleased."

"I'll refrain," he replied with a larger smile.

"Ari's powerful and insane. If he'd found me trying to contact U-Sec . . ." Surefire trailed off, not wanting to imagine what Ari would have done.

She gunned the engine and passed a Corvette as she merged onto I-495 south.

"Whoa, Racer X, why don't you ease up on the accelerator?" Raven held up his water bottle. Now she knew he was feeling better.

"How did Ari find us?" Her eyes flicked to the rearview mirror.

"I think he's tracking us. Not positive how, but with traffic cameras set up in and around DC and security footage from the museum, he had lots of opportunities to monitor us." He took another drink of water. "Plus, if he has someone inside U-Sec, they could've told him about the statue. I'm sure he knew we needed to retrieve it."

"We have to get back. I want answers from Xochi. Now." She switched lanes to pass a tractor trailer with only several feet to spare.

Raven inhaled a sharp breath but didn't say anything. Good for him.

Surefire slowed down and merged into the right lane. "Can we trust Xochi?"

"Yes."

"And you're certain about that? She is married to this thing Ari is trying to raise. What if she's helping him?"

"She'd never do that." Raven finished his water and deposited the bottle in a plastic bag with the rest of his trash.

"Why is that?"

"She hates him. According to Aztec mythology, Tezcatlipoca kidnapped her and forced her into marriage. She has a Mount Everest-sized chip on her shoulder when it comes to him."

Surefire's mind replayed the scene in the Garden and their conversation with Xochi. But there was one thing tucked away in the back of her mind that she wanted answered.

"What did Xochi say to you after she pushed me through the tree?"

Raven shoved his hand through his disheveled hair and then rested it on the back of his head. He didn't answer. Didn't acknowledge her question.

"What did she say?" she repeated the question and slowed the car as they approached their exit.

"She said you were useful to this mission."

"And?"

"And that was all." He stared out the passenger window. His fingertips drummed a beat on the armrest.

Her gut told her he was lying. If he were telling the truth, he wouldn't keep his back to her. "What did she mean when she said I was more than human?"

"I don't know." He shifted in the seat to face her. "How did you get your ability?"

She shrugged and merged onto the exit ramp to I-295 south. "When I turned eleven, it just happened. I never missed a mark. I'd always had decent form, but messed up the dismounts, not landing where and how I should. I had trouble with my hand placement on the uneven bars and missed when switching. My foot wouldn't land properly on the beam, or I wasn't centered on the vault. No matter how much I practiced, my judgment was crap. Then I got better and figured it was developmental, that my years of practice had finally paid off."

Heather had always been a natural gymnast. Surefire was average, ranking mid-range or last in the regional competitions. Then one day she couldn't lose. Until she did, breaking her nose and damaging her knee when she missed her mark for the lamest of reasons—a boy.

"It wasn't because I had grown as an athlete or spent hours at the gym. Once I learned the fundamentals, I excelled at other sports, which I'd never played much before. Everything from bowling to pool to archery—anything that required aim. They kicked me out of a carnival once for nearly clearing out the prizes from their dart games, thinking I'd cheated."

"That must've been fun."

"Actually, it freaked me out. I felt like I didn't know my own body anymore. Later, they tested my blood, and found my skill didn't come naturally. I'd been modified genetically. I was a transhuman. Then I was really scared."

Raven bobbed his head as if turning over what she'd revealed. "We'll ask when we see her, but I can't guarantee a straight answer."

"Ms. Forthcoming, she's definitely not." Surefire refocused on the road. Lines had been redrawn and lanes reflowed because of construction. The exit to Howard Street and to downtown was approaching. Soon they'd be in the city and would need to figure out how to break into the museum and back into the portal, since Ari had informed her that the door in Baltimore was broken and still underwater. This night wasn't getting any easier, and she certainly didn't look forward to dealing with Xochi's cryptic speech and mood swings.

Which reminded her of another strange thing Xochi had said.

"What did she mean by you belong to her?"

Raven's hands clenched then unclenched on his lap. "It's hard to explain."

"Try. Because I need to trust you, and I don't trust her. If you've signed over your soul to that she-devil, then it complicates things."

He let out a breath. "You're absolutely right. I did sell my soul."

Surefire's heart ached at his confession. "Why would you do that?"

"I was faced with death, and I chose life. When you're scared, you don't always read the fine print. She made me an offer to help someone I love, as well as the world." He rubbed his palms across his jeans. "She offered me redemption."

Someone he loved. Was that Kat? The woman whose clothes she currently wore? Something in her gut twitched, and if she didn't know better, she'd say it was with jealousy.

She glanced over at him, and his dark blue eyes—swimming with pain and regret—held hers. The ache in her heart deepened.

"Red light," Raven said.

"What?" Surefire shifted her attention back to the road and slammed on the brakes at the red light at the end of the exit.

"Excellent brakes, huh?" Raven switched the topic. "One of the reasons I bought this car. Stops on a dime." He touched her forearm. "You need me to drive?"

"No, no, I'm good." As long as her heart didn't thud out of her chest from almost wrecking the car, she'd be fine.

He lifted his shoulder then pressed back into his seat.

Her mind wandered again to Ari and what he had done that night. "I still don't understand how Ari changed into my father."

"I don't know either." Raven frowned. "They didn't teach me that cool trick."

"And what's with the roaches and the bugs? It's not like my father and the bugs are somehow related. Unless Ari can transform into anything or anyone at will. I mean, insects, really? They're gross. But it's not like they can hurt you."

Raven's lips cinched together. His expression dropped into one of disgust at the mention of bugs.

"I have a theory," he said. "But I need to ask a personal question."

"It depends on what it is."

"Are you afraid of your father?" Raven asked.

What? The car jerked to the right. Surefire quickly straightened the wheel and hoped Raven figured she veered to miss a pothole and not because she was shocked over his question. A knife to the chest would have been less surprising than what he had asked. She certainly didn't want to discuss with Raven a topic reserved for her therapist. In fact, her therapist had never asked her that question.

"What does that have to do with anything?"

"I'm not sure, but I think I'm onto something."

They stopped at another light, and as the car idled, Surefire considered what he had asked. Searched her heart for strength in admitting out loud what she really felt, because her confession would make it truer, more painful. Raven had been honest with her about Xochi and their relationship, even though she could tell that speaking the truth had hurt him. She wanted to be honest with him, especially if it could help their case.

After a stressful minute ticked by, she replied in a hushed tone, "Yes, I am."

Raven's body stilled. "What did he do to you?"

Surefire stared across the oddly empty intersection. "Nothing. He did absolutely nothing."

"Then why are you afraid of him?" His eyes searched her face as if looking for a clue.

"Because I'm afraid that he'll do nothing again when I fail." Her throat constricted, and she tried to swallow a large lump.

Raven reached out and brushed a piece of her hair from her face. "How do you know that you'll fail?"

She blinked once, then twice as she registered his words. Then she leaned over the console and kissed him.

"Pax, stop staring at me. I'm well. I just need to rest my eye." Oracle lay on the sofa in his office curled up under Pax's jacket. A cold compress covered her forehead.

"Your *eye?*" Pax asked.

"My mind, okay?" She kept her eyes closed and swatted him away. "Go bother Helena for a bit. I'm sure she'll love that."

Pax hesitated. He didn't want to leave Oracle alone even if he was only outside the door. What if she had internal bleeding? A hemorrhage? He'd never seen her react like that—especially twice in one night—to another psychic force. However, again she had refused to go to the hospital—and even in her weakened state she was determined—so they'd compromised on having one of U-Sec's on-call doctors meet them at the office. Doctor Knowe had examined her and given her a clean bill of health. She was merely exhausted and needed to rest, Knowe had said. But until Pax saw a brain scan, he wouldn't be convinced.

"Pax." She pointed at the door.

"All right, all right. But I'll be near the door."

She made an "a-okay" sign with her thumb and finger then snuggled back down under his jacket.

"Did you find out anything?" Pax asked Helena, closing the door to his office partway and leaving a small gap so he could hear Oracle if she needed anything.

"About what?" Helena spun around in her chair. She raised her thinly plucked brows and gave him the stern look of a high school principal. "We have a million things happening right now. You need to be more specific."

"Let's start with the most important and work our way down."

The phone rang. Helena's deep brown eyes flicked to the caller ID display and then back to Pax.

He waved his hand at the blinking phone line. "You gonna answer that?"

"Not unless you can finally explain to Matthews and the FBI the reason your agent destroyed a museum piece and disappeared with a criminal from their Most Wanted list." She tipped her head, waiting for a reply.

"Good point. Let's wait until we have more information."

"I thought you'd agree." She swiveled around in her chair to face the keyboard. "Besides, our office is technically closed. You should be getting rest. Remember when you were a kid? You were prone to bronchitis when you didn't get enough sleep."

Pax looked up at the ceiling in a silent plea for her to get back to business.

"You'll fall sick if you don't take care of yourself, and you obviously don't." She swatted her hand at him then went back to typing.

He looked down at his sweatshirt and jeans, not sure what she meant by not taking care of himself. Except for needing a shower, he was in tiptop shape. He flexed his pectoral muscles and biceps to validate his assessment.

"Then I'd have to hear about it from your mother, and I'm supposed to keep an eye on you."

"Is that why I hired you?"

The computer screen reflected her faint smile. "You tell me."

She appeared to be working on several different documents at once and at the same time droning on to him about his health. Pax bet she didn't make any mistakes. She was a poster lady for multi-tasking. For a woman nearing sixty, she was more on the ball than his twenty-something agents.

"I could ask you about the status of any of my assignments, agents, or contacts, and you'd know. You're better than a computer."

"You do know how to compliment a woman."

"I try." He grinned. "Now, let's start with the statue."

She pulled up several websites on the dual monitors positioned on her desk.

"The statue is of Xochiquetzal, an Aztec goddess of 'flowering' and 'fruitful earth.' She represents love and beauty." She arched a brow at Pax, then added, "A Mexican Venus."

Her finger touched the monitor, so she wouldn't lose her place. Pax peered over her shoulder but didn't get too close. Helena hated when people read over her shoulder.

"She was originally the wife of Tláloc before Tezcatlipoca abducted her," Helena intoned. "There was a ceremony in her honor every year during which a young woman was flayed and her skin worn by a priest. I'm sure that would've been lovely to see."

"Teza . . . Tezca . . ." Pax stumbled on the name. "The god who kidnapped her. Who was he?"

Helena clicked her mouse, moving to another page on the website. "Says here he was one of the original Aztec gods. The tenth of the Thirteen Lords of Day. Whatever that means." Her slim shoulders lifted under her pale blue blazer.

Pax sat on the edge of her desk to see the monitor better.

She scrolled down the page. "He was known as the 'smoking mirror' god and used an obsidian mirror to see into the souls of men and what they feared. Associated with warfare, evil, destruction, and death. Go figure," Helena mused.

"Print out everything you can find on both of them." Pax tapped her desk with his finger.

Helena turned in her chair and shot him a look that reminded him of the one his mother gave him when he ate dinner with his elbows on the table.

"Please."

"That's more like it." She gave his hand a quick pat. "I know your mother taught you manners." She hit print and the printer opposite her desk churned to life.

"Any word on Surefire?"

"No." A shadow of worry passed over her face. "They searched the area and found nothing. The police put an APB out on her."

Helena shifted in her chair and looked him dead in the eyes. "They plan to arrest her for aiding and abetting and destruction of property—among other things. The police in Baltimore are not the most tolerant of transhumans, and the FBI is calling for an investigation into U-Sec's protocols that would allow an agent to go rogue like that."

"Rogue!" Pax belted out. Pressure mounted at the back of his neck. His face flushed hot. "It was obvious she was being coerced. Anyone with sense could see that."

"Take a breath, honey." Helena's formal tone softened to a familiar one. "We need to find her first. Learn what happened. We've known Surefire since she was a little girl. She wouldn't do anything like this without reason. However, these other agencies don't know that."

Pax let out a jagged breath and inhaled a smooth one using the calming techniques he had learned in yoga. It helped, a little.

"Unfortunately, we don't know where to look." Pax crossed his arms again. "How do you find someone who disappears into thin air?"

In all his years of dealing with transhumans, he had never experienced anything like what had happened this morning. Whatever had caused the earthquake was more than human, even a genetically modified one. Strong enough to split the earth, incapacitate Oracle, and make Raven and Surefire vanish. Did Raven do that? Was he that powerful? If so, then Raven must have recently developed these gifts because he'd never exhibited them before. Otherwise, Pax would never have assigned Surefire this case.

Blood pounded in the back of his head. He felt like a toddler trying to cram a wooden cylinder into a square hole. He was missing something, and he was too exhausted to realize what. Soon he'd have Surefire's father to deal with. How do you tell a man that his daughter vanished in front of twenty officers and agents with the criminal Pax had assigned her to capture?

He wished to God one of his partners were here to back him up. They were out of the country, on separate classified assignments. When they had left, the workload had been manageable. He doubted any of them could have forecast something like this happening.

"Have you talked to Pixie?"

"Graham did earlier," Helena responded. "And Pixie said she never spoke to Surefire."

Pax stood and strode to the elevator doors. "I'll check with her personally. Is she still working the switchboard?"

"I believe so."

"Keep an ear out for Oracle in case she needs anything."

"I'm sure she can take care of herself," Helena said to the computer screen.

He pressed the down button and waited. Behind him, the phone rang, and this time Helena answered. The elevator doors parted. He entered and hit the button for the basement floor. Helena's manicured hand shot through the closing doors, causing them to swing back open.

"Paxton." She shoved her thin body between the closing doors to keep the elevator open. Her dark eyes were flooded with alarm. "It's Surefire. Security cameras caught her in the Natural History museum in DC."

Pax dashed out of the elevator, and Helena trailed behind. "The cameras lost sight of her. She had escaped out of a tomb on display in the museum before she reached Baltimore."

"Do you have the video?" He stood behind her desk, barely able to keep still. Finally, a lead they could use.

Helena sat down and opened her e-mail. "Graham's sending it now. I don't know much else except the tomb was part of a Mesoamerican exhibit."

"Forward it to my computer." He ran into his office and flipped open his laptop.

"What is it?" Oracle popped up on the sofa.

"Graham is sending a surveillance video of Surefire exiting a tomb on display in DC. Some kind of Mesoamerican exhibit." He clicked open his email. "That's where she came from before she arrived at the warehouse."

"Then the statue has more meaning than we think." Oracle moved to stand behind him.

Pax picked up the phone and dialed Graham's extension. "And it might be a tip to where she's headed now."

♥ ☥ ♥ ☥ ♥ ☥

Raven's hand cradled the back of her head. His fingers entwined in her thick, silky hair. Her lips were soft, yet forceful, against his own. She knew what she wanted—and he wanted to give it to her. He opened his mouth to hers.

Xochi's necklace vibrated against his chest and sent out ripples of pleasure down past his chest and stomach. Surefire moaned into his mouth. He pulled her closer, undoing her seatbelt. He tightened his fingers in her hair, wanting her to feel how much he desired her.

She smelled clean, like Ivory soap, and he thought soap had never smelled so good. Her lips tasted like cherry lip balm, even better.

Her breasts pushed against his chest. The sweater lifted at her side, and he lowered his hand and caressed the smooth skin above her hip. His hand slid higher under her sweater.

Police cruisers zipped past them through the light. A few early-morning drivers whipped around Raven's car. Someone shouted for them to get a room.

Surefire pulled away. "No."

Raven leaned forward and brushed her lips with his. She placed her hand on his chest and pushed him back.

"No. I don't . . . I . . . umm. I'm sorry."

Sorry for what? Raven wanted to ask, but he was too worked up, too excited. He didn't want this moment to end. He'd never felt anything as potent as her kiss. His body felt revitalized, alive. His heart, which hadn't beat in years, twitched a bit. Or maybe it didn't twitch. Maybe it was the desire that pulsed through his body and caused an odd fluttering inside his chest that he'd never felt before, even when he was human.

A cacophony of honks resounded behind them, and she accelerated through the intersection. Her hands shook as she gripped the wheel.

"That shouldn't have happened. I don't know what I was thinking." She seemed on the verge of tears.

Oh, great. Here it goes, the guilt. It really fed the ego when a woman regretted kissing you.

"But it did happen." He failed to find the right words to soothe her, so instead he spoke the truth. "And judging by that incredible kiss, you want me as much as I want you."

He stared at her, waiting for a response—a denial, an argument, anything. She licked her lips and kept her eyes on the road.

Reluctantly, he settled back into his seat and adjusted himself. He pictured the disgusting swarm of insects so his arousal wouldn't show under his jeans.

"I got caught up, that's all. It didn't mean anything."

Really?

So she wanted to go down that route. "Speak for yourself. But I felt something in that kiss. Something I hadn't felt in a long time, if ever. I'm not going to dismiss it."

Her face flushed pink, and her hands twisted around the steering wheel. "It was just a kiss."

His gaze dropped from her eyes, still avoiding his, down to her lips. He licked his own and could taste a trace of cherry lip balm. He itched to take her one more time. To kiss his way down that smooth cheek to her neck and below.

"No." He tore his eyes away when his body started to react to the too-vivid images playing in his mind. "No, it was more than that, and you know it."

Chapter Thirteen

"Where to?" Surefire changed the subject. Her insides shook worse than gelatin during an earthquake.

Raven studied her and seemed to debate whether to continue discussing their make-out session. To her relief, he chose to accept her change of subject.

"Swing down Constitution, but don't go all the way. We can't get too close. I want to see if there's any commotion outside the museum." He pulled the edge of his shirt down and turned from her to stare out the passenger window.

She made a right at the next light and tried not to think about their kiss.

That proved to be an impossible feat when her body still ached from his touch. And she could still taste him every time her tongue touched her lips. Her face burned hotter. She had never experienced a kiss like that before—full of longing, full of promise.

And it could never happen again.

She'd lost focus, becoming too wrapped up in her emotions and letting down her guard. Which is exactly what had happened at the Olympic trials. It was a kiss then, too, that had caused her to screw up, to lose everything. However, at the time, she hadn't been the one doing the kissing—Heather had been.

With Surefire's boyfriend.

During Surefire's dismount.

In the bleachers right in front.

She bit down on her bottom lip. It had happened over ten years ago, but the memory was still raw and embarrassing.

Now she was letting her emotions get the better of her again. Only this time, lives were at stake, and not a spot on the Olympic team.

How could she have kissed him in the first place?

Raven was being nice to her again. That was the problem. Then she had shared a fear—a painful, gut-wrenching fear—she'd never shared with anyone, not even her sister, and he had responded with the simplest of questions.

How do you know that you'll fail?

It was as if he had more confidence in her than she ever did. No one had said that to her in years. Not since her epic failure at the Olympic trials.

She'd wanted to thank him for it. That was all. It was just an I-appreciate-your-support kiss. At least, she tried to convince herself that was it.

Unsuccessfully.

Besides, wasn't he involved with someone already? Someone whose clothes she wore and couldn't wait to get out of? The sweater itched and smelled faintly of citrusy perfume, a scent she was beginning to loathe.

She set her teeth and concentrated again on the now congested city streets, grateful for the distraction of driving.

Traffic came to a near standstill. The car lurched closer to Constitution Avenue, which was completely blocked by a barricade of police cars. Officers directed traffic up the side streets.

Raven slumped down in his seat as they passed the scene. Surefire turned her head and rested her arm up against the window to block her face.

"Head back to my place." He pointed to the next street over. "I have a plan."

She took a detour down a narrow one-way street and drove two blocks out of the way to reach Raven's apartment. When she pulled into his garage, he told her to park as far to the left as possible.

She climbed out of the car. "How are we getting back inside the museum?"

"Come around to this other side, and I'll show you."

Raven grabbed a crowbar from a shelf. She walked to the passenger side and saw a manhole in the garage floor. Raven used the crowbar to remove the cover.

He pointed down the hole. "We're going underground."

Surefire scrunched her face up. "I don't even want to ask what that smell is. It's a good thing we washed up." She'd be scrubbing this stench out for weeks, and the clothes would have to be burned. At least they weren't hers.

That thought made her smile, just a bit.

Raven grabbed a few items off a workbench and shoved them in his pockets.

"Why don't we just phase?" Surefire asked, hoping for an alternative to trekking through this biohazard.

"I want to save my strength." Raven sat on the edge of the hole with his feet dangling over. "Xochi's necklace helps, but after we landed in Canton, I could tell Xochi's stone was low on juice from phasing both of us. It's rebooted some of its mojo, but I don't want to take the chance of its running out when we need it, since it drains me more quickly to phase us both and especially to hold the phase from here and into the museum. I don't know what to expect once we're there. I'm more comfortable doing it this way." Raven climbed down.

"*Comfortable* is not a word I'd use." Surefire gripped a grimy metal rung and descended. Her lip curled when the stale, putrid odor intensified as she climbed lower.

When she neared the bottom, Raven lifted her down the final rungs so she wouldn't have to drop the distance to the ground. His hands lingered on her sides a little longer than needed, and his chin grazed the top of her head.

With that kiss, she had let loose a huge barrel of monkeys. One that she'd have to seal back up one way or another when this was over.

She moved stiffly away from Raven.

He took out a flashlight, and the beam of light cut through the dark tunnel, sending small and large critters scurrying into the shadows.

"Do you know how to get in from down here?" Surefire made a face as the sewer water sloshed over her shoes. Forget the hot shower, she might need a tetanus shot.

Raven led the way down the tunnel. "I've memorized the layouts of the popular museums and that included any underground drainage or tunnels."

"How are we getting in? Are you planning to phase us through?"

He shined the flashlight at holes just larger than the width of his body spaced out along the walls above them.

"There are several drainage pipes that lead from the original museum basement into this sewer. Some were closed up in the last forty years as the building was remodeled. We're going to crawl up through one of the pipes and break through the seal. It should get us close enough to weave our way back to the exhibit room. Otherwise, we'll have to go to Plan B."

"What's Plan B?" She breathed through her mouth, trying to lessen the stench of animal droppings, decaying rats, and street sludge.

"We'll have to take out some of the guards."

Surefire's stomach dropped. "Take out?"

"Out for dinner and a movie and maybe a little drink." Raven gave her a sly smile.

She gaped at him. "You don't plan to kill them?"

"What did I tell you in the warehouse while you were holding onto the beam for dear life?"

Surefire furrowed her brow. "I don't remember. And I wasn't holding on for dear life. Everything was under control."

"I told you that I won't have blood on my hands."

"Well, then, good." She nodded and then grimaced when her foot squashed down into a slimy hole.

"Though I will make an exception with Ari," he added in a low, tight voice.

They continued forward in silence. The sloshing of their shoes in the muck resounded through the dark and dank corridors. Every now and then, they heard a bus or a truck roll overhead, vibrating the tunnel. Surefire pressed her arms against her body, careful not to touch the grimy walls.

Raven trailed his light over the ceiling. He stopped before a round grate about three feet in circumference at about the level of his head.

"This is it. Can I borrow your knife?"

She responded with a blank stare.

"Didn't you stash it in your bra again?" He winked. "You didn't think I'd miss something like that?"

She sighed. She'd never met anyone, let alone a man, who was so perceptive.

Grateful he'd asked this time rather than grabbing for it himself, she reached underneath her sweater and slipped the butterfly knife out from inside her bra cup.

"Thanks." He shot a look at her chest and gave her his patented boyish grin.

She blushed then grew angry with herself for blushing. She needed to reset ground rules, big time.

Raven used the knife to undo the screws from the grate. He laced his fingers in the grid and gave it a hard yank, popping it off the wall.

He pulled himself up and wedged his feet in a crack for a foothold. He shone the light around the opening.

"I'll lead the way. Stay close."

This was one time that Surefire was happy to be small. It was going to be a tight fit for Raven. She took a few long, deep breaths. The idea of crawling into a dark, narrow tube without knowing what was on the other end or how long it would take to get there quickened her pulse. Sweat trickled between her breasts despite the coolness seeping into the sewers from above.

Raven jumped down and tossed her a keychain flashlight. "This should help a little."

He pulled himself back up and slithered into the hole until his feet disappeared.

When he was inside, he called out, "Do you need help?"

"I can make it." Surefire twisted the tiny flashlight on. She placed it in her mouth and gripped it between her teeth. Using a few small pipes jutting out from wall for leverage, she climbed up and hauled herself into the large drain.

"You in?" Raven asked, his voice muffled. Her face was inches from the bottom of his shoes. If he kicked, she'd get a face full of sewage gunk. She scooted back.

"Yeah," she said around the flashlight.

The pipe was narrower than she'd estimated. Raven slithered his body forward like a snake. Surefire watched the bottom of Raven's sneakers move in front of her. She wedged her arms in front of her head to push through the pipe. After a few feet, her clothes were soaked through to her skin. She didn't want to imagine what with. She rested her forearms in the waste and kept her head craned back. As it was, bits of wet gooey grossness kept flicking up into her face.

The price of saving the world.

The small light held in her mouth swung back and forth as her body rocked from side to side. Her head started to spin, as she struggled to breathe. Maybe it was the acrid scent. Or maybe she was claustrophobic and hadn't realized it until now. This was the first time she'd ever been in such a confined space. She tried to trick her mind into believing the exit was just ahead, just a few feet away. Unfortunately, her brain was not easily fooled.

Raven stopped abruptly. Her forehead banged straight into the bottom of his black Chuck Taylors. Luckily, she didn't lose the light, though her face was now covered with grime. Not a good feeling.

She wiggled back a foot to give him room in case he needed to crawl backward, though she hoped he'd give her a warning. She used the edge of her sweater to wipe the gunk from her forehead and succeeded in adding another layer of the slimy substance to her skin.

Perfect. She'd need a Hazmat team to hose her off after this adventure.

"Sorry, there was a large roach." His voice sounded choked. "It startled me. I have a device that's supposed to repel them, but it got wet."

"Okay." Her brain started piecing a few things together about Raven.

He twisted around to lie on his back.

"This is it."

He lifted his hands and pushed against what Surefire assumed was a metal lid over a pipe perpendicular to the one they were in. The cover clanged to the side of the drain as he shifted it away. He shined his flashlight up through the hole above him.

"It's not too far. If you stand on my shoulders, you should be able to reach the grate. The bars don't look too thick. You could push through. I'm going to move ahead. I want you to crawl forward and work your way until you're standing in this pipe above us. Then you need to stretch out your arms and legs and prop yourself up into it until I can angle myself underneath. Understand?"

"Got it." Her reply was muffled by the flashlight held between her teeth.

He wiggled farther down. When his feet cleared the vertical connecting pipe, Surefire crawled forward and nearly hurled when she noticed rat droppings.

"Uck." She gagged, the light slipping from her mouth. The drain appeared to pitch like a spinning tube in a funhouse as toxic fumes overwhelmed her.

"You'll get used to it."

"Where are we?"

"Not sure. Should just be an empty cellar room."

She tensed. Tiny claws scurried across her shoulder. "That would explain the feces."

Surefire took a quick breath through her mouth and swore she tasted ammonia along with a sweet pungent scent of decaying flesh.

Pulling herself up as far as she could go, she wedged her feet on either side of the pipe.

"I'm in position." She choked back a cough.

He slid into view until his head and shoulders were directly underneath her.

"I want you to place your feet on my shoulders. As I stand, I'll lift you."

She placed her feet on either side of his shoulders, and he hoisted her up. Her fingers grazed the drainage grate above her.

"A little higher."

He clamped his hands around her ankles and lifted her above his head. His arms didn't waver as he held that position.

Her hands hit the grate. She let out a sigh of relief that it wasn't fitted down by screws. She pushed, and it gave. She slid it over the floor, careful not to make any loud noise. She placed her hands on either side of the drainage hole and raised herself onto its ledge. The glow from the exit sign and light from the hallway peeping under the door were the only illumination in the room. She was concentrating so hard on getting out of the pipe she didn't see the metal table above her head.

The top of her head banged into its bottom. A slew of containers—some plastic and some glass—fell onto the floor. A few broke open.

"Uh-oh."

She eased down on the edge of the floor. Her feet hung down the pipe.

"What happened?" Raven called up.

"I knocked into a table. Didn't see it."

"Can you move so I can get up?"

"Shhh." Surefire stilled and listened for any sound of movement outside the room. After a few seconds, she assumed no one had heard the crash.

"All clear," she whispered down the hole and crawled from underneath the table.

Directly in front of her was one of the cases she had knocked over. Her eyes adjusting to the dark, she read the label printed in bold letters: *Latrodectus mactans*. She peered around at another case to her left: *Atrax robustus*. This one had a photo of what looked like a spider taped to the outside.

"Um, Raven . . ."

Her hand touched something large, hard, and furry. It scuttled across the floor.

"What was that?" Raven stopped halfway out of the pipe.

"Are you okay with spiders?"

"What are you talking about?" He pulled himself out of the drain until he was lying on the floor.

"When we were back in Baltimore, when Ari split into that swarm of insects, you looked as if you were about to faint."

He let out a forced laugh. "That's ridiculous."

"I thought maybe he was draining your power. Then I remembered your face when we were in the cavern under the warehouse and Ari looked like Franken-roach. You were grossed out."

"Weren't you? You have to admit that was disgusting."

"And you carry some kind of roach-repellant sonar in the sewers."

"Those things would've been all over us. The sewers are infested with them."

She considered their conversation about what she feared. "Is that why you asked about my father? Had Ari taken the form of something you feared?"

"Fine. Yes. I am afraid of bugs."

She heard a sharp intake of breath.

Raven moved like a flash to the far corner of the room. "Where are we?"

"A room where they've stored their overstock of spiders, I think."

He flattened himself into the corner. "They must've moved things around since I was here last."

"They were renovating the Insect Zoo." Surefire stood and looked around for a light. A small spider crawled over her foot. She kicked it away.

"I'm going to find a light switch. Just stay where you are."

"Not a problem."

Her hand slid over the smooth tile wall. Once in a while something crunched under her foot like she was stepping on M&M's.

"Sorry." She cringed.

"Did you just apologize to a spider?"

"They're living creatures, too. Just because they're creepy doesn't mean they should be respected any less. They help keep the balance of nature as well. You should feel a kinship with them."

"Creepy? More like alien beasts. Some of their bites can kill you."

"As if you have anything to worry about." Surefire flicked on the light and nearly choked.

The floor was alive. Apparently she had knocked over more containers than she had realized.

Raven froze. His face paled.

Surefire swallowed hard. Something crawled up her calf. She kicked her leg and it fell off.

She didn't want to panic. She didn't want to add to the freak-out fest already happening in the corner by the normally cool Raven. She walked toward him slowly with her hand extended. It took all her willpower not to scratch at her arms or kick at the things crawling next to her feet.

"Give me your hand. The door is less than ten feet away."

He looked to the right at the door then back at her. His breathing was more controlled, which was a good sign, but he was still staring at the creatures near him as if they were going to eat him alive.

"I'm good." He exhaled a long breath. He took a few steps forward until he stood in front of her.

"It's stupid." Fear faded from his face replaced by an angry flush. "I can't believe I let this get to me. I'm an idiot."

"We all have our phobias." She reached out and grabbed his hand. "These things are more afraid of you."

"They don't act like it."

She smiled, but the smile faltered when she felt a sharp pain on the back of her leg followed by another one at her ankle.

"What's wrong?"

"Nothing," she replied, though she couldn't keep the discomfort from showing on her face. The bites burned as if flames had sparked against her skin.

"Did something bite you?" His grip tightened on her hand.

She shook her head, but it wasn't convincing. Why was her leg suddenly numb? What the hell were they keeping in here?

Raven scooped her up and hit the door at full pace into the hallway.

"Stay with me," he whispered at the top of her head.

"I'm thine," Surefire slurred, her tongue suddenly too thick to speak, her lips unable to form a simple "f" sound.

He squeezed her close to his chest.

She wanted to ask him how they were going to make it with the museum filled with security guards and police, but she couldn't form words. Her brain was fuzzy, like a static-laden TV.

She closed her eyes when they entered a dark hallway. His footsteps were silent on the marble floor. Voices echoed down the corridor, and he ducked into a bathroom. She wasn't sure if it was for men or women.

The voices passed by, and after a few seconds, Raven popped his head out the door. He started running again and then stopped. She opened her eyes and saw him creeping underneath a video camera.

Cameras?

She thought about the camera in the room when they had escaped the tomb. Had U-Sec seen the footage of her and Raven her leaving the museum? Would Pax be waiting for her here?

That little bit of panic gave her a jolt of clarity. As they crept closer to the stairwell leading up to the display room, she heard voices and footsteps, and she saw bright lights illuminating the floors above.

"We 'on't 'ake it," she slurred some more.

"I should have enough juice to phase us out from this far. But I'm going to clear the room a bit just in case."

She wasn't sure what he meant, and she couldn't form the words to ask. He threaded through one of the exhibit halls until the voices from the stairwell died down to a murmur.

"I'm going to set you down here for just a moment. Don't move."

Don't move? She couldn't even talk, let alone try to stand on legs now engulfed in lava.

He put her down on a carpeted step. Her head rolled back, and she stared right into the jaws of a T. rex hanging several feet above her head.

Was it her, or did the thing move closer? She rubbed her eyes with hands that felt like balloons. She glanced around the room. Raven was gone. He had disappeared before she'd realized it.

Her eyes scanned the walls, and her fevered mind played havoc with her emotions. There were a lot of bones in here, a lot of dead things. What if they all came alive at the same time? Could that happen? It had in a movie she'd seen. Set in a place that looked similar to this room.

She saw a red light. In the far corner. A camera.

A shiver shot down her spine. The pain was getting worse. Her whole body was on fire. Tears poured from her eyes. She wanted to scream but couldn't, wouldn't dare.

Raven was gone, creating whatever diversion he could.

In her panicked, feverish state, she lifted her head. She looked dead in the camera and forced her lips to work.

Raven sped through the museum. Phasing in and out in spurts to conserve his energy, he set off alarms throughout the various rooms and floors. He hoped to split up the cadre of police and guards to opposite ends of the museum to thin out the crowd of officers guarding the tomb's exhibit room.

After the last alarm sounded, he ran back to Surefire. Her glassy eyes stared dead ahead. She didn't make a sound when he picked her up. He almost wished she'd fight him or at least argue about what to plan next. Her silence frightened him more than the spiders had.

This was his fault. He was infused with the power of a goddess, yet those little buggers caused him to panic more than facing a god who ripped the skin off his cousin's face.

Surefire was right. Spiders couldn't hurt him anymore. Nothing could.

Well, almost nothing.

He rubbed her swollen leg. "You'll be okay, Synthia."

He squeezed Xochi's amulet in his hand until the edges cut into his flesh, extracting whatever power was left. A prickle of energy danced along his arm. His body became light and airy, and they both phased out and floated up the center of the stairwell, skimming along the tall totem pole. He drifted toward the stone tomb. Four guards remained in the room. Their attention was focused on the front entrance, not the back stairwell.

Raven moved toward the tomb's wall and attempted to phase through it but couldn't. An invisible field blocked him. He eyed the long spikes protruding from the front, which he hadn't noticed before. Xochi had said he had to verify his identity, and his identity was in his blood. Cutting a look at the preoccupied guards, he positioned himself in front of the spikes and slipped out of the phased form. When they were both solid, he eased Surefire onto her feet.

"Can you hold onto my neck?" he whispered as he bent down to give her access.

She gave the barest of nods then slung her arm around his neck and settled her body against his back. He needed his chest and hands free to allow the spikes to pierce his torso and limbs. He only hoped Surefire had enough strength to hold on.

Behind him, someone shouted, "Stop!"

He heard the unmistakable sound of safeties clicking off.

"Put your hands up."

Raven slowly stood, raised his hands and slammed his palms against the spikes. Shouts grew louder as the guards advanced closer. With Surefire at his back, he assumed they wouldn't take the chance and shoot them. He pressed his body against the center spikes and prayed Surefire would pull through. After their sharp tips pierced his skin, he head butted the top spike.

White light blinded him. He free-fell into a dark, cold pit before blacking out.

♥ ☠ ♥ ☠ ♥ ☠

"The *General* is here to see you," Oracle announced over the speakerphone. Her sarcastic emphasis on "general" was not lost on Pax. Oracle wasn't fond of St. John. Pax wasn't sure if it was something she had read off him or something Surefire had confided to her.

Thankfully, Helena had decided to call it a night—or morning—since it was nearing six thirty. She was even less fond of St. John and wasn't as tactful as Oracle in hiding her true feelings.

Pax filled his lungs with as much air as possible before releasing it slowly, trying to tap into his reserves for composure. He only hoped St. John hadn't brought his wife. He didn't have the patience to battle both.

"Send him in." Pax paused the video he'd been watching of Raven and Surefire exiting the tomb. A blurry, black-and-white version of Surefire's face filled the screen as she stared up into the video camera.

"Paxton," St. John said as he entered.

Immediately Pax stood at attention, even though it had been ten years since St. John had been his commanding officer and five years since St. John had retired.

"Sir," Pax replied. He looked past St. John to the closed door. He let out a sigh of relief that Vanessa wasn't with him.

"At ease." St. John motioned for Pax to sit down.

Despite his words, Pax couldn't feel any ease with St. John's cold grey eyes marking him like a glassy scope at the end of a gun. St. John wore a crisp navy suit and tie, which made Pax feel like a slob in his U-Sec sweatshirt, faded jeans, and tennis shoes.

"How's Vanessa?" Pax ventured.

"As well as can be expected, considering the circumstances." St. John sat down across from Pax. "What happened to Synthia?"

"We're still reviewing evidence."

"What evidence?"

Pax motioned for him to come around the desk. He stood and walked behind Pax with his back straight and hands clasped behind him.

Pax played the surveillance video.

"Again," he barked the order.

Pax replayed it from the beginning.

St. John turned from the laptop screen and stared out the picture window behind Pax's desk. The sun had risen, hanging low in the pastel-colored sky. He didn't say anything for a very long time, just stood and gazed out at the awakening city below.

Pax tapped a pencil on his desk and stared at St. John's rigid back. The silence stretched across the room, stretching his nerves along with it. Pax didn't have time for his power plays. St. John wielded his stony silence as most soldiers wielded hand grenades to break down defenses.

"St. John—" Pax began.

"How did she get there?" St. John interrupted. "Heather told me Synthia was down a well."

A well?

"No, it wasn't a well. We believe Synthia had fallen into a cavern below the warehouse. The police felt an earthquake from the perimeter outside the building where Synthia had pursued Raven. They entered and found a large crack in the floor, as if the ground had opened and then closed over her."

Several seconds ticked by as St. John went back to his reverie.

Pax shifted on his chair and coughed.

"Why did she pursue this target alone?" St. John asked.

"We're not sure."

"How did she end up in the museum after falling through this supposed crack?"

"Again, we're not sure."

"And where's her uniform? She's wearing a leotard in that video. I doubt that is standard issue."

Pax's cheek twitched. He glanced back at the computer screen. "I noticed that, too. I don't understand why she'd wear that."

"For someone who is head of operations, you certainly don't know much." St. John turned his head from the window to regard Pax.

Pax met St. John's cold, interrogating gaze and focused on keeping his blood pressure down and his anger in check. Getting into an argument with St. John was not going to help matters. However, the man wasn't making it easy.

"Where are your partners? Maybe they know something?" St. John demanded.

"They are on assignment. Classified."

"I see." He turned his back on Pax again. "Has this leaked to the press?"

"What?" Pax was taken aback by the question.

St. John spoke in the clipped manner of someone not used to repeating himself. "Has the press seen this video?"

"No. It was sent directly to me from museum security."

"We need to discuss with the museum the consequences of leaking it to the press. I don't want this compromised."

"I already have."

"I'm glad you've done something right."

The pencil Pax had been holding snapped in two. "Sir, this is my operation, and my team is doing their best damn job to get Synthia back."

Pax stood and St. John pivoted around to face him. He noticed St. John had shrunk a bit. His brown hair held more gray, and the hair at his temples had gone completely white. His square face sagged around the edges.

"It doesn't seem like it. Someone from your office called Heather to the crime scene. That is not the protocol. Synthia's identity as a U-Sec Agent was supposed to be kept secret. That was part of our agreement. You were to protect Heather and our family by keeping the media from finding out that Synthia is a *transhuman*."

Though Pax took offense at the way St. John sneered when he said "transhuman," the man did have a point. Pax hadn't realized someone from U-Sec had called Heather to the scene. Because of Heather's—and the St. John clan's—notoriety, Synthia's identity was kept hidden. Society was just getting used to the idea of transhumans. Most people didn't understand what transhumans were, and those who did were afraid of them. As U-Sec had become more well-known and more transhuman crime had occurred, Pax had hired a PR firm to handle public opinion. Unfortunately, that had been a month ago, and he had yet to schedule time to meet with them and review their proposals.

Pax's stomach clenched with dread. If someone had called Heather from the inside, then someone had deliberately broken with protocol. The same someone could've knocked down U-Sec's firewalls and stolen personnel files.

"Did Heather say who contacted her?" Pax asked.

St. John lowered his lids. "A woman, I believe. No name. Why?"

Pax held up a hand, excusing himself for a moment. He hit a button on the phone and paged Oracle.

"Get Pixie on the line."

"Give me a minute." She clicked off.

He had meant to interrogate Pixie an hour ago before he got distracted by the security footage.

Pax faced St. John and steeled himself for a thorough reaming out. "Someone hacked into our network and took Oracle's and Synthia's files before our safeguards kicked them out. I think we were compromised. Perhaps by someone working inside our organization."

"What are you planning to do about it?" St. John's lips pressed together into a thin, crooked line.

"Graham is re-enforcing our firewalls. Everyone working this evening has been spoken to about this issue. However, there is one agent I want to speak with personally. Oracle's tracking her down."

St. John paced across the room. "According to my contacts, earlier this morning, Synthia disappeared with Raven in front of a mess of agents and officers after smashing a stolen statue. Is that true?"

"It's true."

St. John stopped behind one of the chairs in front of Pax's desk. "Why would she help him?"

"I believe she was coerced. If you look at this surveillance video, Raven is carrying her out of the museum. According to the head of security, Raven held a gun to her head before disappearing."

"I was also informed that Raven wasn't holding a gun to her head outside the warehouse. In fact, he was down on the ground. Synthia had an opportunity to take him in, but instead she helped him escape."

Pax set his jaw, determined not to be cowed. He wasn't sure where St. John had gotten his information, but important details had been left out. "As I said, I believe she was coerced. In the lot outside the warehouse, she kept glancing behind her as if someone were watching her. Oracle had detected another presence in the area. We believe something or someone more powerful than Raven had incapacitated her. The same presence Oracle had sensed in the warehouse after Synthia disappeared."

St. John huffed. "You *believe* but you have no proof. We have a bunch of officers who are now saying Synthia is a turncoat. That she's sleeping with the enemy."

"That's not true." Pax's pressure rose. He placed his hands on his desk. "I spoke personally with those on the scene. No one mentioned that theory to me."

"Then they lied to you, because that was the first thing my contacts related to me."

Pax couldn't believe what St. John was suggesting about his daughter. "Synthia is one of our best agents and has usually followed protocol. If she helped Raven escape this evening, then she has a good reason. She nearly captured Raven twice before."

"*Nearly* is the key word."

Pax ground his teeth, too frustrated to respond.

"Synthia has done this before." St. John paced across the room again. "After she failed to make the team with Heather, she became unstable. Depressed. Uncontrollable. She got into drugs and began stealing."

"If I remember correctly, she tried pot once, passed out, and never did it again. Then she stole a pair of designer jeans and got caught, and you made her spend the night in jail."

"You act as if that's normal behavior. Not for a St. John. Not for our family. She lacked discipline. Discipline she had somewhat regained in college, and what I had hoped she'd learn from your establishment. But she obviously hasn't." He shook his head hard. "I want all your people on it. I want her back home as soon as possible. She needs help before she hurts herself, or anyone else for that matter."

Pax's body vibrated with the pent-up rage he was having trouble containing. He was far beyond the breathing techniques he'd learned in yoga.

If St. John expected one-hundred percent from his soldiers, he expected more than that from his family, especially Synthia. When she'd lost her spot on the Olympic team, Pax thought St. John had lost the farm on a horse race. It was as if Synthia's misstep had caused him greater pain than her busted kneecap and nose had caused her. Pax had never understood why, and right now, he was sick of him bringing up her mistakes from over ten years ago.

Like most teenagers, Synthia had made bad choices. She had certainly made up for it in recent years. She'd graduated from college at the top of her class and trained with U-Sec for several years before begging them for a case of her own. With Oracle as her trainer and partner, Pax had known Synthia would be safe—as safe as someone could be in their profession. St. John wanted direction for his daughter's life, and Pax had given it to her.

"I will personally find her," Pax stated.

The phone rang and Pax picked it up, glad for the distraction.

"Yeah."

"I'm forwarding a new surveillance video," Graham said. "It's from the Smithsonian. I spoke to Roy, head of security. He wants you down there asap."

Pax downloaded his e-mail and opened the attachment.

"The video was taken around five thirty this morning," Graham continued.

Pax shot a glance at the corner of the screen. It read seven o'clock.

"Why are we just getting it now?" Pax drummed his fingers on the desk as his computer took its time opening the large video file.

"They sent it around six, but Oliver was trying to get a read on what she was saying."

"For a goddamn hour?" Pax yelled.

"I don't know," Graham responded, defensive. "He said it took a while to make it out."

Astonished, Pax stared at the video playing on his screen. Facing the security camera, Synthia reclined on a step underneath a T. rex skeleton. Her lips moved in exaggerated proportions, as if she were being very precise with how she mouthed the words.

"What did he decipher?" Pax asked.

"He's writing up the report now."

"I want it now. How long does it take? I can make out a few words without even concentrating."

"There's more," Graham said.

"What's more?"

"There's another video. Check your e-mail."

St. John had moved to stand behind Pax. He could feel the other man's presence like a gathering hailstorm at his back.

Pax opened the other e-mail, and the video began playing. It wasn't as grainy or dark as the first. The lights were up in the room and the video stream kept cutting to different angles to catch Raven racing down an aisle between several glass cases with a limp Synthia jostling against his chest.

"Is she . . . ?" Pax started but was too upset to finish.

"Keep watching," Graham said.

On the video, Raven jumped up to a rectangular stone chamber with Synthia hanging across his back and her arms wrapped weakly around his neck. Raven raised his hands as the police officers and security guards raised their guns. Then Raven slammed his body into spikes protruding from the tomb and disappeared.

Pax replayed the video. Synthia and Raven melted into the stone like liquid.

St. John took in a sharp breath. "My God, how did he do that?"

"Any word on her condition?" Pax asked.

"Witnesses said she appeared semiconscious."

"What kind of trick is that?" St. John spoke next to Pax's ear. He leaned over Pax, watching the video with an incredulous look.

"I'm going to see Oliver. Get the museum on the phone. I want access to this tomb. Tell whoever is managing this exhibit to get us as much information on this piece as possible."

"Will do," Graham said.

"Anything else?" Pax asked.

"Only that the statue Surefire smashed is related to this tomb."

"Who told you that?"

"Oliver."

"How the hell would he know?" Pax exclaimed.

"He went on a date with Pixie to see this exhibit and the one on loan at the Walters."

"He's dating Pixie?" *Man, I am out of the loop.*

"I'll let Oliver field that one." Graham hung up.

St. John followed Pax out to the reception area where Oracle sat with the phone in her hand.

"I'm coming with you," St. John stated.

"I didn't expect otherwise."

Oracle hung up the phone. "Can't track down Pixie. She's not picking up her cell, and she's not at her desk."

"We'll deal with her later."

Pax gave Oracle an update on the latest security footage.

"We're heading to DC," he told her.

"Haven't seen the museum in years. I'll meet you in the garage."

Pax made a quick stop at the Tech department to speak with Oliver but was told Oliver had gone to the call center where Pixie was supposed to be monitoring assignments and agents.

When Pax entered the room, Oliver flicked on a screensaver and swiveled in his chair. St. John followed closely on Pax's heels.

"What's up?" Oliver asked with his stoner voice.

Pax figured Oliver had watched *Fast Times at Ridgemont High* too much as a child and idolized Spicoli. Not a perfect choice for a role model, but it did hide the incredible mind Oliver had for gadgets and all high-tech equipment. He could disassemble and reassemble any electronic device in half the time that those who'd created them could. He was instrumental in developing new tools for U-Sec to keep on top of the ever-evolving transhuman crimes.

"You know what's up. What did you learn from that surveillance video?"

"Ohhh," Oliver breathed out. "Oh, yeah. Surefire. Gotcha."

St. John grunted next to Pax. "Is this the type of moron monitoring your agents? No wonder Synthia disappeared."

"Take it easy, dude. It's not my fault she went AWOL. I wasn't even supposed to be here tonight," Oliver said.

"Then why are you here?" Pax bit out, annoyed with Oliver's attitude. "Wasn't Pixie monitoring the systems tonight?"

"I don't know, I guess." He shrugged and looked back at the blank screensaver.

"Where is she?"

"Dunno. We were supposed to meet up and she never showed, so I came here to check on her and she's, like, gone. Can't even reach her."

"Fine. We'll deal with her later. Just tell me what you found. Can you understand what Synthia's trying to say?"

"Uh, sort of. But it doesn't make sense to me."

"Sort of," St. John mimicked with a sarcastic snort. "Unbelievable."

"Show me what you got," Pax said.

"I'm on it." He turned in his seat and began typing. The screen flickered on.

Varying images popped across the three large screens directly in front of him. On the left was the surveillance from the first scene. On the middle, Synthia mouthing into the camera. On the far right, them disappearing into the tomb.

"From what I could tell . . ." Oliver clicked across the keyboard with lightning speed and zoomed in on the center video. A grainy, pixilated image of Surefire filled the screen. "She's . . . uhhh . . . saying something like 'Magic staff and nose raisin good Pez.'"

"Magic staff and nose?" Pax repeated, dumbfounded. Oliver had taken this long to tell him this crap?

"Obviously, she's been drugged," St. John commented. "Probably hallucinating."

"No, she is being very precise with her wording." Pax stared at the screen. "Replay it, slowly."

"Got it. I'll make it loop." Oliver set it up so it looped from the time she started speaking to when she turned her head away.

"And about her being drugged." Oliver spun back around in his chair. "Head of security told me Surefire and Raven entered the museum through a grate in a basement room where they were storing spiders while they renovated the Insect Zoo. Surefire and Raven must've accidentally knocked over a few cages, because the floor was crawling with nasty critters."

"And they think Surefire might've been bitten?" Pax asked.

"Yeah."

St. John swore under his breath. "Do they know what bit her?"

"Not sure. Might be the Australian funnel-web spider. Its venom is strong enough to cause her to go comatose like that," Oliver explained.

"How long does she have?" Pax asked.

"Not long enough if she had a hefty dose."

St. John swore again, this time a string of obscenities Pax had never heard him utter before. "I'm calling in support for this one."

"Withers?" Pax inquired.

"Who else? He can provide military backup, if we need it, and expertise that we certainly need." He gave Oliver a scathing look to punctuate his last remark. "Plus, he owes me one."

"We'll find her," Pax assured him.

"You don't even know where she is. How can you find her, and in time?" He took out his cell phone from his jacket pocket. "No fucking signal. Unbelievable."

He stormed out of the room. A second later, Pax heard the door to the garage slam open and shut.

Pax's mouth went dry and an ulcer started to flare up in his stomach.

"Graham told me you know something about the markings on this tomb."

"A little. I saw this exhibit a month ago." Oliver created a screen grab from the security footage of the tomb then magnified it. "I recognize this image." He moved his mouse to the side and used an electronic stylus to circle the tomb's etching on the screen. "This is of the goddess Xochiquetzal. Pixie kept making a big deal about her. Something about this goddess being an ungrateful bitch. Not sure what she meant."

"That looks similar to the statue Raven stole from the Walters."

"Bingo," Oliver said.

Pax glanced at his watch. Oracle and St. John were waiting in the garage; he needed to go.

"Next time, don't wait to get the report together before contacting me about the video. I needed this sent to me immediately."

"Dude, I just got here thirty minutes ago," Oliver replied. "I didn't even know there was a video until I went through Pixie's computer to figure out why she bailed on me. The first video was in the trash."

"What do you mean the first video was in the trash?" Pax exclaimed. "Graham forwarded it to me an hour ago."

"Ron had resent it after no one replied to him. According to the time stamp, he had sent it to our call center while you were at the warehouse."

"Was it a mistake?"

Oliver shrugged with his eyes downcast.

"Has Pixie been acting strangely?" Pax wondered if his growing suspicions of Pixie were being realized. He never wanted to accuse any of his staff without irrefutable evidence and without speaking with them firsthand. Transhumans dealt with enough false accusations from society. He worked hard to make U-Sec a safe haven for them.

Oliver shrugged again and picked at a mustard stain on his white T-shirt. "Not really. I mean, we started hanging out recently. She just ended a bad relationship. Used to come in with some nasty bruises that she played off. But she wanted to learn more about assembling our gadgets and weapons, so I let her help out, because it seemed to cheer her up." He offered a shy smile.

"You've been showing her your work?" Pax's gut tightened.

"I dunno. It was nice having a chick interested in what I do." He slouched in his chair, not meeting Pax's glare. "I figured it was okay since she worked here."

"It was not okay. No one is allowed in your Tech room unless they have prior permission from one of the partners. What you do is classified as far as U-Sec is concerned. Even from the government."

"I know. I know." Oliver punctuated each word with a guilty nod. "She was just a girl, I didn't think it mattered."

"That's what Samson thought."

"Who?" Oliver looked up at him through his shaggy haircut.

"Never mind. Just don't do it again."

"Am I in trouble?"

Pax hung his head in frustration. Oliver wasn't the first man to be compromised by a woman, and he wouldn't be the last. He was young, a few years out of college. He still had a lot to learn.

"No, just don't do it again."

"I won't. I promise."

"And if Pixie happens to call or drop by, don't tell her anything. I'll deal with her personally." Pax started to walk out the door and then turned back. An idea nagged at him.

"Can you Google what Surefire said into the camera? Maybe cross-reference it with Aztec mythology and anything else related to this case. It might be a long shot, but it's the only thing we've got."

"On it." Oliver swiveled his chair around and started typing.

Chapter Fourteen

Raven's eyes popped open, and the first thing he noticed was a yellow hummingbird fluttering above his face. The second was a canopy of blue and gold fabric draped overhead. The third was Xochi in a purple negligee-style gown. She stood at the foot of a circular feather bed, where he was sprawled, and stared at him with a sensual glint in her eyes.

Xochi? A bed?

He sprang up, lurching backward across silky sheets. A cool breeze blew in from his left through a wall-sized opening that overlooked the never-ending sunset and the lush, green canopy. The breeze prickled up his inner thigh. Startled, he looked down and saw himself exposed in all his glory. He quickly gathered the sheets around his waist.

"Surefire?" he asked, his voice groggy from sleep. He blinked a few times to adjust his eyes. Gold bands adorned Xochi's wrists and head and glowed with their own light source, acting as a spotlight and illuminating her body in the dim torchlight of the chamber.

"Shhh. My sweet huitzilin, my sweet hummingbird," Xochi said as she swayed closer.

The yellow bird whipped away and joined its pals and a few butterflies doing aerial acrobatics around the room.

"Where is she?" Raven squinted. Xochi's gold accessories became brighter as she came closer.

"Resting." She eased down onto the bed next to him and rubbed her small, warm hand across the sheets and up his leg. Wherever she touched, heat radiated through the fabric and danced along his skin. Desire soon followed. His muscles jumped. His groin ached.

Raven tried to twist away, but he was stuck between Xochi and the mountain of decorative pillows behind him. "Is Surefire okay?"

The last thing he remembered was Surefire barely hanging onto his neck before the tomb's spikes pierced his flesh and he blacked out.

"She is well." Her plump lips stretched into a smile. She reached up with her other hand to finger the stone around his neck.

"I see you found my necklace." She leaned close. Her fingertips tickled along his shoulders and unfastened the chain from around his neck. Her hand closed over the necklace, and it disappeared.

The overwhelming floral aroma that infused Xochi's pores—as if she'd bathed in a florist's shop—made Raven's head spin. The odor invaded his nostrils and mouth and traveled down his throat. He coughed, his lungs attempting to expel the odor. Xochi shoved him back against jeweled-tone cushions.

"The first time you came, we had weeks to spend together. The last time, I regretted there was none." Her index finger trailed a light path from his chest down past his bellybutton and stopped where his happy trail began at the top of the sheet still clutched in his hand.

"Now we have a moment before you leave me again." She cupped a hand around the back of his neck, leaned over, and kissed him.

His mouth opened to her forceful kiss. Her power and lust filled him— sensual, exotic, and heady. It tasted like cocoa and cinnamon and tropical spices. Then he thought about Surefire, about Synthia, and the kiss they'd shared in the car.

It wasn't anything like Xochi's kiss.

Xochi tugged the sheet out of his grip and slid it down past his stomach. She kneeled on the bed, straddling him. The sheer fabric covering her torso sifted across his face when she bent over him. The gold plate resting atop her breasts felt cool against his forehead. Xochi rubbed against him, showing how much she wanted him.

He closed his eyes and pictured Synthia making out with him in the car at the stoplight. He had wanted Synthia then, still wanted her in fact. Even though, at this moment, a beautiful, sex-crazed goddess was throwing herself at him, ready to fulfill his every desire. It didn't feel right. Xochi didn't feel right. In one kiss, Synthia had made him feel appreciated, needed . . . loved.

With Xochi, he felt cheap, used, degraded.

Raven pushed away, sinking his head deeper into the pillows. He grabbed Xochi's shoulders and shoved her back.

"No." Raven tried to sit up, but Xochi was a lot heavier than her petite frame let on. "I want to see Synthia."

Xochi sat back on his shins. Her dark swirling eyes studied him with a vacant expression, as if she couldn't fathom what Raven had said to her.

When realization finally dawned on her, the room grew frigid. The birds and butterflies that had silently fluttered about the room streamed out. Her warm, sensual energy reeled back inside of her, leaving Raven with a shiver.

"How dare you." She backhanded him. His head reeled to the side and his teeth cut into his mouth. Blood trickled from his lips.

"And for a human." She sprang from him. Her soft, feminine features hardened with ugly angles of rage.

Raven wiped the back of his hand across his mouth.

"I have killed men for less. Transformed them into scorpions to squash under my heel." Xochi stomped her foot and the room quaked.

Raven started to sit up. She flung out her hand, and he flopped back onto the bed. An anvil resting on his chest would be lighter than the telepathic pressure she forced onto his body to keep him down.

She moved closer. Her upper lip curled back in disgust. Ice-cold energy burned through Raven's veins. He arched his back.

"You have fallen in love with this girl." Her eyes narrowed and stopped swirling. The weight lifted from his body, and he took in a shaky breath. "I can feel it. You are worried about her. You care about her. But does she care about you?"

"I don't know. I hope so."

Her fingers combed roughly through his messy strands. She grabbed a fistful of hair and forced his face close to hers.

"You are willing to tempt my wrath for what you do not know? As I told you before, I will not share that which is mine."

It was Raven's turn to get angry, and his anger made him bold. "I'm not yours."

Red sparks flashed across the blackness of her eyes. "I saved your life. It now belongs to me."

She let go of his hair and shoved his head back into the pillows. Then she spun around and stalked away.

"Is that what happened with Tezcatlipoca?" Raven asked.

Xochi stopped but didn't turn around.

"He stole you from your husband Tláloc and forced you into marriage. Did he have a claim on your life that bound you to him as well?"

She turned so he could see her perfect profile. "Tread lightly, my angry *xicohtli,* my angry bee. Do not sting the hand that gave you life. You may get swatted."

"A simple 'yes' or 'no' would work." He sat up.

Her shoulders drooped a bit. "There is no simple response, and no response I owe to you."

Her hand shot out from her side. A sharp, strong wind formed from out of nowhere and forced Raven back down onto the bed. Vines sprouted from the mattress and wrapped about his limbs, holding him down.

"Stay." Without a backward glance, Xochi left the room through a stone archway covered by a thick drape.

"Don't you touch her." Raven struggled against the vines but his strength was diminished, his powers almost tapped out. Somewhere, perhaps close by, Surefire rested. He feared Xochi was about to give her a rude awakening.

"Xochi!" He pitched against and tugged at the vines binding his limbs. They started to give.

♥ ☠ ♥ ☠ ♥ ☠

Surefire extended her limbs in a nice long stretch that left her feeling refreshed and renewed. She sighed and snuggled back under the silky sheets, nestling into the soft feather mattress for a few more stolen moments of shut-eye.

Her eyes popped open.

Silky sheets? Feather mattress?

She sat up quickly, too quickly. The room swayed. She closed her eyes again and fell back into what felt like a hundred throw pillows.

The last things she remembered were the hard floor of the museum and the sharp teeth of the T. rex looming over her, and then barely holding onto Raven's neck. She cracked open her eyes and saw draped above her head blue, green, and yellow satin fabric, which reminded her of a harem's decor she'd seen in a movie once. To her left, the wall opened to a sun setting over thick fauna. Several monarch butterflies and hummingbirds flew into and around the room from outside.

A gust of wind blew across the bed. She brought the covers up to her neck. She shivered and then peered under the sheets.

She was naked.

Surefire glanced around for Raven. Small torches flickered in the corners of the stone chamber but weren't bright enough to fully illuminate it. Most of the room was in shadow.

"She awakes," a voice boomed from nearby.

Startled, Surefire jumped back and rolled off the bed onto the cold stone floor, pulling the sheets with her.

"Ow." She untwisted the sheets from her legs and peered up and over the edge of the bed at Xochi, who lounged against the cushions with a bemused expression.

"I did not mean to startle you."

"I'm sure you didn't." Surefire scowled at her, though she was grateful to see that Xochi had at least covered up since last time. She wore a ruby-colored tunic adorned with blue and green and yellow feathers that fell in rows like the fringes of a flapper's dress and provided ample coverage of Xochi's goddess-like breasts.

Surefire stood and gathered the sheets up to her chest with one hand, using the other to pull up the sheets at her back to cover her rear. "What happened?"

"I saved your life," Xochi intoned.

"Oh," Surefire responded, taken aback. Then she remembered the spider bite and the excruciating pain of her insides being liquefied or twisted together or whatever havoc the spider's poison had been wreaking inside her body.

"Thanks."

Xochi played absently with the shimmering gold bracelets on her wrists. "Do not thank me. I did it because it was necessary."

"Okay." Surefire looked to the left then right, wondering where Raven was. The room's temperature had dropped several degrees, as if an A/C unit had kicked on. The random birds and butterflies flying about the ceiling began streaming out of the room. Xochi propped herself onto her forearm among the decorative pillows and glared at Surefire with an angry, hurt expression, as if Surefire had just kicked Xochi's prized pet.

"What did you do to him?"

Surefire sucked in her bottom lip, unsure how to reply and concluding that she shouldn't. Her eyes scanned the room for a way out. *Where was Raven? And why had he left her alone with Ms. Psycho Goddess herself?*

When it seemed obvious that Xochi wanted some reply, Surefire clutched the sheet tighter to her chest.

"Excuse me?"

"Raven, what did you do to him?"

Surefire's stomach dropped. Had something happened to Raven? The last time she had seen him was in the museum as she forced her failing arms to wrap around his neck.

"Is he all right?" Worry pricked at Surefire's heart.

"No, he is not." Xochi's black eyes swirled a deep violet. "He is in love with *you.*"

Surefire couldn't stop the smile from creeping across her lips. She started giggling, which morphed into a sidesplitting laugh.

Raven, in love with her?

Xochi had been drinking too much of the ambrosia—or whatever Aztec gods drank to get high. That was the last thing Surefire had expected Xochi to say.

Xochi sat up on the bed, and Surefire could see her shaking but not with laughter, with rage. "You fool girl, what is so funny?"

"I wasn't expecting that." Surefire tried to catch her breath; she was laughing too hard. "Seriously, that is the craziest thing I've heard in a long time. Your feelings are way off."

"Why does she question me? Why is everyone questioning my feelings?" Xochi mumbled under her breath right before her nostrils flared and her body went rigid and she bellowed, "I am not off!"

Surefire stopped laughing. Xochi's power hit her with the force of a hundred little knives slicing across her skin. She stumbled back from the bed but stopped before she went too far. Behind her, the wall opened up to a sheer drop down several stories to the Garden below.

"Raven admitted it himself." Xochi's eyes locked on Surefire for a moment before she looked down at a cluster of marigolds strewn across the blanket near her legs.

Surefire needed to nip this ridiculous assertion in the bud. "I'm sure he didn't mean it."

"Why do you deny it?"

"Because he'd never be in love with me."

"Why not?"

Oh, let me count the ways.

"Because . . . well . . . for starters, technically we just met."

"Love can happen in an instant." She snapped her fingers. "It usually does, and it's usually the human's fault for not recognizing it. Such as you are doing right now."

"Me?" Surefire raised her brows. Xochi was definitely dipping into the sauce if she thought Surefire loved Raven.

"You are in denial. I can feel your concern for him."

"Concern, yes. Love, that's a whole other ballpark."

"You kissed him, did you not?"

Surefire's cheeks heated. She so didn't want to discuss her kissing Raven with Xochi. They weren't exactly on BFF terms. "I'd rather not talk about it."

"I can feel the love streaming from you. It tastes sweet, like chocolate on my tongue." She swung her legs off the bed and stood in front of Surefire.

Surefire glanced behind her at the drop only a few feet from where she stood. Xochi could push her out if she chose. Fortunately, according to Raven, Surefire was useful to Xochi's plans, and Surefire figured this usefulness was keeping her alive at the moment.

"Lust has a very different taste. Bitter. Spicier." Xochi inched closer.

"You don't know how I feel." Surefire shuffled backward.

Xochi reached out her hand and caressed Surefire's cheek. A warm tingle radiated from her touch and quickened Surefire's pulse. "I cannot seduce someone in love."

She laid a kiss on Surefire's throat. The aroma of way too many flowers assaulted Surefire's nose. She coughed and took a few more steps back. Her feet tangled in the sheets. She tripped and fell backward over the edge.

Xochi reached out and grabbed Surefire's wrist, holding her suspended over the drop. Surefire grabbed Xochi's forearm with her other hand, and Xochi tugged her back up with the sheet twisted around her legs.

"Did Raven tell you about me?" Xochi continued the conversation, seemingly oblivious to Surefire almost tripping to her death.

Surefire nodded because she didn't trust herself to form words. Her heart beat faster than the wings of Xochi's pet hummingbirds. With no weapon to pitch, besides the incredibly plush pillows, and no way out, except down the side of what appeared to be a temple, Surefire was a captive audience if Xochi wanted to talk.

"What did he say?" Xochi demanded.

Surefire reached down and untwisted the sheet from her legs then lifted it up to cover her chest.

"He told me about your arrangement. How your power is keeping him alive." Surefire's voice wavered. She was not feeling this heart-to-heart or whatever Xochi had in mind.

Xochi gave a graceful snort. "And that is all? Did he not tell you who I am?"

Surefire shook her head. Xochi's eyes grew wide with indignation.

"I see he does not respect the goddess of love."

"Of wha—" Surefire choked back her words, certain she had misheard her.

"Love, my child. Is not this body, this face, the epitome of love and beauty?" She flung back her head and pushed out her breasts.

Without a doubt, Xochi was gorgeous, an exotic fairytale princess. But her conceit—and emotional insanity—knocked her down a few pegs.

"Sure, I guess," Surefire conceded.

"She guesses." Xochi huffed. Her bottomless eyes flashed violet tinged with red.

Surefire wanted to edge away but remembered the drop-off. She hung her head, unsure how to handle Xochi's hurt pride, and then decided on the truth. "You have to excuse my ignorance, but I'm not feeling any love from you."

Xochi's anger fell away. Her mouth drooped into a frown. Her hand flew up in a dismissive gesture. "I become vexed when my authority, my expertise, is questioned. The anger overwhelms. I am not used to being told that my feelings on the topic of love are incorrect. I am not used to being rejected by a lover."

Xochi led Surefire over to the bed and sat down. She patted the spot next to her to indicate Surefire should sit as well. Surefire gathered the sheet around her body and sat down as far away from Xochi as the mound of pillows would allow.

"Things were not always like this." Xochi waved her hand at the Garden outside. "I was not always . . ." She furrowed her brow and seemed to struggle to find the right word to describe herself.

Surefire could offer several suggestions, though thought better of saying them out loud: bitchy, insane, psychotic.

"Temperamental," Xochi finally said.

Close enough.

"During the world of the Second Sun, I was the giver of life and beauty and love and peace. I used to know what true love felt like. I helped cultivate the spark between humans. Then Tezcatlipoca kidnapped me from my husband and seduced me. I sought to tame him."

The ultimate bad boy.

Apparently, even goddesses can fall prey to them. Surefire wanted to ask what she meant by the "Second Sun," but Xochi continued talking, and given her recent tirade, Surefire thought it best to let her have center stage.

"Tezcatlipoca corrupted me. Humans sacrificed lives to me, bled for me. With their blood, my power grew and I enjoyed it. " She stared down at her hands clasped in her lap.

Surefire scooted farther away into the pillows.

"My husband gave up on me. He married another, and they reside in this very garden—his garden—a refuge for the gods."

Xochi's eyes locked on Surefire's, and for the first time they appeared human, a soft brown flecked with yellow. Surefire wondered if Xochi had been human at one time. "The world has been destroyed and rebuilt several times. Did you know that?"

"No."

"It was before our self-imposed exile. Some gods like Tezcatlipoca became too powerful, and their thirst for dominance became too strong and threatened to destroy the humans and this world we had helped create." She paused for a beat. "Through the portals, I have watched the modern world evolve. I witnessed mankind undermining themselves and the earth, and I desired to atone for my past mistakes."

Surefire's ears pricked up. Xochi atoning for past mistakes sounded familiar and very human.

"When Raven entered my realm, he was the first human male I had encountered in centuries. There are others like me who live here, but we have grown weary of each other. Then Raven arrived, and I sought to use him." She stared outside into the tropical sky.

"I sought to use him to right the balance of the world by restoring spiritual objects stolen across civilizations." She shrugged gracefully. "It is only a stitch in a larger wound but would stave off another purging for a short time."

"Do you mean the world is going to end soon?" Surefire's mouth went dry.

Xochi patted Surefire's leg, suddenly seeming much older than her twenty-something appearance. "Your definition of 'soon' is different from mine. But, yes, one world will end and another will begin. It is the cycle of nature—birth, death, rebirth. And it is already occurring with you and your kind."

"With me?" Surefire pulled back.

"You are more than human. Others label you as *transhuman.*" She shook her head. "Your science is creating a new breed of gods. You're evolving into us, and when humans gain the knowledge of gods, the current world will fall away. It has happened before and will happen again."

Surefire's stomach churned with nausea. Xochi had just handed her another piece to this annoyingly complicated puzzle. She'd have a lot to relate to Pax and the others when she returned home—if she returned home. Xochi said this ending was inevitable, though maybe they still had a chance to stop the next cycle from occurring.

But one apocalyptic problem at a time.

"How can we stop this end-of-the-world crisis?" Surefire asked.

"You must first procure the final skull. It is hidden in the past."

Xochi held up the necklace that Surefire had removed from inside the statue. She leaned over and fastened the tightly woven gold chain around Surefire's neck. The pendant rested just above her breasts.

"This stone contains a piece of my essence. With the aid of the skull you seek, it will allow you to return from the past. Both pieces unlock powers in the other."

Surefire rubbed her thumb over the polished stone. It warmed under her touch. She hadn't looked closely at it when Raven had worn it. Now that she held it, she found it larger than she'd remembered, about the size of her palm. One side was rounded and the other flat with a tiny marigold etched into the milky purple surface. Much like the marigold engraving on Xochi's gold plate.

"Why not give this to Raven?" Surefire asked.

"My priest wore this." Xochi motioned to it. "When he wished to speak with me or journey across worlds, he would simply touch my crystal skull and seek me out. Each god crafted a crystal skull imbued with their own knowledge and energy. To unlock their power, the handler must be human—a chosen human."

"Then I am still human. I thought you said I wasn't."

"I said you are *more than* human. There is a difference. My priests were like you. They were special, more than average men."

"And Raven? Is he still human?" Surefire ventured.

Xochi licked her lips and averted her gaze. "I believe you know he is not."

Even though this wasn't news to Surefire, hearing it proclaimed out loud by Xochi struck a sour chord in her gut. "What about Ari?"

"The magic man is human for now. Through a sacrifice, he has unlocked a quarter of Tezcatlipoca's power and has become the god's vessel. For brief periods, Tezcatlipoca can possess Ari. And Ari can call forth Tezcatlipoca's energy. If he were a transhuman—to use your label—he would have more access to Tezcatlipoca's power. But this *magician* desires power for vengeance. Which is why, I am certain, Tezcatlipoca has chosen him and allowed himself to be awoken and trapped in his obsidian relic, until Ari sets him free. He has convinced Ari to complete the ritual, and this human is deluded into thinking he will possess Tezcatlipoca."

"What will happen if Tezcatlipoca gets the skull?"

"He will possess the vessel, and Ari will be no more."

"And what will Tezcatlipoca do then?"

"Take back that which he believes is his—the world."

This night just kept getting better and better. Surefire didn't want to ask more questions, because the answers were as comforting as a slap to the face.

"But what happens if Ari remains with this godlike power? If we don't snag the skull, Ari will keep the bit of power he's been given. Isn't that better than taking a chance Tezcatlipoca will steal the skull from us and rise again?"

"That magic man doesn't deserve it." Her face hardened. "An ounce of Tezcatlipoca's abilities could cause devastation by any harmless man, let alone one consumed by vengeance and jealousy. Many will die before he is brought down. He will not hesitate to kill those whom you love for disobeying him."

The weight of what Xochi was relaying sat like a ton of cold stones on Surefire's shoulders. If Tezcatlipoca got the skull, the world would be destroyed. If Ari retained his godlike abilities, her family would be destroyed.

Which left one last piece unsaid.

"How will the skull stop Tezcatlipoca?"

"When the final skull is placed with the others, the vessel will be—"

"Stay away from her!" Raven burst into the room through a thick curtain.

Xochi and Surefire stood. Raven ran across the room and skidded to a stop in front of them. Surefire's eyes dipped down from his face to his stomach and then farther still. She couldn't look away. She just stared at his naked body. Yes, indeed, his tattoos did continue lower, much lower.

"If you touch her, you will regret it."

Xochi arched her brows. Her lips twitched into a smile as she stared unabashed below his waist.

"Uh, Raven." Surefire tore her eyes away from his—she had to admit—fairly well-proportioned private part.

"Why don't you cover up?" She tossed him a pillow, a large pillow.

He caught it, and she noticed that the flesh around his wrists and ankles was raw.

"Are you okay?" Surefire motioned to her own wrist.

Raven positioned the pillow in front of himself. He glanced down at his wrists and shrugged. "Nothing that won't heal. And you? How are you doing? I thought you were dead."

He moved to stand in front of her and lifted one arm as if to hug her, then seemed to think better of it and stepped back.

"I got better," she said. Raven gazed at her with such tenderness her heart fluttered. She hiked the sheet higher above her chest. "Thanks to Xochi."

"Humph." Xochi straightened her back. "I am glad one of you appreciates me."

Raven continued to stare at Surefire, and then the compassion lining his face slipped to an expression of regret. "I'm sorry. It's all my fault."

"Don't worry about it. It's fine, really. I understand." The more Raven's tender blue eyes stared down at her, the more the fluttering in her chest increased until it felt as if Xochi's butterflies whipped around inside of her.

He touched her shoulder, and the gentle brush of his warm fingertips caused goose bumps to form on her skin. "No, it's not. I shouldn't have—"

"Enough." Xochi angled herself between Surefire and Raven. Her back was to Surefire, so she couldn't see Xochi's expression, but her shrill tone spoke volumes.

"It is time," Xochi announced. With a flourish of her small hand, the torches lighting the room grew brighter and illuminated a mishmash of leather and feathers and some sort of stone ornaments hanging on the wall across from the bed.

"What is that?" Raven's face scrunched up.

"Your uniforms." Xochi walked over to these so-called uniforms and ran her fingers along the multi-colored feathers.

"Uniforms for what?" Surefire asked.

"You will play the Ullamaliztli to gain the skull."

"The Ulla-what-zee?" Raven balked.

Xochi pursed her wide, plush lips. "An ancient game where you hit a rubber ball at various objects and through rings. You will play to win. The winning team will have the privilege of attending the sacrifice."

"Sacrifice?" Raven and Surefire said in unison.

Xochi shrugged. "The losing team's captain is executed, and the crystal skull you seek is used in the sacrificial ceremony."

"What does the winning captain get?"

"To live," she said matter-of-factly.

Raven and Surefire glanced at one another. His expression reflected the shock she felt.

"You will travel into the past through a portal," Xochi continued. "The final skull was hidden over six hundred years ago. It was never allowed to pass along to future generations. It is locked in time until a human retrieves it." She looked pointedly at Surefire.

"So we're going to travel into the past, play the game, win our lives, snatch the skull from the priest, who will be using it to kill the losing captain, and then pop back home?" Surefire recounted.

"When you put it that way, it actually sounds doable," Raven quipped.

Surefire shot him an incredulous look. "There's one thing. No, a few things that we're forgetting here."

"I never forget anything," Xochi bristled.

"Let's say 'overlooked,'" Surefire clarified.

Xochi hiked a dark brow at Surefire.

"First off, can't Raven just phase out, sneak in, and steal the skull?"

Xochi stared at Surefire with her unblinking black eyes. "Impossible. The skull will seek out any energy from the Old Ones. It will feed off his energy. Raven's powers will be limited. "

"Like Ari did outside the warehouse." Surefire nodded in understanding. "Then that brings me to my next issue. Neither of us resembles an Aztec."

"With these uniforms, you will appear as them."

Surefire stared open-mouthed at the clothes, wondering how to put them on. One item was a thick, corded g-string with large, rectangular pads attached to front part of the cord. It didn't seem comfortable and looked very revealing.

"I will help you don them. What are your other concerns?"

"We don't speak Aztec-ian, or whatever language they spoke," Surefire noted.

"Their language is Náhuatl, and this issue is easily rectified." With a flick of her wrists, small vials capped with glass stoppers appeared in each hand. "One drop of this in both ears will allow you to understand. Drinking this liquid will allow you to be understood."

Xochi handed them the vials and placed her hands on her hips. "Any other concerns?"

"Rules?" Raven inquired.

"You cannot use your hands. Aim for the flat markers and rings to earn extra points or send it through the opposing team's end zone."

"How do we join?" Raven asked. "Will the teams already be in play?"

"At this particular game, both teams were short one member. Your costumes will show your player status. You will be required to join."

"We won't be playing on the same team?" Stunned, Surefire looked to Raven. He shrugged.

"No."

"Is there ever a draw?" Surefire asked.

"Never. The gods will not allow that."

"Will they allow one of us to be killed?" Raven asked.

"Who knows?" Xochi gazed directly at Raven. "The gods can be fickle."

♥　☠　♥　☠　♥　☠

Pax stared numbly at the road blurring outside the windshield and let it lull him into a blank state. He didn't want to feel the pressure of Surefire's possible death looming over him like a weight dangling from a weak chain.

Oracle hadn't said much since they started driving to DC. She kept her eyes on the road even if she couldn't physically see it. St. John was silent, too, sitting in the back seat of Pax's SUV. He had called in a favor from his Army comrade Withers, and he and his specialized team were on standing orders until told otherwise. But he was in the dark as well. Expert troops at his disposal couldn't help him retrieve his daughter—or keep Surefire's identity from being leaked to the press.

Anger twisted Pax's insides, and again he tried to blank out his mind. This case was growing more and more out of his control, and the latest development was enough to send Pax over the edge.

Before they had left U-Sec's garage, St. John's wife, Vanessa, had called in hysterics. A cable news network—a conservative one, not too fond of transhumans—had begun showing a clip of the first Smithsonian security footage with Raven slinging Surefire over his shoulder and running out of the room. Pax had pulled up the broadcast on his smartphone. Blurred images of Smithsonian guards spoke about Raven holding Surefire hostage and then disappearing from outside the museum. There was a shaky low-res video, probably taken from someone's smartphone of Heather St. John speaking with Pax. These were followed by interviews with warehouse workers, some with faces darkened and voices disguised, who attested that Surefire had helped Raven escape from the warehouse.

Pax was going to have a long discussion with Matthews and several others about how to keep evidence about an ongoing investigation from being leaked to the press. It was a topic they had discussed in the beginning of the night with the entire crew, but obviously a few had missed the memo. Pax also considered posting a no-phone policy at any future crime scene overseen by U-Sec.

Reporters were calling Surefire the next Patty Hearst and speculating on why this former athlete was working for U-Sec. *Is she a transhuman? If so, what is her ability? Is Heather, her twin, a transhuman, too?* Pax's cell had rung several times with numbers he hadn't recognized and wasn't about to answer. He had told the office to offer no comment on the case.

However, Heather was already giving telephone interviews, denying the transhuman label—for herself and her sister—and asking the audience to pray for Synthia's safe return and for her sister to do the right thing and turn herself and Raven in to authorities. Sponsorships were on the line for Heather. An unstable sibling making the news could either cast sympathy on her or make people wonder whether she was unstable as well, or more specifically, an unstable transhuman.

Pax's phone rang, and he jerked the wheel.

"Concentrate on the road. I'll get it." Oracle patted his shoulder.

She reached under his right arm and along the front of his jacket. Her long fingers stretched out across his chest and into the inside left pocket. He shifted uncomfortably in the seat and tried not to focus on how warm and inviting her hand felt even through his sweatshirt. He couldn't stop the memories from forming of when she had last touched his chest. Though the last time he hadn't been wearing a shirt.

He shifted in his seat again, grateful his body was too exhausted to react to these thoughts.

She settled back into the passenger seat and touched the phone's screen.

"This is Oracle." There was a pause. "Hello, Oliver. What did you find?" She listened and nodded, and then her brow wrinkled. "Master Stephanos? Who is that?"

Pax motioned for her to give him the phone.

"Just drive. I'll put it on speaker."

St. John sat forward in the back seat.

"Yello, Pax?" Oliver's voice crackled through the car.

"I'm here. You're on speaker."

"Sweet. Umm . . . I think I found something on that magic staff and nose stuff."

"Go on." Pax motioned with his hand as if Oliver could see him.

"I ran a search and came up with some pretty bizarro things and even some porn sites, which I hope I don't get in trouble for."

"Oliver," Pax said forcefully to get him back on track. For all of Oliver's brilliance, he got distracted easily. "I don't care about that. What did you find?"

"I found a magician, Master Stephanos, as in 'magic staff and nose.' We plugged in different phonetic spellings of this phrase and his name popped up: Ari Demetri Stephanos. A few years ago, Fantastic Farrell totally exposed him on a talk show as a psychic hack."

The Stephanos name sounded vaguely familiar to Pax. "So what?"

"There's more. I cross-checked the word 'Pez' with Aztec gods, and there are none, but there is one that comes close. I made the leap after Helena sent me links to the websites she'd found regarding the statue."

"Oliver, you're killing me. Just give us the full report."

"Okay. Right. Stephanos has always been into ancient myths. He's spent like hundreds of thousands of dollars on . . . get this . . . Aztec artifacts. Particularly, the god Tezcatlipoca. As in 'good Pez.' It's a total stretch, but she could be saying 'god' not 'good.' And instead of 'Magic staff and nose raisin good Pez,' Surefire might've meant, 'Magic Stephanos raising god Tez'—as in Tezcatlipoca."

The husband of the goddess from the statue.

"Okay, but what does he—"

"Wait, there's more." Oliver's voice rose in excitement. "My team dug into Ari's background, seeing if we could find any other ties to the case. A few years ago, Ari and his cousin were in this temple in Mexico when it collapsed and supposedly crushed his cousin. But they never found the cousin's body."

"I don't get how this relates to the case." Pax was losing patience. Pieces were starting to come together, but not quick enough to save Surefire. He wanted to end this conversation and begin dissecting what they'd uncovered.

"Ari Stephanos and his cousin used to work for APS."

"The specialty grave robbers," St. John commented.

"That's it, and I found a photo of his cousin. He was arrested some years ago, so we have a mug shot. I sent it to your phone."

Oracle pressed an icon on the phone to download the photo.

Pax's eyes dipped away from the road to the phone. He did a double take at the mug shot of a cocky-looking guy with black hair in his late twenties or early thirties. "Raven."

The only times they had seen Raven's face were at the warehouse parking lot before he phased out, and in the security footage from the Smithsonian museum. He'd always worn a mask during his thefts, so they could never identify him. They had learned his name only when Raven had goaded Tara Kard and dropped that one tidbit about himself.

"Oh, yeah, that's Raven all right," Oliver replied. "Also, found some photos online of him on a snowboarding site. He's sponsored a few teams. One made it to the Olympics. Did some boarding himself. Saw some pics of him getting some sweet air—"

"Oliver, focus," Pax interrupted.

"Right, sorry. Anyway, Raven owned a high-end antiquities business called . . . what else? . . . Ravens Collections, Inc. A legit front for their black market imports. His real name is James Stephanos. He was arrested several years back after an anonymous tip that he worked for APS and was selling stolen art. He hired some top-notch lawyers who got him off on a technicality. Next time he shows is at the dig in Mexico where he supposedly died. Afterward, his business was liquidated and the money given to his sister."

"Where is she?" Pax asked.

"Living on Crete, according to the papers."

"Have Graham track her down. See if she knows anything."

"Sure."

"Any other family?"

Over the phone line, Pax heard the click of fingers typing on a keyboard.

"His parents are divorced. His dad was a doctor in the Army and is deceased. According to divorce records, his mother disappeared one day. Whereabouts unknown."

"Anything else?" Pax asked.

"Ari dropped out of the public eye after Raven's death, and no one's seen him since. He owns a couple of properties and magic shops throughout the country, which are managed without him. He had even opened a museum of magic and torture on Charles Street downtown."

"Magic and torture?" Oracle exclaimed. "Do those really go together?"

"The dude made it work. He tied ancient magic in with the elements of torture. Pixie and I went there on a date. It was wild. A friend of hers worked at the place. The stuff in the back was even freakier than the displays."

"Ask Graham to check it out. And get in touch with Matthews. Tell him what you found out."

"Sure. I also learned two more things. Ari had this major beef with Farrell after the guy sold him out, and Ari swore to fix his reputation. Last week, Ari took out an ad in a magic magazine announcing an exclusive performance of his latest act with a personal invite to Farrell. The show is in three days."

"Did it mention where?"

"It's for industry professionals, and only they can access the information."

"Contact Farrell. Maybe he can tell us something. Have you heard from Pixie?"

There was silence on the other end, and Pax thought they had been disconnected, until Oliver replied flatly, "Nada. But we did find her cell, which is the second thing. Graham went out for coffee and found it in the middle of a parking spot in the garage where Pixie usually parks. She'd made several calls in the previous weeks to the torture museum and other numbers traced to various shops owned by Stephanos."

"You think she was talking with this Ari guy?"

"Possibly. She used to work for him right after she got her abilities."

Pax's hands gripped the steering wheel. That's why Ari's stage name sounded familiar. Before Pixie started training with U-Sec, she had worked as a magician's assistant. Since she could shrink at will to the size of a fairy, she helped put Master Stephanos on the map. Then he tried to scam the world with his supposed psychic abilities, which, according to Pixie, is why she had stopped working with him and wanted to devote herself to fighting transhuman crime instead.

"Thanks, Oliver. You did good. Real good. How did you find out so much in just two hours?"

"I had the Tech team help on the search. That new girl Kathy excels at word games. She figured out what Surefire was saying after we found Pixie's cell phone."

"Give them my gratitude." Pax nodded, proud that his agents were working together to find solutions on their own. It made his job easier. "Now go home and get some sleep."

"My shift is starting soon." Oliver yawned.

"I can't have you putting in an all-nighter. Take today off and come back tomorrow." Pax steered his truck out of traffic and onto Constitution Avenue next to a squad car.

"If it's okay with you, I'd prefer to stick around. I want to see this thing through, then I'll take a few days."

"No problem." Pax hung up.

He rolled down his window and flashed his badge to the officer standing in front of a blockade.

In the seat behind him, St. John began calling in a few more favors.

Chapter Fifteen

Raven stared open mouthed at his outfit in the mirror. He could be an extra from a history reenactment. Mostly, though, he resembled a whacked-out animal hybrid. Red and orange plumes stuck out from a turban-style headdress. Brown fur draped over his shoulders. Deerskin pads covered his shins and shoulders and part of his chest. His face was painted in turquoise to resemble a snake. Adding to this uncomfortable ensemble, he had several inches of blue fabric and animal hide wrapped around his waist and hips, like a low-riding cummerbund, topped with a wraparound stone ornament similar to a yoke carved with snakes, which Xochi assured him was just for ceremony and to be removed before the game. Every time he walked the yoke exaggerated the movements of his hips, making him feel as if he were a drag queen sashaying down a runway. A stone cuff etched with a face that appeared bloated and bruised—Raven hoped this wasn't an indicator of what they would look like after the game—fit over his right wrist, and another with a similar carving was strapped to his right knee. A thong rode uncomfortably up his rear, attached to a cord that wrapped around his waist, from which hung protective leather pads over the sides and fronts of his thighs and, most importantly, his groin.

Surefire appeared even goofier in her getup, which mimicked Raven's from the feather turban and animal hides down to the stone cuffs on her right knee and wrist. Except her outfit, including her face paint, had a monkey theme, which Raven believed appeared more Ewok than monkey. His gaze dropped to the thick leather strap tied tight around her chest, which pushed her breasts up and accented her toned, flat stomach.

Raven swallowed and found himself adjusting the now-too-tight leather padding between his legs. Forget a goofy Ewok, Surefire was more of a sexy barbarian queen.

She cleared her throat, and he raised his eyes to meet hers.

"What are you doing?" She placed her hands on her hips.

There was no denying it. She had caught him in the act. "Staring at your boobs."

Her jaw dropped. He shrugged and tried to give her an innocent look. She slapped his upper arm. So his virtuous expression hadn't been convincing, but it was worth the pink flush peeking out along her cheeks from under her makeup.

"I can't believe you just said that."

He shrugged again. "It's the truth. I couldn't help it. You look hot."

She scowled at him, looking about as menacing as an annoyed parakeet that had mated with a monkey.

He started to laugh, which appeared to frustrate Surefire even more, making the feather on her head flap back and forth with every angry shake of her head. She cracked a smile when she caught her reflection in the mirror.

"Go on and laugh. I don't look hot. I look just as ridiculous as you."

They caught each other's eyes in the mirror, and warmth tickled across his gut. "Trust me, you don't."

He licked his lips. She licked hers. They turned simultaneously to face each other, and Surefire stared up into his eyes. Her expression faded from humor to something he couldn't read but wished to hell he could. The corner of her mouth twitched and her lips parted. He wondered if she wanted to kiss him as much as he wanted to kiss her.

"The vials." Xochi tapped them both on the shoulders with the glass bottles.

Surefire looked away from him, the moment completely lost.

Raven snatched the bottle from Xochi, not even bothering to hide his agitation at her presence. "What is this?"

"Drink. It will allow you to speak and be understood." Xochi rubbed some of the oil in her hands then stuck her fingers into his ears, giving him an oily Willie.

"Hey." He squirmed away and lifted his shoulder to his ear. "That feels weird."

"So you can hear and understand." She turned to Surefire, who cringed at Xochi's oily fingers. She frowned, and her bottom lip puckered in disgust.

"Not really big on the whole ear touching." Surefire took a step back when Xochi had finished rubbing the potion into her ears. She wriggled her own fingers into her ear canal as if to dislodge the oily gunk.

Next, Raven downed the brownish liquid in the glass vial he held in his hand. He gave it over to Surefire who drank it.

Surefire made a "yuck" face and coughed. "That was nasty."

"Yuck!" Raven peeled his numb tongue from the roof of his mouth, where it had stuck from the thick, syrupy potion. "Tastes like sugary, chocolate feet. What is that?"

Xochi lifted her dark eyes to the ceiling. "Babies, both of you." She crooked a finger at them. "Follow me."

Raven motioned for Surefire to go first through the chamber doorway and into the narrow stone passageway. He ducked his head and bent his knees to keep from banging his head on the ceiling. Torches flickered in the corners and lit the way through the twisting corridor and down several flights of steep stairs. His stone yoke scraped against walls, and the grating sound echoed around them—the only other noise in the hallway besides their rubber-soled leather sandals sifting across the gritty floor. Twice Surefire teetered on the uneven steps under the weight of her decorative yoke, and he grabbed her arm to hold her steady. Both times she smiled up at him in thanks and both times his stomach clenched in nervous anticipation.

Anticipation of what, he had no idea.

By the time they exited the temple and started picking their way through the banyan forest, Raven had begun to wonder what he expected to happen between him and Surefire. He hadn't figured himself in love with Surefire even after Xochi's assertion.

He cared for Surefire. Liked her a lot even. Found her incredibly sexy— hell, yeah.

But . . . love?

He wasn't sure what constituted "falling in love." She made him laugh and frustrated him at the same time. She made him feel at ease with himself, yet she challenged him and made him want to prove himself to her. To prove that he was a good person, that he was good enough for her. And ever since they'd kissed, he couldn't stop thinking about her lips against his, how her body molded against his.

Trying to clear this image from his mind, he hopped over a large root. He hoped the ache between his legs would go away, because he couldn't afford any other distractions right now.

Because he couldn't shake from his mind what Xochi had said with such conviction—that he was in love with Surefire—and that notion offered enough of a distraction.

He had never been in love before.

Lust, yes. But love was a foreign notion akin to calling soccer football, which, despite all his travels, he could never get used to doing as an American. It always felt weird, off somehow.

Exactly how he felt around Surefire. Weird and off his game. Xochi had him by a tight metaphysical leash. It was selfish of him to want to act on his feelings for Surefire, and a waste of time to even consider these feelings. They could never have a normal relationship. They could never have a future together.

Xochi drifted over the uneven terrain. Surefire ducked and crawled under a low-hanging branch. Raven leaped over it.

"Show off," Surefire shot back at him.

But, yet, this nagging hope tugged at his heart. It wasn't only because of the physical attraction, of how comfortable he felt around her. She had stayed with him in spite of everything. She hadn't left him. At the warehouse, she'd sacrificed herself, her job, her reputation to help him. She'd stood up to Ari, stabbing his arm at the waterfront when he couldn't react. She'd stayed with him in the museum's storage room. Coaxed him out of his irrational fear. It would've been easy to have left him there. She could've ditched him in the room, found the guards, turned him in. Instead, she'd stayed and risked her life in doing so.

No one had ever done that for him.

No one.

"I'm sorry for what happened in the museum," he said.

"As I told you before, don't worry about it."

A few yards in front of them, Xochi stopped in front of a thick, vine-encased trunk and waved her hand in front of it.

Raven grabbed Surefire's arm. "I want you to know I got your back. I won't let you down again."

"I know." She stared up into his eyes with a sincerity that encouraged him to go on.

"It's just that I had a shitty dad, too." He scrubbed his hand over his face. "Ex-military. An Army doctor, a real hard-ass. He helped found APS, and he's the reason I started working for them. I wanted him to be proud of me, and I didn't want to fail him, too."

Surefire touched his hand as if she knew how hard it was for him to admit this.

"He used to lock me up in our shed and load it with a bunch of nasty bugs to toughen me up. Help me overcome my phobia. After my mom left, it got worse." He paused considering his next words. "But none of his methods helped me get over my fear." He shrugged half-heartedly. "Probably made it worse. Then I watched you get bit and almost die, because of me. And I knew how ridiculous it was to let this phobia rule me. In that moment, I overcame it."

"Can't say they still don't freak me out." He pulled a face, remembering the spiders' legs scurrying over his feet. "But I have a better handle on my phobia now, and I know it's possible to push through it with the right motivation."

The side of her lips quirked up. "Glad something good came out of it."

He grabbed her hands and drew her close. "You have no idea."

Then, as her two-toned eyes searched his face for a clue to what he meant, he knew that Xochi was right. He was falling in love with her.

Xochi cleared her throat. Hummingbirds and butterflies streamed passed them to hold court around their goddess. "We are here."

Surefire pulled away from Raven. Her brow furrowed as she sucked in her bottom lip, and Raven wondered if she felt the same way he did.

Very, very confused.

"I'm ready," Surefire said, her voice tight.

Raven walked up to the trunk. "Same trick as before?"

Xochi nodded and moved her hand over the trunk. The rooted bark parted to reveal a black hole. An undulating drumbeat mixed with animal calls and human voices emanated from the trunk to create an eerie, primal sound.

"You have the uniforms of the players, so they will accept you. Play the game as I instructed, and one of you will be the victor."

"And the other?" Surefire inquired.

"Will be at my mercy." She glared at Raven before she shoved both of them through the hole.

♥ ☠ ♥ ☠ ♥ ☠

Pax, Oracle, and St. John walked around the Aztec tomb under the intense scrutiny of twenty police and Smithsonian guards. The officers were peeved that Pax had ordered them to relinquish their cell phones and were probably suspicious, wondering if they would pull a disappearing act like Surefire and Raven and phase into the tomb.

Pax wished he could. It would make things easier, since the tomb, as far as they could tell, couldn't be opened.

Three sides of the chamber had ornate carvings of serpents with plumes on their heads with human, dog, rabbit, monkey, and bird faces etched in a pattern along each edge. At the front panel, through which Raven and Surefire had disappeared, Pax stooped beside a carved image of Xochiquetzal standing in front of a tree that encompassed the height of the tomb. Flowers resembling marigolds lay scattered by her feet. He studied the black, glossy spikes protruding from the grey stone at points along the tree. Raven's blood had dried to a thin crust on the needle-like tips.

"What are we looking for?" St. John asked.

"A way in." Pax put his ear to the chamber and tapped on the wall. It sounded hollow, but the walls were thick.

"Be careful. No touching." A tall, lanky man hurried up the aisle. His graying hair was combed to the side, and he wore an ill-fitting brown suit. "It's over seven hundred years old. There are only two like it in the world."

Pax pushed against it. "It's solid enough to damage a truck running into it."

"That's not the point. It's the oil from your hands."

He took a handkerchief from his pocket and slapped Pax's hand with it. Pax begrudgingly moved, and the man wiped the place Pax had touched.

"Oil can wear away the hieroglyphics. We take great pains to keep touching to a bare minimum." He stood back with a look of pure admiration. "Marvelous. Don't you agree? Only *two* like it in the world."

"You said that already," Pax replied in agitation.

"We need to get in there." St. John elbowed Pax aside.

"Absolutely not," the man sniffed. "Besides, we had it x-rayed a few months ago. There's nothing inside but a few human remains."

"And I repeat once more. We need to get in there." St. John puffed up his chest and towered over the other man's gangly frame. He stood his ground against St. John though his owlish eyes wavered to the floor.

Oracle angled between the men and stuck out her hand. "I'm Oracle."

He stared at her open mouthed for a few seconds before he regained his composure. "I'm David Jones, curator of the Mesoamerican exhibit."

"Mr. Jo—" Oracle began.

"Doctor," he corrected.

"Dr. Jones, would it hurt to open the tomb just a crack?" She pinched an inch with her index finger and thumb. "One of our agents disappeared through this tomb, and she is very ill. We'd appreciate it if we could take a peek inside."

"It's not that I don't want to open it, but I can't. It has no hinge, no door." He waved his hands around the edges and the front. "There are no seams that we can perceive where one of the panels could slide open. It is one solid piece. We have no idea how the remains—or your agent—got in there, and we have no idea how your agent opened it from the inside. If we tried to open it from the outside, we would destroy it."

He stepped down off the platform and motioned to the plaque in front of it. "It says it right here, if you bothered to read it."

St. John started forward with fists ready to go. Pax placed a hand on his shoulder.

"I know someone who can get us in," Pax assured St. John.

"I won't let you destroy this piece." Dr. Jones positioned himself between Pax and the tomb.

"Oh, she won't destroy it," Pax promised.

Chapter Sixteen

This time Surefire and Raven landed on their feet on uneven dirt at the mouth of a cave. Surefire was getting used to free-falling through nothingness. She teetered from the awkward weight of her uniform, but Raven held her steady. In fact, he was steadying her a lot with the annoying twenty-pound stone yoke strapped around her waist.

"You okay?" He stared down at her with the same unreadable look he'd been giving her since he'd found her alive and well in Xochi's chamber.

"Fine." He continued to regard her in that odd way, so she added, "And you?"

His hand moved from her elbow to her lower back. She froze as his rough palm slid across the exposed skin.

"Been through worse."

She rolled her eyes and stepped away. "This definitely counts as my worst."

She placed her hand on the wall of the cave's craggy mouth. It let out onto a hill that sloped through the jungle, which thinned out midway down. To the right, water rushed down the hill and disappeared under large green leaves. She could hear the soft rumble of water hitting against rocks and then a splash as it fell into a pool. Opposite from them, mountains cut an uneven path across the evening sky. Below them, through a mass of trees and fauna, glowed a sprawling city lit with a multitude of torches or maybe lanterns.

She squinted and craned her neck to peer between a few felled trees and saw patches of farmland dotted with huts around the city limits. Canals snaked through the city's outer rim to the interior, where two-story stone buildings gathered around an impressive stone pyramid with large fire pits illuminating its corners and upper tiers. The peak of the pyramid towered over the treetops. Monkeys and birds screeched in the canopy overhead. Leaves rustled and branches cracked above her. Drums pounded in the distance, accompanied by a faint flute and then the mournful wail of a conch shell.

Surefire took a step back inside the cave. She breathed deeply and was greeted with the rich scent of moist soil and lush plants and rain. A humid breeze brushed across her forehead, which was already beaded in sweat.

"Cool, huh?" Raven leaned on the other side of the cave.

"That's one word for it. I can't believe I'm here. It's surreal. I didn't expect the city to be so huge."

"They were as advanced as many European cities at the time. I can see why the Spanish wanted to conquer them. Plus their massive amounts of gold and the fact that the Spanish were pricks."

For several seconds, Raven surveyed the scene alongside her in silence, then he asked, "Did Xochi hurt you?"

It took Surefire a moment to switch gears from shock and awe over traveling back in time to answering Raven's question, which didn't seem important against the backdrop of the city below.

"No, but I'm sure she wanted to. She was a little miffed."

Surefire let out a nervous laugh, because the thought of Raven in love with her still seemed absurd. Or maybe it was the absurdity of the whole night. Here she was, transported back in time and waiting to play a death match to snag a skull and save the world—not to mention what had happened to lead up to this point. Yet her mind kept going back to Xochi's assertion that Raven loved her. Perhaps the notion of someone falling in love with her—even if that someone was Raven—was the most normal thing she'd heard all night, which made it even more ridiculous.

Honestly, her thoughts weren't making much sense at this point.

"What are you laughing about?" Raven crossed his arms as best as he could with the thick stone bracelet around his wrist and the leather shoulder guard. She had to admit the outfit showed off his lean, athletic body to perfection.

"Just something Xochi had said to me. About what had gotten her feathers ruffled." Surefire gave him a dismissive wave.

"Why was she angry?"

Surefire giggled again when she glanced over at Raven. Those obnoxious feathers sprouting from his turban-style headdress reminded her of a punked-out parrot.

"She thinks you're in love with me. That somehow I stole you away from her." Surefire doubled over and laughed harder. She braced her hand against the wall to keep from tipping over.

"Seriously, can you imagine that? Like we could ever be a couple." She snorted. "That goddess is totally bonkers. I think living for so many millennia has gone to her head." She twirled her finger next to her temple in the universal sign for crazy.

Raven stared blankly at Surefire for a heartbeat then turned and stalked out of the cave.

Surefire stopped laughing.

"Raven, what's wrong?" she called out but he disappeared into the jungle.

She picked her away down the incline along a well-worn path between trees and rocks to keep up. The stupid yoke gave her sides a brush burn as it shifted up and down with every movement of her hips. The g-string dug into the crack of her bottom, and the rough cotton shorts, wrapped around her hips and between her legs, chafed her inner thighs. How she was going to play the game in this getup, she had no idea.

She stumbled and caught herself against a tree. "Wait up."

Raven halted in front of her, his back to her, his hands on his hips.

"I think we go this way." He pointed to the right where the path veered sharply.

"Honestly, Raven, what's your issue?" she asked, even though she knew his issue, had been avoiding this issue, had even tried to dismiss it by making it into a joke. But she hoped that she had read him wrong.

Images flashed through Surefire's mind: Raven gently holding the ice pack against her aching head; his anger at Ari for hurting her; the relief on his face when he found her alive in Xochi's bedroom; and their kiss—how he had defended their kiss, how he had been angry with Surefire for dismissing it.

He cared for her. Had feelings for her. Maybe even was falling in love with her—or at least he thought it was love. Now she had hurt him by making light of whatever he felt for her.

Oh, crap. Oh, crap. Oh, crap.

The drum beat pounded harder and louder, echoing Surefire's nervous heart.

Surefire swallowed a golf ball–sized lump in her throat.

"Uh, Raven."

She toddled over to him and tapped his shoulder. He didn't turn around. Her eyes flicked to the tattoo of Xochi and then lower to intertwining black fluid lines snaking down his athletic legs, forming an image she couldn't make out from her angle.

"Whatever you're feeling for me, it's not real. I mean, Xochi's the goddess of love. I'm sure her power is just making you believe it."

"Believe what?" Raven spun on her. "That I'm in love with you? Which you obviously find amusing."

"No," Surefire backpedaled. "No, it's not funny."

"You're damn right it isn't funny. Do you think I wanted to feel this way about you? I tried to figure out how I could make it work. But, as you so nicely pointed out, we could never be a couple."

His words cut into her. He had thought about them, as a couple. He had actually considered a relationship with her, and he knew it was hopeless and this made her feel hopeless, too, and she didn't understand why.

"Plus, you obviously don't feel the same way, so it's a moot point." He threw up his hands.

Surefire didn't respond. Instead, she rubbed her fingers along the swollen face etched into the stone bracelet at her wrist. She hated to see Raven so upset, but there was nothing she could do or say to make it better.

Raven cocked his head and studied her. "You don't feel the same way, *do you?*"

Her body flushed with heat at the way he studied her with so much hope, so much longing.

What did she feel? Was it love? This giddy feeling every time he touched her. This feeling of wanting to see his stupid, cocky grin instead of his frustrated frown. This comfortable feeling that arose every time she was around him, like she could tell him anything—and she had. More than anyone else.

Of course, there was the technicality of Raven being a wanted man and her being the agent assigned to bring him in. If she even had a job with U-Sec when she returned. If she even had a family after what they would perceive as another major failure when they heard that she'd helped Raven escape from the warehouse lot. As if she cared about that right now. Because the further she was removed from her world, the closer she felt to Raven. And not once did he ever make her feel like a failure.

But she couldn't get past Xochi and her love-goddess powers.

"Honestly, I don't know what I feel, and I don't know what's real."

He bridged the gap between them and took her hands in his. "She's not Cupid. She doesn't make people fall in love. She just encourages that spark to grow, though I doubt she would've encouraged us considering my arrangement with her."

Surefire glanced away from his eyes, as dark and fathomless as the night sky above them. "Your power is from her. How can I believe that you're not emitting some sort of love pheromone to cause these feelings? You definitely distracted Tara Kard and Inferno."

"What?" He pulled away. "I didn't do anything sexual to them. Inferno was sensitive over a gay joke I made, which in hindsight I shouldn't have said. Should probably apologize to him," he muttered the last sentence to himself. "And Tara knocked herself out with one of those Tarot decks that she chucks around. One hit a mirror and ricocheted into her head." He shrugged. "So I took advantage and tied her up. That was all." He spread out his hands in innocence.

He stepped closer, and Surefire stepped back. Her yoke banged into a large trunk behind her and cut into her lower back. Raven rested his hand above her head and leaned down.

"Trust me, that isn't a power Xochi would've given me. I was granted only those abilities essential to my job." His breath slid across her face. His lips with their endearing pout were at eye level.

"I don't know why we're discussing this now." Surefire swallowed down that annoying lump in her throat again. "This isn't the time, and it's definitely not the place."

"You brought it up." His lips touched hers, just a gentle brush, but enough to send a shiver down her spine and to her toes.

She looked up into his eyes and knew he was waiting for her to give him the green light to kiss her again.

"You, over there," a gravelly voice spoke from behind Raven.

Raven moved back and blinked down at Surefire as if awoken from a daze. He turned around, and Surefire watched a man step out from the trees toward them.

He wore a spectacular headdress with plumage that stretched several feet above his five-foot-tall body. Adorning his wrists and ankles were stone bracers. Around his waist was a yoke like the ones they wore.

He pointed with his middle finger, since his index finger was only a stub. "You're dressed to play."

Raven donned a look of nonchalance. He stepped forward before Surefire could even think of moving.

"We are."

"Good." The man's mouth opened into a noticeably non-toothy smile. "We need players for the ullamaliztli."

The man's tight, lean body had seen better days. Joints were swollen where breaks had mended poorly. Scars crisscrossed his well-worn brown skin. On his shoulder was a black tattoo of a sun.

"You're tall." He motioned to Raven. "Good advantage. Glad you are on my team." Then Surefire realized this man's face was painted to resemble a snake like Raven's. A carved serpent's head reared up from the front of his yoke. A stone snake coiled around his wrist.

"And she is on the visiting team. Been waiting for you both." His smile widened across his rubbery face.

Dark eyes twinkled as he elbowed Raven. "What? You lost in the woods?"

"Lost, yep, we were lost all right."

"Glad I found you. They are starting, and we are both down a player."

"What happened to the other players?" Surefire finally found her voice. It was weird watching the man speak. The words coming from his mouth didn't match the movements of his lips. It was like watching a poorly dubbed foreign film. She figured it was an effect of the potion Xochi had rubbed in her ears.

"They died." The man shrugged, shifting the feathered adornment around his neck.

"How?" Her voice faltered.

"One killed by the ball, the other sacrificed." He walked down the hill toward the city, not waiting to see if they followed.

Raven started after him then stopped to look back at Surefire, who had lost the ability to move her legs.

"Killed by the ball?" she croaked.

"Death can happen in football, baseball, even in gymnastics. That's a rough sport, but you made it through."

Yes, she had taken chances in gymnastics, and any sport had its dangers. Hell, driving a car was dangerous in and around DC and Baltimore, where she lived.

"He made it sound normal."

"It can also happen in . . . well . . . uh . . . *Bloodsport.*"

"Are you talking about that Jean-Claude Van Damme movie?"

"You know it?" He seemed impressed.

She sighed. "You're not helping."

"It'll be okay." He took her hand and led her onto a dirt path. "You have me. I'll protect you."

"I don't need you to protect me." Surefire scowled at him. "Considering what has happened to me since we've been together."

"You're having the most exciting time of your life?"

The scowl lifted from her face. She didn't know how to answer that. His positivity caught her off guard. Instead of making her feel stupid for being cautious, for being scared, he was trying to comfort her. Something he'd been doing all along.

"If I live through this, then I'll admit you showed me the most excitement of my life."

"That's incentive to make sure you survive. What else do I get?"

"Another kiss." The words came out of her mouth before she could stop them. Where did that come from? Was she some damsel from a romance novel?

They stopped at the edge of a clearing at the entrance to a dirt causeway that cut across a canal. Several large insects buzzed and skipped across the water. They lost the ballplayer, who had crossed over the canal into the crowded city streets.

Raven gazed down at her. His face was half covered in shadow from his headdress. He was smiling, his mischievous, infuriating grin. The one she was growing to adore.

When he didn't say anything, she took her hand from his. "Never mind."

His eyes continued to stare into hers, fixing her in place. "You know I'll want more than a kiss when this is over."

"Not going to happen." She set her lips, trying to look insulted despite the giddiness that rose again inside her and caused an ache to form low in her stomach and lower still, until the cloth diaper felt even more uncomfortable.

"Come on. Throw me a bone here." He donned an exaggerated puppy-dog pout, which looked ridiculous, yet, made her smile.

She threw up her hands.

"Fine. You're on." It felt good to focus on something other than the death-dealing arena they were about to enter. Plus, it wasn't likely she'd ever have a chance to make good on this promise—even if a part of her was strangely excited about the prospect. She wanted to make him happy, distract him from the craziness as he had been distracting her.

Raven blew out a breath. "Huh, well, you just won this game because there's no way I can focus on anything else now."

♥ ☠ ♥ ☠ ♥ ☠

Raven grabbed Surefire's hand before she could respond and before he could consider what she had just promised. Even though he knew she didn't mean it, had only said it to go along with him. It was bad enough his mind was distracted with images of what could be, he didn't need his body unfocused as well. It was his damn fault for goading her on and wanting to hear her say she'd be with him. Now he had to deal with the consequences.

He led the way over the dirt bridge into the mass of bodies pressing into narrow passageways between bright orange, yellow, and blue cloth-topped stalls overtop vendors selling pottery, baskets, feathers, textiles, and food. Juicy red tomatoes, beans, and corn overflowed from tall baskets. Stone bowls filled with ripe avocados and stacks of freshly baked tortillas lined the street. Aromas of various spices and cooked meats cut through the stale smell of body odor and made Raven's stomach growl and his mouth water.

Women in multi-colored wraparound skirts, some with sleeveless cotton blouses and others with no shirts at all, toted small children and bargained with vendors for food. Men in loincloths, their heads topped with red or pale yellow or blue turbans, stacked the vegetables in the stalls or tended to small animals in cages. They argued and exchanged various items with one another. A few shook hands and surreptitiously took small tokens from each other. Raven wondered if they were betting on the game. Other men wore clothes that marked them as a higher status: elaborate feather headdresses and rich gold and red capes with designs of the sun, moon, animals, and gods. Sparkling gold bracelets encircled their wrists and intricately designed necklaces with emeralds and turquoise hung from their necks. Black tattoos of jaguars and eagles and the sun marked their arms and chests and backs.

People made way for Surefire and Raven. They whistled, hollered and smacked them in an effort to wish them luck. Their excitement invigorated Raven. Much like attending a sports game back home, the crowd's energy was contagious and tempered the apprehension he'd felt when they'd first arrived.

"Wow," Surefire murmured. "This is amazing."

The streets widened as they neared the temple. Vendor stalls and single-room reed huts gave way to two-story stone buildings with courtyards of flowers and pools in between. More people milled about with more elaborate jewels and clothing. Others hung out the windows of second floors to call out to those standing below. Some stopped and stared as Raven and Surefire walked past. He heard a female voice say she was betting on the monkeys, excited to see a woman playing.

A conch shell resounded ahead of them. Its long, lonely wail caused those milling about the streets to hasten toward the temple. Raven followed them, and Surefire hurried next to him. She kept a firm grip on his hand as the streets became more crowded.

Thump. Thump. Thump.

A drum beat an ominous rhythm in front of the throng.

The temple rose in the foreground like a perfectly symmetrical sentinel with the ball court situated at the bottom of its steep stairs. On either side sloped eight-foot-high walls with colorful, detailed paintings of sacrificial rites: blood spouting from a ripped-open chest, a bleeding heart held high, a man trussed up, a lanced tongue, a priest with his arms raised supporting a purple glowing skull.

As they entered the arena, Raven felt a gentle tug in the center of his chest followed by a press of power against his skin, similar to what he'd experienced near Ari. He glanced around the crowd to find the source.

The dirt floor of the court was colored in rectangles of red, green, white, and yellow with a blood-red circle in the middle. Circular stones carved with animal and human faces were placed at measured intervals. In the center, on either side of the court, were two circular rings at the top of the walls. A white line cut between them. Raven studied the rings and noticed carvings of snakes along the edges.

The court stretched about ten feet across and was at least twice as long. People sat and stood around the walls. They shouted as the players made their way onto the field. Men and women wearing brightly colored jewels, feathers, and gold adornments flanked the temple stairs. He assumed these were priests and royalty in their finery separated in upper-level boxed seats from the common people in plain animal hides or cotton loincloths and skirts. At either end of the ball court, men held long sticks with a large drum cradled between their legs.

When Raven and Surefire reached the center of the court, they were introduced to their teammates.

"As far as I can tell, they've never played in this arena," Coatl, the man they had met in the jungle, said. He motioned to their uniforms. "But they are dressed as captains."

"Then let them be captains," Coaxoch, another player, chimed in, and they all laughed.

"Captains?" Raven blurted out, not getting the joke.

"If your team loses, you die," Coaxoch said with a shrug.

Then Raven recalled Xochi mentioning the captains were sacrificed. However, she had failed to disclose the special meaning of the outfits she had given to Surefire and him.

"Did Xochi say anything to you about us being captains?" Surefire whispered to Raven.

"What do you think?" Raven let out a ragged breath. Typical Xochi, leaving out important, death-related details.

"How about you switch outfits with the woman?" he offered to Coatl. "You seem more experienced than her."

"Good try." Coatl slapped Raven's shoulder with gnarled fingers. "But it's too late to change. Besides, I don't plan to meet the gods just yet." He pointed to the top of the temple.

Raven and Surefire looked up to see a man garbed in a long red and gold robe standing at the very top step. Multicolored feathers rose from his headpiece like a feathery halo to rival any peacock. He held the crystal skull— the size and appearance of a large human head—directly in front of his chest. He stood at the edge of the landing and gazed down at the ball court.

There's the power sucker.

The source of the discomforting current bouncing across Raven's skin, trying to burrow inside had grown stronger the farther he'd walked into the arena. Raven focused on keeping this energy out. He already sensed a small bit of his power draining away. He couldn't imagine how weak he'd feel any closer to it. No wonder Xochi had said he couldn't use his abilities to steal it. He doubted her necklace would be much help to him against this force, though Surefire had never fully explained why Xochi had given her the necklace, only that she could harness the power better than him, an assertion that concerned Raven and made him wonder how Xochi planned to use her.

Raven looked up the stairway, and he noticed streaks of deep red dye down its center. On either side of the stairs, rows and rows of skulls lined the top portion and base of the temple. His eyes drifted back to the red stain on the stairs. It wasn't red dye—it was blood.

"Tell me those skulls aren't real," Surefire said in a quiet voice.

"They're not real," he lied.

He scanned the crowd hanging and sitting and standing along the walls of the court. Many had their faces painted to resemble animals such as snakes, jaguars, and monkeys. Mothers held squirming children on their laps. Men laughed and drank from stone goblets. Every now and then a warm breeze carried a whiff of chocolate across Raven's nose.

The crowd roared. Raven looked back up at the man—a priest, he assumed—who raised the crystal skull, now glowing a light purple, above his head.

The conch shell blew, and the people fell silent.

"Tonight begins the festivities of Xochiquetzal!" the priest bellowed from his high perch.

The audience shouted their excitement and pounded their fists on their chests.

The drum again beat out a rhythm punctuated by the eerie call of the conch followed by the soft notes of a flute. Six elaborately jeweled and feathered women, naked from the waist up, entered the court and began undulating their bodies to the music. Their vividly colored skirts swirled around their bare feet, and the patterns blurred together the faster they moved.

Raven soon realized it wasn't just a ceremonial dance. It was a recreation of the game they were about to play. The dancers mimed hitting an imaginary ball. He watched how they swung their hips and used their elbows, heads, knees—never their hands—to bounce the ball against the wall. They threw their bodies to the ground, against the wall, to never let the ball hit the ground. When it did, they all looked down at the player who missed, who dropped the ball. They picked her up, and all five hoisted her above their heads and passed her to the crowd on top of the wall and down the other side.

He glanced at Surefire to see if she'd noticed, too. Her eyes were fixated on the women, and she didn't look happy.

Yeah, she'd noticed.

"Xochi was right. We can't use our hands," he said.

"So it seems," she replied. "And we can't lose."

"One of us has to."

The audience parted again and gave a jubilant shout. In unison, they stomped on the ground and the stone walls with their feet and sticks and any weapons in their hands—a primitive rendition of "We Will Rock You."

The dancers appeared again carrying an elaborate golden tray, which held a black rubber ball a little smaller than a bowling ball.

"Ulli! Ulli! Ulli!" chanted the crowd.

"I'm assuming that's the ball we're using." Raven nodded toward it.

Coatl regarded him. "That's Maxtla."

"Then why is the crowd shouting 'ulli'?"

He narrowed his wide-set eyes, causing his leathery skin to crinkle at his temples. "You really have never played before?"

"No."

"That is our last captain."

All right, so the ball was just larger than a human head.

"There's a head inside the ball?" Surefire turned a shade paler along the edges of her face paint.

"It is good," Coatl responded. "Makes the ball lighter, bounce farther."

"You always want to get a head in the game," Raven added.

"If I wasn't so freaked out right now, that might be funny," Surefire said.

"I try." He lifted his shoulders.

The dancers spread out along the court and began lifting the headdresses off the players. The music became more pronounced, more excited, like a drum roll before a big act. The dancers took off the stone yokes around the players' waists and untied their leather shoes. They removed the players' long ceremonial skirts, feathers, bracelets, and pendants until they were down to loincloths. Most players had knee guards made from leather. Some wore the stone wrist guards and knee guards like Surefire and Raven.

The women moved to Raven and took off his yoke and sandals. They stripped him down to his loincloth and thong with the leather flaps covering his front and thighs. A few smiled coyly and touched lower than needed when they removed his costume. He pulled away, and they snickered.

Raven inspected his leather armguard and stone wrist guard and the circular padded leather draped over his right shoulder. He wore leather shin protectors and a stone cap on his right knee. The cloth lay thickly around his waist with an ornamental leather flap hanging in front of him. He assumed the layered cotton material would help protect his waist and hips from the ball. His torso was otherwise bare, as were the other players.

"I'm not losing this!" He heard Surefire shout, and all the players pivoted their heads in her direction.

The tallest dancer, with orange plumes soaring above her head like a Vegas showgirl, reached for the leather bra wrapped around Surefire's chest. Part of Surefire's concern, he knew, had to be modesty. The other reason was that the bra hid Xochi's necklace.

"Support!" Surefire cupped both hands under her chest. "I need this for support."

The women, who had ample breasts, D-cups to Surefire's B-cups, glanced at one another and laughed. In a huff, Surefire spun on her heel and retreated to Raven.

"Bitches. The only reason theirs are so big is because of *gravity*." She yelled the last word at them, though they had melted back into the crowd.

"Whoa there, partner. Let's save this aggression for the game."

"Oh, you have not seen aggression." She was breathing so heavily Raven was afraid she'd hyperventilate.

"Okay. It's okay." He put up his hands. "Take a few breaths and—"

"And what?"

"We need to plan how to get the skull."

"I thought you never planned."

"Normally, I don't, but it seemed to annoy you before."

She glared at him.

"Or maybe not."

"I don't even know how to begin to plan." Her hands sliced up through the air. "I have a vague idea of how to play this game, but afterward I have no idea what to expect."

"Expect that one of us will snag the skull and one of us will . . ." Raven's words tapered off when he couldn't bring himself to lie or admit the truth.

"Die." Surefire finished the sentence for him and pointed at the mural on the ball court wall of a player with his heart being ripped out.

Chapter Seventeen

Ari watched them load his equipment and supplies onto the plane, ready to pounce if anything so much as tipped toward the ground. Over twelve hours remained until the curtain closed and his opportunity to perform the ritual was lost. In five hours, he'd reach the ceremonial site. That left him with more than enough time to set the stage for Raven's and Surefire's arrival—with the final skull.

That is, if Surefire survived.

Sources at the museum had informed him that Surefire, possibly bitten by a funnel-web spider, had been semiconscious when she and Raven had disappeared into the tomb. If she died, then Raven would need to retrieve the skull by himself. Ari had hijacked Surefire to make things easier for Raven to snatch the skull. Not to mention she'd make a perfect sacrifice. Her transhuman blood was even more enticing than a human's to Tezcatlipoca.

Ah, well. Tezcatlipoca would have to deal with the sacrifices Ari could provide. And Raven would need to figure out how to get the final skull on his own if he wanted to see Kat again, which would be sooner rather than later since Surefire had broken their bargain when she'd mouthed her cryptic message at the security camera.

As if anyone could decipher her message. Ari could barely make out the words, and he was an expert at reading lips. However, he did glean enough to know she'd ratted him out. Surefire had broken their pact, and now Ari planned to make good on his threat.

Was it that hard to keep your word nowadays? Even Ari—who would admit to a few minor personality failings—had planned to uphold his end of their deal. It was the decent thing to do. A man without his word was . . . he couldn't recall the exact phrasing. Perhaps a man without his word was nothing.

Though more likely a man without his word was a woman. Yes, that made perfect sense, since Surefire had just proved it.

His cell phone chirped.

"Yes," he answered.

"It's me, Ari, honey," Pixie's girlish voice shrilled on the other end. Ari held the phone way from his ringing ear.

"Did you get it?" Ari moved away from the plane as the men finished loading it.

"Yes, I did. You'd be so proud of me. I totally dusted—"

"The package," Ari cut her off. "You dusted the package."

"Yeah . . . oh, sorry . . . yes, the package." Her voice dropped when she repeated the words. "I forgot the rule about being on a phone."

Ari hung his head and squeezed the bridge of his noise. Tezcatlipoca's power churned deep inside his chest and oozed along his skin, itching to strangle the annoying life out of her.

Patience.

He could put up with her for a few more hours. Maybe.

He let out a long, exasperated breath. "You *are* using the new phone I gave you? The expendable one?"

"Of course, I ditched the other one earlier. Well, actually, I lost it. But it doesn't matter, it's gone and I'm not using it."

Ari paused at the lost-her-phone part but decided not to press the point. He had more important things to discuss. "What were you saying about the package you picked up for me?"

"Dusted and on its way."

"And the one from earlier?"

"Had to call in a few favors. Friend of a friend of a friend of a friend, and now I'm in über debt to them. Have to send them a crateful of designer duds from the States. Apparently they're worth sweet bank over there. Did you know that?"

No, he didn't, and he didn't care. "Is it finished?"

"Packed up and on schedule to arrive when we get there. Proud of me?"

He pinched his lips together. He hated giving solicited praise.

"Yes," he ground out.

"And her? Will I be able to dust another . . . ahh . . . package? Because I can't believe she sold you out like that. You know, I never trusted that chick. Always seemed into herself if you ask me. Even too busy to join my book club."

"What?" Why did she always drone on about things? If he didn't need her help, she would be the one sacrificed to Tezcatlipoca.

"I started a book club at U-Sec, and she totally blew me off."

Ari exhaled a long-winded sigh. "You can do whatever you want when this is over."

She squealed, and again Ari moved the phone away from his ear. "Really? Oh, thank you!"

"We're getting ready to take off. I need you and the package here now."

"Sure thing. And tell Tezzy I said hi." She hung up.

Ari stared at the phone and blinked. *Tezzy?*

Tezcatlipoca's power pulsed through his veins. It bubbled under his skin down to his groin. He dropped to his knees and folded his arms into his chest. A sadistic mixture of acid-like pain and desire filled every crevice of his body.

He might have to find another assistant. Soon.

♥ ☠ ♥ ☠ ♥ ☠

"Surefire disappeared in here. Far out." TimeTrap trailed her fingertips along the outside of the tomb.

Dr. Jones slapped her hand down.

"Read the sign." He pointed to the glaring red text at their feet: "Do not touch."

She shrugged and whirled back to Pax. Her straight dark bob whipped across her cheek. "You want me inside there."

"Yes," Pax replied as patiently as possible even though his patience had left town an hour ago as they'd waited to locate TimeTrap. A freak laboratory accident during her days at MIT had given her the ability to bend space and time. Unfortunately, she was hard to track down, especially on her days off. She loved the 1960s, and, judging by her go-go boots and the pot smell lingering on her psychedelic dress, she loved it too much.

She lowered her tortoise sunglasses, which covered the top half of her long, oval face, and pinned him with her brown—and bloodshot—eyes. "What's in there again?"

St. John shoved Pax aside. "Listen. I need you in there now. I need you to find out whatever you can about where Synthia is."

TimeTrap leaned against the tomb and pushed her sunglasses up her nose. She looked past St. John to Pax.

"Who put 'the Man' in charge?" She made air quotes with her fingers when she said "the man."

"The man?" St. John exclaimed.

"This is Surefire's father," Pax said.

"Oh." She looked St. John up and down. "Explains a lot."

St. John glowered. "What the hell does that mean?"

"Nothing, daddy-o." She patted his right cheek.

St. John turned beet red. Pax swore steam would start streaming from his ears any moment.

"I don't even know why Pax let you come here. You should be suspended. You've obviously been smoking a narcotic." St. John's lip curled in disgust.

"What I do with my days off is my business. And *when* I was, it was legal." She then added under her breath, "And if it weren't for people like you, it still would be."

St. John jabbed a finger at her. "This woman is in no condition to be supporting us."

"She's the only one who can help." Pax did his best to hide his embarrassment over TimeTrap's appearance. He needed answers now, and she could get them.

"Yeah, I am the only one. So get over it. Plus, grass helps me tune out and tune into the cosmic forces better." She wriggled her hands in the air above her head. "Though it's pretty much out of my system now." She sighed. "Bummer."

A vein in St. John's forehead began to stand out. Pax searched the room for Oracle to back him up and maybe placate St. John, but she was in a deep conversation with the head of security, who reminded him of a seventies actor he couldn't quite place.

"But if you're chomping at the bit to expel me from U-Sec," TimeTrap continued, "and from helping you tonight, I do have a prescription for it." She reached into the sparkly black clutch she carried and took out a small rectangular piece of paper. She waved it in St. John's face.

"We don't have time for this." Pax grabbed TimeTrap's elbow and led her away from St. John, whose hands were fisted so tightly they started to lose color.

"Dr. Jones gave us the x-rays of the tomb." Pax shoved the printout into her hand. "Can you use this to find your way in?"

She took off her glasses, pursed her lips, and stared at the image on the paper.

Pax raised his eyebrows. How long did it take to review a simple layout? "We don't have all night."

"All right, already. Take a chill pill. I got it." She handed him her sunglasses, her purse, and the printout. A second later she called out from inside the tomb.

"Gah, this place hasn't been cleaned in eons." Her voice penetrated the tomb's wall. She let out a muffled cough.

Several officers scattered around the room let out curses and words of shock over TimeTrap disappearing then reappearing in the closed tomb. Pax heard someone utter, "Freak."

Jones's eyes grew as large and round as his glasses. He cupped his hands and yelled against tomb, "Don't touch anything."

From outside, they heard a dull crack.

"Oopsy-daisy," TimeTrap chirped.

Jones hung his head and looked about to cry.

"Oh, it's nothing. Just some dead guy," she called out.

"Do you see anything?" Pax asked.

"I forgot my flashlight."

"You want mine?"

"No worries. A few small cracks are letting in some slight. But there's nothing to see. Just four walls and . . ." A loud bone-crunching noise resounded through the walls. "Dead dudes."

"Don't move anymore," Jones's voice wavered. "Just get out of there."

"Crazy," she said. "There is something. I'm feeling it. Some kind of whacked-out energy field above my head."

"What's it like?" Pax prompted when she became silent.

"Total blackout. I mean, my eyes adjusted somewhat to the dark but this area above my head is like a black hole, and it's swirling."

When she heard TimeTrap speaking from inside the tomb, Oracle stopped talking with the guard and moved next to it. She closed her eyes and rested her hands on the wall. Her face went blank as she opened her mind. "Pax, this isn't good. I'm losing her brain patterns by the second. Something is in there with her."

"Get out of there now!" Pax ordered, frantic. He was not about to lose another agent.

"I can't." She sounded panicked. "Oh, God, it's swarming around me. It's blocking me from teleporting back out."

Without hesitation, Pax took several steps away from the tomb.

"What are you doing?" Jones squeaked out seconds before Pax barreled into the tomb's side, causing a crack to form. Bits of stone streamed off it.

"Don't!" Jones sprang forward. St. John grabbed him from behind by the arms and wrenched him back.

The security guards and police officers stationed in the room inched closer. A few officers reached for their stun guns, but they didn't have a clear shot with Dr. Jones, St. John, and Oracle surrounding Pax.

"Her brain waves are weakening," Oracle pleaded, her gray-white eyes moist and swirling with black smoke.

Pax backed up again, farther this time. St. John positioned a struggling Dr. Jones at Pax's side, using him as a shield from the police.

Oracle ran behind Pax with her arms raised out at her sides. "Don't shoot!"

Guards yelled for them to move and for Pax to stop.

Let them shoot him. He didn't care. Pax wasn't losing another agent tonight.

From inside the tomb, TimeTrap screamed. Pax sprinted forward. He hit the tomb the second time with his shoulder, and it crumbled. A blast of wind streamed out and knocked him back a few steps. He staggered forward against the gust and the frigid, black cloud that followed it. Behind him, he heard officers shout at one another and a few yell out in fear. Soles of shoes screeched across the floor in retreat.

"Kali, are you there?" he asked, using her given name.

Oracle trailed him as he stepped over the stone pieces at his feet.

"She's still here," Oracle whispered.

Behind him, Jones bemoaned the desecration of the sacred piece.

"Priceless," he sobbed.

"Bill me," Pax countered.

He heard a moan followed by a pale hand waving just beyond the rubble.

"That was so cool," TimeTrap said weakly.

Pax stomped over the tomb's crumbled remains. He grabbed her hand and leaned down to pick her up.

Her head lolled back and forth against his arm. "Totally sick."

"You're going to be ill?" Oracle asked.

"Maybe. The room's spinning. But, man, what a trip."

Pax raised his brows. "She's fine."

"What *was* that?" St. John stared up at the ceiling.

Pax looked up as well, expecting the black cloud to be circling over their heads, but there was nothing but the ceiling's lights.

"I have no idea," Pax replied.

TimeTrap raised her head and looked pointedly at St. John. "It was a dimensional portal, silly. Duh."

Chapter Eighteen

The conch shell let out another weary cry, echoing the hopelessness Surefire felt. This was no joke, no dream, no reenactment. Their lives were at stake, and after the dust settled, one would be the victor and the other dead.

She couldn't tear her eyes away from the colorful, graphic painting of a figure dressed similarly to the priest holding aloft the skull atop the stairs. However, in the painting, instead of a skull, he grasped a bleeding heart.

Would it matter if Raven lost his heart? A heart that no longer beat? Would it kill him since he wasn't technically alive?

Sadness sprouted like a weed across her chest, making her eyes water and her throat close. She wasn't certain if she was sad over one of them possibly dying, or over Raven already being sort-of dead.

The field cleared with only the players remaining. Surefire's team shouted for her to join them on the other side of the central line. Raven rubbed her shoulder and wished her luck before jogging over to join his team. She wiped away a tear before turning to walk across the field.

Her teammates, Huitzilin and Itzli—both with faces painted in the same monkey motif as her's—made it known they weren't thrilled to have her on their team. As Surefire approached, Huitzilin spat on the ground and glared at her with his one good eye; the other was swollen to the size of a small lime. He twisted and turned his torso to the left and right. His joints let out a disturbing series of pops.

Itzli welcomed her with a blank appraisal. His face was handsome even with the decorative paint. His high cheekbones and full lips softened his prideful expression. His wide-set, intense eyes trailed up from her feet to her face and made her squirm as if he were assessing not just her ability but her looks. Surefire wondered what he saw, if he saw an Aztec woman or past the outfit to who she really was under Xochi's spell. Without comment, he turned his back on her and began jumping up and down, shaking out sinewy arms and legs covered in a myriad of yellow and brown blotches. Several female voices cried out his name. He ignored them, keeping his focus on a man in a cloth tunic rimmed in gold wearing an ebony-and-red feather headdress.

Surefire watched this thin, regal man stride into the center of the field with the ball held above his head. The crowd chanted, "Ulli. Ulli. Ulli."

He gestured to the players, and they moved to various areas of the field. Surefire assumed he was the referee.

She looked around at the other players to understand their positions on the I-shaped field. The perpendicular goal areas reminded her of end zones in football. Huitzilin walked backward into the center of their goal area. Itzli and Surefire placed themselves about five feet from the center line.

Her muscles surged with adrenaline. She took a few focusing breaths and stretched out her legs, one and then the other. She bent over and grabbed her ankles and pulled her head down to her shins to work the kinks out of her back.

Treat this as any other competition. Play to win.

She'd figure out the rest later. At least, she hoped she would.

Raven's side she dubbed Team Snake based on their common face paint. A scarier mascot than her Team Monkey, since their facial art looked more comedic than deadly.

Surefire concentrated on Team Snake lined up opposite from her and tried to block out the boisterous spectators, many of whom sat on the eight-foot-high sloped walls on either side of the field. Raven leaned over and placed his hands on his thighs. He caught her eye and blew her a kiss. Butterflies flittered across her gut despite the anxiety twisting her insides into a pretzel.

She lowered her gaze to the ground. She didn't need any diversions.

A short note sounded from the conch shell somewhere above them. The ref tossed the ball into the air. Raven's team skidded forward and slammed the ball toward them with a flat stone paddle. Huitzilin raced toward the ball before it reached the goal area. He threw himself into the wall and hit the ball with his shoulder. It bounced higher onto the wall. Spectators pulled their legs and feet back to avoid getting hit. Itzli ran forward and, using his hip, directed it to Surefire. He shouted for her to send it down field. Surefire moved her elbow under the ball, her body anticipating the speed, force, and angle needed to send it back over the center line past the other team.

"Son of a bitch!" she screamed when the ball slammed into her harder than a punch from Pax.

She grabbed her elbow and rubbed it. She'd been expecting to be hit by a dodge ball not a five-pound medicine ball.

They scored a point, though she wasn't sure how.

Raven mouthed, "Are you okay?"

In frustration, Surefire spun away. Now she knew why Itzli's skin held a patchwork of bruises, and Huitzilin's eye stood out like a puffer fish, and Raven's teammate lacked most of his teeth.

That ball was a deadly weapon.

The Snakes gained possession of the ball, and Raven kneed it directly at her head.

She ducked.

The ball went into the Monkeys' goal.

And the Snakes scored.

Half the crowd cheered and the other half booed. Then something hit her head. It felt like a banana peel.

"What are you doing?" Itzli yelled at her.

She grinned. "Self-preservation."

He pointed to the priest frozen at the top of the hundred or so stairs. He still held aloft the skull as if it were personally presiding over the games.

Itzli didn't need to say anything else.

A moment later the ball whizzed by her head. It bounced against the stone wall and ricocheted toward her. She sprang forward and landed on her side. Angling her hip, she cringed and cursed and passed the ball to Itzli. He swung his arm around and shouldered the ball into a marker that resembled a stone lollipop.

The crowd shouted. The ref threw up his arms. The Monkeys were awarded another point.

Surefire decided the best defense was a good offense—even if it meant looking like her blotchy teammate when it was over. She only prayed to make it out with all her teeth and no internal bleeding.

One of the Snakes lobbed the ball straight up into the air. It arced down toward her side of the line. She ran forward and skidded in the dirt. Pebbles and grit dug into her bare feet and burned her heels. She pushed back the pain and stuck out her good knee. Raven careened into her and shoved her to the ground. Her bad knee twisted underneath her. He hit the ball into the Monkeys' marker and scored a point for his team.

He put out his hand to help her up.

"What was that?" She slapped him away and hobbled up on her own. She kicked out her throbbing knee.

He grabbed her elbow and yanked her close. "You can end the game by getting the ball through that ring."

He pointed to the ring above her head.

"Why didn't anyone tell me?" She kicked out her knee. The pain subsided to a dull prick.

"You're a woman. They think you can't do it."

"Really?" She straightened up and eyed the stone ring with a trio of snakes carved around the edge. The circle was barely larger than the ball.

Raven backed away to his side when the ref yelled and made the universal, and timeless, motion for off-sides.

"What about you? You'll be sacrificed."

"If you get it in." He winked at her.

Surefire stared at the ring. She studied it. The ball rebounded around the Snakes' side of the court. Raven and his teammates passed it back and forth from shoulder to hip to knee then back to the Monkeys' end zone. Huitzilin swung a stone paddle and slapped the ball high against the wall and back to the Snakes' goal line.

Raven nodded at Surefire. She knew the next time he controlled the ball he'd pass it to her.

For easy targets, she'd let her body feel out the correct movements. For a difficult target, she liked to drop into the zone where everything else faded away. No more catcalls from the crowd. No more scent of spices overlaying body odor. No more pain throbbing in her hip and elbow and knee.

Getting into this target zone invigorated her. Gave her a jolt of energy like a shot of espresso. Before her falling out with her father, when they'd been close, he'd take her to the Army base where she'd perform for the other officers by downing pool balls into pockets and then eventually shooting targets with various weapons. All accomplished with perfect precision. She remembered the pride she had felt when her father beamed at her after these performances. He'd affectionately announced to the other officers that she was "his girl."

Of course, neither her father nor the officers would've killed her if she missed.

Her eyes followed the ball. Her feet shifted about ten feet away from the red centerline that ran below the ring until she felt the angle was almost right. She'd have to make adjustments depending on how Raven lobbed the ball to her—the momentum, the trajectory, the height all determined how she positioned her body to hit the ball through the ring.

Raven's teammate passed him the ball. He threw his shoulder into it and the ball shot through the air with the speed, it seemed, of a cannon ball.

She saw and felt the ball coming toward her. Her muscles tingled and itched. Her heart rate slowed. Goosebumps prickled across her flesh. She jumped forward and turned, jutting her side out. As the ball slammed into her hip, she moved a half-inch to the right. The pain barely registered. Time appeared to slow. The ball hit the wall, spinning forward at the precise angle toward the target.

It sailed through the stone ring.

She refocused her eyes and looked around and wriggled her fingers in her ears. Something was wrong. Torch flames crackled. Birds and monkeys screeched from afar, but there were no other sounds. No jostling of bodies. No catcalls. No drum beats. She gazed up at the spectators sitting on the walls and those lounging in their box seats. Everyone gaped at the ball rolling to a stop on the other side of the line as if it were possessed.

Then, moving as one beast, every head turned to her, and the crowd erupted into one cacophonous scream. The drums beat. The conch shell blew out a victorious sound. Huitzilin and Itzli scooped her up between them and hoisted her onto their shoulders. They both grinned at her. Itzli kissed her thigh, which was a bit odd and uncomfortable. Huitzilin apologized for his rude welcoming. She could play with him anytime, he told her. He squeezed her thigh a little too high, and she wondered if there was a double meaning in his invitation. She struggled to get down but they had a mean grip on her lower legs, pinning her in place.

Across the field, men in long, colorful robes grabbed Raven by his arms. His teammates melted into the crowd. For a brief moment, she met Raven's eyes before they dragged him up the long steps to the priest still holding the crystal skull at the top of the stairs.

She tapped Itzli's shoulder. "I need to get down."

"You do not walk. You are being honored."

Itzli and Huitzilin plowed through the tight crowd. Some spectators stretched out their arms and extended their fingers to paw at her legs, rub her skin, touch her feet.

"What's happening?" she asked.

"You will witness the sacrifice," Huitzilin replied. "And have a piece of his heart."

"Oh." Surefire paled. She balanced herself on their shoulders as they ascended the stairs. On either side, in what she considered the box seats, the upper class paid her homage by throwing gold bracelets and rings at her.

Xochi's pendant sat like a lump between her breasts underneath her leather wraparound bra. Xochi had told her the necklace could return them from the past, but she had left out the most important part.

How?

♥ ☠ ♥ ☠ ♥ ☠

Six priests jostled Raven into the temple's high chamber. At the far end, a wall opened to the blue-black sky above. They dragged him toward an obsidian stone table in the center of the room and pushed him down until his back and head slammed into the cold, hard surface. He struggled against their calloused, vise-like hands, but their strong fingers dug into him and held him down.

Raven tried to phase out or tap into his strength to knock them off. But the skull was somewhere in the chamber, and its energy pulled at him like a noose wrapped around his soul. It tugged away, trying to choke it out of him. Its force became exponentially stronger the closer Raven came to it. His muscles ached and weakened. He stopped fighting against the priests and focused instead on blocking the vampiric force feeding on his power.

The skull's pull grew more demanding. Even though the men obscured his view of the room, Raven knew the high priest drew nearer to him with the skull.

He concentrated harder and was surprised when some of his power pumped back into his body. Pitching on the slab, he knocked two of the men off him. They leaned forward and threw their whole weight into pinning him down.

Encouraged by this bit of strength, Raven concentrated even harder to regain his powers. It was difficult, akin to sucking a too-thick milkshake up a thin straw. His forehead beaded with sweat from this metaphysical tug-of-war. The priest walked closer, and the power overwhelmed him. It was too much. He couldn't fight it anymore.

From a corner of the room, he heard knife blades chinking together. He cringed. If those murals surrounding the game field told the true tale, then he knew what that sound meant.

They were planning to cut out his heart.

He could heal. That was true. However, a missing heart, even one that no longer worked, might not be a wound from which he could easily bounce back. Xochi had said he would retain some of his abilities around the crystal skull, but she hadn't been clear on what.

A knife landed with a clank next to his head. He turned and came face to sharpened face with the knife's pointy black tip.

That is going to smart.

The high priest took his place at Raven's head. He cradled the skull in the nook of his arm. The lower priests continued to stand guard with three on either side of him, though they had loosened their grip on his throbbing limbs. A priest to his top right picked up the blade. To Raven's left, a priest let go of his shoulder to grab a gleaming gold bowl adorned with a rainbow of jewels. At least his heart would go out in style.

He heard a murmur of voices just outside the opening to the room. A shuffling of feet followed, and then Surefire's voice asked about Raven.

Her two teammates lowered her from their shoulders and guided her to the bottom of the sacrificial table. Surefire's mismatched eyes grew wide. In the torch-lit room, he watched her tremble.

"Raven?" she ventured.

"Do not speak," the priest barked from above Raven's head.

Raven gave her a reassuring smile, but he was certain it didn't reach his eyes. Surefire's frown deepened.

"My priests and I are the only ones permitted to speak. I am Acacitli, presider of the ceremony. Priest to the great Xochiquetzal and Xochipilli."

"Good for you," Raven replied. "Now, can we get on with this? I have a date with Xochi, and I hate to keep her waiting."

Acacitli slapped him.

"Ow." Raven moved his pounding jaw back and forth.

"Do not speak her name in jest." Acacitli held up the skull. He closed his eyes and began intoning a vow over and over again. Raven couldn't understand the words even with Xochi's magic liquid translator. The priest spoke in tongues.

Slowly, the pale purple skull filled with an opaque light that morphed into an illuminated cloud, swirling and churning and building into a mini-thunderstorm. The priest opened his eyes, and his pupils and irises had been replaced with the same swirling gaseous light from inside the skull. His voice became stronger, more emphatic as he continued repeating the odd, guttural words.

The lower priests on either side of Raven began repeating the words. They, too, lowered their lids, and when they snapped back open, their eyes contained the same violet light.

"Raven," Surefire whispered.

"The pendant." He nodded to her chest.

The priest to his right leaned forward in a trance, his movements robotic. He ran the edge of the blade over Raven's chest and scraped a shallow cut. Warm blood trickled down his chest.

"Now," Raven mouthed to Surefire.

She reached under her leather bra and took out the pendant. She rubbed her thumb over its smooth surface. Her eyes closed and her lips moved as if she were meditating.

He stared at the pendant, hoping some magic force would erupt from it and transport them out of there.

Nothing happened.

Behind Surefire, two compact, muscular guards slithered from out of the shadows and grabbed her arms. Her eyes flashed with surprise then fright.

This wasn't part of the deal, at least not what he recalled. Raven struggled to remember Xochi's exact phrasing on what would happen after the game: *One will be the victor, and the other will be at my mercy.* He'd be damned if Xochi had turned the tables, leaving Surefire at the mercy of her whims.

Raven strained against his captors to sit up. One of the priests pressed the blade to his throat. Reluctantly, he eased back down.

Surefire threw herself backward and squirmed. Tugging with both arms to escape, she kicked out her foot, and the man to her right grimaced then twisted her arm back. The man to her left forced her hand out to a priest at the end of the table.

"Calm now. We mean you no harm." Another priest made a small slice in the center of her outstretched palm. "A small offering of thanks is all she requires of the winner."

Surefire flinched as he squeezed several drops of blood from the cut into a golden cup.

"What are you doing to her?" Raven shouted.

The blade at his throat sliced a shallow cut against his skin.

"No!" Surefire reached across the table, her hand dripping blood onto his legs. The two guards yanked her back.

The priest removed the blade from Raven's throat. The cup containing Surefire's blood was passed to the middle priest, who dipped two fingers inside and leaned over Raven, drawing a mark over his heart.

Raven couldn't see what the man had drawn. Whatever it was, it set Surefire in motion. She smashed her head back into the man still twisting her arm. He grabbed his nose and let go. She swung her free hand around and slammed her palm into the man holding her left hand.

The priests surrounding Raven didn't notice Surefire's escape. Or maybe they didn't care. They kept their weird, whirling eyes focused on Raven and the knife piercing his chest.

"Stop!" Surefire screamed and reached for the useless pendant again, pressing it into her bloody hand.

The knife's blade dug deeper into Raven's skin, and he shut his eyes tight against the intense sting. His eyes watered. His throat constricted. His muscles clenched against the agonizing pain ripping through his body as the blade cut deeper.

Around the periphery of the room, a few people gasped. A whisper started low then multiplied into a drone of voices as it rounded the room.

"No!" Surefire shouted when the blade began working its way into his sternum.

The searing pain increased and rose to a level Raven had never felt before, didn't think he could endure. He arched his back. Warm blood streamed from the wound and down his sides and toward his stomach. The priests tightened their hold on him. He swiveled his head back and forth.

He glimpsed the room from around a priest's feathery robe. Warriors and various temple servants dropped to their knees. They weren't looking at the high priest, they were staring past him, past Raven to Surefire.

He whipped his attention back to Surefire, and his eyes widened. Stars exploded across his vision, and the room faded to gray before coming back into focus.

Was he hallucinating, or were Surefire's features changing into someone else's?

Xochi's?

♥ ☠ ♥ ☠ ♥ ☠

The pendant warmed in Surefire's hand, growing hotter by the second until her skin started to singe and she let it go. She looked at her hand, no longer cut or stained with blood. An eerie purple light emanated from the pendant, matching the skull's violet vortex. A mild electrical current flowed through Surefire's body. Every inch of her flesh, every bone in her body, hummed with this energy. She closed her eyes and took a breath. She smelled lilac, lavender, and a multitude of flowers. When she opened her eyes, the room was bright, not the uneven darkness of the flickering torches. The light came from the people in the room. Each person's body glowed. The priests surrounding Raven were so bright with an opaque light she couldn't make out their features, just their outlines. Yellow lights shown from the torsos of those kneeling. They looked as if a child had colored over their images and gone way outside the lines.

"Synthia," Raven gasped her name.

Her gaze met his, and the shock on his face caused her to panic.

What's happening?

You are my conduit. Xochi's voice echoed in her mind.

"Oh, no, no, no," Surefire responded out loud in a hushed tone. "This wasn't part of the deal."

You promised you would do what it takes.

"But I didn't think it would be this."

Surefire's right hand rose in front of her face. It twisted from side to side on its own. Surefire willed it back down. She didn't want to be Xochi's human avatar.

What is an avatar? Xochi asked.

Stay out of my head and my body. Surefire pushed with all her will to dislodge Xochi.

Xochi slammed back with a punch to Surefire's core. This punch came from inside, an explosion of power that made the worst PMS cramps seem like a tickle. Surefire doubled over. Her torso throbbed. Vomit burned up her throat.

Do you want to save Raven? Xochi inquired in a calm tone, as if asking if she wanted a drink.

Surefire watched the blade disappear into Raven's chest. His eyes rolled back into his head, but he remained conscious. His face creased with pain. His teeth ground together.

"Yes," she whispered. Her eyes teared up. Her heart hurt as if the blade had pierced it.

Then let me in.

But won't the skull steal your power as well?

It is filled with a piece of my essence. It will be drawn to me.

Then why did it weaken Raven?

The stronger force draws the power from the weaker. Raven is not stronger than the power within the skull. When I fill you, we will be the strongest, but it won't last. Your blood on the pendant binds us for a short time. Blood from a true sacrifice binds us forever.

I don't know about this. Xochi wasn't on the top of Surefire's "trust list." In fact, she wasn't in the top fifty.

Let me in, Xochi's sultry tone purred.

I can't.

Raven screamed. Blood spurted from the wound and soaked his chest.

Let me in now! Xochi's voice screeched through her mind.

Surefire clutched her aching head. "Stop hurting me. I'll do it."

At that moment, she'd do anything to stop Raven's agonizing screams—even surrender herself to Xochi. She exhaled and let down her guard. Power poured up her spine then flowed back down to her extremities. Xochi pushed Surefire out of the way to the back of her own mind. Surefire was present, yet not. The sensation was like watching a video shot from someone else's point of view with Xochi in control of the camera.

She was trapped in her own body. Xochi's energy, so all consuming, possessed her limbs, and she could no longer move them. She'd been relegated to observer status from inside her own head. Panic gripped her, and she wondered if she'd ever break free and have control again.

Then she remembered the necklace Ari had worn and how Tezcatlipoca had changed Ari's appearance and spoke through him. Was this what he'd felt when Tezcatlipoca had possessed him? Was Xochi prepping Surefire as Tezcatlipoca was prepping Ari to enter into their world? Was this a trick? Had Xochi set up Raven and Surefire for this moment?

Xochi glided Surefire's body around the obsidian slab toward Raven's head. Surefire's hand shot out and grabbed the wrist of the priest cutting into Raven's chest. Immediately his light faded to a weak yellow. He blinked his eyes several times before he staggered back from the table, leaving the blade in Raven's chest.

His befuddled appearance turned to horror.

"Xochiquetzal," he invoked and fell to his knees.

She reached across and grabbed the priest holding the gold bowl. It clattered to the ground. He tripped backward and fell as well, mumbling the goddess's name. The other priests let go of Raven and dropped prostrate to the ground.

Xochi turned her attention to Raven. His aura glowed differently than those of the others, with a spectrum of blue, green, violet, yellow, and white. Surefire stared, transfixed, as the colors pulsated and circled around the shape of his body.

"Synthia, is that you?" Raven asked.

"Yes and no," Xochi answered using Surefire's voice.

She grasped the handle of the blade. Raven placed his hand atop hers.

"Your eyes," he croaked.

The high priest stood transfixed, holding the skull over Raven's head, still repeating the ancient words. He never noticed the ceremony had long since been over.

"I am going to remove the blade," she said.

He nodded.

She pulled, and Raven's body arched upward. "Ugh, couldn't you have counted to three?"

He hacked and sputtered. Dark liquid poured from his stab wound and appeared as an inky smudge against his multi-colored aura. Shocked, Surefire realized this dark liquid was blood. His hands covered the deep slice to no avail. Xochi guided Surefire's hands over his. He let go and slowly lay back. His blood heated her hand and ran in between her fingers. Xochi pressed down. Her power trickled down Surefire's arm like tiny rivulets of lava. Surefire wanted to scream but couldn't move her lips or use her voice. Her skin, her organs, her veins were on fire, and any minute might combust. Xochi's power pumped over Raven's wound, and it began to close under her fingers.

Xochi lifted Surefire's head and grabbed the high priest's arm. He released the skull, and she caught it inches before it landed on Raven's face.

The high priest blinked. When his eyes finally focused on Surefire, he ran screaming out of the chamber.

Coward, Xochi spat at the retreating priest.

"Synthia," Raven whispered with uncertainty.

His voice tugged at Surefire. A tingling sensation grew inside her chest, expanded out through her torso to push against Xochi.

The goddess wasn't about to relinquish control. She leaned Surefire's face down to Raven's and pursed her lips.

No! Surefire reeled. That bitch was not going to use Surefire's body to kiss him.

Surefire gathered her will. She focused on the stinging sensation traveling down her limbs to her extremities and visualized squeezing Xochi's energy out. Something akin to nails scratched down the inside of Surefire's skin, trying to hang on. Surefire gritted her teeth and pushed past the pain. Xochi was almost gone, she could feel it.

That fickle goddess didn't own this body, Surefire did. Xochi's burning power faded to a warm mist followed by a cool elation. Peace flowed through Surefire. She suddenly wanted to touch Raven, wanted to feel his lips under hers, wanted to hold him—to be with him. Now.

She placed her left hand on Raven's face and kissed him.

Raven pulled back, and his words were so low and soft, she could barely hear him.

"We need to go."

"Home." With her right hand, she clutched the skull to her chest and touched his lips with her own.

The world faded away.

Chapter Nineteen

When they returned to the office, Pax poured himself a cup of coffee, black. He downed it and then drank another. His stomach growled. He glanced at his computer's clock, just after two in the afternoon. With the nonstop morning, he'd forgotten to eat breakfast and lunch. He grabbed a protein bar from his desk drawer. Not much, but better than nothing.

On the edge of his desk, Oracle sat sipping one of those high-octane energy drinks that wreaked havoc on Pax's stomach. She faced a wall covered with LCD televisions tuned into news stations from around the world to listen for any new information. TimeTrap slept on his office couch, where she had passed out after eating two bags of chips and a package of jelly Krimpets from the vending machine. St. John had left to check on his wife, who was hysterical and unable to get out of bed and had called him home. Pax was certain to get an earful about that drama when St. John returned.

Pax checked his e-mail and then his cell phone for the thirtieth time in the last fifteen minutes to see if Matthews or anyone else had uncovered any new information. On the drive home, Pax had called and filled Matthews in on what had occurred at the museum. Graham had already spoken with Matthews and gotten a warrant to search Ari's museum in Baltimore. Search warrants for transhuman cases were easier and quicker to obtain than standard warrants for reasons that grated on Pax even though he was grateful to have something work to his advantage at the moment.

Once more, Pax ticked through a mental checklist in case he was missing anything.

They couldn't track down Raven's sister yet. At this moment, Ari and Pixie were their main leads. Unfortunately, none of their combined contacts could locate either one. They hoped Ari's local museum yielded a clue. The police were also checking flight records of large and small airports and attempting to trace Pixie's calls to Ari's phone. Matthews had volunteered to run interference with the FBI on Pax's behalf to give him space to find Surefire.

Pax figured Matthews wanted to make up for losing one of his agents. It was a start.

Matthews had continued the search for the officer who had intercepted Surefire's original call. Checking flight records, they'd found he had boarded a flight to Athens, Greece, at six this morning—a trip his wife had no knowledge of.

The only good thing that had come out of this disaster was finding a truckload of artifacts Raven had stolen. A few were from the Smithsonian's various museums, so their recovery somewhat placated the staff's anger over Pax destroying the tomb. Though several security guards had been obliged to haul Dr. Jones away after he'd begun chucking bits of the crumbled tomb at Pax. He hadn't thought a reserved man like Jones could have such a temper.

It wasn't like the tomb was the only one in the world.

"Anything?" Oracle shifted around on the desk and motioned to his laptop.

"Nothing of interest." Worn out, he slumped in his chair and considered another cup of coffee. His stomach protested the idea.

Oracle sat back on her hands and closed her eyes. Pax turned his attention to the televisions. Heather St. John's face flickered across a screen as a cable news network began an interview with her from a plush, modern living room.

That was fast. Her public relations agent must be working overtime.

"How long has your sister worked for U-Sec?" the reporter asked.

"Several years." She beamed at him with a TV-perfect smile.

"Can you tell us about U-Sec? We understand they employ transhumans. Is your sister one?"

"I've answered that question already for Katie."

"But what is Synthia's job at U-Sec?"

"She's an agent, Tom. She works to protect the interests of our corporations and our country."

The reporter nodded and glanced down at the papers in his lap. "But what was she doing on this case with a suspect called Raven? He's wanted by the FBI. And I understand Interpol is looking for him as well."

"Tom." She shook her head while maintaining her model smile. "I'm only going to say this because I want to quell rumors. My sister was hired by U-Sec as a favor to my father. Levi Paxton, one of the founders, served under my father in Afghanistan. He hired Synthia to give her something to do. You see, she . . ." Her smile wilted at the edges. Her eyes teared up as if on cue. "She had a breakdown after failing to make the Olympic team with me."

Pax tensed. "Can you believe this dreck?"

"It's a shame."

They cut to a video of a teenaged Synthia performing her balance beam routine. As she began her dismount, her foot slipped and she fell forward. Her knee and then her nose smacked against the beam.

"I'm sure it was hard for her to watch you go on to win all those medals," the reporter prodded.

"It was difficult. And I think that led to her later issues."

"We've had conflicting accounts about this case. Some say she was kidnapped. Others are saying she was helping Raven. What is the truth?"

"I don't know. She was assisting on this case and just got caught up." She shrugged and looked down at her hands.

Pax figured she'd win an Emmy with this performance.

"I just want her to come home safely." Tears trickled down her cheeks.

The news program cut away from Heather to show a grainy video of Raven disappearing into the tomb with a barely conscious Surefire draped around his neck. Next they showed Pax destroying the tomb, which segued into another segment: "What is U-Sec, and are we safe?"

"What the hell does that mean?" Pax shouted at the screen. "This is the thanks we get? Just last week, they ran a piece on us unmasking the Laser Killer and how we saved the city. Now we're the bad guys?"

"Whatever sells more ads," Oracle replied. "Nothing personal."

"And who leaked those videos to the press? Roy's going to get an earful for this screwup. In fact, I may have him fired. As head of security for that museum, he should know this is unacceptable."

The phone rang, and they both looked at it. Pax didn't want to answer it. If it was a reporter, he was liable to do or say something they could really report on.

Oracle picked up. "Yes?"

She huffed and rolled her eyes. "Helena, he's here. I'm just helping out, since you had gone home to take a break."

Pax took the phone. "Yeah."

"St. John's on the phone. Miss Vida Pierce herself is missing," Helena intoned.

"Who?"

"Heather St. John. The one and only. Thank the Lord."

Pax felt guilty for being a touch happy about the development. Helena transferred St. John to his line.

"Heather's gone," St. John stated.

"So I heard."

"What are you going to do about it?"

"How is this my fault?" Pax shouted back, then added, "Maybe she's spewing more crap about Synthia on TV."

"Cut the shit, Pax. She was at Hunter's house. They wrapped up the interview with CNN two hours ago. She was taking a shower while Hunter was watching the game. He heard her scream and ran to the bathroom. She was gone—the shower was still on. He has that place tighter than Fort Knox. No one can get in or out of there and not be videotaped."

"Any clues."

"Dust."

"Dust?" Pax pulled the phone back from his ear.

"Yeah, Hunter saw dust that sparkled in the light floating in the air. Then he said something about Tinker Bell."

"Tinker—what?"

"A fairy-fuckin' princess. Trust me, I ran drug tests immediately, and he came clean."

"Pixie dust," Pax pondered out loud.

"What are you saying?"

Pax placed his elbows on the desk and rubbed a hand over his forehead. Though all clues had pointed to Pixie's involvement, he had still held out hope of another explanation. It killed him to find a betrayal of this magnitude at his company, a place Pax and his partners had built on trust.

"The mole is Pixie Chick. Her given name is Bella Markowski."

"Pax, when this is over . . ." St. John trailed off.

"I know."

"I'm coming to your office now."

Pax hung up and leaned against his desk. All those years spent building this business, spent recruiting and training and securing the facility. How had he missed her? How had he missed what she was capable of? Pixie had passed all the tests. She came from a fairly stable home. She had never committed a crime. She had even started the office book club.

"Did you have any idea?" he asked Oracle.

"Not a clue." She lowered her eyes to the desk. "She was effective at blocking me out. Some transhumans are, but not because they have something to hide. I try not to read anyone's thoughts without provocation."

Next to his laptop, his cell phone rang. Matthews's number popped up on the screen.

"What did you find?" Pax answered.

"Not much." Matthews sounded as tired and frustrated as Pax. "We're checking out a hard drive we found in the museum's back office. The place had a lot of Mesoamerican artifacts on display, which fits in with our case: ceremonial knives, human skulls, some blood-stained robe worn by a priest. Bizarro stuff like that."

"Makes me wonder whether Ari could be somewhere in Mexico."

"That's a possibility."

Pax considered another possibility, which still seemed impossible to him. "Do you think Ari is really trying to raise an Aztec god?"

Matthews paused for a beat. "If you'd asked me a few days ago, I'd say maybe he *believed* he could do it and was delusional. But with everything that has happened . . . Surefire and Raven disappearing into the tomb and from the warehouse lot and Oracle being overtaken by an unknown psychic force—" He stopped mid-sentence then asked, "How is Oracle?"

"All right."

Oracle waved at Pax and mouthed for him to tell Matthews "hello." He spun in his chair, putting his back to her.

"Glad to hear that." Matthews's voice perked up, and he cleared his throat. "Getting back to the museum. We did find something else, though I'm not sure how—or if—it relates."

"I'm listening."

"So far, from his hard drive, we learned that Ari had done a lot of research into these crystal skulls. In fact, he owned a few, which were missing from his display cases. Then I remembered hearing about a crystal skull stolen from the British Museum of Man not too long ago. I did a search on those skulls and came up with another one missing from a museum in Paris, stolen last month. Several more were reported taken from private collections."

"How are these related to our case?"

"According to legend, there are thirteen crystal skulls in total and various theories about ceremonies involving the skulls, including speaking with gods. One describes the end of the world if they are brought together in a certain configuration."

"And you think Ari might be using them to potentially raise this god?"

"It's a thought."

Pax tried to digest this new theory, but it wasn't going down well. This added another layer to an already complicated scenario. "I'll consider it. Did you hear about Heather St.—"

"Pax, I'm getting something." Oracle jumped off the desk. She darted over to the window and placed her hands on it.

"I'll call you back." He hung up on Matthews then bolted off his chair to stand next to Oracle. "What is it?"

Her eyes narrowed. She took a deep breath. "Can you feel it?"

"Feel what?"

She leaned her forehead on the window. "A vibration, like a metaphysical ripple. Something that doesn't belong here just dropped into our world."

No, it couldn't be. Pax's stomach sank. Those ancient gods didn't exist.

"What do you think it is?"

"I'm not sure, but the energy does feel similar to what I felt in the warehouse." She turned to Pax. "We have to track it down."

♥ ☠ ♥ ☠ ♥ ☠

The priest's scream, the spectators' chants, the drum's rhythmic thumping all faded into a comforting silence before Surefire and Raven materialized onto a springy mattress with Surefire's lips sliding across Raven's. The weighted crystal skull rolled out of her hand and thudded onto the floor.

Other than those details, Surefire had no idea where they were, and she didn't want to open her eyes to find out. She only wanted to keep kissing Raven. Because the more he kissed her, the more the world dropped away and the horror of the night became a hazy memory.

Raven's mouth opened and his tender lips pressed against hers in sharp contrast to the strong fingers digging into her sides, pulling her closer. Her tongue slid against his, and he tasted sweet and salty and she wanted more. A shudder worked its way down her spine. Her skin tingled wherever his fingers strayed—over her shoulders, her lower back, her stomach.

Raven wrapped his arms around her. His skin, which had always been warmer than hers, burned against her shoulders, stomach, and arms. Her fingers tangled in the locks of his hair and knocked the turban off his head. The stone bracer on her knee cut into her skin; a prick of pain rose up her leg. Bruises on her elbows, her thighs, and her shoulders throbbed. She didn't care about any of those aches and scrapes. She only cared about the way Raven's hands massaged down her back to just above the leather padding around her waist. He hugged her to his chest, and his muscles twitched and hardened under her.

Xochi's pendant scraped across Surefire's chest as she moved higher and straddled Raven's torso. Now a cold stone against the bare skin above her leather bra, the amulet no longer channeled Xochi. Though a tiny, annoying voice warned Surefire that this was a trick. Her desire for Raven, the way his touch made her shiver and her skin sizzle at the same time, and the ache low in her belly were products of Xochi's power forcing her emotions into overdrive.

She tamped down the nagging voice. It didn't matter. Nothing mattered except this moment.

A phone rang next to the bed.

A phone?

She started to pull back, but Raven held her to him.

It continued to ring four more times then stopped. She cracked open her eyes and turned her head. Raven kissed her cheek, down her neck. His stubble scratched a path across her throat to her shoulder. Her eyes adjusted to the dark. From the side of the bed, light peaked in around drawn shades. Moving boxes filled the room. Red numbers on a digital clock on the nightstand showed that it was two o'clock in the afternoon. Next to that, a photo of her family stared accusingly at her.

Oh, no.

Raven flipped her over and stretched out to cover her. He kissed her ear, and she moaned. He sucked the base of her neck at the sensitive slope of her shoulder, and she shuddered.

The phone rang again. An annoying tap on the shoulder from the real word. The excited butterflies in her stomach turned into nervous bees.

"Wait," she pleaded against his lips, though she didn't stop kissing him.

He ignored her, and his tongue delved deeper into her mouth, caressing hers.

She pulled away. "We can't."

"Why not?" He slid his right hand over the leather wrapped around her breasts.

Back in time, far away from her sister's condo, from her bedroom, from her family, and from U-Sec, she and Raven were possible. What they were doing was possible.

Now her mind reeled. Panic rose in her chest. Her sister could be home. Someone could be watching, waiting for them.

"We can't," she stated again with more force.

"I don't understand." He raised his lips from her neck. His face paint no longer resembled an abstract snake but a Rorschach inkblot from her hands and lips running over it. "You want me. I want you. We're both adults."

"We're at my sister's place. She could be home."

He craned his neck. "Heather," he shouted. "You there?"

They both listened for a few seconds to the silent condo.

He stared back down at her. The edge of his mouth cocked into a smile. "All clear. You want me to hang a bra on the door or something?"

She narrowed her eyes, and he hung his head in resignation. Letting out an exasperated breath, he dragged his body off her and kneeled down by her legs.

"What's wrong?" Raven adjusted the loincloth between his legs. He proceeded to shed the leather shoulder pads.

Where to start?

She sat up and untied the bracer from her knee then removed the one on her elbow to buy time to consider her answer and cool her overheated body, but she couldn't stem the nervousness rattling her core.

"For starters, Ari is about to unleash a god and end the world," she said in a fast, furious tone. "I just made a high priest run screaming out of a temple before we materialized in my bedroom. And you're still on the FBI's Most Wanted list, so, technically, I'm harboring a fugitive at my sister's condo to add to my growing list of crimes."

"And none of this turns you on?" He gave her a devilish smile.

She huffed. Of course, he wouldn't be worried about this situation. He had nothing to lose. She arched a brow and met his eyes, deeper and bluer than she'd ever seen them. Damn, how she loved losing herself in his eyes. When he stared at her, she felt important, desired, like she was the center of the universe.

A universe about to be destroyed if they didn't focus on coming up with a plan.

"We have time." He motioned to the clock on the nightstand. "The Aztec feast day starts at midnight. We don't want to deliver the skull too soon. In fact, the later, the better. Less time for Ari to perform the ritual and more time for us to figure out how to stop him."

"How will we find him? We have no idea where he is."

"How did we get here?" he asked.

She furrowed her brow. "I said I wanted to go home."

"Yes, and then . . ." He motioned with his hand for her to continue.

"Then I touched your lips and the skull."

"We have a winner." He leaned forward. His fingertips tickled a path across her stomach. Her skin broke out in goosebumps. His hand moved lower and slipped under the leather belt.

"So, it worked like the ruby slippers? There's no place like home and all that," she offered.

"Yep."

Before his hand could move farther under the loincloth, she grabbed his wrist. "What did I look like at the ceremony?"

He removed his hand and scrubbed the other down his face. "I'll never understand how women can turn it off and on so quickly."

He rolled off her onto his back and stared up at the ceiling.

"Because we think with our minds, not our privates. Answer the question."

He laced his fingers behind his head. "Your eyes were black and your skin had this purplish hue. You smelled like Xochi, like tropical flowers, lavender. Your features even changed. At certain angles you looked like her."

"Is that the reason for all this?" She flapped her hands.

"All what?" His eyes flashed up at her.

"You coming on to me."

"If I'm not mistaken, you kissed me first."

"I obviously wasn't in my right mind." The annoying voice of reason she had stamped down came roaring to the forefront of her mind. "I was possessed by the goddess of love or lust or emotional issues . . . whatever she is. But she took over my body like Tezcatlipoca controls Ari using an amulet like this." She flicked up the necklace around her neck.

Raven shifted onto his side to face her. "She possessed you?"

Surefire nodded. "It was the only way to save you."

"Do you still feel her inside?" He searched her face.

"No." She removed her turban and shook out her hair. It fell in a knotty mess onto her shoulders. "But I was scared. I still wonder if we can trust her. It took all my strength to force her out, and she didn't want to let go."

Because Xochi wanted to use Surefire's body to touch Raven, get close to him. Anger boiled low inside her at the thought of Xochi using her like that. She wondered if that anger had helped her fend off Xochi.

She unclasped the necklace and set it down on the nightstand just in case Xochi had any more urges.

"I appreciate what you did." Raven cut a glance at his chest, and Surefire's eyes fell to the red slash above his heart, slicing through a wing of his raven tattoo. "I had no idea you had to go through that to save me."

"It's fine. I'm fine. It's over now." She slumped against the headboard and untied the leather band around her waist.

"Thank you." He lifted his hand and touched her cheek. She tried to ignore the flush following his touch, but it blossomed and moved lower down her chest.

"Just returning the favor." She wanted to close her eyes and rub her cheek against his palm, so warm and comforting against her skin. Instead, she pulled away and scooted across the bed. She needed to focus, and every time he touched her, she lost herself, her control, her reason.

"Are you still weak?" she asked.

"I don't have all my abilities. I can't phase out or do any powerlifting. This skull is sucking at me like a very big, very persistent tick."

"Xochi said the stronger power feeds on the weaker one. That's why the skull didn't affect her possession of me."

He closed his eyes. His features clenched in concentration.

"What are you doing?"

"Trying to block it or even suck some of the power back into me like I could somewhat do with Ari." His eyes popped open and swirled black and blue and violet, his pupils and irises liquefying and then swirling together. He blinked and his eyes returned to normal. "It takes a lot of willpower, but with practice I might block it at least."

Surefire scanned the boxes and tried to remember where she'd packed her work clothes. In a few days, she was supposed to move into a new apartment. Now she wondered if her new home would be a jail cell. She started to slide out of the bed when Raven grabbed her wrist and stopped her.

"Where are you going?"

"To get changed."

"No, you're not." His fingers trailed up her arm.

She stared fixedly down at her hands clasped in her lap. She couldn't chance a look at him because this feeble control she'd gained would be lost. "This can't happen."

He yanked her down onto the bed. Her breath caught in her throat. He held her hands up over her head and lay on top of her. She couldn't move, tethered to the bed by his strong hands and body pinning her down. Even with the skull tapping into his abilities, he was preternaturally stronger than any man she'd been with.

This just made her heart beat that much faster. How would it feel to have such power make love to her?

He lowered his head so his lips were just above hers, not quite touching.

"When I had that knife stuck in me, I got through it because of you. Your promise that we could be together helped me focus. Now, I'm telling you, get out of your own way so we can enjoy a few moments of pleasure before the shit hits the metaphysical fan."

I got through it because of you. Her mind warned her it was a line. Her body, flushing and aching in places where she didn't have any bruises, was ready to screw logic.

Her conscience made one last ditch effort. "It's impossible."

"For us to be together?" His brows lifted. "If you're worried about Xochi," he stopped, uncertainty creasing his forehead, and Surefire wondered what Xochi had said to him about their relationship, if Xochi had threatened him away from Surefire.

"I'll deal with her." He smiled reassuringly.

"What about Kat?"

"Kat?" His eyes squinted in bewilderment.

"You know, the only-woman-you-ever-cared-about Kat?" Fury and—she hated to admit it—jealousy tore through her veins and tensed every muscle. She squirmed under his grip. How could she forget about Kat?

How could he?

His features pinched in disgust. His upper lip curled. "*That* Kat?"

"Yeah, the one who keeps her clothes at your place?"

"Oh, no." He made an ick-face. "You're talking *Flowers in the Attic.* That's a real turn-off."

"Kat's your sister?" It was Surefire's turn to look confused.

"Yes, and you thought she was my . . . Oh, wow. No."

"Sorry, I just assumed, because I never heard anyone talk about a sibling in that way."

"I practically raised Kat." He let go of Surefire's hands and moved off her. "My mom bailed on us when I was ten. Kat was only five. My dad had no idea what to do with a girl. I think she resembled my mom too much for him to deal with her."

"I'm sorry." She eased up and crossed her legs.

"It is what it is." He shrugged. "I made sure she was safe. I put her through college and then grad school. And kept her in the dark about what Dad and I did for a living. Part of my deal with Xochi is that my sister would be taken care of. That I could still see her. After my dad died, she was all I had left. Well, all I cared for. Ari was always a narcissistic prick."

"Does that explain things?" He faced her expectantly.

"Yeah." She reddened, embarrassed for thinking the worst.

"For the past few years, I've been by myself. The last relationship I had was with an upstanding woman who turned me in to the cops out of spite. She loved me for my money and hated when I wouldn't spend it on her. It's not the first time a man misjudged a woman."

"Then what happened?"

"Ari hired some hotshot lawyers and got the charges dropped with the intention of me paying him back by helping with the temple heist in Mexico."

"Which is how you ended up here."

"And now you know the rest of the story." He waved his hand in the air.

She eased back against the headboard and then picked up the picture of her family set on her nightstand.

Raven had shared a bit about himself, and she wanted to return the favor. Something about him, his calmness or his openness, made her want to share as well.

"What's wrong with this picture?" She handed it to him.

He studied the image of her father, mother, and sister with Surefire, who was in her young teens. The women were dressed in ball gowns. Her father in a tuxedo. They stood in the interior of the White House with a tall, ornately decorated Christmas tree in the background.

"Besides the bad hair?" he noted.

"Aside from that." Her mom had insisted they keep their hair short in a Peter Pan cut. Less hassle when performing.

She pointed to her face. Raven peered closer.

"Your eyes are the same color. Did someone touch up the photo?"

"No." She placed the frame back on the nightstand. "My father made me wear contacts so my eye color matched."

"Why?"

"Because he wanted us to be perfect, down to the way we looked."

"That's a lot of pressure for a young girl." Raven squeezed her hand.

"Tell me about it. He and my mom expected even more from us when competing. For my mom, it was her reputation on the line. She was an Olympic medalist turned coach who ran a gymnastics school. Heather and I were walking advertisements for her school." She crossed her arms and blew out a breath. "My father must've had a lot of money tied up in the school or maybe something else on the line. I don't know. He was more upset than my mom when I didn't make the team. At least she told me years later that she forgave me. My dad on the other hand . . ." She lifted a shoulder. "Our relationship was never the same."

"What happened that day?" He propped himself onto his elbow and looked up at her.

"My sister happened." She sighed then stared down at her duvet cover, decorated with purple and beige abstract flowers. "I was dating this guy, Seth. I'd met him on the gymnastic circuit. Knew him since we were kids. I saw him behind my parents' back, which was hard, trust me. They kept close tabs on us. Heather was jealous. She was jealous my dad and I were close. She was jealous that I'd started winning gymnastics competitions, even though I couldn't care less about the sport. I only did it to make my parents happy."

Surefire ran a finger along the back of Raven's hand, over the fine black hairs on the back of his fingers. "So, during my routine, she took Seth into the stands in my line of sight and made out with him. I saw them, got distracted, and missed the beam during my dismount. I broke my nose and blew out my knee, ending my career."

She touched the bump on her nose. "And now you know the rest of my story."

"Sounds like the women I've dated. I'm sorry."

Surefire bowed her head and shrugged. "Heather didn't realize it would turn out the way it did or how it would affect the family. And, in her own way, she's tried to make up for it. Of course, if I had gone on to win any medals, they would've taken them away."

"Transhuman testing." Raven nodded. "Several athletes have been fined and stripped of their medals in the last few years."

"They weren't testing at the time I was competing, but now it's standard practice, just like steroid testing. The Olympic committee made it retroactive and is reviewing videos from up to twenty years ago and forcing some unnaturally good athletes to take the test."

"How did you find out you were a transhuman?"

"I was required to take the test before I could enter college. Now health insurance companies are making applicants undergo testing for genetic enhancements. Unfortunately, it's causing discrimination, especially when looking for work. U-Sec employs many transhumans with no interest in law enforcement, because it's the only place they could get a job."

"I hadn't heard about that."

"Most on the outside haven't. The media has been more focused on the dangers posed by transhumans than their benefits to society or any discrimination."

"How did it happen to you?"

She shrugged again. "I don't know."

Though a part of her did know, and she wasn't ready to say that possible fact out loud. She reached over and placed the family photo facedown on the nightstand.

"It's strange," she said. "I never pictured you like this. I just pegged you as a—"

"Sociopathic criminal?"

"More like a selfish, egotistical con artist."

"Don't get me wrong. I was never a saint. I stole because it gave me a lifestyle I couldn't afford otherwise. It made my father happy—which was rare—to have his son working with him." He dropped his eyes and ran his hand over the duvet. "And I was good at it. It was easy. It gave me a rush. Still does."

"How do you feel about it now?"

"It was wrong what I did. I returned what I could from my former life, but I'm atoning for my sins now." He let out a cynical laugh. "In fact, I'm atoning for my sins at this moment. The first woman I ever truly wanted, and she doesn't want me. I can't think of a more apt punishment."

Surefire pivoted to sit on the edge of the bed with her feet dangling above the floor. "I didn't say I didn't want you."

"Come again?" He tried to don an innocent expression that didn't work on him. His eyes were too intense, rimmed with dark lashes that should've made his eyes softer but made them deeper, more seductive. His body was all male, down to his well-defined abs underneath his ink and the dark trail of hair starting at his bellybutton and disappearing under his loincloth.

She blushed when his lids lowered and a wicked smile played across his lips, hinting at the not-so-innocent things on his mind.

"You heard me." She tore herself away from his heated gaze and hopped off the bed. "But it's just that . . ." She struggled to say what went against everything she felt. "It's not right."

He sat up and she had to look away, upset by the hurt clinging on his handsome face. "If I wasn't this creature bound to Xochi, would it change your mind?"

Surefire put her back to Raven and focused on finding clean underwear in a half-packed suitcase on the floor. "I don't care about that. I mean, it sucks about Xochi's hold over you. But I'd never consider you some sort of creature."

The bed creaked behind her. His feet hit the floor with a soft thump. She felt him standing behind her, looming. His body heat radiated against her back. She felt small, vulnerable, and she didn't know why.

"If I wasn't a wanted man, if you weren't a U-Sec agent, then this would work. You know it would. We're not that different."

Surefire sucked on her bottom lip. He was right. On many levels, they were the same. They had both ended up in this mess because they wanted to please someone else. Wanted respect. Wanted love. They'd both made mistakes and were trying to atone for them.

If Surefire gave in and slept with Raven and anyone found out about it, how would it look? What would they think of her? What kind of agent would she be, sleeping with her target? It was bad enough she'd partnered with him to stop Ari. Her reputation and motives were already in question by the authorities, her bosses, and—she knew deep in her gut—her family.

"There's another bathroom in the hall, around the corner. You can use that one to clean up. Then we'll head out."

She walked into the adjacent bathroom and closed the door. And immediately regretted it.

She stared at her reflection in the mirror. The face paint was smeared and smudged from Raven's kisses. No longer a monkey but a bluish blob.

She turned on the shower to let it warm up. Then she grabbed a washcloth, dampened it with cool water and began scrubbing her face—harder and harder until her cheeks were red and the paint was washed away. She would forget about Raven. About how he made her feel. About how she wanted him. It was wrong to feel this way, to even consider being with him in the midst of all that had happened, was happening. All that was about to happen.

These weren't the actions of a U-Sec agent, of a St. John. She'd disappoint Pax, her father, maybe even herself.

Raven knocked on the bathroom door. She turned off the faucet and dropped the cloth. She wiped at the tears streaming down her face. She hadn't even realized she'd been crying.

"Do you have a towel I could use? I don't see any in the guest bath," he asked through the closed door.

"Just a second." She grabbed an extra set before throwing open the door.

Raven looked down at her and squinted. His brow creased when he met her eyes, which were stinging from tears she struggled to hold in. "What's wrong?"

Her heart melted along with her guard when he looked at her with such care and concern. Damn it. That's why her body warmed when he was near and why she was willing to give in to desires she'd otherwise ignore.

She couldn't remember when anyone had looked at her in that way. Had bothered to ask how she felt. Had even cared about how she felt.

She grabbed his arm and yanked him inside the bathroom. She wanted to kiss him. Now.

She stood on tiptoes and brushed his lips with her own.

He put his hands on her shoulders and gently pushed her down. "What's this?"

"I changed my mind."

His body stilled before he inched closer, and she stepped back. Any trace of worry disappeared from his face. He seemed taller, stronger than she'd ever perceived him before. His presence filled up the bathroom, made her breath hitch in her throat.

His eyes flicked with a purplish light before darkening to a deep blue. He leaned down so his lips were against her ear. His voice deepened into a low growl.

"Once we start, I won't stop this time."

She touched his smooth chest and traced the raven tattoo with her index finger. His muscles twitched underneath her fingertip.

"I wouldn't want you to, James," she whispered.

♥ ☠ ♥ ☠ ♥ ☠

He covered her mouth with his. She was so much smaller than him, seemed so fragile. With Xochi's powers, he needed to be gentle. Hold back, so he didn't hurt her.

But he didn't want to hold back. He wanted to feel everything, wanted her to feel how much he desired her.

He reached down and picked her up. She was light, yet curvy. Soft. So soft, even with her well-toned legs and arms, that he wanted her skin pressed as close to him as possible. Her hair tickled his chest and shoulders. She returned his kiss with a feverish intensity he hadn't expected, making his desire burn hotter until every touch, every kiss made him insane with the need to be inside her. He propped her up on the granite sink. His hands palmed her small breasts. Under his palm, he felt her heart beating steady and strong and sure. For a second, he swore his heart pumped out a minuscule beat in response.

He sucked on her neck and ran his thumbs over her nipples. She groaned. The ache in his groin intensified. He'd explode if he didn't take her. Now.

She spread her legs. He tore off his loincloth.

"Synthia."

"Do it." Her voice was urgent.

He ripped off her leather bra and then her loincloth. His fingers played with her, testing her. She was ready, and he was beyond ready.

He slid inside her. Her head fell back, and she moaned louder with every thrust. His hands wrapped around her sides, forcing her closer and holding her in place. He kept his pace measured. Somehow he pulled back on the throttle.

"Harder," she begged.

"I don't want to hurt you."

Her fingers entwined in his hair, forcing him to look at her. "You won't."

"You have no idea." He pulled her hair back and kissed her neck. The bruise from Ari had faded.

He delved deeper and harder, but still didn't unleash himself totally. He wouldn't hurt her even it meant never experiencing the full extent of his strength in bed again, as he could with Xochi.

That didn't matter to him. Being close to Synthia was all that mattered.

Raven lifted his eyes to stare into her two-toned ones, like shiny jewels, half-closed as she arched her back. Beautiful. Erotic.

Hot water cascaded from the shower and heated the room. He kissed her neck again and licked a line up her moist skin. She shuddered against him. He couldn't hold back anymore. The orgasm crested, and he let himself ride it to the climatic end.

Panting, Synthia leaned back with her head resting against the mirror, clouded with steam. "That was amazing."

He rested his head on her shoulder, which was moist with perspiration. She gently scratched her nails down his sides. He edged down to her nipple and took it into his mouth. She drew in a breath.

He picked her up, and she wrapped her legs around his backside, holding him inside her. Walking to the bedroom, he kissed her mouth, so sweet, so intoxicating. Slowly, he grew hard again inside her. Her nails dug into his back. He knocked over a stack of moving boxes before he eased her down onto the bed.

"Again, I want you again," he whispered.

Pax's truck barreled down St. Paul Street. Oracle leaned forward in the passenger seat with her hands against the dashboard. They had been driving for over forty minutes, weaving in and out of Baltimore's streets from their offices on Route 40 as Oracle honed in on the odd disturbance and directed Pax.

"Pull over."

Pax slid his truck into a parking spot to his right. Oracle jumped out and stood in the middle of the pavement with her arms outstretched and her head held back. Several people walked by, making a large circle to avoid her.

Oracle hopped back into the truck. "Drive. We're going in the right direction."

They hit a few lights and two construction zones that detoured them onto a bumpy side street before merging onto Light Street.

Fifteen minutes passed, and Pax could see Pratt Street a block ahead.

"We're at the harbor. Which way?" Pax's fingers tapped the steering wheel.

"Pull over in front of the Pratt Street Pavilion," Oracle said, without hesitation.

He turned onto Pratt and whipped into a spot reserved for emergency vehicles in front of the pavilion. An officer appeared from behind a pole and waved his arms at them.

Oracle opened the door.

"Sir, you can't park here." The officer jogged over to the passenger door.

Pax took out his U-Sec identification. He handed it to Oracle, and she held it out to the officer. Pax glanced at the man's badge: Officer Paul Stevens.

"We're working with Detective David Matthews, Criminal Investigation Division, Transhuman Unit," Pax stated.

Stevens studied Pax's ID then handed it back. "I know Matthews. Do we need to secure the area? Is there an immediate threat?"

"None so far. We're following a lead." Pax wasn't sure how else to describe it or even explain it.

"Keep me posted. I'll inform the other officers about what you're doing. Let me know if you need backup." He motioned for them to exit the vehicle and then stepped away to call it in on his radio.

Pax wanted to remember this officer's information. Most on the force cringed when they encountered U-Sec. Stevens didn't even bat an eye.

Oracle was already walking toward the water. With a few long strides, Pax caught up to her and took her hand so she could see. She pulled him around the building and down the pier where the Constellation was docked.

"Over there." She pointed across the water.

Pax squinted in the sunlight glaring off the harbor and wished for his shades. "Can you be more specific? Federal Hill? Or maybe the marina? Fort McHenry is to the left, but I can't see it from here."

She moved forward toward the edge of the pier. "Around there. Perhaps between them. I'm not sure, but I'm feeling a tug from that direction. It's stronger here."

Pax scanned the area from the Science Center to a marina to a seafood restaurant. Then it dawned on him. "Heather owns a condo at the Harborview just across the water. For the past few months, Synthia's been living with her. Do you think she's there?"

Oracle nodded. "It makes sense. She could be back in this world, and this odd disturbance could be blocking her from me. I've learned my lesson about opening up fully with a presence like this around."

They walked briskly back to the truck. Pax made a few phone calls for backup and the last one to St. John. If Synthia was there, he wasn't losing her again.

♥ ♀ ♥ ♀ ♥ ♀

Surefire pulled her U-Sec uniform from the dryer. As she did, her sister's cat, Prada, purred against her leg and looked longingly up at the fabric clutched in her hand.

"Not this time." She shoved the cat away with the side of her foot. "Damn furball."

"I need clothes and shoes." Raven poked his head into the laundry room wearing only a towel wrapped around his waist.

"Across the living room is my sister's bedroom. Hunter keeps some of his stuff there. Not sure about his sizes though."

"Hunter Thompson?"

"Yeah, why?"

Raven groaned.

Surefire blinked, confused by the disgust on his face. Then she remembered. "Is it because he plays for the Ravens?"

His lips twitched, and he looked down. "I guess his funk won't wear off on me."

"Are you serious?" She'd never understood men and their sport's team obsessions.

Raven shrugged and walked away in the direction of her sister's room.

She pulled her mask from the dryer then reconsidered. The sole reason for hiding her identity was to keep her family safe. Dozens of officers and guards, not to mention security cameras, had seen her face. She didn't want to turn on the news, afraid of what she might find.

Oh, shit. She stood abruptly, and her stomach dropped. *Heather.*

If the public saw Surefire working for U-Sec and that she was a transhuman, did they believe Heather could be a transhuman as well? Were Heather's medals and sponsorships now in question?

Pushing the thought aside, Surefire ambled out of the laundry room and into the hall. Her sister could handle herself. She always had, even if it meant throwing a sibling under the bus. Surefire would cross that road when she came to it.

Surefire shut the door to her bedroom. Her eyes trailed over the boxes near the doorway. Some were knocked over, their contents spilled.

She blushed and hugged her U-Sec uniform to her chest.

What have I done?

Xochi had said her power only encouraged attraction to grow from what was already rooted. Could she even trust these feelings to be real? Even now, with him in the other room, she missed him. His warmth, his tenderness. She wanted his arms around her. Just the image of his hands on her body sent a tingle across her chest.

Good Lord, what was wrong with her?

She slipped into her one-piece black uniform. It was formfitting to allow ease of movement, like rock-climbing clothes.

She needed to nip these feelings in the bud at once. She'd had her fun. Blew off steam. Now she needed to focus on the task at hand. Anything between them would only be a distraction. This time it wasn't some trifle like a medal at stake, it was the fate of the world.

Besides, it wasn't as if they could ever be together as a couple with the white picket fence and yard with yapping dogs and pool parties and summer cookouts and vacations down the ocean.

After the stunts she'd pulled recently, she'd be lucky to have a janitorial job at U-Sec, if she didn't end up in jail. Raven would go back to Xochi, since she literally held his life in her hands.

It was easy to forget that part. Considering how the world viewed transhumans, she hadn't felt particularly human in a long time.

Her eyes watered, and she nearly tripped over the skull, which was lying on its side staring straight up at the bed. Nothing swirled inside the crystal. Its empty sockets stared upward from the top of wide, delicate cheekbones. She peered more closely and wondered whether that bone structure could be Xochi's. It was smaller up close than she recalled, about the size of her own head.

Prada rounded the corner of the bed. Her back arched when she bumped into the skull. She let out an irked meow and ran into Surefire's open closet.

Maybe the crystal skull did have its merits.

The television clicked on in the living room, followed by the whir of the microwave. Raven must've found her leftover steak from the other night, when Heather had forced Synthia on a blind date with Hunter's friend.

That had been a big mistake. Apparently, the jock had trouble with a woman beating him at pool. If he hadn't been so obnoxious about it, she might've thrown a game to ease his ego.

She sat on the bed and slid on her fitted shoes, made especially for climbing with enough support for running as well. She opened the drawer in the nightstand and grabbed her backup utility belt. It didn't have all the bells and whistles of the one she had discarded in the Garden, but it did have her dart gun, which might come in handy when confronting Ari. She slammed the drawer shut, and the phone fell off its base and onto the carpet.

She stared at it, afraid to touch it. It had been over twelve hours since she had last talked to anyone from U-Sec or even her family. It might as well have been a lifetime ago as far removed as that world seemed to her now.

She picked up the phone to hang it up as Raven whipped open her door. He wore one of Hunter's fitted white T-shirts and distressed designer jeans, a bit baggy on him, and dark leather tennis shoes. He saw the phone in her hands, and before she could explain, he ran across the room and tore it from her grasp.

"What did you do?" he demanded, low and spiteful.

She swallowed. "I . . . uh . . ."

"They're dead."

"Who?"

"Look for yourself." He lifted her up by her arm and pulled her into the living room.

On Heather's large television was a grainy video of Surefire at the museum, lying on the step, mouthing into the camera. She grabbed the back of the sofa as her knees wobbled. In her haze, she'd forgotten about the museum.

"Why?" Raven glared at her. "I told you not to. You have no idea what Ari will do." His voice sounded hollow, disapproving. No love. No lightness and caring. Nothing. He'd turned it off just like that. Because she hadn't listened. Because she'd made a mistake. Because she'd failed him.

"I was scared," she admitted, too ashamed and angry with herself to argue.

"It's too late." He gestured at the TV. On the screen was her sister being interviewed. Surefire couldn't hear her sister's words as a male voice spoke over the video feed. *"This is a shot of Olympic gold medalist Heather St. John being interviewed just three hours ago about Synthia St. John, her sister, an UltraAgent, who went missing last night while tracking a transhuman thief known for several high-profile international heists and most recently several thefts in our local museums and from local collectors. Heather St. John disappeared from the Chevy Chase home of her fiancé—Ravens' quarterback Hunter Thompson. We will have more information on this startling turn of events when the police make it available."*

Raven clicked it off.

"I caused that," Surefire said softly to herself and dug her fingers into the sofa's low-back cushion, afraid she'd pass out. Her heart sank with the realization that because of her, Heather was in danger. Surefire had broken her promise, and Ari had taken her sister. "What about your sister?"

"Missing. I just tried calling her apartment. Her roommate said she disappeared from her bedroom."

"Oh, God, I'm so sorry."

He shoved past her and headed to her room. She trailed behind him. "What are you going to do?"

"I've got to find Ari now." He grabbed the skull and closed his eyes, but nothing happened.

"What the hell?" He threw the skull down on the bed. "It worked before."

She reached down and picked up the skull. It felt heavier, or maybe she was just weaker.

"Remember what you said earlier? We need to touch. I'm the conduit." She put out her hand to him. His hand remained fisted, as if he didn't want to touch her. He stared at the skull and wouldn't even glance up at her. She looked away, pain squeezing her heart at his coldness.

From the living room came a loud knocking on the door.

"Synthia, it's your father. Open up."

Raven reluctantly bent forward and placed one hand on the skull. His other hand clasped Surefire's.

It still didn't work. He dropped her hand and ran his over his face. She recalled the other part of the equation.

"We need the necklace." She grabbed it from the nightstand. Clasping it around her neck, she tucked it into her uniform. "It's what makes me the conduit."

The knocking grew louder, echoing across the condo, followed by the sound of the latch unlocking.

Surefire touched his arm and then the skull, and the room dropped away.

Chapter Twenty

Pax hung back in the private elevator foyer with Oracle. They were crammed behind five police officers Matthews had sent for backup. Next to Pax, TimeTrap yawned and leaned her head against the closed elevator doors.

In front of the group, St. John thumped his fist on the door of Heather's condo.

Pax's forearm throbbed where Oracle held onto him with a death-grip intensity. She drew this strange force to her like a magnet to metal, and they weren't sure why it affected her so strongly. As they closed in on the source, the disturbance pressed against her psychic shields, trying to burrow inside her mind. When they had entered the building, Oracle had had to fight to keep the suffocating force out. Pax had told her repeatedly to stay outside or take a cab back to the office. She had refused his request—no surprise there. Oracle was Surefire's mentor, and she wanted to be here if they found her. It was bad enough she couldn't open her mind to search Surefire out, and Oracle didn't want to desert Surefire when she needed her the most.

Because when the police found Surefire, they planned to arrest her.

Pax prayed Matthews could get the warrant overturned or buy time until they spoke with Surefire first.

Oracle's muscles seized, and he thought she'd crack from the strain. An image of the room tinged with an odd purplish haze materialized inside her grey-white eyes. She snapped her eyes shut.

He began to second-guess his decision to let her stay. When her body trembled, he feared she was losing the battle.

"Oracle, I want you to go." Pax hit the down button.

She shook her head and pressed her lips so tightly together they paled to a milky pink.

"It's your father. Open up." St. John banged three more times before unlocking the door and shoving it open.

Pax nudged Oracle in front of the elevator.

Oracle's eyes popped open. The violet haze clouding her vision dissolved to white. She let out a gasp. Her muscles relaxed. She released Pax's arm.

St. John charged through the doorway with the police in his wake. Pax lost sight of him in the crush of bodies funneling into the condo's entranceway.

"Heather!" St. John yelled. His commanding voice echoed inside. "Heather, are you here? Synthia?"

"It's weakened." Oracle stepped back and propped herself up against the wall.

"What's going on?" TimeTrap lifted her sunglasses and eyed Oracle with trepidation. She pushed away from the elevator doors just before they slid open. "Is she okay?"

"I'm good." Oracle waved both of them off. "Give me room to breathe."

Pax and TimeTrap scooted back. The elevator pinged, and the doors closed behind them.

Oracle fanned herself with her hand. "Whatever it is, it's weaker now. Not fully gone. Just not as intense. Like when someone passes through a room with a strong perfume. It continues to linger even after the person leaves."

"And Synthia?" Pax asked.

Her shoulders slumped. "I don't know. I'm not about to open up."

Oracle inhaled a deep, chest-expanding breath before letting it out, slow and controlled. "See if you can find Surefire. I want to regroup. I'll be right behind you."

Pax hesitated, until Oracle glowered at him. "As I just said, I'm fine."

Pax nodded, eager to get inside. He turned and walked through the doorway into another foyer. Just past this entrance hall, he watched the police spread out across the great room and canvas the area. Several broke away from the group, guns drawn, and disappeared into a room to the left, off the main living area.

His gaze skimmed over the soaring ceilings, polished dark wood floors, and posh modern living room, way larger than his first apartment, which opened up to a wall of windows overlooking the sun-brightened cityscape and harbor.

No doubt Heather's sponsorships paid well. Too bad she might lose them, if they didn't clear Synthia's name. Though that wouldn't matter much if Heather turned up dead. Pax quickly cleared away that thought.

He walked into the great room, and his stomach growled in response to the tasty aroma of steak. Someone had been cooking recently. The scent permeated the room.

Pax peered into the open doorway to his left. It led into an enormous, court-sized master bedroom that carried the minimalist theme of the great room. This decor caught him off-guard, because he expected a frilly, over-the-top princess theme to Heather's bedroom, not a platform bed flanked by boxy nightstands and a plain mahogany trunk at the base. Just beyond the open door, photos peppered the pale blue walls in thick wooden frames. He squinted when he noticed a black-and-white photo of Synthia kissing Heather's cheek—or maybe it was Heather kissing Synthia's cheek—at about ten years old.

An officer stepped between Pax and the photo and reported that the room was clear. Nothing amiss.

"Where's St. John?" Pax asked.

The man motioned his head toward the hallway off the dining area. "In Surefire's room."

Pax continued through the great room toward the kitchen and formal dining area, which narrowed into a hallway. If the great room was larger than his first apartment, he could probably fit his current townhouse inside this entire condo with room to spare.

TimeTrap sauntered in past Pax and flopped down onto the grey, sterile sofa in front of a super-sized flat-screen television.

"Nice digs." She blew out a bubble and picked up a tabloid magazine from the dark wooden coffee table.

"What are you doing?" Pax demanded.

"Ahhh . . . reading a magazine." She held up a two-page spread and pointed at a photo of a couple embracing. "Hey, here's Heather and Hunter. I really don't know what he sees in her."

"Put that down *now*. I need your help finding Surefire."

She pushed her shades up onto her head. "Thought she wasn't here."

"No one said that."

"She's not here." St. John marched into the living room from the hallway.

"See, told you." TimeTrap settled back against the sofa with the magazine, and Pax thought his blood pressure couldn't pulse any higher.

"But I found this." St. John held up what looked like a cloth diaper and leather bra. "In the guest room where Synthia's been staying."

"Wow, someone likes to role play," TimeTrap piped in.

St. John jeered, "Are all your agents this insolent?"

"For their sakes, no." He gave TimeTrap a heated look that reflected the frustration burning through his body.

TimeTrap held the magazine up to her face and began reading it with exaggerated interest. Pax pushed past St. John and jogged down the hall and into the room St. John had indicated belonged to Surefire.

His eyes shot to the sheets in disarray. He picked his way over a few moving boxes tipped onto the floor. Various clothes and personal items spilled over the cream carpet. Next to the bed lay a ripped-up cloth similar to the one St. John held in his hand. Piled up next to it were various leather pieces and stone bracers with red and yellow feathers peeking out.

"This wasn't here before," Pax said to St. John, who had followed him into the bedroom. After Synthia had disappeared, Heather had allowed U-Sec's agents to search her condo, and no one had noted any strange costumes.

Pax poked his head into the adjacent bathroom. A crumpled white towel lay on the floor with another hung up unevenly. Both were damp. Drops of water clung to the shower head.

With officers stationed outside the building, Surefire had to have entered the condo by a different entrance and left the same way. Or maybe . . . Pax's eyes darted around the room, searching for another explanation for their disappearing act.

Then he saw it.

"I think she was here," Pax said.

"Synthia?" St. John asked with no shortage of incredulity. "Why didn't she notify us?" His gaze landed on her bed, and his gray eyes turned to steel. His hands wrung the leather pieces together. "Maybe she is involved with that Raven character. If she did this to us, I'll kill her."

"I don't really blame her. Raven is hot." TimeTrap plopped onto the bed. "Twice in a row, he made the Top 10 Hot Transhumans list that us girls put together."

"One more word." St. John stood shaking in the doorway and pointing the leather bra at her. "One more godforsaken word from your idiotic mouth, and so help me you'll find yourself trapped in a—"

She disappeared.

"Damn it, Stephen. We need her." Pax met his harsh gaze with one of his own.

St. John huffed. "A lot of good she's done us so far. My dog would've been more helpful and more respectful." He finally glanced down at the bra he had used to threaten TimeTrap. He threw it to the ground with a disgusted grunt.

"TimeTrap knew the black cloud was a dimensional portal, and she may know what that is above us." Pax pointed at the ceiling, where a cloud of white smoke was beginning to thin out.

"A portal through space in our universe." TimeTrap appeared on top of a wooden dresser. She gazed up at it. "It gives off a different vibe. More positive. This one's not sucking my power away like the dimensional one. I can work with it." She laced her fingers and cracked her knuckles, ready to tackle a project.

"Are you willing to play nice, General Jarhead?" She removed the sunglasses from her head and placed them on the dresser.

Pax was relieved when St. John ignored her quip and replied, "I want my daughter back."

"Find Surefire." It wasn't lost on him that St. John had used the singular form of "daughter."

"Yes, sir." She saluted Pax.

TimeTrap maneuvered around the boxes and grabbed a chair across from the floor-to-ceiling windows. She raised her skirt higher on her thighs so she could lift her legs and stand on the chair. However, even with her platform boots, she couldn't reach the swirling white cloud.

"Wait. Do you have your locator?" Pax asked. Oliver had created a device to track her, even in different time periods.

"I left it at home." She spread out her palms and bit her bottom lip. "Sorry, I was off the clock this weekend."

Pax moved to stand under her. He pulled out a digital wristwatch from his inside jacket pocket. "Wear this. It's got a GPS built in. If you're still in our time period then we can at least find you."

She took it out of his hand and stared at the flashing red light. "It doesn't really match my outfit."

Pax didn't offer a reply, hoping to God she was joking.

Her frosted pink lips stretched into a toothy smile.

"Paxie, you're such a stiff. Of course, I'll wear it. It's very mod." She slipped it around her wrist. "Can you give me a lift?"

Pax wrapped his hands around her calves over her patent leather boots.

"Just raise me up a tad, but don't sneak a peek. I'm not wearing any underwear."

"What?" Pax's gaze shot up to her face.

She shrugged and gave him an impish grin. "Like I said, I wasn't on the clock."

"Christ almighty," St. John swore. "And my daughter's life is in her hands. Unbelievable." With that, St. John shoved past three officers rubbernecking in the doorway and left the room.

Pax lifted her up.

"Report back the first chance you get." He wasn't certain she heard him, because a second later the portal sucked her up and away, and everyone could see she was indeed going commando.

As soon as Surefire's hand touched Raven's arm, the skull glowed and a white light encircled them. It pulsated, throbbed, and grew to cover their bodies—a sentient being attaching itself to them like a second skin. Raven had the sensation of being ripped apart and put back together, but it happened too fast. There was no pain, merely a stinging sensation in his muscles down to his bones.

He didn't remember this ripped-apart feeling when they had travelled from the past to Surefire's room, although he'd been distracted at the time with the knife wound and her lips on his and all that.

Raven pulled his arm out of Surefire's grip and held the skull tight to his chest. His eyes skimmed the dimly lit room where they'd materialized. It had a low ceiling and three stone walls, with the fourth wall opening into a hallway lined by lit torches. They were in a temple's inner chamber—not unlike the one Ari had led him into years before.

Without a word, he turned from Surefire and ran down the corridor. All he wanted was to find his sister and stop Ari. He should've known Surefire wouldn't keep her promise. She was a woman. It was a given.

A prick of guilt stuck like a thorn in his gut. He tried to ignore it, but a part of him couldn't blame her for what she had done. He had left her alone and in pain, dying under the jaws of a T. rex skeleton, no less. She'd been scared. What else should she have done?

From the winding corridor behind him, Surefire shouted for him to stop. He continued on his forward trek, though his gait slowed slightly.

And what about him? The thorn grew larger until guilt nudged out his anger. If Surefire's crime was breaking a promise under duress, his was far worse. He had taken advantage of her. He had caved in to his desires—desires which caused a strange tightening in his chest and many other places anytime he thought of her, looked at her. They could never have a real relationship. He could never give her the life she deserved. Not with him bound to Xochi. Not with Xochi pulling the strings. Not with Xochi's essence keeping him alive.

But Surefire made him forget all that. Maybe that's why he fell for her. She made him feel normal again.

He rounded a sharp turn, and by some trick, the corridor grew longer with his every stride forward. Did this hallway ever end? He'd turn eighty before he reached another chamber.

Something large buzzed his ear. A bumblebee? A dragonfly? He swatted at it, and the thing landed on his back. Four thick legs clung to the white, overpriced T-shirt he'd snagged from Hunter's drawer in Heather's apartment-sized walk-in closet.

Raven knocked the insect off, not wanting to lose focus. Nothing was going to stop him from reaching Ari and finding his sister—not even an enormous bug with a vise-like grip.

"Raven." Surefire's voice echoed behind him. "Wait up."

The corridor cut to the right, and her words faded away. In his hand, the crystal skull heated and started to glow with a purple, opaque light. He slowed down, growing weaker as the skull grew brighter. Losing a pint of blood would be less draining than being near this energy-sucking skull. He closed his eyes and concentrated on reeling his power back in.

A sharp nail tapped his shoulder.

"How did you catch up so fast?" Raven spun around, expecting to see Surefire, and nearly dropped the skull.

"Hello, James," the woman chirped in a voice he used to find cute and perky but now found contrived and annoying.

"Bella?" He nearly choked.

She twirled before him in a too-short silk robe of yellow and light blue that flared out from her skinny thighs to reveal gold, sparkly panties. Two paper-thin wings—made from what looked like pink nylon and carbon fiber—were folded against her back, and he couldn't tell if they were attached by a harness under her dress or directly to her spine.

"Call me Pixie." Her girlish voice sounded twelve even though she was pushing thirty.

Surefire's light steps echoed from the corridor behind Pixie, who tossed back her black kinky hair and winked a pale green eye at Raven. She moved to his side to face Surefire as she jogged to a stop in front of them.

"You didn't look . . ." Surefire leaned against the wall while she strove to catch her breath. ". . . like you were moving that fast."

She narrowed her eyes and looked Pixie up and down. "What are you doing here?"

"You know each other?" Raven asked.

"She's an UltraAgent," Surefire replied.

"*Was* an UltraAgent." Pixie straightened her back, looking too pleased with herself. "I've switched teams."

Surefire's lips set into a determined line. "Then you're the reason Ari knew my identity. You're why my sister is missing."

Surefire's hand fell to the dart gun holstered on her belt.

Pixie darted behind Raven.

"Ah-uh." She wiggled her finger while she peeped over his shoulder. "Although, did you even check your weapons this time? Not very agent-like to run off without making sure things aren't hosed before you need to use them."

Surefire set her jaw. Her lips tightened and her eyes narrowed, reflecting the tension Raven could sense building inside her.

"Have you met my ex?" Seemingly oblivious to the ticking bomb in front of her, Pixie rubbed Raven's arm.

He pulled away. Her touch and her insinuation made his stomach churn with disgust. "Don't listen to her."

"What are you talking about?" Surefire's hand hovered over the gun.

"Raven and I were once lovers." She emphasized the word *lovers,* so that it hung in the air long after she spoke.

Raven shrunk back when he saw realization, then pain, creep across Surefire's face. Bella, or Pixie, whatever she called herself now, was making their relationship appear more important than it had been. The only thing memorable about their time together was her handing him over to the cops.

"What do you mean?" Surefire's brow wrinkled.

"Well, he's a boy and I'm a girl. Really, do I have to recite the birds and the fairies?"

Surefire pushed Raven out of the way and, with one smooth move, slammed Pixie up against the wall, pressing her forearm against her windpipe.

Pixie shrunk down to about six inches and flew to the ceiling.

"Big mistake, bitch," her tiny voice squeaked.

Pixie threw out her hands, and gold dust glittered and fell from her doll-sized fingertips. The shimmering particles obscured Raven's eyesight. Pixie, Surefire, and the corridor faded into a golden haze. He inhaled, and the glitter burned down his windpipe. He struggled to breathe; every breath created a scorching sensation in his lungs. Clutching the skull, he put out his hand to find the wall, Surefire, anything. Repeatedly his hand swiped through the cold, gold mist, to no avail.

His head spun. Black spots floated across his vision. The skull slipped from his fingers, but he didn't hear it hit the stone floor. He mouthed Surefire's name, because he didn't have the breath to speak it.

The black spots grew until they obscured his vision, and his mind clouded. Before he lost consciousness, Raven could've sworn he heard another voice calling Surefire's name from somewhere down the hall.

♥ ☠ ♥ ☠ ♥ ☠

As Pax entered the living room, an agent flicked on the television. One of the twenty-four-hour news channels blared across the screen, rerunning the interview with Heather and recounting how they didn't know anything yet. They flashed to footage of Hunter's home and the officers standing guard outside. They mentioned Synthia as well, with experts commenting on her mental state and throwing out terms like Stockholm syndrome.

Enough.

Pax needed air, space. He stepped into the private elevator foyer where Oracle stood with her arms crossed, leaning against the wall.

"Pax?"

"Yeah."

"Thought it was you. I recognized your cologne."

Pax smiled to himself. Years ago, when they were first dating, Oracle had bought it for him as a birthday present. It was still his favorite.

"What are you doing out here?" He propped his shoulder on the wall next to her.

"Same thing you're doing." She treated him to that brilliant, white smile of hers. He always joked she could do toothpaste commercials.

"It's stuffy in there. Too much hot air."

"Considering the main source of it is downstairs making a phone call, I'd think the air would be clearer."

Pax snorted at her joke. "Who's he calling?"

"I believe it was his army contacts from what little I could make out before the elevator doors closed. Readying the troops for when we get a signal."

Pax reached into his pocket and pulled out a pack of gum. He offered a stick to Oracle.

"Have you taken a break yet? Maybe put into play some of those relaxation techniques Lily taught us last week?"

"Why are you asking me this?"

"You used to smoke when you were anxious and tired. Now you chew gum." She took the stick he held out to her.

She knew him too well.

"I'm afraid you might get an ulcer."

"And you're not stressed out?"

She lifted her slender shoulders. "I'd rather funnel that energy into something productive."

"Like what?" His voice rose through his exhaustion, finding insult in Oracle's statement when she only offered help. Why did she always have to talk to him as if she knew best? "And what could be more productive at this moment? It's been over forty-five minutes since TimeTrap got sucked into the portal and the cloud disappeared, and we haven't gotten any signal. I thought she might even pop back here. Maybe take one of us to Surefire, if she'd found her."

"Give it time. You should learn to allow yourself a few moments to just breathe." She softened her voice.

Just breathe?

What was he doing now? What was he doing every second of every day? Breathing.

Pax chewed vigorously on his gum for a few moments, which calmed him down more than any of Lily's yoga techniques ever did.

"It's not just TimeTrap," he admitted, because if he didn't, he was going to burst. "I don't understand Surefire's behavior. Before Pixie's deceit, I would've said Surefire was never capable of betraying us." He softly banged his head back on the wall. "Christ, Cassandra, I just don't know anymore."

"Well, I do. I've been around that girl enough to know that her one driving force is to be accepted, to prove to her parents, her father, once and for all that she's not a failure. I would bet that whatever is going on with Raven has to do with protecting those she cares about. If Ari is behind this, as we suspect, he might've threatened her life or her family or yours. Even you thought she appeared coerced at the warehouse."

"Yeah, but looks can deceive. I've been off my game on this one."

Her nostrils flared, and Pax knew she meant business. "Pixie had lots of friends at U-Sec. She dated Oliver, who gave her access to his tech room. Whether it's Ari or someone else, Pixie could've given him information about a number of our employees, not to mention our weapons. She could be an independent contractor, selling this information to the highest bidder."

Pax pushed off the wall and paced the small foyer. Damn it, why hadn't he thought of that? He'd had Graham secure the firewall when they'd learned about the breach. However, he hadn't considered what an insider like Pixie would know about U-Sec.

"Get Helena to send out a memo to all our agents. Tell them about the breach and to be aware, especially those who worked closely with Pixie. However, right now, our focus should be Surefire's family."

"Officers are at the St. John home. I'll check out any other friends or relatives who may be targets." Oracle took out her cell phone, then stopped. "There's also Raven."

"Raven?"

"With all that's occurred, I just remembered that Oliver phoned me while you were inside the condo. Raven's sister was reported missing by the Greek authorities. Same way as Heather. Disappeared out of her locked bedroom."

Pax stopped pacing and stared into Oracle's gray-white eyes.

"It's possible Raven is being coerced as well as Surefire."

The GPS tracker clipped to his belt gave off a resounding beep. "Check into that," he ordered before pulling out his own cell phone.

He dialed U-Sec and Oliver's extension.

"Yello." Oliver picked up.

"It's Pax. We've got a signal."

He heard the frantic sound of keys clicking on the keyboard.

"Ahhhh," Oliver let out as he clicked around. "Got it."

"Forward the coordinates to my phone. I'm notifying St. John."

"It's coming from central Mexico. Is Pixie there?"

"We believe so."

"Tell her to kiss off for me, will you?"

"Roger that." He took the elevator down to the first floor, where St. John sat in the lobby, speaking on his phone. Pax grabbed St. John's shoulder.

He stopped his conversation and pulled the phone away from his ear.

"Central Mexico. I'm downloading the coordinates now," Pax stated.

St. John nodded and spoke into his phone. "General Withers, get your troops prepped, we're going airborne; we're heading across the border. Notify the President of Mexico and our ambassador that we have a potential hostage situation."

Chapter Twenty-One

Ari's eyelids flitted open. The room blurred before slowly coming into focus. Four walls fashioned from stone blocks surrounded him, the one on the far left angled up to the low ceiling. Several tall lights lit the room. A doorway opposite from where he sat led to a corridor lined with flickering torches. Next to his closed laptop, his glass-topped desk held a vibrant feather headdress that he had never seen before. Behind those items, a black crystal skull faced him with empty sockets which swirled with a quick flash of red.

Awareness oozed back into his skin. An arm draped around his shoulder. A weight on his thighs where someone sat. Cool breath tickled his ear.

Pixie lounged on his lap. Her robe was undone to reveal a gold shimmering bra and panties underneath.

"What's going on?" He pushed her off his legs.

"Ari." She stumbled back and yanked the robe tight across her chest. "I was just conferring with Tez about our new guests."

"Tezcatlipoca was here." Ari jumped to his feet. His desk chair flipped over behind him at the sudden movement.

Awareness tingled back into his extremities. He grasped the pendant around his neck. It was hot. He didn't remember calling Tezcatlipoca. Normally he let down his shields and summoned the god's powers to allow him to take over. However, ever since they had arrived at Tezcatlipoca's temple with the skulls, the god had been coming and going as he pleased, using Ari's body as he pleased.

Ari did a double take at his naked chest. Last he remembered, he wore pants and a button-up shirt. Now a cotton sarong edged in gold was wrapped around his waist. Leather sandals hugged his feet. Gold bracelets encircled his arms.

When did I change clothes?

Pixie skittered around the desk and tied her robe. "He wanted to make sure things were on track. I told him we were cool."

Ari eyed her as she pushed back pieces of frizzy hair from her face. All the while, her pea-green eyes stayed focused on the wall behind him.

"How long have I been out?" Dread crept up his back.

Pixie pursed her small mouth and lifted her eyes to the ceiling. "A few hours, maybe? I don't know. There was so much to do. We've been majorly busy."

Ari leaned forward, placing his hands on the desk and struggled to keep the fear from showing on his face. He didn't want Pixie to know that this wasn't part of the plan, that he hadn't allowed Tezcatlipoca to take over his body.

"What have you accomplished?" he asked in an even tone.

She edged around his desk like someone approaching a watchful dog, unsure whether it would attack or lick her face.

It would be the former, if Ari didn't need Pixie's help tonight.

With a sideways glance, Pixie eased next to him and then opened his laptop. Security footage from cameras around the temple popped up on the screen. One showed Surefire and Raven strung up in a cell, both with their heads hanging down, unconscious.

"We secured Synthia and James. Oh, I mean Surefire and Raven." She giggled nervously. "I was never good with code names. Thought theirs were kinda lame anyway. Soooo . . . Tezcatlipoca broke off pieces from his slab and made cuffs, then Raven couldn't phase out. That god is pretty smart," she beamed proudly. A little too proudly. "Not that Raven could do much anyway. Those skulls are totally sapping his power."

And pulling a number on me as well. Ari watched the screen as she enlarged the view of the ceremonial chamber.

"Skulls are in place as well as sacrifices, who should be awake just in time to die, which will make things much easier for us. That new dust you created for me works like a charm." She patted his shoulder, and he jerked away.

"Who's that?" He pointed to a corner of the screen at a woman. He bent lower, certain his eyes were deceiving him. Why was she dressed like an Andy Warhol groupie?

"Oh, yeah, her." Pixie blew out an annoyed breath. "That's Kali, known as TimeTrap. She's an UltraAgent. She must've come through the portal Surefire and Raven took to get here. I wouldn't worry. Tez had fun messing with her." Pixie laughed and blushed.

Ari shot Pixie an annoyed look, but she didn't notice. She smiled serenely to herself, and her eyes glassed over as if reliving an inside joke.

"TimeTrap made it up to the surface once. I figured she was going to travel back to the main office to get our boss, but Tez stopped her. Worked some magic using the skulls to keep her tied here. Ha!" She threw back her head, enjoying the prank more than Ari thought necessary. "She's been lost for a bit, trying to get back to the surface, but she can't. She keeps popping here and then there within the temple and then ending up in the same spot again."

She giggled. "We had a laugh watching her get more and more pissed as Tez kept her going in circles. Oh, that god's a trip."

Not any more pissed than Ari felt listening to Pixie drone on. Pixie called one of the most powerful beings in the world a "trip" and acted as if they were drinking—and Ari was suspecting maybe something more—buddies.

"Oh, and we have company setting up camp." Pixie brought up another screen from a camera stationed outside the temple ruins. "We were just trying to decide what to do when you came back around."

Military trucks and soldiers littered the ground above them. Mexican soldiers were erecting a large canopy and unpacking their vehicles.

How had they found them?

TimeTrap. She must have a GPS tracking device. Tezcatlipoca wasn't smart enough to have anticipated that one.

No worries. Ari planned to turn this challenge into an opportunity. He glanced at the time on his laptop. The ascension ceremony would begin soon, and then he could test his newfound powers on these soldiers. It would be perfect. It would be more than perfect.

"Wait a minute." He pushed away from his desk. "You said I was out for a few hours. It's closer to six."

Pixie backed up, her palms held out. "Three hours. Six hours. Time flies when you're busy prepping for your boyfriend to become a god."

Before he could respond, she shrunk down and squeaked in a diminutive voice, "I'll check on our guests for ya."

She flew out of the room.

He righted his chair and then dropped down into it. He wasn't losing control. This was normal. Tezcatlipoca had increased powers because of the skulls. This had once been his temple. His obsidian mirror, the conduit of his power, was located here. It was understandable that Ari would lose some control. However, after the ascension, he'd have Tezcatlipoca's abilities and the god would be in *his* control.

A niggling feeling clenched his gut. A feeling that the ceremony wouldn't go as planned. That Ari was missing—or ignoring—something. Raven's voice rang through his head. *You're the one who's been played, my man.*

Ari shoved these doubts away and clicked open his email. Everything was under his control. Besides, he had too much riding on this ceremony to stop now.

Thirty RSVPs from fellow magicians for his exclusive show filled his mailbox. All had replied yes.

Pride welled up inside. He'd prove to them yet that he deserved to be in the ranks of the best. His mistakes would be forgotten. He'd blow them away with his act—real magic. No parlor tricks. No transhuman abilities. The real, supernatural deal.

He'd be a sensation. They'd beg to learn from the best. But no one could emulate him. No one could steal his tricks, because they were taken from a god. He'd be the only one. The one possessing true magic.

He clicked on the latest response from the Fantastic Farrell.

He'd be there. Backstage. Wanting to see firsthand what Ari claimed he could do—along with the million-dollar prize money given to the magician who could prove real magic existed. Ari really didn't care about the money. Wasn't doing this for the money. Because with the power of a god, he could and would have everything he ever wanted.

Ari would give Farrell an act he'd never forget and make him regret ever having disparaged Ari's name.

He read a second email from Farrell, who was concerned because someone from U-Sec had contacted him about the private show. This hadn't deterred him from attending. In fact, it made him even more interested in seeing what Ari had to offer.

Thank you, U-Sec, for adding a bit of sensationalism. What every good entertainer needs. Maybe he should have his assistants wear U-Sec uniforms for effect.

He typed a note to tell Pixie to make this last-minute change.

His phone alarm went off, indicating that the time was nearing for the ceremony. His skin itched with a current, buzzing just underneath, waiting for release. His muscles tightened in anticipation. Heated energy rose from his chest and exploded outward to his limbs.

Showtime.

Chapter Twenty-Two

Pixie stood on the other side of the black bars in the prison room with her arms crossed. She wore a satisfied expression of a cat who had eaten the prized canary—with a side of catnip.

Surefire longed to smack the smug look off her face. Unfortunately, both her arms were chained above her head.

"Hang tight," Pixie joked in a girlie voice. Surefire had no idea why guys fell for that contrived cuteness.

"Tez will need you in *achiton cahuitl*." Pixie beamed, looking even more pleased with herself. She bent toward the bars as if she were sharing a special secret. "That's Náhuatl for 'in a little bit of time.' Tez taught me that."

"Tez?" Raven asked, hanging from another set of chains across from Surefire in the cramped cell.

"Tezcatlipoca. Pu-leeze. You don't think I'd waste my time with Ari, do you? He didn't have any real powers. Now a god on the other hand," her pink nylon wings fluttered, and she clutched at her heart, "That's a fairy's best dream."

"You're not a real fairy." Surefire pointed out. "You had those wings surgically added."

"Do I detect jealousy? Hmmmm?"

"Jealous of a girl who can imitate a gnat?" Surefire huffed. "No."

"Did he tell you his sob story?" Pixie leaned on the bars. "I heard it all from Ari after *I* left *Raven*. His cocky act is all just an act. You know, his momma leaving. His sister the only woman he ever cared for. Blech. Pathetic."

Surefire hazarded a glance at Raven. If looks could kill, Pixie would be splattered across the hallway wall. Raven struggled against the cuffs around his wrists, but the cuffs weren't forged from iron like hers; they were made from shiny black stone—similar to the pendant Ari wore around his neck. Even in the dim light of the cell, she could tell Raven's face had grown gaunt and he was straining with the effort to keep the opposing force from draining his strength.

"Where's my sister?" Raven ground out.

"And Heather?" Surefire interjected. "Are they okay?"

"Until the show begins." Pixie's lips twisted into a sadistic smile that put Surefire's every nerve on high alert.

"What do you mean?" Raven demanded.

"You'll see soon enough."

Surefire's head throbbed, and she screwed her eyes shut against the dull ache. Whatever magical dust Pixie had used to knock them unconscious had given her a worse hangover than a night out with TimeTrap.

"How long were we out?" Surefire rested her head against the cool stone wall.

"Don't worry your pounding brain about that. In a short while, you'll be asleep forever." Pixie snickered at her lame dig.

"Why are you doing this?" Surefire implored.

Appearing to seriously mull the question over, Pixie tilted her head and gazed up at the ceiling. "Opportunities. A god can offer way more growth opportunities than U-Sec ever could. Besides, a girl has to look out for herself in this world, because no one else will. Thought you of all people could relate."

With that, she shrunk down and flew away.

"Where's a fly swatter when you need one?" Surefire mumbled to herself.

She stretched her back and shook out her hands, which were numb from lack of blood. She could feel Raven's eyes on her, but she wasn't in the mood to meet his gaze and hear whatever he had to say. Of course, her being chained across from him in the eight-foot-by-eight-foot cell made it hard to avoid him.

"Don't believe Pixie. There was nothing between us."

"Does it matter?" Surefire fixed her eyes on the bars of the prison cell. "There was nothing between us either. Just a moment we got caught up in. That's all."

Surefire told herself she wasn't going to cry. Damn him, she wasn't going to lose it. If she was hurt, it was only because she'd betrayed herself, not because she was developing feelings for him. She deserved it. She couldn't expect anything more than what she'd gotten from him. She'd deluded herself into believing that he cared for her. If he really did, would he have turned his back on her so quickly without waiting for an explanation?

She didn't want to believe love was something she had to prove to someone. She already had that with her parents.

"We only dated for a week at best," he said.

"I don't care."

"I didn't know she could shrink."

"I don't care." Just the thought of Pixie touching him, of him touching her intimately and enjoying it made her sick, made her want to scream, and this compounded the anger and humiliation she already felt.

"I'm sorry," he said.

Surefire jerked her head up at his words, not expecting him to say that.

"I said, *I'm sorry*. I overreacted. You didn't know what would happen." He sighed. "You didn't know what Ari was capable of. You were scared. I would've done the same thing in your position."

Surefire wasn't sure how to respond. He was apologizing for hurting her. She wasn't used to this. "You're right. I was scared. The pain was intense." Damn her teary eyes. "I didn't think you could help me."

"It was my fault. I got you hurt."

"You didn't mean to. It was an accident."

A few seconds ticked by, then he said, "We can leave together after this is over. At first, I didn't think it was possible. But I want to be with you, and somehow we can make it work. We could start a life together."

Her heart did a somersault at his words. He wanted to be with her. Stay with her. Wanted to have a life with her. For a moment, she let herself relish in this fantasy before reality broke through to stomp all over her lovely parade.

"What kind of life? We'd be fugitives. It would never work."

"Never say never."

She tugged on the chains. A screw popped out of the shiny metal bracket attached to the ancient stone wall. She tugged again. Raven saw what she was doing and started pulling on his.

"So, what do you think?" Breathing heavily, he threw his body forward.

She stopped tugging to rest her wrists, which were starting to chafe. "I can't go with you. They'd think I pulled a Pixie. I want to explain to them what happened. I want to tell them what Xochi said."

He slumped back against the wall. "What did Xochi say?"

She rubbed her left then right wrist. "Just that the world's going to end because of transhumans."

His chains rattled as his arms fell limp. "She said that?"

"She didn't go into details, but I plan to find out more after this is over."

"I hadn't heard anything about that."

She shrugged. "So you see why I want to stay."

He yanked again, and a screw popped loose and tinged onto the floor. "Then I'll stay, too."

"What?" She stopped in mid-pull.

"I'm staying. I can't let you take the fall for this."

"But your mission. The artifacts. Xochi."

"It can all wait."

She stared into his eyes, darkened by the shadowed chamber. "One of us has to return the skull. It can't remain here."

"Then you go." He slammed his arms down, and the left chain popped off the wall. He winced.

Leaning his shoulder against the wall, he caught his breath. "I'll explain what happened and then leave. I doubt they have any prison that could hold me for long."

"You could try explaining everything to the authorities and the museums. You may be able to reach an agreement if they understand."

"They'll never relent." He rotated then flexed his left arm in a stretch.

"Even if they knew the world is at stake?" She wedged her feet against the wall behind her and leaned forward, pushing out with all her strength.

"They wouldn't care."

"You don't have a lot of faith in people."

His shoulder lifted slightly. "I was on the wrong side for too long. I became jaded. I justified my actions. That's how you can continue committing crime if you have a conscience. And, trust me, most have none."

"Like Ari." Another screw fell out and dropped to Surefire's right.

"He has one, somewhat smaller than most. The problem is his pride. He wanted to be something he wasn't. He wanted to be special and have these abilities that seemed to come so easily to others. Then transhumans went public, and traditional magic wasn't much in demand. He needed to reinvent himself."

"Then where does Pixie fit in?"

"She worked as Ari's assistant."

"Huh." Surefire considered this. "I remember her mentioning she'd worked as a magician's assistant but didn't know it had been Ari."

"I hadn't realized she could shrink." Raven wedged two fingers into the cuff on his right hand. "It makes sense now with the tricks Ari was able to perform with her."

"She wasn't born that way. Her mother was a scientist working to reduce subatomic particles."

"And whose mom isn't?" Raven joked. "Was Rick Moranis involved somehow?"

"No." Surefire let out a weak laugh. "But there was an accident. Somehow Pixie got mixed up in it and then suddenly she could shrink at will. Her mother retired over what had happened. She tried to make Pixie normal again and nearly killed her in the process. In the end, Pixie's mom destroyed the machine and her research."

"No more incredible shrinking women," Raven mused.

"I think one's enough."

"Amen to that." Raven took in a deep breath before throwing his weight out from the wall and pulling down on his right arm.

Surefire strained her upper body forward against the chains. Then she walked her feet up the wall at her back. She jammed her feet in two cracks. Her arms leveled out and blood flowed to her hands and provided a small bit of relief.

"Do you still have the necklace?" Raven asked.

"It's under my uniform. Why?"

"Is it heating up? Any vibrations?"

"Nothing right now." Surefire tucked her head down so her mouth was directly over her chest. "Testing . . . one . . . two . . . three. I don't think there's anybody back there."

Raven burst out laughing. The juxtaposition of his whole-hearted laugh against the starkness of the dungeon and their situation wasn't lost on Surefire.

"That was good. Almost as funny as your Kafka comment earlier."

"Oh, that." She snorted. "My ex loved bizarre, creepy stories. Collected the classics. *The Metamorphosis* was one of the few I'd read. Freaked me out for months."

"I bet."

Surefire pushed her feet against the wall and strained forward again until both wrists burned from the effort. Several more screws dropped out before the chains finally popped off the wall. She fell forward onto the floor. Her right wrist twisted underneath as she caught herself.

"Ow. Crap." She rolled onto her butt and cradled her wrist to her chest.

"What's wrong?" Raven looked down at her.

"I think I sprained my wrist." Surefire tried to rotate her hand, but the biting pain stopped her. "Ah, yeah. That's it."

Raven drew back and strained against the final chain until it popped off the wall. Grit and crumbles of stone streamed onto the floor.

Surefire touched the tender skin and couldn't find any broken bones. Definitely a sprain.

"Here. Use this." He dropped to his knees next to her and again struggled to catch his breath. When his breathing evened out, he ripped off his white shirt and tossed it to her.

She looked from his lean muscular chest to the crumpled remains of the shirt in her hand then back to his chest. Her face flushed when she remembered how smooth and warm his tattooed skin felt under her fingertips. She wasn't sure how she could be turned on with the stabbing ache in her wrist. She was glad for the shadowed room, so he couldn't see the heat creeping across her cheeks.

"Never seen someone actually do that in person. I assumed it only happened in pornos and *Incredible Hulk* movies."

"You know which one I'd prefer." He turned his attention back to the cuffs around his wrists. "Edward Norton was so buff when he morphed into the Hulk."

She smiled to herself.

"Wrap it tight around your wrist but not too tight to cut off circulation. It'll act as a splint until we can get you an x-ray," he said.

Surefire nodded then cringed when she tried to push the metal cuff up her arm. There wasn't much play. She could move it only a fraction of an inch at best. There was a keyhole on top but without the tools in her utility belt, which Pixie must have snatched when she was out, she couldn't break it open. The iron chains clanged at her sides and weighed down her arms, adding at least an extra ten pounds each. She wasn't sure how she was going to escape this cell and find her sister carrying this awkward weight on a sprained wrist.

Stepping on a corner of the shirt, she pulled up with her good hand and ripped it in half. Carefully, she wrapped the soft cotton around her tender wrist and then wound it up her hand between her thumb and index finger. Raven's scent, earthy yet sweet, clung to the shirt and drifted across her nose with every movement. She raised the bandaged hand to her nose and breathed in and then immediately felt ridiculous.

What was her problem? Was she in high school hugging her boyfriend's jacket? No, she was stuck in a dungeon, who knew where, with her sister—and the world—in danger.

She glanced over her shoulder to see if Raven had noticed, but he was too busy working his fingers under his cuffs, trying to figure out a way to get them off. He picked up one of the chains and flattened his hand against the wall.

"Is that a good idea with your power tapped out?" Surefire interrupted him as he swung back the chain.

"It's worth a try." But he dropped the chain and hopped forward, arching his spine. Twisting around, he craned his neck trying to look at his back. "I think Xochi is sending me a message. My back is tingling."

"Move to the bars near the torchlight so I can see it better." Surefire motioned him closer, her marshmallow-looking hand glowing against the shadows.

On his lower back, near his side, the tattoo of Xochi's statue faded from his skin. In a slow reveal, an outline of a person formed in its place, followed by a head with straight, dark blonde hair flowing past narrow shoulders, then a chest covered in a black form-fitting shirt. The nose formed with a slight bump in its center. Surefire's mouth went dry. Next came the eyes—one blue, one green.

Surefire stumbled back, her head spinning. Why was her face materializing onto Raven's back? Around the figure's neck appeared the pendant as it hung around Surefire's neck. However, in the tattoo, red liquid dripped from it.

Blood.

The priest's words came back to her. *A small offering of thanks is all she requires.*

That was how she had called Xochi before. Her blood activated the pendant.

"What is it?" Raven eyed her with concern.

"It's me." She turned her non-bandaged hand over and looked at the blood drying around her wrist under the edge of the cuff. "She wants me to use my blood to activate the pendant."

"Do you think it's safe? Remember what happened last time." Raven watched her over his shoulder as she scraped a nail along her wrist to reopen the wound.

"It's our only shot."

"Oh, there you are." A low female voice intoned on the other side of the bars.

Surefire and Raven jumped. Surefire's heart almost leapt out of her throat.

"I've been wandering around for hours looking for you. I think something was messing with me." She shivered. "Thought I'd never find you in this maze. And, trust me," she pointed to her platform boots, "not made for walking."

Surefire's jaw moved up and down, but she couldn't form any words. Her brain was too busy taking in TimeTrap's dark eyes lined thickly with black eyeliner and her tall, lean, pale body clothed in a block-patterned dress and white patent leather boots.

"Kali . . . I mean . . . TimeTrap, how did you get here? How did you find us? Are the others with you?" Surefire finally managed say.

"They're coming—I hope." TimeTrap tapped what looked like a watch on her wrist. "And to answer your other questions: I followed the ions left from the portal in your sister's condo. Pax called me in when you and Raven disappeared from the museum. Unfortunately, I passed out on Pax's couch and didn't have time to change before we got a read on you."

"Who's this?" Raven asked.

"This is TimeTrap. She's a U-Sec agent and my—"

"How do you do?" She sauntered up to the bars and stuck her hand through them.

Raven shook her hand, though he glanced at Surefire with his eyebrows raised, probably wondering why an extra from an Austin Powers movie had been sent to save them.

"My, you look even tastier in person. Really, you should've been number one."

"Excuse me?" Raven pulled his hand back.

"TimeTrap is here to help us. She's wearing a GPS device, and Pax, hopefully, is on his way." Surefire pointed to TimeTrap's wrist.

"Right." Raven blew out a breath.

"I teleport via Q-T, quantum transference. Bend space-time to get from point A to Z and then back to N if necessary, but I don't travel to the past in *our* universe. Grandfather paradox and all that," TimeTrap said with a flick of her wrist.

Surefire had forgotten about the grandfather paradox, even though TimeTrap constantly reminded her of it whenever she spoke about her time-travel ability. Had they traveled to the past of their Earth or into a parallel universe from The Garden? Did Xochi and her kind know a way around this paradox?

"How did you create those portals, anyway? We measured nano-sized ones at MIT, but they formed and went in seconds." TimeTrap snapped her fingers. "My power doesn't create them, I'm sort of—"

"I'll explain it after we're out of here and the world hasn't ended," Surefire interrupted her.

"Considering you're both stuck in this dungeon, I'm assuming Raven's not the master baddie?" TimeTrap asked.

"He's on our side," Surefire replied.

"Can you teleport other people?" Raven asked.

"Why?" She leaned into the bars and put her hand on his chest. "Someplace you want to go?"

"Hey, give the man some space." Surefire nudged her back.

"Sorry, I forgot you had a little tête-à-tête."

Surefire widened her eyes. "What?"

"Don't worry. It was just your father, Pax, and the police in your room with the crumpled sheets and discarded clothes next to it. I'm sure no one jumped to any conclusions." She waved her hand dismissively, though she was having a hard time hiding her devilish grin.

"This is just perfect." Surefire banged her head against the bars.

"None of that will matter if you don't get us out of here, and we don't stop Ari," Raven interjected.

"Ari?" TimeTrap pulled back, then her eyes widened. "Oh, that magician guy. Pax thought he was up to no good. Don't worry. I got you covered."

TimeTrap disappeared then reappeared within the cell and grabbed her friend's arm. Surefire closed her eyes before floating through cold, silent space. She opened them when her feet touched the floor of the torch-lined hallway with the cuffs no longer attached to her wrists. Raven stood next to her, unchained as well.

"Have you seen my sister or Ari?" Raven asked, color slowly returning to his face.

"Unfortunately not. This place is a total maze. I did find a way out and got to the surface long enough for Pax to get a read on my location. I'm hoping to find it again now that I've found you."

"No," Raven replied. "I'm not leaving without my sister."

He swung his head from one side of the narrow winding corridor to the other.

"Could be that way." TimeTrap flicked her hand to Raven's right. "I came across a huge chamber with an enormous black rock and—"

Raven took off without waiting for her to finish.

"Of course, I could just pop you over there. If I've seen it once, then I can travel to it," TimeTrap called out to his back before he disappeared around a bend.

She shrugged and turned to Surefire. "Starting a new fashion trend?" She motioned to Surefire's bandaged hand.

"Sprained wrist. Long story."

"Long story, I'm sure." TimeTrap smirked knowingly. "I can imagine how it got sprained."

If Surefire's cheeks flushed any hotter, she could fry an egg on them.

"Shall we get this party started?" TimeTrap held out her hand.

"More like crash one." Surefire took it.

"Even better."

"Before we go, I need to ask you a favor."

TimeTrap lowered her heavily shadowed lids and regarded Surefire. "Depends on what it is. This is my weekend off, you know. Well, it *was* my weekend off."

"Get Raven out of here. If Pax and the crew show up, Raven can't be here. He needs to return the skull. It can't remain here, and you're the only one who remove it from our world."

"What about you?"

"I'll stay back. Take the heat. Explain to Pax what went down. Hopefully, they'll go easy on me."

TimeTrap pursed her pink-shaded lips and nodded. "I'll try. Whatever energy that held me back from returning to the surface and popping to Pax drained my phone's battery and even the GPS unit. I'm hoping Pax got a read on me before it went dead. That bad mojo is pretty strong, and I can't guarantee it won't be back."

"But if there's an opportunity?" Surefire peered imploringly up at her friend.

"I'm here for you, girl." TimeTrap squeezed her hand. "Just fix me up with one of Raven's hot non-criminal friends, will you?"

Before Surefire could respond, the corridor fell away into a black void through which TimeTrap tugged her weightless body. Then the darkness lightened, and she found herself in a chamber nearly five stories high at its peak. To her right, steep wide stairs led toward a dark doorway. In the center of the room, twelve crystal skulls were arranged on the floor in a pattern Surefire couldn't discern from her angle. Each flickered with a soft light reminding her of a jack-o'-lantern.

TimeTrap's smooth forehead creased. "Those skulls weren't there before."

"And neither were those women." She pointed toward the opposite side of the room at an oblong-shaped obsidian slab, the size of a mammoth foot, polished to a smooth sheen so it shone like a black mirror reflecting the room in a perfect dark contrast.

On either side of this obsidian rock, two women hung chained to the wall. Their arms and legs were spread out, so they formed an x-shape against the grey brick.

"Oh my God." Surefire sprinted forward toward the woman on the left.

Raven bolted into the chamber from an entrance across the room and ran up to the woman on the right. "Kat!"

"Heather." Surefire reached up and grabbed her limp, cold leg and screamed, "Heather!"

Chapter Twenty-Three

The helicopter crested the mountain, and Pax shifted in his seat, wedged between the window and General Withers. Rugged terrain straight out of a classic western movie passed beneath the helicopter's lights. The uneven land soon smoothed out into a plateau with patches of green mixed with tan, reminding Pax of camouflage.

Was this land hiding something? His agents? Raven? An ancient god raised from the dead?

Pax made a sour face.

Now he knew he was losing it. Ancient gods didn't exist. It was ludicrous to entertain that idea, and he couldn't believe he'd even brought it up to Matthews earlier. Whatever was going on could be explained—rationally.

How? He had no idea. But an ancient god rising up to destroy the world? That was straight out of comic books or a 1980s movie. Hadn't Bill Murray starred in something like that? Marshmallows were involved and a possessed refrigerator.

He rubbed his forehead, pressure mounting at the base of his neck. Apparently, he had left his sanity back at Andrews Air Force Base.

"We're here," the pilot's static voice crackled over Pax's headset.

Pax peered out the window. The landing lights fell on several vehicles—Humvees and military-grade Jeeps—parked near a green tarp pulled tight over a makeshift base.

Pax lifted his eyes to the blue horizon as the helicopter descended. A cluster of lights glimmered in the distance.

President Diaz had briefed them in Mexico City when they had first landed. General Brigadier Felix Reyes would meet them at the site to oversee the operation and the Americans in his zone. Diaz had made it clear they weren't happy to host U.S. troops in their country on such short notice or to allow them to carry weapons on their land, either. The Mexican government was granting them a "personal favor"—whatever that meant—though Pax was certain Diaz would enlighten him when this mission was over.

As it was, Pax had kept his team to a minimum and brought only St. John and Withers along with two of his troops, Johnson and Calloway—young, eager soldiers Withers was priming to handle transhuman incidents. For once, Oracle hadn't put up a fight to come with him. She was exhausted and decided to take her own advice and rest, so she could help Surefire when they found her.

And they would find her, she had assured Pax.

He wasn't holding out hope. He was tired and numb and for the last few hours he'd been operating on auto-pilot. He could hardly remember the trip out here and just snippets of conversation between him and Withers. A conversation accompanied by a few barely audible grunts from St. John, who had impressed Pax by napping in the midst of this chaos during their flight from DC.

"That might be the farming community Diaz told us about." Withers' voice cut through the headphone's static. He nudged Pax's arm and pointed at the lights where Pax had been staring. "On the coast is where my wife and I vacationed for our fortieth. Amazing resort. You should take Cassandra there."

"Sure." Pax wasn't in the mood to remind Withers that they had been broken up for a year. For whatever reason, Withers could never remember they weren't together or maybe he chose not to. He loved to lecture Pax on the wonders a good woman could do for him.

As if he had time for a relationship. He was lucky to find time for sleep.

The helicopter teetered, then came to rest on the ground.

"We'll find them, Pax." Withers smiled, showing off straight pearly teeth under a thick white mustache; the tan skin around his clear, blue eyes crinkled. "We got a good team here."

"Thanks, sir." Pax was always amazed by Withers's upbeat and friendly tone. He had more tours of duty than Pax could recall, and many of them in the toughest war zones, ones that left good soldiers with post-traumatic stress disorder. If Pax had an ounce of Withers' easygoing nature, half his problems would be solved.

They removed their headsets then disembarked, hunched over to jog away from the helicopter. The blades whirled to a slow stop above their heads.

A man stepped out from under the tarp, flanked by two soldiers carrying assault rifles. He wore a general's hat with one star and a gold emblem in its center that Pax couldn't make out. His uniform was clean and crisp, tailored to his small frame. Gold buttons and multi-colored insignia stood out against the dark fabric of his jacket. His light brown, baby-smooth skin lay across delicate features—too delicate for a man, yet not quite feminine.

Androgynous.

His green eyes were sharp and direct and regarded Pax with the intensity a boxer gives his opponent.

He walked forward and extended his hand to Pax.

"You must be Levi Paxton." The man spoke in perfect English with no trace of an accent.

"General Reyes, I presume."

Reyes inclined his head and shook Pax's hand.

"Call me Pax." His hand jerked as Reyes squeezed it in greeting. He hadn't expected to feel a jolt of pain from the general's handshake.

They let go at the same time. Pax turned away to introduce his team and to cover up the shock he knew was etched across his face. Despite Reyes's lean build, he was strong—transhuman strong. Judging by his aggressive handshake, Reyes wanted Pax to know it.

After the introductions, Reyes led them into the makeshift base. In the center were several folding chairs and a table with satellite imagery and geographic maps of the territory spread across it.

"As you can see, we've been studying the area, trying to determine where your agents could be. This is a farming community with a few resorts scattered nearby, nothing more."

Without a word, St. John approached the table and paged through the maps. He squinted before drawing a battery-operated lantern closer and leaning over the pages. The light blinked off then back on again.

"General Reyes," Pax began.

"Call me Felix." The edges of his mouth quirked up. "We're all friends here, are we not?"

His words came out as a challenge, not a statement.

"Of course," Pax replied, too tired to take offense at Felix's tone. Pax needed his help, and he planned to be as congenial as possible to make sure he got it. "We are grateful for your assistance. But we're not mistaken. We picked up our agent's signal in this vicinity."

"Could her GPS unit have dropped from somewhere? Gotten lost? Or maybe the signal is off?"

"No, this agent followed a special route to get here." Pax wavered, unsure how much Felix had been briefed on. "She's a . . ."

"Transhuman," Felix finished for him.

"Yes."

"I have met a few in my day." He stared fixedly at Pax.

"I'm sure you have." Pax met his pointed look and held it. "You're talking to one right now."

"I know. I've heard the stories." Felix grinned. However, his eyes, the cool green of a jaguar's, still shown with a combative glint that was beginning to wear on Pax.

He didn't know what game Felix was playing, and he didn't have the time or patience to find out. He inhaled a long, deep breath. As usual, it didn't help.

"I don't give a damn what you heard about me," Pax said in a tone he hoped conveyed his seriousness. Instead his words came out loud and angry. The soldiers stationed at the corners of the tent started forward.

Felix raised his hand, and they held their positions.

"I'm here to find my agents. If you have a problem with me, then I'll be happy to discuss it when this is over. But right now, I need your help. No games. No stories. No posturing. Just your help."

"I did not mean any offense," Felix said. "I meant it as a compliment. Your reputation precedes you."

Pax didn't believe him, but it didn't matter because he needed his help. "Then let's get back to saving my people."

"President Diaz spoke to me about your case. And this Raven your agent was assigned to arrest." Felix's gaze flicked to St. John, still studying the maps. "You believe he's with her."

"Yes."

He nodded then folded his arms. "I heard he died at the Pyramid of Quetzalcóatl."

"So they say."

Felix lifted his hand and stroked his chin. "Did you know that since Raven started his thefts, several lost icons have turned up at the Museo Nacional de Antropología in Mexico City? Significant religious relics thought to have been destroyed or stolen by APS, which he used to work for."

"No."

"You should."

Pax stamped down the irritation prickling up his back. He didn't like the condescending way Felix spoke to him. As if he were privy to an essential fact, and Pax was too much of a thick-headed American to understand it.

"Perdón, General Reyes." A solider entered the tent and walked up to Felix, interrupting their conversation. In Spanish, he quickly addressed his commander. Felix whipped his head toward the open flap of the tent as the soldier spoke. Pax could make out a few words from his high school Spanish class, enough to know that a truck was approaching their small base camp.

Suddenly, the lights in the tent flashed on and off and on again. Two lamps in opposite corners, including the lantern on the table, burnt out. St. John cursed and took out his cell phone to use as a light to continue reading the maps.

As several soldiers tried to power the lights back up, Pax followed Felix outside to check on the intruder. Withers stepped up to Pax with his two men in tow.

"Came from the cluster of homes we saw from the helicopter." Withers nodded to the headlights cutting through the night and bouncing along the dirt road.

Felix's men stood guard, rifles pointed at the fast-approaching vehicle.

"What's going on?" St. John came up behind them.

"We have a visitor. And he's in a hurry, considering he's kicking up more dirt than a Dervish," Withers commented.

A soldier handed Felix night-vision goggles. He peered through them before saying to Pax over his shoulder, "I think it's Alvaro Vega, owner of the farm. We questioned his tenants earlier, but he wasn't home. Maybe he will have your answers."

The rusted pickup truck came to a dusty stop several feet from the parked vehicles. A squat man with a horse-shaped face and cowboy hat jumped out of the driver's side. He shouted and pointed to the passenger seat.

Felix's men advanced. After they looked inside, a soldier called out to Felix and motioned him over.

"There's a sick woman in the truck," Felix translated for Pax.

The driver flailed his arms in a fit for Felix to hurry up. Pax and Felix ran over to the truck, and Pax heard the man say his name was Alvaro. That was all he could catch, since Alvaro spoke so fast that his words came out like a string of low musical notes. Felix nodded and leaned inside the passenger door as Alvaro continued to speak. The withered woman rolled her small head back against the pitted headrest. Her long white hair fell in wisps around her overly lined face. She murmured what sounded like a chant. Felix bent over her, his ear close to her mouth.

Then he stood up abruptly and called out to his men, who carried the woman out of the truck and into the back of a Humvee.

"What's wrong?" Pax asked.

"Her name is Anarosa. She is a *curandero*—a healer. She said there's a presence here, an evil seeping into our world. Her sisters have felt it as far as Playa del Carmen."

Realization dawned on Pax. "Get her out of here. This force nearly killed one of my agents. If this woman has any telepathic abilities, it could harm her. That's probably why she's affected and we're not."

Felix narrowed his eyes; his hand pinched his chin as he mulled over Pax's words. Finally, he yelled to his men. Two soldiers jumped into the Humvee and tore away back down the dirt road.

"Is there something more you'd like to share?" Felix's thin lips pressed together.

"What did President Diaz tell you?"

Felix glanced over his shoulder. At first, Pax thought it was at his men, but then Felix looked past them to a rock formation jutting out of the flat ground.

"I didn't believe him," he said in a voice so low Pax had to move closer to hear him. "When you've seen what I have, you no longer believe in fairytale monsters. Men are devils enough."

Alvaro approached them, his eyes drawn to the same area Felix continued to stare at. He pointed two stubby, crooked fingers and started to speak in his whirlwind manner. This time Pax caught the words *gringo* and possibly *disco,* but he had to be mistaken.

St. John stalked up to them, interrupting Alvaro. "What's going on with that woman?"

"Anarosa is sick," Felix replied in a clipped tone.

"What does she have to do with us? And this guy?" He flipped up his arm at Alvaro. "Who's he?"

Felix looked from Pax to St. John then back to Pax, as if determining who was in charge. When he continued speaking, he addressed Pax. "This is Alvaro, the farmer I mentioned before. He owns the land we're on. Earlier he saw a white woman over by those rocks. He thought he imagined it because she wore a," his soft features cinched in confusion, "disco outfit. Then she disappeared, and he got the call about Anarosa falling ill and did not investigate further."

"It had to be TimeTrap, my agent." Pax started toward the rocks. "It could be an entrance."

"There's more." Felix grabbed his shoulder, and again Pax was taken aback by his strength.

Pax pivoted around, and this time he didn't hide the shock on his face.

Felix dropped his hand. "Several months ago, a group of Americans were excavating at that site in the middle of the night. Alvaro was visiting family in Mexico City and heard about it the next day. He reported it to the authorities, but they did not respond. He thinks the local police were bribed. During the incident, one of his workers went missing. They found his body a week later. Drained of blood."

"You said there was nothing but farms around here."

Felix shrugged and kept his focus on the rocks and away from Pax's accusatory gaze. "I didn't think it was important. As far as I knew, it was a rock formation, until archeologists recently discovered that they were remains of a temple. Although many locals claim it is an ancient altar. I wasn't aware of any entrance, just a pile of rocks."

"We need to check it out now. It's our only lead."

"It is a sacred place to our people, Pax. Protected by our government. Outsiders are not permitted near it."

"Too bad." St. John, who had been listening silently to their exchange, marched forward toward the rocks.

In unison, the Mexican troops released their safeties with a click and aimed their weapons at St. John's back. In his peripheral vision, Pax saw Withers and his soldiers slowly reach for their weapons.

"General, call off your men." St. John stopped though didn't turn around or raise his hands.

"With all due respect, you are in my arena." Felix reached into his pants pocket.

Pax shot a knowing look at Withers, who motioned his men to stand down. The last thing they needed was a gunfight with the Mexican military. Besides, they were outnumbered, and as Felix had mentioned earlier, they were in their country. They had to respect the rules, as much as it pained Pax, who knew deep down in his churning gut that those rocks held the answers he needed.

"If I give you access to a sacred site," Felix took out a pack of gum from his pocket and popped a small, square piece in his mouth, "what is the United States willing to do for us in return?"

Chapter Twenty-Four

"Heather, can you hear me?"

Surefire tugged on the gauzy white dress sweeping between Heather's outstretched legs and flowing to her calves. Metal bands secured her ankles and wrists to the wall. Long sleeves stopped halfway down her arms, forced out to her sides by the metal cuffs. The billowy sleeves hung down from her shoulders to her elbows and gave the appearance of wings. Against the gray stone wall, she looked like a snow angel in the middle of grimy slush.

"Heather," Surefire said again, louder and more desperate.

A chill cut across Surefire's torso. Her sister couldn't be dead. No, she wouldn't let her die. As much as she'd hated Heather in the past. As much as she cursed her for what had happened. As much as Heather's personality could grate on her nerves worse than the sharpest nails on a chalkboard.

They were family, sisters, twins.

The chill crept higher as she stared into Heather's pale face—her own face—a lifeless mask.

"Wake up!"

Heather's head lolled from one side to the other. She groaned.

Surefire's ragged nerves eased in relief. Heather was alive.

She ran her fingers over the wall to find a foothold to climb up. The ache in her sprained wrist intensified, but she ignored it and jammed her fingertips into several cracks to find a secure grip. Then she noticed horizontal slits in the stone above Heather's ankles, which were shackled to the wall. Underneath each foot, a granite bowl-like object protruded from the wall. She looked up and spied vertical slits above Heather's forearms and similar bowls below.

Standing on tiptoes, she peered into the closest receptacle. Dark red crust coated the inside around a hole where the bowl intersected the wall. Surefire's chest tightened with worry. Her sister wasn't hanging there as an angelic accessory.

"I'm going to get you down." Her eyes darted around the room for a table or chair to stand on. But aside from stacking the skulls, there was nothing to use that would enable her to reach any higher than Heather's foot.

"Somehow," she added quietly.

Heather raised her head. Her eyelids fluttered open. Her dull green eyes stared vacantly down at Surefire. "Synthia?"

"It's me."

"What happened?" Heather asked in a voice raspy with sleep. "I thought we lost you."

She tugged at her arms once then twice. Her eyes flashed an acidic green, no longer dull but wide awake with fear.

"What the hell?" Heather sputtered. "Oh, God." She bucked her body but the metal cuffs held her in place.

"Get me down," she managed to scream through clenched teeth.

"Calm down. I'll get you out of this."

"Calm down?" Heather screeched.

Oh, boy. Why did she say that to her?

"I'm chained to a wall—I don't know where—with a sister last seen half-dead, hanging over the shoulder of a criminal, who vanished inside a stone box. Plus, I've got a splitting headache. And you're telling me to remain calm?"

Surefire placed her hands on her hips. "Fine. Freak out for all I care, but remaining calm might help your headache, while I figure out how to get you down."

Heather blew at the choppy strands of blonde hair that had fallen into her face. "Hurry up. I have to pee."

"I'll do my best."

"And Syn," Heather added.

"Yeah." Surefire glanced up, not even bothering to hide her irritation at Heather's tantrum.

"I'm glad you're okay."

Surefire nodded, surprised by those words and unable to remember the last time Heather had said anything remotely comforting to her. Apparently waking up kidnapped and chained to a wall had softened Heather a bit.

She inspected the cuff around Heather's ankle. There was no lock. The metal band appeared welded into the wall with no release mechanism. Maybe TimeTrap could pop Heather out like she had for Surefire in the dungeon, if she could find her. She craned her neck and scanned the chamber for her co-agent and friend. A few minutes ago, Kali had been beside her; now she was gone.

She glanced over at Raven, who was standing with his head held back, speaking to his sister Kat, strung up in the same position as Heather. Kat nodded then winced when he tried to pry his fingers into the metal band at her ankle.

"How did you get here?" Surefire asked Heather.

"I don't know." She squeezed her eyes shut then opened them again as if trying to focus. "I was taking a shower, and the water started to shimmer like gold or silver. Whatever. Almost like someone sprinkled that annoying shiny confetti people stick in birthday cards. Next thing I know, I'm dressed in a gospel-choir gown, chained to a wall, with my sister screaming my name and giving me a massive migraine." She squeezed her eyes shut again. "Can you dim the lights or something? It's gotten brighter in here."

"I'll do what I can." Would it be wrong to knock Heather out again?

Surefire whirled around when she heard what she thought was a horse galloping up behind her. Then she spied TimeTrap jogging then hobbling across the room. Her boots not made for running either.

"A couple of things." She limped closer and held up two long fingers.

"First." She lowered a finger. "There's a computer connected to the walls. I think it might unlock these brackets. But it needs a password." She lifted her hands, palms up. "Breaking computer codes is not my bag, babe. Too bad Oliver isn't here."

"Who's this?" Heather frowned down at TimeTrap.

TimeTrap looked up at her with unabashed annoyance. "Kali?"

Heather stared blankly back as if TimeTrap had replied in Chinese.

TimeTrap blinked. Her lips cinched in disbelief. "Synthia and I work together. A year ago, all of us went out to Hampden, and you ticked off a large Baltimore hon during HonFest. I popped us out of there before you had your scrawny butt handed to you."

Heather's frown deepened.

"Dear Lord, how many people does she know who can bend space-time?" TimeTrap let out an exasperated laugh. "I vote we leave her derrière up there."

"I heard that," Heather exclaimed in a surprisingly loud voice, considering she nursed a migraine. "Just because I don't remember you is no reason to be a—"

TimeTrap dragged Surefire away from Heather and her rant and over to the skull circle.

"Sorry about that. She's been drugged," Surefire said then reconsidered. "Though more likely she's just being her normal self."

"Don't care. We got more immediate concerns." TimeTrap held up two fingers and pointed at the ceiling.

Surefire looked up and saw a black cloud about the size of a Hula-Hoop swirling directly above the skulls. Within a few seconds, it grew to the radius of a round dinner table. A breeze kicked up in the room—a gathering summer storm—blowing strands of hair across her cheek.

"What is that?" Surefire asked.

"The second thing I needed to tell you. It's like a black hole. Dimensional portal to be specific. It sucked my power away the last time I encountered it, when I tried to find you in that tomb at the Smithsonian. It's blocking me. I can't transport anywhere or anyone when that portal's near me."

It expanded as wide as a truck and lowered as it grew. Inside the obsidian slab between Heather and Kat, a similar smoky substance appeared and began to form into the spinning shape of a hurricane cloud. Wind gusted from the four corners of the room and whipped past them, sweeping Surefire's hair into her eyes. She twisted the strands into a ponytail and stuffed it into the back collar of her uniform.

Besides the whistle of wind past her ears, the swirling black mass made no other sound. She expected claps of thunder or the deafening roar of a tornado as the smoky cloud funneled down into a vortex between the skulls. This strange silence made it more foreboding, like they were waiting for a giant boot to drop.

"What's going on?" Raven called over to them. "Can you get my sister down?"

"I'm being blocked." TimeTrap pointed to the supernatural whirlwind. She told him about the computer system linked to the walls and the password. He ran to the back side of the stone wall.

"Sorry, Kat," Surefire said to Raven's sister.

With a weak smile, she gave Surefire a thumbs-up. Her easygoing response reminded Surefire of Raven, along with her wavy black hair, which mimicked his, except hers flowed past her shoulders and disappeared behind her back. She even had the same slightly pouting lips within a softly angular face, serene like Mary from a painted Greek icon. Especially when compared to Heather, who was throwing an adult-sized hissy fit.

"Ugh, honestly, Synthia, you really need to dim the lights. They are getting brighter." Heather flailed against her restraints.

"Then close your eyes and—" Surefire stopped when the room brightened exponentially, forcing her to squint. "What is that?"

"Not sure. But any time ancient skulls start to glow, it's not a good thing," TimeTrap replied.

A phosphorescent white light blazed a trail along lines etched into the floor crisscrossing the skull circle underneath the mini-tornado. The light ricocheted off each skull, bouncing from one to the other like a Day-Glo pinball. Surefire's eyes followed its trail until it ended at a crystal skull, glowing with a soft violet light, on the opposite side of the circle—Xochi's skull.

In unison, the skulls pulsated and hummed. Their inner lights grew from the twinkle of a birthday candle to the roar of a fire that consumed each so you couldn't make out any distinct features. Each skull emitted a different color of the spectrum that merged together in the center to form a black beam. This dark shaft cut through the tornado hovering above and then curved into the black, shiny slab situated between Heather and Kat. Purple, yellow, green, white, and blue flashes of light illuminated the black beam at random intervals—multi-colored lightning against a menacing storm cloud. A shape materialized in the center of the stone slab. A shadowy head and torso.

"Trippy," TimeTrap whispered.

Raven ran out from behind the wall and took in the otherworldly light display. "What's going on?"

"I think the skulls' energy is feeding into the portal and making it grow," TimeTrap explained.

"Then we need to stop it." Surefire surveyed the skulls. What would happen if she moved one of the skulls from the circle? Would it break the connection or act like a ticking bomb, where cutting the wrong wire could cause it to blow?

"Synthia, do something. Please," Heather wailed. Surefire wasn't certain if it was the fear in Heather's voice or her uttering "please" that prompted Surefire to lean down and reach for the nearest skull.

TimeTrap grabbed her forearm.

"That wouldn't be good, babe," she said. "You'll probably get sucked into the portal and ripped to shreds."

"Trying to sabotage my man's plans?"

They turned simultaneously to the squeaky voice and the small body flittering above them.

"Pixie?" TimeTrap blurted out just in time for Pixie to enlarge her fist and hit her square in the cheek. She teetered on her platform boots before collapsing onto the ground.

Surefire and Raven leapt forward with their arms outstretched. They grabbed for Pixie. She flew out of reach a foot above Raven's head.

Pixie shook out her now Barbie-sized hand. "Always thought Kali had rocks in her skull."

Surefire jumped up. Her hand swiped up at Pixie and just missed her. Pixie flew several feet above her and laughed. As she ran forward, Surefire's foot kicked a rock. Without another thought, she scooped it up then dropped it when pain surged through the joints in her hand. She'd forgotten about the sprain.

Pixie swooped down and grew to midsize in the air. She rammed into Surefire's stomach.

"Umph!" Surefire toppled backward. Her head slammed onto the hard, uneven floor at the edge of the skulls. Her right hand flew up and back. Stars exploded in front of her eyes. Her hand burned, sucked into the icy tornado formed within the skull circle. Sand and grit sheared across her skin. She yanked it from the whirling vortex. The makeshift bandage around her hand had disintegrated. Her fingers were red with too many scrapes and cuts to count. Bits of torn flesh hung from her knuckles. A few nails were missing, replaced by pools of blood. More blood seeped from wounds, soaking what remained of the cotton cloth around her wrist.

She squeezed her trembling hand to her body. Warm blood soaked her uniform through to her chest and down to her stomach.

Pixie let out a tiny shrill scream. Surefire's head popped up, and she saw Raven pinching one of Pixie's wings. She thrashed from side to side and tried to claw her doll-sized fingers down his face.

Using her left hand, Surefire picked up the rock she'd dropped. She stood and her vision wavered. Pixie and Raven appeared to merge into one before splitting apart again. She dropped the rock and bent over. She couldn't focus with the throbbing, nauseating pain in her hand.

Surefire glanced up, and her eyes locked onto Raven's. His face clenched with determination. He pulled back and used Pixie's force to spin her around into the wall behind him. Her head smacked into the stone and bounced back, leaving a red smear on the wall. He let go, and her body slumped onto the floor.

He ran over to Surefire, who dropped to her knees next to TimeTrap. He squatted down next to her.

"She okay?" he asked.

Surefire felt her pulse; it was steady.

"Unconscious."

"And you?" He took her bloody hand in his.

She winced. "I'll deal."

"We need to wrap that up." He looked down at his naked chest. His eyes drifted down to his pants. He gave her a half smile. "Maybe we can rip a piece off Heather's dress."

"Good idea." She tried to smile but ended up wincing again.

He kissed her forehead.

"Synthia, are you okay? That hand looks nasty." Heather continued to tug against her restraints. The flesh around her wrists had turned pink with the effort.

"It's all right," she lied, as she cradled it against her chest.

"Is this Raven?" Heather wriggled her fingers at Raven, who was walking over to her.

"Bingo," he answered.

Her eyes narrowed to slits.

"The *criminal* who disappeared with her inside the stone box," he confirmed in response to Heather's suspicious appraisal.

"And we've joined forces," he ripped a piece of fabric from the bottom of her dress, "in more ways than one."

Heather hiked her meticulously plucked brows at Surefire. She knew what Raven meant. What Surefire had done. The accusation was written all over Heather's flushed face.

Surefire averted her gaze to Raven as he jogged over to her with the cloth. He wrapped it tight several times around her hand.

"Better?"

She did her best to give him a reassuring smile without wincing. Slamming her hand into a car door would hurt less than this firestorm of pain.

"How about you? Are the skulls draining your power?" His skin looked a shade lighter but his blue eyes were still dark and clear, and he hadn't wavered when he'd flattened Pixie against the wall.

He lifted his shoulder. "I'm keeping it out, for now. But I can feel it tugging at me."

He glanced toward his sister then back at Surefire. She sensed he wanted to make sure Kat was okay but didn't want to leave Surefire's side. The black beam streaming into the slab blocked Kat from their view, and Kat hadn't made a peep since he'd dispatched Pixie.

"Go, check on Kat. I'll be fine." She summoned the strength to smile again, this time a broader one.

Raven seemed to buy it. He told her he'd be right back and then sprinted under the black shaft to the other side.

A fever spread down her arms and to her legs and feet. She feared infection as her body trembled and her skin tingled. She turned hot then cold then burning hot again.

Surefire staggered over to her sister and collapsed against the wall by her feet.

"You slept with him, didn't you?"

"Yeah, I did." Surefire didn't have the patience to care about what Heather thought or what she knew. "Is there a problem?"

Heather remained silent for a second. Then her tense features relaxed, as if she'd decided it wasn't worth battling over.

"You look sick."

"Thanks, Captain Obvious." Surefire's mouth went dry. She clawed at her chest, now on fire. She needed to get out of this uniform.

"You always get cranky when you're sick," Heather joked. At least, it seemed like she was joking, trying to put Surefire at ease.

Surefire figured she'd misread Heather, because another voice was speaking at the same time. In her head, calling her name.

Synthia.

"If Raven can . . . ugh," Heather thrashed against the restraints, "get me down, then I can help you."

Heather stopped squirming. "Syn, we need to get Raven. We need to get you out of here. You look sicker, almost purple, which is not a healthy look."

Then again, Surefire could be delusional with pain, because the voice spoke her name again. Seemed to whisper in her ear. She went completely still, trying to figure out where the sound originated.

"Synthia, stay with me. I don't want to lose you again. I thought you'd died back in the warehouse. I could've killed Pax when I found out you were missing, and then he just blew me off."

Synthia! The voice boomed throughout her head, strong enough to crack her skull.

"I'm sorry," Heather went on, pleading with her now, as if she were afraid of what she was witnessing. "My agent made me give the interview. I don't know if you saw it, but they were afraid of losing money from my sponsors. I'm sorry, Syn. For everything."

Surefire unzipped her uniform down to her chest. Xochi's amulet emitted a purplish light underneath the streaks of blood covering it. The blood from her hand had soaked through her uniform and activated the pendant. It was Xochi's voice calling her name.

"Oh, shit, that can't be good," Heather murmured.

Surefire lifted her head. The amulet grew hotter and brighter between her breasts. A mild electrical current traveled from her chest and over her shoulders to the back of her head.

"Is that Ari, as in cousin Ari?" Surefire heard Kat say from the other side of the black cloud.

"Part of him is," Raven replied.

From the opposite side of the chamber, Ari entered the room in a headdress adorned with brightly colored feathers and a cotton sarong edged in gold. It draped from his hips and ended at his ankles. In his hands, he held another crystal skull, larger than the others. Its gleaming polished surface reflected the black mass, now tinged with red, streaming from the middle of the skull circle.

"Welcome to the most amazing—and final show—of your lives!" Ari announced with true showman-like flair.

His shape wavered between a roach, Surefire's father, a human-sized bee—at which Kat screamed—to a clown. A very disturbing clown with a large red nose to match a broad, red mouth and wearing a yellow-polka-dotted satin outfit.

TimeTrap lifted her head, took one look at the clown and then lay back down again, her eyes squeezed shut.

Surefire wished she could do the same.

A multitude of spectral images peeled off Ari and into the whirlwind. One looked like a frog; another a rat; another an old, hunchbacked man. Surefire assumed these were phobias; belonging to whom, she had no idea. The kaleidoscope of fears spun around the center of the room and disappeared into the ceiling.

Once more, Ari shifted into her father. Then he stopped just outside the circle of skulls, and the image fell away to reveal Ari's prideful face and a way-too-pleased-with-himself smile. He looked from one to the other as if expecting applause.

"How did he do that?" Heather asked Surefire, then her voice rose to a shrill. "How the fuck did he turn into our dad?"

Surefire tried zipping up her uniform, but the zipper stuck. Using her uninjured hand, she squeezed the pendant tight into her palm to keep it hidden. The vibrating energy pulsed back down her spine and encased her skin up her arm and down to her toes. The scorching pain in her bandaged hand dulled to a numbing ache.

"You don't have to do this," Raven said.

"Come on, James, that's so cliché to say. As if that line ever stopped anyone. I wouldn't be in this position if I didn't think it was necessary. And, of course, if you and Synthia hadn't gotten the final skull for me."

Surefire peered under the spiraling dark mass spilling into the onyx slab. She could see Raven's feet and legs, but the black beam blocked his upper body from view. He eased forward toward Ari and out of view on the other side of the skull circle.

"What's he talking about?" Heather whispered.

Surefire ignored her question, too focused on figuring out what Raven was doing. Well, trying to focus. Her body hummed with the energy of a washing machine on the spin cycle, making it difficult to see straight.

An onyx altar rose up from the floor in front of the black slab and underneath the funnel. Blades emerged from the slits above Heather's forearms and ankles. They bent forward like metal fingers poised to slice.

Kat pleaded for Ari to stop.

"I apologize for bringing you into this, Kat. You can blame Synthia for that one. She gave me no choice."

"You had a choice all along." Raven bolted from the other side of the skull circle.

Ari held up his hand, palm out. Raven stopped in mid-leap. He strained against an invisible force that surrounded Ari. Raven's face reddened and his muscles tensed. He pushed forward as if against a brick wall to reach his cousin. He managed to step one foot closer. Then Ari twisted his hand, and Raven flew upward through the air, pitched with such a force, he looked like a discarded sock puppet flying across the center of the vortex and into the onyx altar. His back cracked against its edge. Blood trickled from red scrapes that marred his skin. His jeans hung in tattered shreds. A bloody bald spot appeared on the back of his head where hair had been ripped from his scalp. His body sagged onto the ground.

Kat shrieked. Heather spat a few obscenities and pushed and pulled against her restraints.

Lilac and lavender scents drifted across Surefire's nose, so strong she could taste their floral odors, pungent and bitter.

Xochi's voice echoed across Surefire's mind. *It's time, Synthia, for a sacrifice.*

Ari turned his attention to her. "Surefire, if you would be so kind as to lie on the table. I need three *human* sacrifices to begin."

He transferred the skull to one hand, and in the other he produced an obsidian dagger similar to the one the Aztec priest had used on Raven.

Xochi's amulet burned under the death grip Surefire held it with. The vibrations along her skin turned into liquid heat, rolling down and covering her body with a metaphysical hot wax. She didn't remember that sensation from before.

Synthia, you need to let me in.

She had no idea she was keeping Xochi out. She hadn't the strength to stand, let alone keep an ancient god from possessing her.

I'm too weak. I've lost a lot of blood. I don't know if you can use me.

You are my vessel.

I don't like the sound of that.

Avatar, then?

Surefire rested her head against the cool wall. *That's not any better.*

Ari stepped around the crystal skulls and made his way toward Surefire and Heather.

He will be weakest as the transference begins. But I need your body to finish him.

You mean sacrifice *my body.*

You promised to do what it takes.

Ari pointed the shiny, sharp blade at her while his other hand cradled the skull, which continued to swirl with a black smoky substance tinged with red and now with flashes of violet. She met Ari's eyes. His irises were black like the knife in his hand, and the slab filled with the gray smoky figure and the table underneath where Raven now lay covered in blood and still not moving.

You don't have to remind me again, she told Xochi.

Surefire let go. Of her body. Of her mind. Of her anxiety and fear and pain. She relaxed her tight, stressed muscles. She released the strangled breath she'd been holding. She emptied herself of all thoughts and emotion until all that remained was a shell.

Pointing the knife at her like a wand, Ari flicked it toward the sacrificial table. He made the movement again and then again. He stepped closer and swept his arm out to the side.

"Why can't I move you?" Ari's eyes drifted away from Surefire to the skull in his left hand. The red flashes had given way to a purplish light.

Surefire closed her eyes, and when she opened them—correction, when Xochi opened them—the room glowed. The details were more stunning, like comparing a black-and-white television with an HDTV. She could make out cracks in the stone on the ceiling high above. She could count the individual feathers in Ari's headdress. She could see the pores on Ari's skin. Auras encased everyone's body. Heather's was white. Raven's had dulled, his myriad of colors fading fast. A smoky gray cloud outlined Ari's body.

"You hold no power over me," Surefire said, though she didn't really say it. Xochi said it through Surefire's mouth.

It felt weird, wrong. Xochi's grip on Surefire's body seemed stronger, tighter than during the Aztec ceremony. Surefire started to worry that she wouldn't get her body back. She'd never get Xochi's essence out. Maybe it was the skulls. Maybe the skulls made Xochi stronger, like they fed Tezcatlipoca's power. Maybe Xochi could use the skulls to take over Surefire and coming back into this world.

"Who are you?" Ari stumbled back. His befuddled expression fell away. His lids closed and then lifted to reveal black orbs with a sheen of red pulsating through them. His body grew more muscular and taller.

"Xochiquetzal, I hoped you'd join me," he said in a deep, booming voice.

She moved forward, and beneath every step a blade of grass or a small flower sprang up.

Heather gasped behind her. "How are you doing that?"

She ignored Heather and regarded Ari. "How could I not? You are my husband. I go where you go." She brushed passed him, and a cool bolt of energy shot through Surefire's body. She walked to the edge of the skulls.

"You married this douche? When did that happen?" Heather blurted out.

"Silence!" Surefire pointed at Heather. A vine snaked out of the wall and covered Heather's mouth. Her muffled scream echoed through the room.

Could you give me that power? Surefire asked Xochi.

Xochi turned her attention back to Ari or Tezcatlipoca or whatever he was at this moment. She stepped between the skulls and made her way to the center.

"Surefire." Raven stood at the edge of the skulls. Dark red smudges covered his body, distorting his tattoos. Dried blood caked his hair and along his cheeks. His jeans hung in shredded strips over red-streaked legs.

He reached out his hand and grabbed her shoulder. Ivy snaked around his ankles and pulled him back until he fell. "Leave her out of this. Her body won't survive it."

Is this a good idea? Surefire concentrated on moving her feet and stepping back from the skull circle, but she couldn't budge her limbs. In fact, she couldn't feel her limbs or her body anymore.

She started to panic. *TimeTrap said we would be destroyed if caught in this vortex.*

I'll keep you safe, Xochi answered, though she didn't sound reassuring.

The wind whirled and whipped across her skin, but Surefire couldn't feel it. It was as if she were watching all this transpire from a video monitor in another room, except she had no idea where this room was located. The world grayed out before they reached the center of the supernatural tornado—an empty space about four feet in diameter.

Tezcatlipoca, controlling Ari's body, followed her into the center of the skulls.

"We'll rule again. We'll walk amongst the mortals again as it was in the beginning," he said.

"We will be free, my hummingbird," she whispered and raised her hand to touch his cheek. Power arched between them and flowed from the skull he held in his left hand to pass through Surefire's body. It stung and felt tantalizing at the same time and made Surefire relieved she could feel something.

"We need a sacrifice of three to open the portal and bring us fully into power," he said.

Xochi lifted Surefire's hands, and the vortex floated above their heads. She did a half turn and flung out her arm in Raven's direction. Grass and flowers sprouted from the floor underneath him. Vines snaked around his body and dragged him to the altar.

Raven struggled to tear the plants off, as the vines pulled his body closer to the obsidian table.

"What are you doing? Stop!" he cried out.

"You are mixed with the blood of gods, Raven, a more potent blood than mortals. Your sacrifice will make the connection even stronger. Our worlds will be one," Xochi said.

"It will destroy our world. The world we were working to save," Raven shouted back.

"You were trying to save it. I gave up on the world long ago." She snapped her wrist, and the blade flew from Ari's hand to hover over Raven's heart. "We gave up this world for the humans, and now it is time for our return."

She turned back to Ari who wore a euphoric expression, a combination of love and lust and obsession, which would've made Surefire's skin crawl if she was in control. He reached out and encircled her waist. His head bent down and met her lips in a slow, lingering kiss that burned with a force that cut through Surefire's veins and made her want to scream, made her want to writhe in pain. She struggled against Xochi's hold on her, against Ari's forceful grip. She managed to push away from Ari. Xochi slammed her back far inside herself until the world became smaller, as if she'd been moved from the front row to nosebleed seats.

Surefire's mouth opened and welcomed his demanding kiss. Her body melted into his arms and held him close. Xochi slowly lifted Surefire's arm, and her fingertips grazed the smooth, cool surface of the skull. Overwhelming feelings of love, lust, longing poured forth from her body, making her head spin with these extreme emotions, making her heart ache under the pressure.

Power shot forth from the crystal and smacked into her with the brunt force of a bullet. Pulling on her last ounce of strength, Surefire slammed forward, and her essence poured back into her arms, her hands, her legs, her torso. For a split second, she had control.

Ari's lips ground into hers with a violent possessiveness that frightened her. His fingers dug into and bruised her backside, forcing her into him as if trying to merge their bodies. His arousal pressed against her abdomen from under his sarong.

Xochi smacked her spirit back inside again. No matter how hard she tried, she couldn't force this spiritual squatter out of her body.

Surefire begged her to stop. Xochi ignored her pleas and continued her unearthly lip-lock with Ari.

Surefire's heart thumped in her chest, hard and quick. It strained to keep up with this love goddess's endorphins surging through her veins. It was too much. Her heart was going to give way. She knew it.

The sounds of Kat's wails, of Heather's muffled shouts, of Raven's struggles dropped away.

Her body went numb until she felt nothing. Not the press of Ari's lips or the power surging from the skull or the disgusting feeling of Xochi rubbing Surefire's breasts against Ari's hard muscular chest.

Then her vision faded into a gray smoky cloud, and nothingness consumed her.

Chapter Twenty-Five

St. John stood firm, not turning or making any movement of surrender.

"What will it be?" Felix arched his brows at Pax. "What will the United States do for us?"

"I'm not the president," Pax responded. "I can't promise what's not within my power."

St. John shook his head. Pax could only imagine the irritated expression on his face. At least he kept his mouth shut.

"U-Sec." Reyes chewed thoughtfully on his gum. "Your help. No questions asked. When we need support."

So this was what Diaz had meant when he said they'd owe his government a favor. Pax wondered if they had been set up, if Diaz had known they'd need to dig into protected, sacred land to find his agents and that Pax would have no other choice but to agree to their demands.

"I promise my help when you need it. No questions asked."

Felix grinned, a quick flash of white against his flawless bronze skin. "I appreciate you being so accommodating."

He shook Pax's hand, and this time Pax squeezed harder than needed. Felix's grin fell around the edges.

"Raul." Felix swept out his arm, and the soldiers left their positions and filed in line in front of St. John, who turned and glowered at Pax. His face was redder than a pepper even in the shadowy light.

Pax had no desire to deal with his issues.

"Gentlemen, follow us." Felix set out in front of his troops.

Withers and his soldiers brought up the rear behind Felix's men. Pax strode up to St. John, who waited for him. His face hadn't lost any of its angry flush.

"Not a word." Pax walked past him behind Withers.

St. John made a noise. Something between a growl and a sputter.

"What?" Pax turned around, allowing St. John to catch up. With the choking sounds coming from St. John, Pax was afraid he'd stroke out if he didn't speak his mind.

"Unbelievable. They just held us hostage, and you know it." St. John had sense enough to keep his rant to a harsh whisper. "This is bullshit."

Pax was looking back at the vehicles when an uncomfortable feeling passed over him. Something in their environment had changed. The night suddenly seemed quieter, darker.

"We need to play by their rules for now," Pax said.

"For now," St. John echoed, with a grunt. "I don't trust these guys. And I want them to know we will personally deal with our lawbreakers—especially Synthia."

The short hairs on Pax's neck stood on end. "We don't know her side yet."

"Do you think I want to believe this about her? She's my daughter. But what she's done and failed to do has put others in danger." He stared into the distance, past the soldiers, past the stone altar, as if looking for Synthia's innocence in the rocky hills surrounding them—and not finding it. "By all accounts, she's aided a criminal."

"Oracle believes she was coerced." Pax knew St. John had exceedingly high expectations for his children, but this judgment was way beyond strict parenting. "She thinks someone could've threatened you and the rest of her family, which is why Synthia went along with Raven."

"Then she didn't do enough to protect it. Her sister is missing because of her." St. John started forward when Withers and his team fanned out amongst the brush. Pax kept pace with him. "I only wanted Synthia to have the best advantages in life, but when given the opportunity to excel, she failed. I expected more from her, Pax."

"You'd rather find her guilty without trial?"

"No, I won't throw her to the dogs without hearing her out. I'll pull as many strings as needed to get her out of this mess. But even I have my limits."

Pax glanced over his shoulder and noticed that the lights under the tarp had gone out.

"Besides, what Synthia and Pixie have done has only made it harder on U-Sec."

Pax's attention snapped back to St. John. "How so?"

"Transhumans are already on uneven ground with society. Most have no idea what U-Sec is. They see it as a specialized security firm dealing with transhuman crimes. They don't want to know the freaks work for you or that two of your own have become turncoats. A public relations nightmare is what we have here."

"What are you suggesting?" Pax stopped, and St. John stopped as well, his face unreadable as clay.

"Pixie pays for her crimes to the fullest extent of the law. And if we learn Synthia's actions were not done in the best interest of our country, then she joins Pixie. We show we have zero tolerance for traitors with superhuman abilities."

Pax couldn't deal with this now, and he couldn't believe St. John was even suggesting it.

"What does your wife have to say?" Pax asked, letting the bitterness he felt weigh down his words.

"Vanessa doesn't know about my decision. She's already had enough stress tonight to put her in the grave. She doesn't need me digging it for her." St. John took a breath. "I talked to your partners, and they agreed with me."

"They didn't say anything to me." In fact, he hadn't spoken with them in over a week. They were both working a top-secret case that even he wasn't privy to.

"I spoke with them before we left Baltimore. Sean said to do whatever I believed necessary."

Pax doubted St. John had showed his partners both sides of the coin. Neither Sean nor Gloria would have any of their employees convicted without a trial.

"I explained to them how it wouldn't be good for business. You have a government contract to consider. And you have to think about your employees. Many couldn't conform in the private sector. And we're not about to let them roam the streets on their own."

"Are you saying my employees would be targeted?"

"I'm saying that unless they are directly monitored by us, I don't trust them."

"Us?"

A sardonic smile stretched his thin lips. "The government. More specifically, the Department of Defense special committee I advise that contracts U-Sec. Why do you think we allowed you to form U-Sec and put you in charge of these transhumans? Because you hold some *secrets* about underground government experiments?"

Pax didn't reply. In fact, he couldn't reply, because he had to focus all his energy to keep his fist from flattening St. John's patronizing face.

He hazarded a glance at Reyes and his soldiers, who were circling the stones for a way in. He needed to be over there, not discussing this ridiculous mandate from St. John.

"You're an asset to our country. You're a threat to others. And, without a doubt, we need U-Sec. Every day, we are uncovering more threats to our nation that have nothing to do with terrorist cells or crime syndicates. Supernatural threats I never knew were possible. We need the abilities UltraAgents can wield. The stronger and more diverse your team, the more you can help your country."

Pax opened his mouth to interrupt St. John and demand that he elaborate on what he meant by supernatural threats. Then he reconsidered. He didn't need more distractions. His anger had reached the boiling point with this inane conversation, blurring his focus until all he could see was red.

"But you're also a ticking bomb." St. John pointed a thick finger at Pax's chest. "The nuclear gorilla in the room to be monitored and caged, if needed."

"And you're willing to cage your own daughter?" He slapped St. John's hand down.

After a moment of deliberation, he replied in a somewhat remorseful voice, "We all have to make sacrifices for the greater good. It's what we do as soldiers and citizens. If she's a menace to our country—to U-Sec's stability—then yes."

"The question still remains how she became a transhuman." Pax turned from St. John and headed toward the rocks.

"Watch your step, Pax. You're treading on dangerous ground."

"This conversation is over. I have a job to do. Nuclear gorillas to save." Over to Pax's left, the lights in the distance blinked off. A ding resounded from his pants pocket. He reached in and saw a warning on his cell phone's screen. *Low battery.* Then the phone shut down.

A revolver went off, followed by shots from an assault rifle. Pax dove down onto the ground against a thorny bush and took out his gun from the holster over his flak vest. Reyes shouted in Spanish for his man to stop. But the solider ran away. He threw down his assault rifle and let out a panicked scream. His arms flailed. Pax could see something trailing close behind him, followed by several more shadowy *somethings.*

Frogs?

No, it couldn't be.

Pax eased into a sitting position, gun cocked and ready to fire. Around the rock, Reyes's men had fallen back. Some began shouting, and a few fired their guns at the ground. Reyes shouted orders to his men to regain control, but they took off in opposite directions. Pax couldn't see Withers or his two soldiers. He assumed they were under cover, determining their next move. Pax looked behind him and saw St. John's thick head pop up from a low bush.

One of Reyes's men ran past Pax screaming about rats. A second later, Pax saw rats the size of small dogs streaming across the brush as if trailing the Pied Piper.

A few more shots went off in the distance. Pax stayed low and inched ahead. Another solider waved his arms frantically. A flock of birds—crows or gulls, Pax couldn't tell—descended on the man. He fell to the ground.

"Withers," Pax yelled.

He heard rustling and then an "over here."

Pax hustled toward the hand waving ahead of him. A few more shots rang out close by.

"What the hell is going on?" Pax reached Withers, who was flanked by Johnson and Calloway. They had taken position behind a squat tree with a maze of low-hanging branches.

"I don't know. They're delusional. Maybe got a whiff of some sort of peyote."

"I think it's more than that. One of Reyes's men ran past me followed by a shitload of rats. They certainly looked real."

"What do we do?" Withers asked.

"Cover me." Pax squinted, trying to adjust to the dark night of the new moon. "I need to find Reyes. Looks like most of his men have scattered. Several have dropped their weapons. But stay here. If there's a toxin being released near the tomb then I don't need my entire team exposed."

St. John crawled up behind them. "What's the plan?"

"Pax is going in." Withers inclined his head. "We're covering."

"Fine by me, but I hope Reyes knows our agreement is under reconsideration given this incident." St. John moved off to the side and disappeared into the shadowy brush.

"I'll give you the signal when it's safe." Pax eased ahead, remaining in a crouch.

Besides a few panicked cries in the distance, the immediate area had fallen eerily quiet. No more shouts. No scurry of small animals. No crunch of boots along the uneven ground.

A blanket of silence covered the area and hung like a cold, wet weight over Pax's head.

He held his gun out. Finger resting on the side above the trigger. Ready to fire.

"Reyes! Felix!"

He reached the cluster of rocks. The formation towered two stories above his head. Gray boulders of varying sizes lay stacked on one another, giving the impression of an ancient stone house complete with a slab angled across the top to create a roof.

He flattened himself against the rocks and slid around the structure, looking for Felix or a way in.

"Felix!"

Then he saw it. An ashen, sunken shape more withered than Anarosa crumpled on the ground in front of a pitch-black slit between the rocks.

"Pax," a brittle voice whispered. "Pax, it's true."

"Felix?" Pax dropped to the ground next to him.

He grabbed Felix's hand then dropped it—shocked by the paper-thin skin barely covering his brittle bones. Felix's hat had tipped off to the side, and his thick, black hair now glowed with a white sheen. His delicate features sagged with dried-up, leathery skin.

"What happened?"

"It's true," he repeated, gazing past Pax up at the starry sky.

"What's true? Felix, what happened to you?" Pax wanted to touch him, shake him, make Felix look at him and give him an answer to what had to be an illusion. But he was afraid to touch him. Afraid Felix would crumble to dust.

"Tezcatlipoca," he wheezed. "Tezcatlipoca."

The name Surefire had mouthed into the camera. The legendary husband of the goddess depicted in the statue. The god Ari had spent so much money and time researching.

"What about him?"

"He sees into your heart. Your fears." Felix's eyelids fell closed. "He knows your fears."

"What I fear has already happened." Pax stared into the crevice between two boulders, barely wide enough for him to pass through, if he angled himself sideways.

Pax stood and gave a signal to Withers and his men to approach. A few feet from Reyes, he spied night-vision goggles. He scooped them up.

St. John, Withers, and the two soldiers rounded the rock formation.

"Jesus Christ." St. John shuffled back when he noticed Reyes's prone body.

"Our fears," Pax explained. "Whatever is in there," Pax pointed to the slit, "makes our fears a reality."

"Shit." Calloway backed away.

Withers cut a look at him and he moved back into position. "Sorry, sir."

"What do we do?" Withers asked.

"Be prepared. Leave your phobias at the door. Blank out your minds. It's possible this thing can read our thoughts. We don't need to give it more ammunition."

"Agreed," Withers replied.

"Is that it?" St. John wiped his brow with the back of his hand and then pointed to the crevice.

"Yeah."

A hopeless scream streamed forth from the opening and prickled over Pax's skin like biting grains of sand.

"Move!" Pax sucked in his breath and pushed his way through the rocky slit, several feet long and growing wider as he pressed further.

Withers, Johnson, and St. John followed Pax, with Calloway bringing up the rear. The fissure opened up into a room, and Pax pulled on the night-vision goggles, illuminating the shadows into a sickly green. He stood in a square chamber with a low ceiling and a steepled doorway directly across. Hieroglyphics similar to those on the tomb of the Smithsonian lined the top and sides of the door. He ran over and looked into the doorway. Steps dipped steeply from the entrance and around a sharp corner.

Behind him, a man shrieked with terror. A grinding sound echoed in the chamber, which shook with the force of a minor earthquake. Pax grabbed the stone doorjamb to steady himself. Sand and bits of rocks streamed into the chamber. Withers jumped out of the crevice into the room and ran to the opposite side. Coughing, he bent over. Johnson tumbled into the room with St. John pushing him through. The crevice closed behind them.

"Where's Calloway?" Pax asked.

Withers shook his head, his face downcast. "Might've been claustrophobic, and whatever is here sensed that. Though how he made it this far in the Army, I don't know. Maybe this thing exploits even our minor fears."

"Anyone else experiencing any phobias?" Pax looked around the room, his eyes stopping on each man. They shook their heads.

"I had an odd feeling right before Reyes's men went nuts. Like a weight pressing against me. It didn't feel right to me. That's why we held back. I don't sense it anymore." Withers took a long breath. "It's like it withdrew."

Withers took out a small flare from a hidden pocket and lit it. Pax took off the goggles.

"Maybe Calloway wasn't claustrophobic. This place could be booby-trapped," St. John offered.

"Good point. Stick close. I found steps leading from this room. We should keep moving."

Pax placed a hand on Withers' shoulder. "I'm sorry."

He looked down at the floor then back up to Pax, his eyes cool and his expression decisive. "Calloway knew the risks. We all do."

Withers gave Pax another flare, which he lit and carried to the only doorway. Pax motioned for them to follow him. The steps were uneven, and the corridor was damp and slick. When he got to the bottom, he flattened himself against the wall and snuck a look around the corner. More of the same thing. Steep steps followed by a sharp turn. So far, the corridor was solid. Aside from the damp walls and several sunken steps, everything appeared well preserved. How far they needed to go to find the source of the scream, he had no idea.

Another wail tore up the stairwell. Drenched with fear and louder than before, it set off every alarm in Pax's body. The person sounded in pain, and Pax didn't have the patience to be safe anymore.

"Let's move."

He bounded down the stairs, blindly rounding each hairpin corner. The stairs ended at a triangular corridor lit by torches. He tossed the flare to the ground and sprinted forward.

Withers shouted behind him to wait, but Pax ignored him and continued running. He only stopped when he reached the end of the corridor, which emptied onto the landing of a steep, wide stairwell spilling down into a tall chamber several stories high. At the bottom of the stairs was a ring of skulls lit up in a rainbow of colors, reminding him of cheesy Halloween decorations.

In the middle of the skulls, he could make out two figures embracing within a swirling black mist. This mist funneled upward and angled into a large black, polished slab. On either side of the slab a woman hung chained to the wall. Small knives hovered over their wrists and ankles. Immediately he recognized Heather's light blonde hair. He didn't know the dark-haired woman, who let out another long, wailing scream that made Pax's skin prickle. Then he noticed a man lifting a knife off a crudely chiseled stone table and walking toward the circle of skulls.

Raven.

Pax double-timed it down the steps.

♥ ☠ ♥ ☠ ♥ ☠

It's not Surefire.

Raven told himself that again and again and again.

But it didn't matter. Seeing is believing, and what he saw was Surefire making out with Ari in the middle of the swirling gray cloud—and enjoying it.

Rubbing her chest over his, grinding herself against him like an oversexed co-ed at a bar.

It made him sick, enraged, and . . . hopeless. So hopeless he'd stopped struggling against the vines wrapping tighter and tighter around his arms and legs until his limbs throbbed and then numbed.

It's not her.

The knife hovering over his chest pricked his skin, and it didn't matter. Nothing mattered.

It's not her.

His heart couldn't buy whatever his logic tried to sell. He turned away toward the shiny slab between his sister and Heather. Inside the dark, mirrored surface, a shadowy embrace played out. Smoky forms took shape. Xochi, wearing a headdress with two thin plumes sprouting out from the center. Gold bracelets wrapped around her forearms, and her plate-sized necklace lay over a sheer purple dress. And then Tezcatlipoca appeared. Bands of thick turquoise were painted across Tezcatlipoca's eyes and mouth. A plumed headdress rose above his head adorned with yellow, red, and white feathers surrounding a gray circular disk. He was tall, lean, muscular—a poster child for mesomorphs—with a simple red cloth wrapped around his narrow waist and hips, which was the only simple thing he wore.

Another circular emblem, the edges painted red and white around an empty black center, hung around his neck and settled at his stomach. More gold and multi-colored feathers than Raven could count wrapped around and hung from his legs and arms and hairless torso, enough to make any tropical bird jealous.

Their images wavered, and he saw Surefire's face instead of Xochi's and Ari's face in place of Tezcatlipoca's.

He stared at the dark slab, and the ghostly figures faded in and out like a television channel with poor reception. The knife twisted and dug deeper into his chest. He didn't care, because what flashed across the screen was worse than the sharp prick of the knife's point working its way into his sternum.

Surefire and Ari were in the mirror. They weren't kissing, they were shouting. At least, their mouths were open, pantomiming a yell for help but not making a sound. Their ghostly forms spun around as if confused.

No!

Raven strained against the vines.

These gods were trapping Surefire and Ari as they had been trapped. Xochi was switching places with Surefire like Tezcatlipoca was attempting with Ari.

Kat's high-pitched scream echoed again, followed by a muffled cursing bout from Heather. He craned his neck and saw drops of blood dripping into the stone chalices below Kat's forearms and feet. He bucked against his restraints.

"Xochi, stop!" Raven arched his back. A spasm seized the muscles along his spine. He flopped onto the table to catch his breath.

The images reflected in the polished slab became clearer, surfacing from a deep, murky lake. They flickered between Surefire and Ari then Xochi and Tezcatlipoca and then back again. The vortex spun harder. From inside the stone, Xochi's image pulled out of the kiss, and Tezcatlipoca lowered his head to suck on her neck. His attention was focused solely on her body; she locked eyes with Raven.

The knife withdrew from his chest. Raven's torso pitched upward. He clenched his hands at the pain following in the knife's wake, the sting of a giant spike being removed.

He heard the knife clatter onto the table next to his side. The vines holding him down shriveled and dropped away. He clutched at the slit in his chest, a wound that would've killed an average man; it merely made him feel human, vulnerable, weak.

Warm blood seeped around and coated his fingers, making them sticky as it began to dry. His stomach churned from the pain. A sour taste oozed across his tongue. His head spun as he eased up. He stared at the knife on the table, its pointy tip aimed at Ari's back. And he knew what he had to do. What Raven had told Ari he'd do, if the god himself didn't do it.

With a shaking hand, Raven grasped the knife and closed his eyes. He concentrated. Hard. So hard he felt the veins on his neck engorge with blood as if he were struggling to bench a heavy weight. He reeled in the skulls' energy swirling around him, which took every bit of his remaining strength. Invisible swaths of cold wind encircled his body, electrified with the skulls' powers. This vampiric energy snapped along his skin, feeling for a way inside to draw out Raven's power and merge it with theirs.

He strained against this energy suck and reversed the flow, like slamming on the brakes and throwing a speeding car in reverse. He drew what he could inside to heal himself until the room stopped spinning and the gash stopped bleeding. Shutting out the energy stream, Raven slowly opened his eyes. He wasn't fully healed, but it was enough to get the job done.

He leapt off the table toward the skull circle, toward the whirling vortex, toward Ari.

"Stop!" a male voice boomed. Its authoritative tone surprised Raven and halted him in his tracks.

He half-turned and looked up.

A man the size of a linebacker raced down the steep stairs on the other side of the chamber. He wore fatigues and a flak vest and held a gun that could've been a toy in his large hands.

Pax.

Behind him, three men in fatigues—one younger and two older—filed out onto the landing.

"Heather," one of the men, resembling an aging pit bull, yelled.

"Daddy," Heather cried, the word muffled by the vine gagging her mouth.

"Stop." Pax jumped down the last several steps with his gun locked on Raven. "Drop the knife."

Raven glanced from Pax to the two soldiers positioned on the landing. They leveled their weapons at Raven and slowly descended the steps. He raised his hands but didn't drop the knife. Between the skulls continuously trying to suck his power and his trip through the vortex of death that almost shredded off his skin, he wasn't certain he'd recover from a well-placed shot to the forehead. He had enough strength for a one-way trip through the whirling circle, and he couldn't afford to lose an ounce of it.

Heather's father bounded down the steps, around the skull circle, and over to her.

"You son of a bitch," her father bellowed at Raven from the other side of the skulls. Raven couldn't see his face through the gaseous funnel, but his tone spoke volumes. "Get her down *now.*"

"I can't." Raven glanced from the slab to Surefire standing in the vortex then back to the slab.

Xochi's eyes bore into his from inside the black mirrored surface. Her frustration, her impatience sped through him. He knew if he didn't act soon, then he'd have two gods entering the world instead of one.

And Surefire would be gone—forever.

"You heard him." Pax stared down the barrel of the gun aimed at Raven's head. "Release them."

Before Raven could plead his case, a squeaky wail rose behind them.

Pax's eyes stayed fixed on Raven's when he uttered, "Pixie, I have two men covering me. Don't move."

"That bitch." Pixie ignored Pax's warning and sprinted toward the skull circle.

"Pixie, don't do it." TimeTrap pulled herself up from where she'd been lying. "That's not Surefire."

"I know that. It's Xochi, the skank. She had her chance; now it's my turn."

Pax's brow furrowed, but he didn't drop his cool blue eyes from Raven's. "What are you talking about?"

"You'll see *achiton cahuitl*," Pixie replied.

"No!" TimeTrap bolted toward Pixie. She put out her hand and reached for Pixie's arm.

In a blink, Pixie shrunk down and out of TimeTrap's grasp. She swooped into the vortex. In another blink, her body was torn into shreds as if she'd flown into a jet's turbine. Bits of Pixie chum flew through the air and onto Pax's face. He raised his hand off the gun and wiped the debris from his eyes.

Now!

Xochi's command tore through Raven's veins. His body vibrated with renewed energy. He twisted around and looked down at the crystal skull next to his feet. Xochi's skull. The one they had stolen from the past. Pale purple light spilled forth, carrying Xochi's power in a violet beam that eased over and covered his skin in a purplish hue. Before the skull had sapped his power; now it replenished him. His wounds itched and began to heal. His muscles tightened and pulsed with restored strength. Xochi was diverting the power, her power, from the skull and into Raven.

The soothing vibrations stopped. The current cut off. But Raven's power bar wasn't fully recharged. His gaze flicked to the granite slab. Xochi's image faded, replaced by Synthia's terrified face in vivid Cinemascope.

"What just happened?" Pax stared at the slab. "Was that Surefire?"

TimeTrap hobbled up to Raven to stand between him and Pax. "Don't shoot him. It's Ari. He needs to stop Ari."

With TimeTrap distracting Pax, Raven surged forward and into the skull circle. He stepped over the skulls, bracing himself for the pain, bracing himself to be chopped into little bits like Pixie. The wind tore at his tattered jeans and borrowed sneakers, stronger than before. What felt like shards of glass ripped across his exposed skin. He squinted and bowed his head and pushed forward. His jeans were soon gone, although small bits clung to the open cuts across his skin. He forced his hand down to his groin to keep what remained of Hunter's underwear snug over his privates.

His ears rang. Blood ran down his face like beads of sweat. He held the knife tight to his palm even though a meat grinder was going to town on the outside of his hand. Xochi's recharge hadn't been enough to fully protect him, but it did strengthen him, allowing him to push past the pain. He felt nothing except anger—anger at Xochi for endangering Surefire, anger at having to watch this prick of a god use Ari to kiss his way down Surefire's neck and run his tongue between her breasts.

Raven remembered how her skin felt under his lips, under his hands. Smooth, tender, and inviting. How she tasted. Salty and sweet and more potent than any drug he'd ever had.

Ari had no right. Tezcatlipoca had no right.

He stepped into the eye of the storm, coming up along their side. Surefire turned and pivoted, positioning Ari's back to Raven. Her eyes remained closed, as Ari continued to kiss and suck at her neck.

Rage flared inside Raven's chest. He hated his cousin for what he'd done to Surefire, his sister, himself, and the others who had lost their lives in his selfish pursuit of power—of real magic—to make up for his inadequacies. As if he were the only one to ever have any.

Raven leapt the short distance and grasped Ari's shoulder. He ripped him from Surefire. Her eyes popped open. She staggered back.

Ari's eyes bled from black to his human brown before widening in realization. He pawed at Raven. His hands slipped off Raven's blood-slicked flesh, and Ari lost his balance.

He toppled into Raven.

"This *is* personal." Raven plunged the knife into his heart.

He ground it down to tear the vessel into pieces.

Ari's face contorted in pain mixed with disbelief. "You wouldn't . . ."

His voice faded into oblivion. His body slumped. His eyes rolled back into his head.

"Guess again." He yanked the blade out and threw it to the floor.

The skull slipped out of Ari's hand. Raven caught it before it hit the ground. The vortex gave one last turn. It sucked Ari's body from the floor. His lifeless form shot over Surefire's head and slammed into the obsidian slab, which cracked down the center and shattered into pieces onto the altar.

The vortex dissipated. The ringing in Raven's ears stopped, and the room fell quiet. The gag across Heather's mouth wilted away. The metal clasps holding Heather and Kat opened.

Cradling the skull, Raven sprinted forward and caught Kat with his free arm. He inspected her wrists, sliced and bleeding. He placed the skull on the floor and then tore strips of fabric from her dress and wrapped it around her wounds.

"Can you stand?"

"I'll be fine." She motioned for him to put her down. After he set her down, she immediately took his arm and began inspecting his cuts.

On the opposite side, St. John caught Heather and lowered her onto the floor.

Raven watched the fear then awe spread across Kat's face as she took in his abrasions, bad enough to send him to the hospital, if he were still human.

"You need to get out of here." Kat tipped her head toward Pax, who kept his cool eyes trained on Raven. His gun was lowered, but his hand remained tight around it.

Raven met Surefire's eyes as she stood on shaky legs in the center of the skulls. A lump formed in his throat and guilt tugged at his chest.

She nodded at him in understanding. He started toward her. He wanted to touch her, embrace her. Make sure she was okay.

The moment Raven moved away from Kat, Pax aimed his gun at him. "Don't go near her."

"Stay where you are." To Raven's right, across the circle of skulls, St. John raised his weapon. His eyes bore into Raven's with an animosity he gladly returned.

"And get some clothes on for chrissake," St. John added.

Raven looked down and finally realized why he felt a breeze along his butt cheeks and between his legs. The elastic from the underwear remained loose around his waist, and pieces of cotton flaps hung down the front, barely covering his family jewels.

Behind him, he heard fabric ripping. Next, Kat came around and tied the bottom portion of her dress around his waist like a sarong.

"Jealous?" She pressed her lips together and glowered at St. John.

His jaw ground back and forth, but he didn't respond.

"Will you let my brother do what needs to be done? He just saved our lives, so back off." She limped in front of Raven and flicked back her long black hair.

"Kat, don't do this," Raven said.

"Move out of the way." Pax lowered his gun when Kat stepped between him and Raven.

Defiant, she raised her chin and held her ground.

"I don't have a problem arresting you as well." St. John's aim never wavered.

Raven edged Kat out of the way, out of the line of fire from St. John's gun. That man was lucky he was Synthia's father. That fact was the only thing holding Raven back from taking St. John's gun and breaking his hand for threatening Kat.

"Dad," Surefire ventured.

"Don't." He pointed a finger at her while still holding the gun on Raven with his other hand. "I saw what you did."

"It wasn't her," Pax argued. "Even I could see she was possessed."

"Daddy." Heather pulled herself up and leaned her shoulder against on the wall for support. Bright red smudges blossomed along the front of her white dress where she cradled her bleeding arms. "Pax is right. It wasn't Synthia."

"I don't care. She knows what she's done. What he's done." He swung his arm around to point at Raven. "What they've done together."

"When we get back to the states, we'll discuss this," Pax said.

"Raven needs to return this skull." Surefire bent down and picked up Xochi's skull. "And to be safe, he should take both of them. The one Ari had been holding." She motioned behind Raven. "I believe it belonged to Tezcatlipoca, the monster behind all this."

The skulls continued to glow. Their inner lights flickered and pulsed—powered by one another. Raven could feel their energy tugging at him. He felt lightheaded, a combination of blood loss and the succubus skulls. Since Xochi had left the building, her skull in particular had been tapping into his reserves. He tried to focus on reeling in their power, sucking at them as if from a metaphysical straw, but he only had the strength for so much. He needed to get away from the skulls and out of the room.

"No," St. John said. "Raven doesn't leave."

Surefire turned to Pax to plead her case. "These skulls can't remain in our world. It's not time for them yet."

Pax moved to stand just outside the skull circle, closer to Surefire. "You can explain everything later. Right now, you're coming with us. We need to sort this out, especially with the Mexican government. We need to tag all this for evidence."

"She's right." TimeTrap laid her hand on Pax's shoulder before leaning over to unzip her boots.

"Stay back. Behind me." Pax angled away from her.

"No." She kicked off her boots.

TimeTrap shot an unconcerned look at the soldiers standing on the bottom stairs, their guns still drawn and focused on them. She moved in front of Surefire but stayed outside the skull circle.

TimeTrap wriggled her toes. "Much better."

"What are you doing?" Pax demanded.

"Don't you see them glowing?" She jabbed her thumb over her shoulder at Surefire and the skulls. "In fact, they're giving off a current that's messing with the mojo of our world. It's not right. That's the reason Oracle got hosed. Like a disturbance in the force. It's keeping me from popping out of here. My abilities are null and void right now."

She shared a look with Surefire that Raven couldn't read.

"No," St. John asserted again. "I want all this," he motioned to the skulls, "collected and brought back for investigation. I want these two," he motioned to Raven and Surefire, "separated and placed in holding cells. And arrest these jokers for obstruction." He bobbed his head to indicate Kat and TimeTrap, then looked over at the two soldiers standing several feet behind Pax on the bottom stairs.

The soldiers didn't move at St. John's order. Raven sensed a rift in the ranks.

"Sir?" The other older man, a dead ringer for Paul Newman, asked, "What are your orders?"

Pax's jaw twitched.

"Withers, I gave you an order." St. John squared his shoulders.

"You did, Stephen," Withers replied. "But you're retired as my general, and this is Pax's operation. We answer to him."

"I'm warning—" St. John began.

"Johnson, check on Ari." Pax interrupted St. John.

The young soldier walked over to the crumbled slab where Ari's feet stuck out like the Wicked Witch smashed by Dorothy's house. He felt Ari's leg and gave it a squeeze. Then he pushed at the stone lying on top of him. It didn't budge. He dipped down and peered underneath. "I believe he's dead, sir. He's unresponsive and starting to get cold. It will take several men to move this rock off him."

"Now what, Pax? Since you're in charge," St. John sneered.

"Oracle felt the disturbance. Back in Baltimore, she sensed something that didn't belong. I believe them," Pax said.

"Bullshit," St. John shot back. "If these skulls hold the key to something powerful then we need to protect it. We need to keep it in our hands before someone else gets it. This is a matter of national security."

"They don't belong to you," Raven interjected.

St. John's finger tightened over the trigger. "Don't you talk. Don't you say another goddamn word."

"Pax?" Raven met his eyes, guarded and cold, but at least not borderline insane like St. John's. "We can't just remove them from this room. They need to be taken from our world. This," he swept his arm over at the group of skulls, "is not meant to be yet."

Pax kept his gun ready, though lowered, which Raven assumed was because Kat remained next to him. It made him respect Pax even more.

"What do we need to do?" Pax asked.

"Synthia and I need to return the skull to the past."

"That's a crock. A convenient crock of shit at that," St. John grumbled.

Pax gave him a look that would make most men want to run home to their moms. St. John cleared his throat and averted his gaze.

"We'll come back," Raven offered before he considered the logistics of returning from the past without the aid of the skull as they had done before. Was there a portal that allowed them to reenter this world? He hadn't noticed, and Xochi hadn't mentioned it.

"Somehow," he added.

"Humph." St. John shifted his feet.

Pax began, "If we—"

A violent quake cut off whatever Pax was about to say. Dirt, grit, and pieces of stone blocks dropped from the ceiling. Pax and Kat covered their heads. Withers slipped and smacked his back on the bottom stair. Johnson fell into a crouch along with Heather, who plastered herself against the stone wall where she had been hung. TimeTrap dodged a chunky rock and slid onto the floor then curled her long legs under her.

St. John kept his gun positioned on Raven. Though his arm trembled with the vibrations of the quake, his dead, determined glare dared Raven to move, to cover himself, to help Surefire, who stared transfixed into Xochi's skull clutched in her hands. It glowed and pulsed a soft violet that matched the ethereal glow emanating from the blood-streaked necklace around Surefire's neck.

Swaths of energy encased Raven, tugging, it seemed, at his soul to add fuel to the ever-expanding metaphysical fire roaring to life in the room and surrounding the circle of skulls—the ceremonial circle where Surefire continued to stand, oblivious to the gathering supernatural storm around her.

She needed to ditch the skull. She needed to get out of that circle and away from Xochi's skull.

"Synthia," Raven hollered. She didn't look his way or acknowledge him or even acknowledge the room falling apart around her.

Something was wrong. He had to get her out of there.

The skulls' tiny lights roared to the size of large flames. Tezcatlipoca's skull slid from behind Raven and into the place where Xochi's skull had been set. Light poured out from the goddess's skull, spreading over Surefire's skin, coloring it an unnatural purple.

"You can't have her." Raven vaulted toward Surefire. A muffled pop echoed across the quivering room, followed by a sting in his right shoulder. He stumbled back and grabbed at the torn flesh.

"The next shot goes in your head." St. John marched forward with his gun lowered, held between his hands.

"Stephen, drop it now." Pax pointed his weapon at St. John.

The tremors subsided, but the floor continued to vibrate under Raven's feet as if a cargo train was passing by outside the walls.

"Pax, you'll have to shoot me, because I'm not letting this asshole near her." St. John stopped a few feet from Raven and raised his gun again.

"Don't you see what's happening to your daughter?" Raven yelled.

"What?" St. John ground out.

"It's a transference of power from the goddess. Synthia will be linked with her."

St. John's grey pebbly eyes lit with understanding. "Like Ari? Will she have that kind of power?"

A cold pinch twisted Raven's gut, and it wasn't from the vampiric energy encircling him. The realization of what St. John meant, what he was planning to do, what he was planning to give up to see a demonstration of the power overflowing from these skulls enraged him.

"Fuck you." Raven dove to the side and into the circle.

Two loud pops went off simultaneously.

♥ ☠ ♥ ☠ ♥ ☠

Not again.

Surefire felt Xochi's presence rise up inside her. First the nostril-filling scent of lavender and a multitude of flowers. Followed by a lick of invisible flames that started at her toes and burned past her calves and thighs to spill between her legs. Then it rose higher until the heat enveloped her, cutting her off from the world until the only sounds she heard were her short, shallow breaths and the erratic beats of her heart.

At least she controlled her body. Could feel her fingertips buzz with the energy pumping out of the skull. Could tilt her head and peer down at Xochi's necklace, glowing with a purplish hue and reflecting the light of the skull, which pulsated in her hand, mimicking her heart's frantic rhythm.

Dark, shiny drops of liquid covered the necklace and matched the deep-red splashes across her chest and hands. Even her hair was wet, several strands sticking to her cheeks. The ends started to crust with what she believed was dried blood. As far as she could tell, she wasn't cut or gashed as Raven had been when he entered the vortex. Her shredded hand was almost healed from the goddess's power. Xochi had shielded her when she had walked through the cutting wind, which meant the blood belonged to someone else.

Ari.

Raven had stabbed him as she had stumbled back from his embrace and back into this world from a gray, shadowy place. The portal had sucked Ari's body into the slab, and he had flown over her head, spraying blood down on top of her.

Uck! She was going to vomit.

"Fuck you."

Her eyes shot up at the sound of Raven's voice. Through a purplish haze, she watched him leap into the circle. His hand reached out but stopped short of touching her.

She squinted and tilted her head.

Why isn't he moving?

He hung in the air, half in and half out of the skull circle, stuck in mid-reach. His arm was outstretched. Frozen fingers, raw with chewed-up skin, splayed half a foot away from her arm. Inches from his head was suspended a small object. She focused on it, and her vision magnified until she saw the microscopic pits in its shiny surface.

How did I do that?

Fear swam in her chest at what she had just done, at what she'd just seen.

A bullet.

She retraced its trajectory to the gun held in her father's hand. A puff of smoke drifted above the muzzle. On the other side of her father stood Pax, his gun smoking as well. But her father's body blocked what she knew had to be another bullet. This one meant for him.

What the hell?

Her insides shook as if she'd drunk ten cups of espresso. A giddy excitement formed low in her belly and traveled even lower, where a pleasurable throbbing grew between her legs.

She was horny.

Xochi, what's going on?

This oddly timed sexual feeling freaked her out more than the hyperactivity or the microscopic vision or the magical pause button activated in the room.

My power. You are accessing it. Xochi's voice poured through her head in her sultry purr.

What? Accessing it?

Let me describe it as you may understand: downloading it.

Surefire pulled a face at the technology reference. *But how?*

Ari's death has secured our connection. Just as Ari had sacrificed a human to secure himself to Tezcatlipoca. Officially, you are my avatar. A sacrifice of three would allow me to fully possess you.

I don't like this.

That doesn't matter. It is, so it is.

Images flashed through Surefire's mind. A visual mash-up of sex, bloodshed, flowers, insects, animals, births, deaths, human sacrifices from Neanderthals to the dawn of *Homo sapiens* sped through her thoughts too quickly to process, as if someone had hit fast forward on a history documentary. Then there appeared images of worlds she'd never seen before: red suns, purple skies, and a multitude of people.

No, not people. Something else. Something more. Something definitely not human.

The scenes blurred into one another until all she saw were multi-colored streaks that caused a headache so strong she squeezed her eyes shut.

What's happening?

As my vessel, you can open portals when in a completed ceremonial circle. As I said, it is akin to downloading a computer file.

How do you know about computers?

Through the portals, I've watched the world evolve and humans gain knowledge lost for centuries that only the gods had possessed. But I can see your memories as well, and I can see how you view the world. And soon you will have my memories, my knowledge. Each skull allows access to a different file, depending on which is placed in the center. You are unlocking mine. Soon you will have all the knowledge of love, lust, death, happiness.

No, no, no, no, no. Surefire shook her head hard with every "no." *Make it stop.*

She could tell Xochi was smiling even though she couldn't see her.

It may be more than your feeble brain can take, since you are not ready. It takes years of training in using my power, being my vessel. And even then . . .

Her words tapered off into silence.

Tell me how to stop it.

Power flared up and singed her veins. Surefire dropped to her knees. Her muscles seized. She was certain her head would explode any minute as her body imploded with the power pushing at her insides. She tugged at her hands wrapped around the skull. Her fingers cramped from clutching the skull so tightly, but her hands wouldn't budge from the skull. She couldn't let go; a supernatural glue held them in place.

You must learn respect. Xochi's voice pitched higher. Surefire was certain cracks had formed in her skull from the shrill sound.

"I'm trying to save the world here. Set aside your pride," Surefire spoke aloud through gritted teeth.

Xochi's power pulled back. A tide that had been drowning Surefire now ebbed away, allowing her to breathe.

A singsong sigh drifted over Surefire's body. *I won't have my vessel destroyed just yet.*

Xochi swung Surefire's head back around to Raven. She focused her eyes on his handsome face clenched with determination to reach Surefire. *The longer I possess you, the more I feel what you feel for him. What he feels for you. And I am reminded how I, a goddess of love, have not felt this emotion in over a millennia.*

Xochi sighed again. *I will not do to you what was done to me. I will not keep you apart from him.*

What are you saying?

Remove the skull from the circle and return it to the past, Xochi replied, making it sound as simple as returning a defective item to a store.

Without hesitating, Surefire rose then teetered to her feet—awkward since she couldn't use her hands for balance. She pitched herself into Raven. She leveraged her feet against the ground and shoved with all her strength against his shoulder. The skulls' energy formed a heated gelatinous field around the perimeter that slowed them down. Thankfully, it wasn't the whirlwind created by Tezcatlipoca's skull.

It didn't hurt but felt as if she were pushing through warm pudding. She strained against Raven until he tumbled back and she fell on top of him. Xochi's skull dropped from her hands and rolled onto the floor. Its light dimmed to a dull flicker.

Someone hit the play button and the room came alive. A bullet whizzed over them. Raven sat up. His confused eyes found Surefire's.

She gave him what she hoped was a reassuring smile. Raven glanced up over her shoulder. His face registered shock before he cried, "Get down."

He shoved her off him. She fell onto her back and lifted her gaze to find her father marching at them. If Pax had unloaded a bullet on him, as she'd assumed, he must've missed. Only several feet from them, her father aimed his gun at Raven and squeezed the trigger again.

Hypnotized, she watched as a bronze streak sliced through the air on its way to burrow into Raven.

Her hand shot up, guided by an inner force, and caught it in front of Raven's forehead.

His eyes crossed as he looked up at her hand, holding the bullet aloft inches from his face.

Remnants of Xochi's energy coiled inside her, pressing against her skin along her forearm to her hand, which closed tight around the bullet.

She couldn't process what she'd just done or how she'd done it. A deafening silence descended over the group. Surefire could feel the weight of every pair of eyes looking at her. Their fear, their wonder, their shock cut through her.

Her father stopped a foot in front of her. A satisfied expression plastered across his boxy face, which seemed more lined and soft with age than she'd remembered. It was the satisfied expression from when she had won her first gymnastics competition, when she had gotten her first perfect scores, when she had outdone his men at the shooting range.

Her dad raised his gun at Raven for the last time.

"Stop it." She threw out her hand and released the force of Xochi's power, as if releasing a Frisbee from her curled fingers. Raven got caught up in the power surge, and she heard him slide behind her across the floor.

Two other guns discharged across the chamber as Xochi's power slapped St. John in the middle of his chest. He dropped his gun. He flew back and Surefire watched two bullets from Pax or maybe Withers zip past her father's head before he smacked against the ground. Then he skidded across the uneven floor on his back.

She wanted him secure and envisioned vines encasing him. A second later, green vines slithered through cracks and wrapped around his legs and arms, pinning him down.

She rose and stalked over to him. The bullet burned in her fisted hand. Out of the corner of her eye, she saw Pax starting toward her.

"No." She swooped her hand up to her side and pictured vines growing over Pax's feet.

Pax stopped. He struggled to lift his feet but thick, flowery vines had wrapped around them up to his calves. He pulled one foot free, but as soon as he set it down, more grew over it, faster and thicker than before.

"Synthia, please," Heather pleaded, not making a move from the floor where she slumped. Her arms and legs covered in blood, she looked pale and frail.

Surefire blinked. She'd never thought of her sister as frail before.

She turned her attention back to her father, lying several feet in front of her, not even struggling against his restraints.

He grinned, and she couldn't remember what it was like to have him smiling at her.

It made her heart shiver.

"I knew those skulls had power. Now we can harness it. Perfect it." He stared at her, and she could almost see the gears churning behind his shining gray eyes.

"And destroy the world doing so," Surefire replied. "It isn't ours to have. It isn't time. Judging by your reaction, I can see why Xochi said we aren't ready."

"We're ready. Just look at you."

"It almost destroyed me. I pulled out in time."

"But you could learn to harness that power, couldn't you?" He tried to sit up, but the vines wrapped tighter and higher around his arms, matching her rising anger. "Look what you just did. The strategic possibilities of what you could do and what others could be trained to do are endless."

"Others?" Surefire exclaimed.

"Monitored by the right people, our soldiers would be indestructible with this type of power."

Surefire's voice lowered with determination when she replied, "I'll be damned if I let anyone else become this. This power is meant for peace, not war."

She let her words drown in the contempt pumping through her veins. "We are *so* not ready."

His thin lips pulled up in a sneer. His eyes lost their excited glint and darkened to the dull grey of a winter storm. "You don't deserve it. Just like you didn't deserve to be a transhuman. Your sister did more than you ever would, and now I wish . . ."

"What do you wish, Dad, tell me?" Surefire prodded. "You used me for your own experiments to make me better—a winner. I had always suspected it, and your actions just now confirmed it."

He grunted and shook his head. That disapproving look she had come to know made an encore appearance.

"You lost out because of a godforsaken little prick. You were given the opportunity to be someone, and you screwed it up. And now you're doing it again. Christ knows some of it's his fault." He glared over her shoulder at Raven, who now stood at her back. "Another prick."

"Thanks for leaving the 'little' part out," Raven tossed back. He dropped his voice when he spoke next to her ear, "We need to go. I've got the skulls."

She nodded but kept her attention locked on her dad. He wasn't getting away with making her feel inferior—ever again.

"I am someone whether or not I use my transhuman ability." She squatted in front of him. "Whether or not I keep this newfound power locked away and become a peace-loving hippie."

"Whoot!" TimeTrap shouted in agreement behind her.

She tossed the bullet into his lap and stood.

"Like it or not, I am your daughter." She turned from him. "And if that's not enough to make you care, then you don't deserve to call yourself my father."

"I'm ready." She met Raven's deep blue eyes, full of compassion, hope, respect, and love. What she should have gotten from her father, but what she got from a stranger, a thief, a man who understood second chances.

"So am I." He leaned forward and brushed her lips with his. Energy arched between them. Her lips tingled. Heat pooled again low in her belly—and this time it had nothing to do with Xochi's power. He deepened the kiss as if he felt it, too, and wanted more.

The chamber faded around them. She heard someone call out her name. But she wasn't sure who.

Chapter Twenty-Six

She sank into a pool of warm water, never taking her lips off Raven's, which continued to slide over hers. She heard the playful splash of a waterfall behind her. Drops bounced up and sprayed over her hair. Finally, she pulled back from Raven and drifted down under the water.

Peaceful. No more gunshots. Whirlwinds. Shrill goddesses. Only the numbing sound of the tumbling water.

She rubbed her hands over her face, her hair, her neck, her chest. She opened her eyes to a greenish light reflecting moonbeams across the ripples overhead. Below her was inky darkness. Two objects drifted past and disappeared below her feet.

Xochi's and Tezcatlipoca's skulls.

She unzipped her uniform and pulled out her arms, and the top part floated to her waist. She came up for air in front of where Raven was treading water.

"Your chest." She traced her finger along the ugly gash over his heart.

He reached up and wrapped her hand in his. She noticed the skin hanging in shreds on the back of his hand. Tendons pulled tight as he gripped her.

"Kiss me again," he whispered, his voice as raw as the tattered skin over his body. "Whatever is inside of you is healing me."

She kicked her feet and rose up to meet his lips. She concentrated on pushing the energy buzzing in her veins out and into him. She pictured a current, a purple electric field arching from her body and into his. She focused until she felt it drawing away from her and flowing into him.

He pulled her tight to him. Her small, soft breasts smashed up against the muscles in his chest, which grew stronger and harder the longer they kissed. She arched her back and wrapped her legs around his waist.

His makeshift sarong dropped away. Keeping one hand on her, he tore off the remnants of his underwear.

They floated through the water. Kissing. Caressing. Their flesh slick and cool. Drowning in the feel of each other's bodies, of the power vibrating through them, intensifying with every kiss, every touch, until it felt like she'd explode.

They floated under the small waterfall, a heavy shower spray, and then Surefire's back hit a smooth outcropping of rocks. Raven's hands dropped to her hips. He ground against her. Between her legs.

"Synthia."

"Don't say anything." She didn't want to talk. She only wanted to feel, to kiss, to make love. Because if they stopped, if they spoke, she'd have to confront what had happened in the chamber and what was happening to her now with the power surging and energizing every cell so that everything—the cool liquid swirling around her, the mossy rocks, Raven's hands massaging her sides—became more intense than anything she'd ever felt.

"I can do that." He yanked down her suit and lifted her up on the rocks.

Without another word, he slid into her. Slow and easy, completing the connection. Pleasure rocked up from her stomach and pranced along her skin. This warm buzz made her head spin and her body shake with a euphoria that seemed too much.

She moaned. Her nails raked along his shoulders. How could she contain the heat, the intensity that threatened to erupt from every inch of her body? She had no idea. But she didn't care. Because as much as it overwhelmed and scared her, she wanted more. She wanted all of him. She widened her legs almost to a split to force him farther inside. As deep as he could go.

"You don't have to hold back anymore."

Raven groaned against her neck. His movements became quicker, more forceful. He didn't hold back.

His fingers dug into her lower back. He pulled away and stared into her eyes as his grew wide and dark and swirled with a purplish tint. His lids dropped and he drew in a quick breath.

His body quivered with a spasm that matched her own. One that vibrated into the rocks and the pool around them. His heated breath danced along her ear and down her neck and mixed with the cool, soft breeze drifting across her from the jungle.

"I've never felt anything like that." He swallowed against her shoulder.

She buried her head against the side of his face. His stubble scratched along her cheek.

"Yes." That one word was all she could get out, still shaking with a few aftershocks.

Raven leaned back. He cradled her cheek in his palm. "How do you feel?"

She didn't acknowledge his question. She was too busy looking at his chest. It was smooth and perfect without even a scar to show for the nasty gash that had been there minutes ago. She turned her head and reached for the hand caressing her cheek. That, too, held not even a wrinkle where the flesh had been stripped away.

"I don't understand."

"You rebooted me." He flashed his trademark smile. "You're like my health pack. A walking, talking, love-making health pack."

She let out a weak laugh. "Never been called that before."

"What happened back there?" He smoothed back her wet hair. "What did Xochi do to you?"

She laid her head against the rock and let his hand slowly caress her hair. It calmed her, especially when she knew she had to confront the reality of the situation.

"I'm Xochi's official vessel or avatar or priestess." Surefire's face pinched. "Or maybe file server. I'm not sure. She keeps using different metaphors. It's confusing and annoying. Especially when I'm sure she has no idea what half of them mean."

Raven stopped caressing her and rested his hand on the back of her head. She couldn't tell from his blank expression if he was in shock or confused or just plain angry.

Maybe a combination of all three.

When he didn't reply, she added, "I'm to Xochi what Ari was to Tezcatlipoca before he tried to transcend into an actual god."

"Synthia, I'm sorry." His hand dropped away.

He started to shake, and it had nothing to do with the cool air kicking up from outside the pool.

"It's okay." She reached out to him.

"No, it's not. She had no right to do this to you."

"It was an accident."

"Yeah, right." His upper lip curled, and his eyes darkened until they appeared more black than blue. "Nothing is ever an accident with her."

She touched his arm; his skin twitched. His hands lay fisted on the rocks as if he wanted to smash them or anything within his grasp to release the rage building inside.

"Can you reverse it?" he asked without a shred of hope in his voice. He knew the answer.

She stroked the pendant, surprised to find it hot. Static energy danced along her fingertips. She moved her hands around the chain to feel for the clasp. It was gone. She grasped the stone and tugged as hard as she could until it dug into the back of her neck. Maybe she could break it off. An arc of power stung her hand. In the center of her palm a red mark formed where her skin burned.

"I don't think so." Her palm itched while her skin healed and the wound faded away.

Tears ran down her face. She wasn't sure where they came from or why. Once they started, her whole body shuddered with what Heather always referred to as an ugly cry.

"Synthia." Raven drew her back into his arms. He kissed the top of her head. "It'll be okay."

"I can't go back. I don't even know what I am anymore. Where I belong." She sniffed. "My father wants to use me as a weapon of mass destruction. I just tied up my boss—with a plant, no less. And I was supposed to be in my sister's wedding. Oh, God, we were going to pick out dresses next week. Then there's my new apartment. I'm going to lose the security deposit for sure." The floodgates opened wide, and along with it came every possible thought of everything—minor or major—in her life that was going to change.

"Shhh." He slid up onto the slippery, wet rocks then pulled her out of the water and cradled her. She bent her legs and sat in his lap. He felt so big and warm and safe. She wanted to stay there forever.

"What did you do?" She rubbed her eyes. "When this happened to you?"

"My situation was different." He rested his chin on the crown of her head. "I was scared. I have to admit it. It took a while to readjust, leave my old life. Get used to being superhuman."

She smiled at *superhuman*.

"You're not in this alone. We'll figure it out together. Whether Pax forgives you or not. Whether you get to wear an overpriced and unflattering bridesmaid's dress or not."

She snorted. "You must've seen Heather's choices."

He wrapped his arms tighter around her. "It'll suck at first. I'm not going to sugarcoat it."

She was grateful he avoided mentioning her dad and what he had done and said. Just the thought of it brought fresh tears to her eyes. How she could ever face him again she didn't know. He had used her and was unabashedly planning to use her once more. No wonder he had been so incensed when she didn't make the Olympic team. His prize experiment had failed. She wondered if her mom knew and figured her mom had enough pain to last her for some time. She never needed to be told.

"We need to go back, when you're ready."

She nodded against his chest. "I know. I want to discuss what happened with Pax. He deserves an explanation."

"I need to make sure Kat is okay. Then figure out what to do with the artifacts they found in the warehouse. Talk to Pax about what needs to be done."

She yawned, exhausted. "How do we get back?"

"I'm sure we'll figure something out between the two of us." He touched the stone pendant, and a pleasant current raced along her skin.

"In a little while." He kissed her.

Surefire lifted her arms to encircle his neck, and when she did, she felt his heart let out two gentle beats against her chest.

Epilogue

Pax stared at the hours listed on his timesheet on the computer monitor. The numbers blurred into one another until he couldn't tell a one from a four from a nine. What he did know is that he hadn't slept a full night in over thirty hours. Or was it was forty? Or maybe it was pushing fifty? Hell, he didn't even know that.

He saved the file and thought about doing it later when he was less distracted, tired, anxious. Whenever that would be.

A day ago, he had left Mexico after suffering through an intense interrogation by the Mexican military and government, followed by a thorough reaming out by the U.S. ambassador and several agents who hadn't been forthcoming about the agency they represented. They had wanted a report last month, so he'd spent another day churning out a one-hundred-or-so page novel recounting Raven's international theft ring that morphed into an occult ceremony that left several people dead, several more injured, and several others missing, including a U-Sec agent and their original target, Raven.

From his debriefing of TimeTrap, Heather, and Kat, they had confirmed that Raven had been working for their side. Ari had been behind the murders, kidnappings, skull thefts, and attempted murders. He had set up and used Raven and Surefire to find the final skull to finish the ceremony and ascend to this godlike state of being.

Pax had thought it all a crock of shit when he and Matthews had discussed this possibility before his trip to Mexico. Although he had toyed with the idea in desperation, it had still seemed ridiculous. He'd seen transhumans with powers that amazed him, but they were science-produced anomalies. Their DNA, their cellular structures, had changed to give them super abilities. He'd never seen anything like what he had witnessed in Mexico.

The contained tornado. The images fading in and out of the stone slab. The skulls lighting of their own accord.

Then there was Surefire, Synthia.

She had been possessed. A pale purple light had covered her skin. Her eyes had reflected and glowed with the same color. Then she'd caught a bullet.

He couldn't believe what he'd seen. He had been too stunned to react until she'd thrown out her hand and her father had slid across the floor. Pax had been afraid she'd do something she'd regret. He'd moved to stop her, and with a flick of her hand, she'd made vines sprout from the ground next to his feet, strong enough to make him struggle to break free and give him bruises.

Then St. John. Her father. He had let it happen to her. He had tested her. He had seen the potential in her newfound power. He had wanted it.

Pax began to wonder if along with contracting U-Sec for defense cases—and monitoring U-Sec's agents as St. John had admitted—if the DoD agency St. John worked with was still experimenting with DNA, trying to craft the perfect soldier, as they had tried with Pax before the experiments had been outed by outraged religious groups and shut down. They didn't want their tax dollars being used to improve God's creation. Children of man, not of God is how the religious right labeled transhumans.

Many of the transhumans working with U-Sec had sought out private gene therapy to get their abilities, some had been caught up in accidents that had altered their DNA, and others were unsure why their powers had manifested.

This side of St. John concerned Pax. He worried for the safety of his agents, that they could be compromised in the name of strategic defense.

Pax didn't even know how to deal with, let alone control, powers supernatural in nature. He hadn't believed it was possible. Oracle had once mentioned that the more she opened her mind and the more she used her ability, the more she tuned into things she believed were not of this world—maybe from another dimension. She couldn't be sure, but she had considered that this next evolution of mankind was creating an imbalance. A disturbance between what we know to be supernatural and our reality.

At the time, Pax had thought her power was going to her head.

His phone dinged on his desk. As if reading his mind, Oracle texted him with her voice-activated phone: "Meet in lobby in 15. Graham's driving you home. Get sleep."

Pax texted back, "Ok."

He rubbed his forehead. His joints ached, his eyes blurred, and he felt like he had aged forty more years.

Which made him think of General Reyes. He'd heard he was getting better. The spell from the god was wearing off, and he was returning to his normal self. He wanted to see Pax when he was well. No doubt to make good on Pax's promise.

But first, he needed sleep. Pax pushed back from his desk. He scooped up his keys then reached for his cell phone, which began ringing.

St. John.

"Yeah," Pax answered reluctantly.

"Any news?"

"No." Pax sat down again. "Between Reyes's troops and our people on the case, I hope to hear something soon."

Silence.

"I'm heading home," Pax broke the silence, wanting to end this conversation. "If you have anything else, we can discuss it later."

"Pax, I'm sorry."

Pax pulled in a breath. He hadn't been expecting St. John to say that. He couldn't recall that he ever had before.

"I'm not the one you need to apologize to."

"I saw this as an opportunity for her. For the country. I knew—"

"What did you know, Stephen?" Pax's hand shook holding the phone. He was trying very hard not to squeeze his phone into pieces. "Hell, I didn't know what was going on. What those skulls were capable of."

"There are things we need to discuss. Threats to our country my group has found that have nothing to do with transhumans."

Pax's head swam as the pressure built in the back of his neck. "I can't talk about this now."

"We need those skulls."

"You know what was decided. We split them between our countries. It's the only way. They can't be together."

"When you find Synthia, we need to get those skulls she took back. It's a matter of security."

The desk phone buzzed, and Helena's voice rang clear, "Pax, you have company."

"Gotta go." Pax hung up on St. John, grateful for the distraction, but hoping Helena could work her secretarial authority and make his untimely visitors go away.

He pressed the speaker button. "Tell them I'm busy."

"You don't want me to do that."

The door opened and in walked Surefire and Raven. She wore a strappy tank top and faded jeans. He wore dark blue jeans and a black T-shirt.

They looked like two young friends out enjoying the warm afternoon.

"Pax." Surefire ran over to him and threw her arms around his neck. She squeezed, and the purple stone hanging around her neck pressed against his lower chest and felt oddly warm through his shirt.

"I'm sorry," she whispered.

He patted her back, too shocked to do much else. Raven stood in front of his desk, his tattooed arms at his sides. He gave Pax a faint smile.

Pax patted Surefire's back and let her go.

She leaned against the side of his desk. Her dark blonde hair was pulled up in a ponytail. Several strands had broken free and framed her face. There was nothing different about her that he could sense. The same old Surefire, small, cute, and feisty.

And more powerful than anyone he knew.

"We came back," she announced.

"Like we promised," Raven added.

Pax glanced from one to the other while he considered what he wanted to say. His mouth opened once, then twice, and nothing came out. Between a lack of sleep and everything he'd witnessed in Mexico, and now Synthia sitting across from him, looking her cute, peppy, normal self, he was certain he was about to lose his mind. He'd never been at a loss like this before.

Surefire motioned for Raven to sit down, and they both plopped onto the two chairs facing his desk.

"Where have you been?" Pax finally regained his senses.

The couple shared a look before Surefire replied, "Returning both skulls to the past, where, hopefully, they'll remain. I meant it when I said we aren't ready for that kind of power." Her mismatched eyes sought out his for agreement.

"I understand. But what about you? And him?" Pax jerked his head at Raven.

"I need time to figure out what happened to me." She glanced at her outstretched hand resting on the arm of the chair. "What I'm capable of. Raven is going to help."

"I bet he is," Pax said before he could stop himself, one of the hazards of not having any sleep.

Raven's lids lowered over his dark eyes. Pax could see the familial resemblance to his sister—his wavy black hair, a bit unruly, like the attitude he struggled to hide on his face, the sides of his lips quirked up in a challenge.

Surefire placed a hand on Raven's. Pax could tell Raven kept himself in check for her.

"Where's Kat?" Raven asked.

"Should be on a plane back to Crete today. We had no reason to hold her."

"She's okay?" His lips softened along with his eyes.

"We checked her out. Just surface cuts and bruises."

Surefire rubbed Raven's hand. "We'll tell you everything, Pax. That's why we came back. There are things you need to know."

"And you need to know about what I've been doing these last few years," Raven said.

"You want me to get you off, drop the charges for cooperation." Pax was unable to hide the annoyance in his voice.

"Something like that," Raven replied, carefully.

"I don't know what I can do." He rubbed his eyes, burning with exhaustion. He needed sleep.

His phone dinged with a text from Oracle saying she and Graham were in front of the building. He clicked off when his phone announced another message. He glanced down at the screen and saw another text. This time Oracle questioned whether Surefire was in the building. She sensed an odd energy.

"Whatever you can do is appreciated." Raven nodded. "Once you hear what we have to say, I think you'll understand."

"And Heather? And Kali?" Surefire piped up.

"Both good. Heather's recovering but hasn't slept since you left. You might want to see her."

"Yeah," Surefire agreed with reluctance. "I should."

"Kali has taken time off. Not sure when she'll be back." Pax placed his elbows on the desk. "Your father. He's looking for you. He called just before you arrived."

She sat still for a moment, not even blinking. In fact, she didn't seem to breathe. Raven rubbed his thumb over the back of her hand.

"He's worried about you. He wants to apologize."

Surefire sucked in a breath. "He can start by letting me go, by leaving us alone. I'll see my mom. I won't tell her everything, just let her know I'm safe. But I can't . . . won't . . . talk to my dad."

Raven stared at Surefire, and the tenderness Pax saw in his eyes caught him off-guard. Could he trust this guy? According to his agents and Heather, who wasn't apt to like most people, Raven was a good man. He'd sacrificed himself to save them, Synthia, the world. Synthia had proven herself in battle as well.

"Whatever I can do, I'll make happen," Pax conceded. "We'll get the paperwork in place. Propose a deal to clear your names, if they take it."

"Thank you." Her eyes were wet in the corners. She motioned to the door. "You should go to her. If I know Oracle, she doesn't like to be kept waiting. Tell her I'm sorry for everything."

"Tell her yourself." Pax stood. "When you're ready. You owe that to her."

"I do." Surefire and Raven stood up at the same time, in sync. "We'll be back next Monday."

"We promise." Raven gave him a quick smile. He grabbed her hand, and they disappeared before Pax could respond.

He walked out the door, past Helena to the elevator. "Be back next Monday."

Helena poked her head into his office. "Where did they go?"

"Where did who go?" He stepped into the elevator as his phone dinged again with another text. He didn't bother to read it.

"Is that how it's going to be around here?" The doors began to close on Helena, who was standing with her arms on her hips and her eyebrows raised.

"For now."

About the Author

When J.T. Bock was a child, she wanted to be James Bond or Indiana Jones or a vampire hunter or Wonder Woman. Whatever brought her the most action, adventure, and romance while playacting on her stage—otherwise known as her grandmother's basement. Now J.T. has assembled her own team of action heroes, supernatural creatures, and maniacal villains and set them on adventures far from her basement to exotic lands and alternate dimensions.

From a secret location outside of Washington, DC, J.T. conjures these pulse-pounding tales to share with those kindred readers looking for an exciting escape. Her alternate identity enjoys spending time with her workaholic husband and their sidekick rescue dog, traveling to interesting locales, running her graphics business, and enjoying life to the fullest with an amazing group of family and friends and a good glass of wine.

Check out J.T.'s latest adventures and find her by flashing her initials in the sky, opening up her favorite bottle of Pinot Noir, or visiting her on the web:

Official website: www.jtbock.com

Facebook page: www.facebook.com/J.T.Bock.Author

Twitter: @jtbockcom

Questions? Suggestions? Random thoughts? J.T. loves hearing from readers, fellow dreamers and pop culture geeks. Leave a review on Amazon or Goodreads and email jennifer@jtbock.com, so she can personally thank you for your support.

Transcrime doesn't take a vacation, so why should Pax?

After the incident in Mexico, an exhausted Pax is ready for a vacation. He plans to fish, eat steamed crabs, and enjoy cold beers at his bay house just a few short hours away from the office. Unfortunately, Felix Reyes has other travel plans for Pax. He calls in his favor and asks Pax to stop a transhuman Mexican cartel leader who is distributing a drug with irreversible effects—the power to turn men into women.

And this female cartel boss has unfinished business with Pax.

Coming soon to an online book retailer.